The
Tramp

the TRAMP

BOOK ONE OF THE BOUND CHRONICLES

SARAH WATHEN

The Tramp

ISBN-13: 978-1-942938-00-2
ISBN-10: 1-942938-00-4
Library of Congress Control Number: 2015901762

Cover art by Sarah Wathen
Edited by Peggy DeKay and Andrae Lamar
Interior design by Sarah Wathen

www.sarahwathen.com

Give feedback on the book at:
layercakeproductionsllc@gmail.com

Twitter: @SWathen_Author

First Edition
Printed in the U.S.A

acknowledgements

Special thanks goes to Her Last Boyfriend, for creating a concept album so aligned with my story that one can't exist without the other. I'd also like to thank my editors, Andrae Lamar and Peggy DeKay, for helping my book become so much more than it would've otherwise been. Heartfelt gratitude for experts in their fields, medical examiner Rachel Lange and glass artist Fahan Sky McDonagh: you made my characters authentic and my scenes accurate. Most of all, I'd like to thank my mom, for supporting every crazy artist scheme I've had since I was a kid, and my husband, the idea guy and the reason I write in the first place.

Warning: Adult language and situations may make this book unsuitable for less mature audiences. Parental discretion is advised.

For Bill.

prologue

Summer.

"Go on. Get outta here, John." His grandma shooed him out the door with her broom like he was a stunned sparrow, trapped and ready to defile her sparkly kitchen. He was too polite to scowl, but he should have; his mother never shooed him. His dad had deposited him in Shirley County two nights before, on the first day of summer vacation, and no sooner had Dad pulled away than Grandma Pearl had snapped off the television and claimed the computer was "on the blitz."

"Set some bugs on fire or make some mud pies, but you aren't wallowing around in here."

John had no intention of wallowing anywhere, but he wasn't sure where to start roaming. The country was so different from the crowded city streets that were usually out of bounds for seven-year-olds. He set his hands on his hips and looked to his right, down a dusty dirt road that wound towards the river to the west. He had never gone that way without his mom or dad, but he knew how to find the key to their private family boat dock overlooking the rapids. The problem was he didn't want to play by himself.

"Don't go to the river, just stay around here and find another kid or something," Grandma Pearl shouted through the screen door, reading his mind.

How does she do that? It was a skill John wanted to learn. He stuffed his hands in his pockets and turned his head in the opposite direction, to the neighbors' house up the road. He knew the McBride family that lived there through stories and vague memories of holiday weekends, but he couldn't remember anyone by name. There were always plenty of kids around at family gatherings, but the house seemed pretty quiet just then. He looked at the rambling ranch house, wishing he didn't feel so weird and abandoned, when a glinting light over the white picket fence caught his eye.

Is that water from a hose? No—it was spraying crazy in all directions, like a... like a Wet Willy?

John had seen one in a commercial once. Focused on the place, he could discern faint music blaring from a radio. "Lucy in the sky-y with di-a-monds..."

Then, he heard a loud whoop and the maniacal, high-pitched laugh of a pixie.

"What the f—mmmph?" John sometimes bleeped himself. Even alone, a pottymouth just seemed too wrong. Even though pottymouths felt so good to think.

Feeling less weird, and more curious, John tramped up the road to find out what the fmmmph was going on at the McBrides's. As he neared the yard and looked through the wooden fencing, he could see a skinny girl, about his age, sporting a bright yellow and white striped bathing suit, and clomping around in red rain galoshes. John couldn't see much point in the boots; he watched her dive with complete abandon onto a flooded Slip-n-Slide, and the water sloshed out the tops of her shoes when she rose to her feet. Then, as she bounded over to dance a kind of stomping polka under the lunatic rain of the plastic-haired sprinkler, he understood. Obviously, one needed boots for such a dance.

Like a berserker, but not naked. John made a mental note to find out what female berserkers wore, if there ever were any in the Vikings lore book his dad read to him. Mesmerized by the show, John suddenly vaulted in the air and screamed like a berserker himself when a huge dog slammed against the fence. Jaws snapped and spit flew out of the creature's mouth. A hellhound!

The girl screamed and leapt across the yard toward the dog. "Randal! Down, boy," she hollered, pushing her soaked hair out of her eyes and wiping her snotty nose.

John was on his butt, in the dirt, his red Converse tennis shoes like exclamation points at the end of two jutting legs. He couldn't even think of a word to bleep. The girl shouted over the cacophony of barking dog mixed with Beatles jam, "You better move back onto the street, kid. I taught him to do this if a stranger comes up to the gate."

Street? It was a dirt path, but John scrambled up to stand with his pride in his throat. He stepped backwards a few paces until his sneakers met the packed earth of Riverbend Road. He didn't like being called a "stranger," and he didn't remember the pint-sized, water-soaked redhead. She must be a part of the McBride clan, though. In a small town everyone is tied together in dozens of ways: by a sibling or a mother or a best child-hood buddy. The city was different: everyone's disconnected even though everyone lives close together. That was one of the reasons he felt so out of place in Shirley County—he didn't know everyone who knew everyone else. John considered backtracking and going to the boat dock by himself.

The redhead was cooing at the hulk of a dog, stroking his back. The mastiff, which easily outweighed her by a hundred pounds, calmed and made low purring sounds in his throat like he was a cat ready to curl up on her lap. She straightened up to appraise her guest, her eyes roaming over him, boldly.

Her eyes were black. Weird.

She was pretty. John felt his cheeks burn and then a weird tingly feeling crept up his crotch. He shifted his weight and scratched places that didn't itch. She watched him, more comfortable in the country quiet than he could ever imagine being.

"Hi, I'm Candy," she finally belted out, with a wide, friendly smile. "This is Randal."

"Uh…I'm John." He put out his hand, starting to approach the fence again, but he snatched it back when Randal lurched forward with a slobbery warning growl. Candy had a strong grip on his collar and, in no danger herself, giggled confidently. Her laugh was gleeful—contagious—and John grinned despite himself.

"Cherry lollypop?" he asked.

Her brows knitted in confusion.

John gestured to her tangled hair, all twisted up and pinned around her head in long braids. Whoever had tried to tame it that morning had lost the battle. The ends stuck out, higgledy-piggledy, her long bangs framing her face in wild matted disarray. The effect was a perfect half-chewed lollypop on her pale slender frame. "Maybe tangerine," John reconsidered, pondering the color of her hair and cocking his head to the side—she wasn't quite a carrot top.

"Huh? Oh—candy. Ha ha, so funny." Candy mussed her uncivilized head and then pointed to his. "You're a Lemonhead, then."

Not bad. His nicely combed hair was already frizzing and curling up around his temples, rounding out his blonde head, just like the cartoon on a Lemonheads candy box. He could feel it fuzzed around his temples and he hated that. His pressed blue polo, buttoned nearly to the top, completed the look. He unbuttoned a button. They both chuckled; their hilarity gaining intensity as Candy snorted and clapped her hand to her mouth with a loud wet slap.

"Laffy Taffy," John accused.

Candy let her knees buckle, sinking to the muddy grass, and grabbing her crotch. "Stop, I'm going to pee."

"Oh—sorry." John cast around for an adult, an outhouse, something.

"Don't worry, we can wash off." She tore off across the lawn towards the sprinkler. "Come on, he won't be mean if you come through the gate."

John knew he should get soaked too after the hellhound jump scare. He shoved his hands in his pockets and shifted his damp shorts around. *Whoops.*

Randal had settled down and didn't spare him more than a passing glance as he came through the proper gate. He stripped off his polo, kicked off his shoes, and ran headlong into the Wet Willy before Candy could notice that his shorts were already wet in the one telling spot. She couldn't have noticed much, already dancing in the sprinkler, closing her eyes and singing at the top of her lungs. John leaned over and sent muddy water flying against her skinny white legs. She tackled him first, and then brought him back up to dance, her cold, water-logged hands insistent. Randal jumped in to snap at the whirling tubing, got sprayed and whipped in the face, and jumped back out ad nauseam. He tired of the water play after a while, and slouched over to blend with the wooden shaded porch. His eyes rolled back in his head and his muscular haunches twitched in a dream state. Guard dog indeed.

Candy suddenly froze, gasped, and grabbed John's arms. She held him still under the tinkling rain of the sprinkler. "Hey, wanna go look for rubies in the creek?"

"There are rubies in there?" John was surprised, but he already trusted in Candy's superior country girl knowledge of the great outdoors.

"Oh, yeah. Sapphires, too." She nodded, wide-eyed, and moved in closer to conspire, "My Uncle Pat told me he found a sapphire this big," her hands cupped to hold an imaginary goose egg, "when he was my age, and he sold it for a million dollars."

"Wow."

"I like rubies better though—they're red. Hold on, let me go put Randal inside."

She turned off the water. The wiry plastic mini-hoses collapsed to the ground as the last of the water dribbled out the end of each tiny tentacle. She meant to leave John on the porch for the quick dash inside, but her grandma insisted they both come in for a hug and a sandwich, before setting out on their expedition. John was happy to oblige, starting to feel a fondness for red himself.

After lunch, they left the big house through the back door and headed through the yard towards the dense woods. Randal stayed behind, to John's relief. The kids walked past a wooden play set, complete with slide and clubhouse, which John admired longingly. He wondered where all Candy's cousins were that day. The place seemed so quiet, not the usual bustling beehive of the large McBride family. As they climbed up a rocky narrow path, into the trees, Candy explained that one of her cousins was graduating from college that weekend and that most of the family were at the ceremony. She had complained of a stomachache, but really only dreaded the lacy dress she would have been forced to wear had she attended the party. Grandma Catherine preferred to stay home and get things ready for the inevitable family celebration at the homestead, which followed all important McBride Family events.

"Somebody has to watch Uncle Tommy, anyway," Candy remarked with a wave of her hand, referring to her uncle who even John remembered. He was large and kind, probably older than John's dad, but he seemed like a child in pre-school.

The pair grew hushed as the evergreen forest closed in around them. They stepped carefully over loose earth and around algae-covered boulders, still slippery from a recent rain, and the air felt moist and heavy as they approached the creek. John spotted a patch of bright orange mushrooms sprouting around the base of an enormous pine tree.

"Which alien planet sent those as spies?" he wondered aloud.

Delighted, Candy decided that they must find clues to lead them to the mushroom spaceship, which set in motion a competition to find the crustiest yellow lichen. No rubies or sapphires were discovered that day, but John did find a bright red ladybug that he swore bit his nose, despite Candy's protestations that "fairies" don't bite. Candy found a profusion of blue flowers with yellow sunny centers and John helped her thread them into her braids—long since tumbled loose, falling like thick ropes over her skinny shoulders. After hours of searching, they found a scummy brown crawdad that scuttled away into a deep black hole. Almost as good as an alien spacehip. The day grew warm and the afternoon hummed with contentment as the two children picked through woodsy treasures.

In what seemed like the blink of an eye, to children lost in their own invented world, the day rushed headlong into sunset. With a despondent look through the trees at the failing sunlight splashed over a nearby field, Candy announced that they had to get back before her grandma whipped her good. Proclaiming the road around would be faster than going back the way they had come, Candy led them through the trees and they emerged on the far side of the woods. Barefoot from wading in and out of the creek and scrambling sure-toed over slimy rocks, John and Candy sat in the grass just outside of the little forest, pulling shoes back on over muddy feet.

"Candy," said a deep, quiet voice.

John jumped and Candy yelped.

"Oh my gosh. You scared me, Uncle Brian," she said, grabbing her chest. John turned to see a tall thin man in faded jeans and a worn plaid flannel shirt: cuffs unbuttoned and gaping wide at his wrists. He was walking up the road towards them. "Where'd you come from?"

"Candace, you need to come with me. Right now." He was gruff and stony-eyed, expecting immediate compliance but not exactly angry.

"Am I in trouble? It's not dusk yet, we were on our way back home."

John watched her fidget and guessed she was later than she had promised to be.

"It's okay if you come now. I can get you home faster in the truck," her uncle said, smiling and jerking his thumb back over his shoulder where his old blue pick-up idled on the side of the state road, about a hundred yards away.

"In the truck?" Candy stood up and craned her skinny neck to look around him at the waiting vehicle. Its door was ajar. "What's wrong?"

He held out his hand and flicked his fingers, impatient and distracted. "Just come with me. Now."

"Okay, I guess. Come on, John," said Candy, leaning over to haul her new friend to his feet.

Uncle Brian barked, "No. Just you. Let's go—now."

"But…" Candy let go of John's hands, pink blooming across her face. "His grandma lives right next door to Grandma Catherine."

"We're not going to Grandma Catherine's. Your mom wants me to bring you home." Her uncle clenched his jaw and gestured towards the truck again.

Something was weird. Candy had told John all about staying at her grandma's house. She would have the whole family room to herself, with her brothers and all the cousins away for the night. They had talked about a sleep-over. She looked uncertainly from John to her uncle, clearly not wanting her fun weekend to end, but also not wanting Uncle Brian to be mad at her. The pick-up's engine ticked out tense seconds. John strained his vision and could just see the limp figure of another kid asleep on the bench inside.

Candy followed his line of vision and perked up. "Andy's with you?"

"Yes. Everything's fine, sweetheart," Uncle Brian said, his tone softening and his smile returning.

The smile looked forced to John.

"Okay. Well…bye." Candy dove in to embrace John, who had been standing next her with a frown. She squeezed his waist, then leaned back and shrugged, "You just follow the trail around either way. It leads you right back to your grandma's house. Or mine. It just circles the woods. Sorry." She turned to walk with her uncle, without taking his hand.

"I can find it," John said, not entirely certain that he could. But the unfamiliar trail was not what was setting his nerves on edge. That kid in the car looked more passed out than asleep; and John didn't like the way Candy's uncle smiled with his mouth but not his eyes. Creepy. He thought about saying something, but only managed to return Candy's own soft, "Bye."

John watched her walk away, her cut-off jean shorts still damp and muddy in the rump, and her coppery braids twisting down her back, trailing blue flowers with every step. She got into the cab next to her "sleeping" cousin, pinned between him and that Uncle Creepy, and waved from behind a filthy window. Her uncle slammed his door, avoiding John's gaze. Then, the ratty truck spun its wheels hard, and they peeled away off the grassy shoulder, tires squealing on the asphalt. John gasped and trotted over to the road to see them racing away in a cloud of dust.

"No…"

He sprinted home, his feet pounding the packed earth and his lungs choking on their exit.

§

"I'm sure," he told his grandmother, "Candy called him 'Uncle Brian'."

"John says it was *Brian*, not Pat, that picked her up," Grandma Pearl insisted into the phone receiver. She had been in the middle of making their usual Sunday dinner with Aunt Beth when John burst through the door. Dinner sat forgotten on the stove. "Yes, Sheriff—that's right. Candace Vale, little Candy. She must be about seven…"

John's aunt patted his hand and pushed the glass of juice towards him once more, urging, "Honey, you need to drink this. You need to calm down."

John was sure they put Benadryl in the juice to make him sleepy, but he wasn't having it. He arrived on the scene huffing and puffing, after sprinting for over a mile, but he was not in a panic. He needed to know what was happening in that nasty old truck; with that man with the oily smile. He needed to know that Candy was safe and he had a queasy feeling in his gut that she was not. His report of the strange episode had been greeted with blanched expressions from both his grandmother and his aunt. When his Uncle Dan, who had been chatting in the den with Grandpa, heard what they were talking about he raced out the door and jumped into his jeep, rambling on his cell phone. John's cousins were loitering in the side rooms and hallways, lurking around corners and eavesdropping.

"So, you said Brian told her that you couldn't come with them? That Candy's *mom* told him to come?" Beth wrung her hands under the table. "No, that doesn't sound right…" She trailed off, beseeching her mother with her eyes.

"No," Grandma Pearl snapped. "Damnit, I know for a fact that no one in that family has seen or heard from Brian McBride in over two years. He is dead to them."

part one:

moving on & holding back

chapter one

"We're lost."

Shannon strained her eyes to peer down the winding mountain road. The trees were dense and she could only see a few yards in front of her as they rounded each bend—bushy Fraser firs, towering oaks and wide-leafed maples. Blood red and dazzling orange maple leaves would be the crowning glory of an autumn drive, but in summer bugs swarmed the sticky air and dense trees were suffocating. The road was two-lane, but narrowed as they progressed. Their rented Dodge Durango smoothed out the curves and inside the cab it was quiet. Not like Shannon's roiling gut. Her composure wrenched away with each turn, her fingers biting the seat cushion. But at least they were finally descending.

"We're lost, aren't we?" She looked at the side of her husband's clean-shaven face, daring him to take his eyes off the road again.

"You're sure this isn't on the map?"

"Kevin. We left the map at the cabin. Remember? You said the GPS would be fine."

"Well, what does the GPS say?"

"It says the road is under construction and to turn back, that we're lost."

"Come on, the GPS didn't say that," he chuckled. He was calm while her nervousness rose like bile, threatening to spew forth. She hoped he got plenty of splatter when it did. "Shan, this is the best part of a vacation, finding all those less traveled nooks and crannies. This is where the real people live, not like the campgrounds or furnished log cabins. If you want to really know a place, you have to get lost now and then. Not that we're lost."

"Kevin, come on."

"Let's play the alphabet game again," said Maddie, their youngest, nestled in the back seat. She fought her seatbelt to tuck her legs under her bottom, the better to bounce in anticipation.

"Maddie honey, there aren't any road signs to play that game." Shannon had become increasingly alarmed about the lack of signage for the last several miles. Leave it to the kids to highlight her fear with the game that had been driving her crazy for two days.

"Mommy, are you okay?" Madison was a sensitive child, and honed in on her mother's mood like she had a PhD in Stressed Out Bitch, so Shannon always had to be careful to keep her cool.

God, I wish I had a glass of Cabernet in my hand right now. "Mommy's okay, sweetie." She reached back and squeezed her daughter's knee. "Daddy's right, it is fun to explore new places."

"Oh, Shan. Look at this." Finally out of the stifling forest, the ridge opened up on one side to reveal a beautiful valley below. Patchwork fields of kelly green, wheaty gold, and bright buggy-lime; woven together with the hard lines of black asphalt highway and concrete thru-streets. The bucolic pattern was stitched through with the lace of white gravel parking lots and tree-lined streets, dotted with brick, stone and wooden dwellings. It was a village, nestled in a valley and hidden from view—until that moment. Her mood sky-rocketed and she rolled down her window, hoping to catch the scent of flowers, or maybe the call of a bird.

"Wow. It's absolutely perfect, babe," she sighed. "How could this not have been in the travel book? Look—a sunflower field."

Kevin stroked his chin. "I told you. You just have to get off the beaten path to find the jewels."

"Hands back on the wheel please." She allowed a smile, but they weren't on level earth yet.

Nearing the valley floor, Shannon got a clearer view of the land and she gazed around solemnly, watching the mountains rise up on either side. Soaring summits encircled them; their jutting baldness stark compared to the lushness at their feet. The channel of parceled lowlands was long and narrow, lying between two parallel mountain chains; the mountains were stone behemoths, separated like the ancient arms of some half-buried giant that had fallen, clasping his hands overhead in unanswered prayer.

"Okay. You were right, oh sage, and noble patriarch. Never will I doubt you again." Shannon laughed and replaced her sunglasses, shaking her hair out into the fresh air.

"Uh, Mom. You're blowing all the pages around back here. Close the window."

"Hey, young man. Don't take that tone with your mother."

Shannon rolled up her window anyway. At least he was communicating. Her teenage son had been sulky for most of the trip and it was wearing on everyone. He had made a techno-nest for himself in the wayback, surrounded by pillows, snacks, comics, and his iPad and headphones. He missed most if not all the scenic drives.

"Thanks, I could smell the cow patties all the way back here." Like most of Braden's conversation those days, his words dripped with sarcasm.

"Brady, please."

"What's a cow patty?" Maddie asked, her chipper voice in stark contrast to her brother's affected gloom.

"It's cow shi—"

"Braden!"

"Pottymouth! Mommy, that's a pottymouth!"

"Yes, it is, Maddie. Thank you. Son, you better add a quarter to the jar."

Braden whined. "It's not a pottymouth if I'm talking about the real thing, Mom. I mean that's a noun, not an expletive. Right, Dad?"

Something about that made Shannon smile inside; he wasn't as grown up as he liked to pretend. *Oh, we all just need to relax and stretch our legs outside.*

"You can say 'poo-poo,'" Maddie offered.

"Big kids don't say 'poo-poo,' stupid," her brother explained, waxing didactic. "You won't understand until you're my age."

Fourteen is so ancient, son. Shannon repressed her smirk, keeping her voice even with an effort, "No name calling, please."

"If you feel inclined towards the scientific, Brady, just say feces. Not the other." Kevin smothered his own amusement and risked a conspiratorial glance at his wife.

"Well, feces then. See, Maddie? All those brown patches out there in the cow fields are feces," said Braden, jabbing a finger at the passing turds.

"Ew, gross."

"It's just natural, you two." Shannon knew their side trip into the country town could go awry any second. "What happens when you eat, huh? Cows have to eat, too. And when they do, sooner or later, they defecate."

"Yeah, and then we eat *them*," her son quipped.

Shannon could have slapped him. She held her breath, watching her daughter's face in the rearview mirror, waiting for the inevitable next questions from her sensitive six-year-old.

"Cows?" Maddie's eyes opened wide, with both wonderment and horror; focused on the peaceful giants slipping past her window and chewing their cud.

Shannon sensed her husband's foot growing heavier on the gas.

But Braden was on a roll, "Well, where do you think burgers come from? Meatballs, hotdogs—although lots of hotdogs are pigs."

Shannon twisted around to give her son a warning look, and felt a pang of regret, seeing the new knowledge settle onto her daughter's features.

No questions yet; she gazed out the window in silence, but Shannon bit her lip to see a tear sliding down her daughter's baby-plump cheek. In the end, they were obliged to stop the car, and approach the fence, so that Madison could apologize to the cows for having eaten their brothers and sisters and mommies and daddies. Braden said something under his breath about all cows not being so closely related, and Shannon felt her insides clench with the effort to keep her cool. She knelt beside her daughter, and hugged her, explaining that those cows there were likely dairy cows: "See how there are only a few, and all of them are mommies? They're lucky to have such a wonderful green pasture and fresh grass to eat." When a member of the herd grew curious, and drew near to the fence, the whole Derrington family got the willies—they were so huge up close—and instinctively headed for the car in unison.

After a few more minutes drive, they neared the heart of the valley and approached what looked like a town square atop an enormous hill. Shannon exhaled with relief. She was glad for a bit more civilization and hoped for something to eat. The more meatless, fake and packaged, the better. Three sides of the square were enclosed by brick, and trees abounded, but she could see stores and maybe a restaurant.

"This looks pretty neat, but it feels like we're looking at the back of everything." Kevin absently checked his gas level and range.

Shannon pointed to a break in the enclosure. "Keep on driving around, I think the road turns uphill there."

"Aha, there we go…"

A narrow steep avenue veered off the main road. Shannon saw with dread that they were headed up into more dense wood. She preferred the open sunlit valley much more than the endless switchback mountain roads that had crowded her vacation. As their path darkened under the heavy canopy of leaves once again, she realized she had felt safer in the open valley, bathed in sunlight. Her hands gripped the seat as the big SUV engine powered up the incline. Without warning, the trees cleared and the road leveled off. To the side was a small gravel parking lot.

"Let's check it out," said Kevin, squeezing her leg in comfort. Brady made a barfing noise from the wayback, always disgusted by parental fondling of any kind.

"Please, let's just stop." Shannon struggled to swallow the biting reply that threatened issuance as surely as the contents of her stomach. They were near the summit, she was sure of it, but the lot looked like a safer alternative and gave them a chance to get their bearings. She could see that the road ended a couple hundred yards away at a tall ornamental gate with a "No Trespassing" sign. A sizable house lay beyond, mostly hidden by trees.

Kevin had his pick of half-a-dozen parking spaces, and he slowed the car to a gratifying stop. They faced a low brick wall with a little wrought iron door. On the other side, there was tree-lined path that led to a bricked courtyard. Shannon craned her neck and saw a dazzlingly blue open sky through the trees. If there was a god, he had earned her gratitude. She hoped there were antique shops or a place to find a few good souvenirs. There wasn't much in the way of shopping at their rented cabin and Shannon was dying for some money-spending fun to take the edge off. "Cool guys, let's check it out."

"Agreed. I'm up for an adventure. How about you, kids?" Kevin shut off the engine and got out, whether the kids were up for it or not.

"Is there food?"

"Well, we'll never know until we explore, Brady."

"I'm starving, Dad."

Without turning back, "There probably is food, Son. Let's look around." More resistant to Braden's barbs than Shannon, he ignored the whining and headed for the entrance to the square. "Hmph. Buffalo Square, Est. 1927. Neat, guys."

Shannon tried to mimic his confidence until she heard her son comment on his hunger for a fat, juicy hamburger, and Madison started to mewl. "Nobody's getting a hamburger—not today. Maddie I think I see a fountain."

Shannon held out her hand to her daughter, turned a cold shoulder to Braden, and the two girls caught up with Daddy at the gate.

"There *is* a fountain. Let's make a wish, Mommy!"

"Okay, and guess what…" Shannon saved a secret cache of travel surprises in her purse, for trying moments, and the occasion seemed worthy. "I have a special wishing coin, just for you, just for this very special fountain that we found in this secret place. Come on, I'll show you when we get there."

The courtyard was tiered to accommodate the steep grade of the hill; Shannon fought the urge to shout a warning, as Madison skipped over to the fountain in the center of the square and perched on the concrete seats that ringed the fountain.

"Here you go, my special girl."

Madison gasped at the shine of the silver dollar when her mother placed it in her palm. The thing cost over twenty bucks online, but it was worth it to see the look on her daughter's face. "So, do you think it's maybe a secret fountain?"

"I think it must be. It's so quiet up here, and see how the trees are so thick around us? I bet there are elves in those trees and they use those branches as their whisper network." Shannon noticed with a sinking heart that the fountain was dry. To head off disappointment, she pointed up, "Look, did you see that? A yellow fairy."

"I see it! Yellow means friendship—she's a friendly fairy, Mommy."

The "fairy" was a yellow butterfly. Yet, what was more magical than a butterfly appearing right when you needed one? "Okay, so make a wish and make it a good one."

Her eyes scanned the square for her son. Braden was headed for a bronze buffalo that stood in deep shade, guarding an imposing building in the style of a French manor house. The building was cloistered in a tangled nest of ancient oaks so deep and dark the back of it disappeared in shadowy, clinging green and brown. A monotonous drone of locusts pressed down around her, the waves of noise so thick and wet she could almost feel its weight on her back.

Braden squatted down, dwarfed next to the buffalo statue. "I guess it's called Buffalo Square because of this."

Kevin snapped a picture.

Already bored with the buffalo effigy, Braden stood back up and wrinkled his nose. "It smells funny here."

"Oh son, that's nature. Fresh country air."

"Doesn't smell very fresh to me. It smells like something rotting."

"Old places tend to have a little more mildew here and there, Brady." Kevin draped an arm over his son's shoulder and walked him around the edge of the courtyard, gesturing around them and speaking in low tones. A gentle attitude adjustment. Shannon wondered how one of her children could be such a ray of light and the other such a wet blanket. She shrugged inwardly and followed their progress around the square. There were several Victorian houses converted to storefronts; their present state only hinting at their former splendor: a bait and tackle store, a bookshop, an inn, and a small post office—all empty and dark from the looks of it. Closed.

Something in the gutter in front of the bookstore caught her eye.

"Huh, what's that?"

Leaving Madison to count the multitude of coins already thrown into the fountain, Shannon walked closer to investigate what turned out to be an abandoned doll lying face down. It slumped over the curb with its head and neck scrunched against the pavement. She felt an urge to help the poor little thing. She loved old-fashioned dolls and that one was the kind of china doll that her grandmother used to make. It had porcelain hands and feet, with black-painted Mary Jane shoes, and its tufted eyelet dress and pinafore looked handmade. She picked it up, turning the doll over to look at its face.

She dropped it with a start. "Oh my god."

The doll's forehead was broken, most of its delicate face gone, and someone had stuffed the hollow porcelain head with ground meat. The meat had begun to rot and was seething with maggots. The doll lay on the ground staring up at her with one lolling eye, the putrid meat spilling out onto the sidewalk like ruined toy brains. The maggots roiled, in panic, worming into the blood-encrusted plastic hair. Shannon clapped a hand to her mouth, then realized she had touched the vile thing and shook out her hands with a groan.

"What is that, Mommy?"

"Honey, go with your brother. Braden, take your sister with you."

She was satisfied that the sharpness in her tone was not lost on her son, by the look on his face. "Okay. Come 'ere, Maddie," he said at once, waving her over to him. He led his little sister away, keeping her talking about coins and wishes, and Shannon's heart swelled.

Kevin approached, looking concerned. "What's up, babe?"

"Why did it have to be hamburger meat?" she asked her husband in a hushed voice, pointing to the horrid mess. "Maddie has a baby doll just like that."

"Ugh. Yeah, that'd give her nightmares. I think it might give me nightmares, come to that," Kevin admitted, holding his hand over his nose and mouth. "Let's kick it into the bushes, so she doesn't see it when we come back through here."

"Who would smash a little girl's doll and stuff it with hamburger meat?"

Kevin sighed, probably wishing she'd just drop it. "Look, Brady and I spotted a grocery and maybe a restaurant down that side of the hill. Seems like there's more going on down there, why don't you and the kids go investigate while I peek in at that bait and tackle store? It might be open, I saw someone inside."

"Okay." Shannon hauled in air to calm her nerves and caught a whiff of decomposing meat. She pulled hand sanitizer out of her purse and doused herself with it up to her elbows, then headed for the opposite corner of the square. Stepping down the wide tiers and rounding the fountain, she found the kids playing in the shade of camellia trees. Maddie was smelling fat country roses planted in a huge whiskey barrel.

Certainly much nicer in this quadrant. She drew nearer and the trees cleared in front of her. *Oh yes. There's my blue sky.*

Madison balanced on a wooden bench next to the courtyard wall. "Hello, Mommy. This is Mr. Brave." She jumped down and skipped over to a brightly painted statue of a Native American chief, with a feathered headdress sprouting high above his brow and flowing clear to his moccasins. He stood next to a carved wooden gate and as Shannon approached and looked down, she found the gaily-painted buildings that had first coaxed them to stop.

"Now this is more what we were looking for, right guys?" Shannon pushed open the gate, which advertised, "Welcome to Big Joe's," in every color of the rainbow. Big Joe's sat crouched below the surface of the walled terrace like a living thing. Climbing stairways and threading passageways connected a network of cribs and cubbyholes, each painted in constant fiesta. While the rest of the plaza was ringed in muffled shade and stifling air, Big Joe's rolled down the hillside in the sunshine and opened onto fresh breeze and a roaring river below. "Why, I never even realized there was a river along there, did you guys? What a surprise—let's check it out."

"I hope there's food."

"Oh Brady, can't you see there's a grocery there? Of course there's food." Shannon swatted him on the rear, her spirits soaring with the sweet wind and the promise of shopping. She ushered the kids forward to begin their descent. "Careful, you guys, it's steep. Madison, hold onto the railing."

The first building in the cascading array of stores was a restaurant. Considering Braden, Shannon figured that was the best place to start. But the doors were locked.

Shit.

Madison raced ahead with exclamations of delight, barreling down a cobbled path shaded by hanging flowerpots. Braden voiced his habitual displeasure and the vision of a braying donkey danced in Shannon's head.

"Hold on, I think I see someone inside." Shannon waved to a portly older woman in a kitchen apron who walked past the front door, but the woman sidled by without recognition. She continued towards the back of the room, her long braid swinging back and forth over her sizable rump. Shannon could clearly make out dining tables set for customers, and she rapped on the glass doors, but the woman disappeared. "Well, I never."

"Mommy, there's somebody out here," Madison called from around the corner.

Following her daughter's summons, a splendid multi-level patio came into view, its timber floor flanking at least a third of the restaurant and offering a panoramic view of the river. A young man was sitting in a chair near the outside railing, his feet propped up and his arm cradling the sketchbook in his lap. Shannon could see her daughter had interrupted his drawing, but he was turned toward her with one elbow cocked on the back of his chair, smiling and squinting into the sun.

Wow, a friendly face. "Hello, there. We're sorry to disturb you."

He shrugged without comment, shaded his eyes, and winked at Madison. He looked maybe a few years older than Braden, though his eyes seemed to tell a different story, somehow wiser than his age.

"We were hoping to get something to eat around here. Will the restaurant open soon?"

"Not until dinner." His voice was deeper than she expected. Deep and arresting.

Shannon cleared her throat and looked at her watch. "Darn, it's only half past two."

He glanced towards the restaurant, his face unreadable. "Pretty big crowd at dinnertime, though."

Was he joking? "It *is* quiet around here," Shannon said. Not wanting to insult the locals, she added, "But quite beautiful. Are you from around here?"

Repugnant: "From Shirley? No."

Thought I heard a Northern clip. Shannon was grateful for a respite from the local twang that garbled most conversation. "Is that what this town is called? Shirley? We didn't see a name on the map."

"Hey, there you guys are."

"Daddy!" Maddie ran to Kevin like she hadn't seen him in weeks.

Turning to find her husband staggering towards them with an unruly armload of fishing gear, Shannon pulled a nylon bag from her purse and stuffed Kevin's smaller purchases in. The young man returned to his sketchbook, his dark hair hanging over his face to block out their presence.

"So, let's hit that grocery and move on," Shannon said, suddenly feeling ridiculous and unwelcome.

"You meet a local?" Kevin boomed. "Hi there, how's it going? Put 'er there."

"Hello." The artist offered his hand, looking rueful at his charcoal-stained fingers, but Kevin grabbed them in a hearty shake.

"I'm Kevin, and this is my wife Shannon," Kevin pushed her forward to shake hands, "and my munchkins, Brady and Maddie."

"Nice to meet you." He didn't add his own name.

Braden nodded curtly, but Madison bounded towards the stranger and strangled him in a neck-hug. He held his sooty hands clear and returned her squeeze with his elbows, glancing at her father in question.

Kevin nodded towards the river. "Good fishin' here?"

"You wouldn't want to fish in that beast." He shook his head, looking out over the rushing water. "Class V rapids. Plenty of people have died trying to run those." He tapped a charcoal pencil against his thigh. "Unless you're a grizzly bear…I wouldn't go in for salmon, no matter how pink the flesh."

The young man gazed across the river, careless of the pall he had cast with his bizarre reflections. Shannon looked closer at his drawing in progress. She might have chosen bright blues and greens—maybe some earthy reds and browns—for the gorgeous vista across the rapids. Yet, he opted for stark black, capturing the ferocity of the river and ignoring its beauty.

They all watched the rapids for several heartbeats.

Kevin spoke first, "The bait and tackle staff wasn't too helpful, but the counter girl gave me this map. What kind of smaller off-shoots are there from the river—lakes or creeks—for the newbie?"

The young man accepted Kevin's map and spread it out on his lap to get his bearings. "Most of the best fishing spots in Shirley are privately owned, so I wouldn't bother with those unless you want to lose an ear." Braden stiffened but Madison, oblivious to the unsettling remark, gawked at the side of the stranger's face where his strong jaw-line met a dangling silver hoop earring.

Oh God, tell me I don't have to worry about boy-craziness just yet.

Kevin pointed to a green splotch below the valley. "How about down south there? That's technically wilderness, so no one can own that land. Government preserves, right?"

"Yeah, but don't be expecting strawberry jam."

"That's a good one." Kevin thumped the kid on the shoulder, producing a dumbfounded cough as he steadied his drawing pad. "But, I can fish there legally, if I have a license."

"Probably. I don't fish."

"Well, let's do it, babe," Kevin exclaimed, turning towards Shannon with a face full of adventure. "I have a license; we have all our camping gear in the Durango. We're prepared for anything. Let's get off the beaten path."

"Pretty far off." The young man raised his eyebrows, dubious. With a lazy shoulder shrug, he returned his attention to the river.

Shannon felt embarrassed, for no reason she could see. "But the cabin, Kev."

"We can be back at the cabin tomorrow, we've paid for the whole week in advance. Let's just do it."

Shannon looked to her kids. They were busy finding debris that had blown onto the deck and chucking it over the rail. She examined the map. The wilderness area didn't seem too far south. If things didn't pan out, they could always retrace their steps and at least the tiny town was civilization. There was that inn up in the courtyard that couldn't be too booked. "Okay. But let's make sure to stock up on groceries before we leave."

"Great," Kevin cheered, smothering her with kisses as Braden gagged behind them.

"Good luck," Shannon heard the young man mumble, quiet in a way that set her nerves on edge. She glanced over to see compassion for a split second, before mossy green eyes found his drawing again.

"Yay, let's get out of Buffalo Square," muttered Braden.

"Come on, troops." The kids followed him away from the river.

Shannon lingered. "What is it? Don't think we tourists can handle a little wilderness?"

He shrugged, working the charcoal into the paper with his fingers. "You seem like nice people." He kept his eyes on the opposite bank, then picked up his pencil again to fill in the details of his drawing with abstract swirls and tangled edges. "Shirley's not a nice place."

"What do you mean, exactly?"

"It doesn't like strangers. I should know."

"It?" Shannon felt like an intruder since she arrived, even though this kid was the first person she had actually spoken with so far. "You mean the local folks?"

"Well…" He rested his pencil on his lap and scratched the back of his neck with his other hand, leaving a powdery black smudge on clean skin. "Them, too. But I didn't mean the people—"

"Yo, Sam! Happy hour ain't gonna get too happy 'til we drop our load, man. The Buffalo's got her legs spread and waitin' for—" A man, who had sent his lewd announcement ahead of him around the side of the restaurant, stopped short as soon as he saw Shannon. "Oh, I'm sorry, ma'am."

Sam. "Don't worry about me, I could use a happy hour myself right about now."

"Oh, no happy hour in Shirley County, ma'am. But, we're always happy around here, right Sam?" The guy displayed a condescending grin, the kind her dad called: "Shit-eating."

Shannon raised an eyebrow. "You don't say."

"Break's over, pal."

"Yeah I know." Sam was already gathering his things, stuffing a pack of cigarettes in his shirt pocket and dusting his hands on his jeans, no longer willing to meet Shannon's gaze.

"Well, thank you for your advice, Sam," she ventured.

But his eyes never returned to hers as he joined his colleague. They clumped across the deck towards the back of the restaurant.

Almost helpful…. Shannon let out an exasperated breath and decided to forget the cryptic remarks, well acquainted with the moodiness of teenagers; if he was a teenager.

She turned towards the stairs, jogged down, and forced pep into her stride. "Oh well. Kids."

Her mind fixed on picking out ice cream flavors, she went to find the others, peering down little alleys and niches between the tiny buildings. A woman was leaning from around a corner straight ahead, but she ducked out of sight when she saw Shannon.

"Um, excuse me? Can you please tell me where the ice cream..." Shannon trailed away, seeing that she was talking to thin air once she rounded the corner. It was an empty dead end. No door. No window. No exit. *I know I saw a woman here. With black hair to her waist. So exotic, in such a Podunk little town—*

"Go away." It was a whisper on the wind, barely audible. But Shannon whirled around as if that woman had screamed it. There was no one behind her.

"I scream, you scream, we all scream for ice cream, you scream..."

Shannon jumped and grabbed her chest, then chuckled at her reaction to her daughter's song.

"Well, at least I know where Maddie is." Her laugh came out as a nervous titter. She hurried toward the cheerful sound, looking over her shoulder at nothing.

chapter two

Madison was standing in front of a small bungalow with a candied pink and yellow door and an unlit neon sign in the window, encouraging passersby to, "Have a sip. Take a lick." Feeling a little dirty, in a kiddie-porn sort of way, Shannon pushed the door open to venture inside.

"Dad's looking for the shop person. There's no one here," Braden called over his shoulder. He stalked off down the path, kicking stones and bending down now and again to grab one and peg a bird. An indignant crow hopped away from him, squawking.

The store was at least cooler, air-conditioner dry, and Shannon filled her lungs in relief. She smelled burnt coffee, old leather, and books. The place was part ice cream parlor and coffee shop, part library and game room. Two walls were lined with bookshelves that met in the corner, the store separated by a wide hutch crammed with board games. One side was a festival of overstuffed chairs parked next to marble and iron ice cream tables The other was strewn with beanbag chairs mostly hidden from Shannon's view. She wouldn't have minded crashing on a beanbag with an ice cream cone, but she had a feeling the place was closed. Just like everyplace else.

Why bother having a shopping area where the stores are always closed? Small towns drive me insane. She crossed her arms over her chest and frowned all around, her hair frizzed and her patience gone. "Kevin, where are you?"

Behind the shop counter, she could see a fancy cappuccino press—unmanned, of course. A faded silkscreen print claimed that, "Joe's swirl will blow your whirl," next to a lonely soft-serve machine and tubs of ice cream under frosted glass. Kevin appeared from behind the counter, apparently having cased the back room unsuccessfully, his hands raised in surrender. Shannon banged the counter bell, wincing, as the action stung her fingers to the bone.

"This is the rudest little shithole I've ever had the misfortune of 'discovering.'" She was embarrassed by her air-quotes. It was so very Braden of her.

"That's a pottymouth, Shan."

"Let's get the hell out of here before I say a worse one, then."

A teenage girl snorted and bit down on her knuckle to stifle her laugh. Her companion raised a finger to his lips, barely daring to breath in their covert location behind the hutch. The two had been absorbed in their game, she on her belly, knees bent with her feet in the air as he sat cross-legged opposite a chessboard—concealed, when the tourists bustled in with self-righteous demands.

"The grocery was definitely functioning and staffed when I passed it," Kevin said as he opened the door. "Let's just get some supplies and hit the road."

"Fine."

The door banged shut behind them, the whines of children and their strained parents fading into the summer heat.

"Was that rude of me not to spring up and fulfill their every desire?" the girl asked in mock innocence.

"No, but you're definitely a sugar-honey-iced-tea hole."

"You're disgusting, Louis. How would you know, anyway?"

"Touché, Candy, my dear."

"Are you gonna move, or not?"

"Yes, Snappy Snapstress. Give me a minute here."

She had already given him at least twenty and she could tell he wasn't going to figure a way out of her trap. "Your knight is growing mold on it."

"Don't help me."

"I'm trying to help myself." Candy rifled her shaggy red hair in frustration, and rolled onto her back. She squinted her eyes at the cracks in the ceiling, transforming them into a network of roads on an old yellowed map, and began composing a story in her head to entertain herself. The bell banged on the front door again and she heard the conversation-in-progress between two men pour into the store.

"…not saying the prohibition is a bad idea, Greg. I'm just wondering if you're fighting a losing battle. I mean, where is it getting us?"

Great, who's that? Candy scooted her sneakers in closer to her butt to make sure they were still hidden from the latest intruders.

"I'm weary of the rhetoric, Dave…"

"It's Pastor Dave," she whispered to Louis upside down, worried when she saw her friend's enthusiastic nod. "I'm gettin' the hell out of here."

"What? What about our game?"

The baritone voice went on in the other room, "… and there is something rotten growing here, my friend. Alcohol feeds it like an evil nectar. We have to stand united against it. Don't tell me you're turning away from the calling."

Ew, Mr. Davis, too? She finally recognized the second voice as that belonging to her and Louis's high school guidance counselor. Greg Davis was definitely someone she had no interest in chatting up. There were still two weeks before school started and Candy intended to relish them. "You win," she said and handed Louis her king.

She flipped over on all fours and crawled over to spy around the side of the hutch. The two men had their backs to her. Candy ignored her friend's disapproving pout, blew him a kiss, and donned her backpack.

"Turning from that particular law is not turning from God, Greg, and I think we'd all do well to remember the difference. It's the people of Shirley who are my concern, not the politics."

"Explain to me the difference, Dave."

She didn't care who she was abandoning; she wasn't hanging around to hear more of that. Feeling like a naughty puppy dog, she scuttled past the narrow opening and into the back room. Louis swatted her on the butt as he rose to greet the newcomers and Candy almost stood up to kick him in the balls.

"Hi, Pastor Dave," she heard him call as she slipped out the backdoor.

"Whew. Escaped the shepherd-longing-for-a-lost-sheep look," Candy sang to herself. The kid who was working the counter frowned at her over his cigarette. "You got customers, Chris."

"Aw man…" He stubbed his butt out in the dirt. "Alright, alright."

"See ya later." She headed for the restaurant with spirits soaring on adrenaline. *Bye-bye, Pastor Chipmunk.*

Her smile faded as soon as she thought it; the youth pastor's friendly round face and slightly bucked teeth filled her with guilt. She heard other kids using that nickname for him but it was crappy and he didn't deserve that. She liked him and his youth group actually was fun. But. She just didn't think she believed in all that church stuff anymore. As soon as she had turned sixteen, she excused herself from the Wednesday night youth group carpool. She told her dad she could drive herself, but of course she never drove to church.

"Better stuff to do…" Having conquered the stairs and mounted the patio deck outside Big Joe's restaurant, she surveyed the area from her superior vantage point. The grounds were empty. Inside, she could see Mrs. Mendez wiping down the dining tables for the dinner hour. Otherwise, it was a ghost town: only one car in the parking lot and no delivery truck to signal Sam's presence. She had hoped to run into him, but apparently there was no shipment scheduled. She saw a chair pulled close to the railing overlooking the river and, in a sudden gloom, she plopped down on it. She kicked up her feet and wondered how she would fill the rest of her afternoon, since a rendezvous with her new favorite person seemed unlikely.

'Oh, poo," she mimicked Louis, in wholehearted agreement with his earlier sentiment. "Sam, where are you?"

She met him earlier that summer, not long after the last day of school; he was part of the crew hired by her Grandma Catherine for refurbishments on the old McBride homestead. Sam was one of the painters. Candy wandered into her grandma's kitchen one afternoon and found him lying on his side, one elbow on the floor, his head turned nearly upside down. A silver earring lay against his five o'clock shadow and one arm was arched over his head to pull out a delicate, unwavering corner edge of paint. She fell in love right there. Or, at least she fell in love with his painter's hands, and his biceps were hard not to notice. He was concentrating hard, chomping gum and rocking out to his iPod, so he didn't know she was there. She made sure to hang around pretending to be busy, though, hoping he would notice her at the close of the workday.

He did, and that's when she noticed his eyes. Green. So green and they darted away from hers whenever green locked with black. She worked up her courage in Grandma Catherine's downstairs bathroom, pinched her cheeks and rubbed her lips to make them cherry red. When she finally sidled over and casually asked Sam if he ever painted anything else, besides walls, he had turned adorably awkward, admitting to drawing: "mostly weird stuff from my imagination." Candy recognized a budding artist when she saw one and she encouraged him to talk about his drawings. He just smiled and asked her for her phone number. She was confused, yet happy to supply it.

Later that night, she got his text, "some of my stuff".

She gasped as she clicked through the attached files; there were half a dozen photos of his bedroom wall, adorned with some of the most passionate, honest, horribly beautiful drawings she had ever seen.

When she saw Sam the next day, she presented him with a gift box of charcoals and asked him to meet her at the gas station; there was only one in town and it happened to also be her dad's mechanic shop. About a twenty-minute walk, in the mountains south of the shop, there was an ancient rotting one-room cabin. Her twin brothers, Simon and David, had discovered it their sophomore year of high school, one day when they skipped class, and they used it as a party hideout until they graduated. When they left for college, they passed on the secret location to their younger brother Max. Max told Candy about it the previous summer, right before he took off himself. She had been using it for a place to get away and write poetry, or read, preferring solitude over a party. She had a feeling Sam might like it, too.

She had led Sam in through the sagging doorway, sweeping her arm wide and grinning, "I would be honored if you'd decorate my walls in the artistic tradition of your bedroom."

He had stepped in behind her, ducking under the low arch and investigating the moldering room with a wry smile. "This palace is all yours?"

"Honestly, I think it belongs to the forest now." There was a tree branch growing through a gaping hole in the ceiling. "But they let me stay here a lot."

Sam sat down on the old resident loveseat and leaned back, crossing his ankles in front of him and watching her, his eyes glinting with mischief. "You know what that's gonna cost you? Hiring a master artist like myself?"

"I'll be happy to pay it."

Her brothers always called the hideout The Shack but she and Sam called it The Palace. They started meeting there to make art, trading walls back and forth in collaborative paintings. Candy loved what she called, "battling with paint." Especially with Sam.

She sighed and glanced around the restaurant grounds once more for any sign of Sam.

"Nope."

Leaning back in her chair, she settled in for a daydream instead of the real thing, more disappointed than ever to be sitting alone on the deck of Big Joe's.

chapter three

Amanda Jameson clicked away from the Wicca training website when her mom breezed into her room.

"What are you doing in here alone? The Davises are here, why don't you go out and play with Molly?"

"Mom, I think I'm a little old for 'playing.'"

"Yeah, fifteen-years-old is ancient. You're being rude, go get your suit on."

"I have my suit on."

"Well everyone's by the pool—they're grilling hotdogs."

Amanda snorted. *How ironic.*

She snapped her laptop closed and tossed her swim cover-up onto her bed, grinning at the pool party scene that she knew was waiting for her. Her brother Tristan had been dating the same girl for over three years and had yet to score. "Poor guy's balls are probably about to explode," she mumbled, walking down the hallway to the glass door leading outside. She paused long enough to watch Ashley Davis skip past Tristan, giggling, her breasts bouncing in a baggy swimsuit. Tristan reached out an arm, to grab her as she went past, but she slapped his hand away and screamed. Amanda chuckled and stepped out onto the pool deck.

"There you are. Hey, Mandy." Ashley gave Amanda a full body hug. Tristan's cheeks went red over her shoulder.

"Hi guys," Amanda said, pulling back and looking the buxom senior girl over. Her full-coverage suit was surely meant to be modest, but the plain white, wet fabric was thin and showed every detail underneath. *Girlfriend's got an impressive bush.*

"Mandy, come sit by me," Ashley's little sister called from her lawn chair. Molly had already smothered herself in tanning oil; every square inch that was allowed to be exposed. The Davis girls' father was extremely strict. Amanda was surprised they were even allowed to wear swimsuits at all.

She readjusted her own skimpy string bikini, flashing a smile at Tristan's friend by the grill. "Hey, Will."

"Hi."

His petite blonde girlfriend scowled next to him.

"You want me to grill you a dog?" the enormous linebacker asked.

"Thanks, but I think Tristan already has a wiener grillin'." Amanda bit her lip to keep from grinning.

"Shut up, Amanda," her brother said, flouncing into a patio chair.

"Huh?" Will was one of the nicest guys you'd ever met, but totally clueless. The blonde rose up on tip-toe to kiss him, just about climbing onto his back in the motion. He growled and pretended to bite her neck, scooping her into his arms.

"Stop it. You animal," she squealed, then tossed her head back to give him better access.

Tristan settled his dark sunglasses onto his face and started gnawing his nails. Ashley sat on the low stool in front of him, right between his knees. "Tristan, will you put more sunscreen on my back?"

"Uh. Yeah, sure."

Amanda couldn't stop her smile from spreading as she dumped her stuff by the lawn chair next to Molly. She untied her sarong and let it drop to the ground, never worried about looking fat next to her old friend. Molly rolled over to roast her front side for awhile, and Amanda pictured a pig with an apple in its mouth, being rotated on a spit. "Hey. So glad you guys could come over."

"Can you believe summer is almost over?" Her friend squinted into the sun. "I'm gonna work on my tan every chance I can get before school starts."

Yeah, tan cellulite is much more attractive than pale cellulite. "I know. Me, too."

"Hey kids." Mom popped her head through the sliding glass door. "I'm going down to Buffalo Square to pick up a couple things. Y'all need anything?"

"No. Thanks, Mom," Tristan muttered, his voice strained.

"No thanks, Mrs. Jameson."

"I'll take some more Coke. And more chips?" Will called, before she disappeared back inside.

"Coke. Chips. Okay, bye kids. Tristan's in charge, Amanda."

Yeah right. Amanda smirked. Tristan squirted more creamy lotion into his hands, with a loud wet spurt, deep concentration darkening his features.

Will's girlfriend stood with a hand on her hip, shaking a finger at him in mock condemnation, "You are so rude. Me want coke. Me want chips."

"I'll show you rude." Will's hand shot out like a viper. He pulled her bikini string as she screamed and dashed away.

"You asshole," she laughed, covering her bared breasts with her hands as she jumped into the pool. Will was right behind her. Water sloshed over the sides and sprayed supine Molly, who was closest to the pool. She squealed, and Amanda almost lost it the sound was so authentically piggy.

"Let's do a chicken fight," Ashley cheered. "Tristan, get in the water with me. Put me on your shoulders."

"I've got to go to the bathroom," he said, making for the house.

"Got to relieve yourself, bro?" Amanda said under her breath. She rifled through her magazines for a good one. *Dum-dee-dum, show's over.*

chapter four

She looked at the Oreo cookie on the wall.

"I didn't know an Oreo could tell time." But, as she watched, the licorice whip second-hand started ticking backwards instead of forwards. "Of course it can't," she giggled.

"What's so funny?" She turned to see her cousin Andy had woken up. Finally. They had been waiting forever.

"You're funny, Funny Face," she said, as Andy's smile morphed into her Uncle Brian's scowl, his rusty beard-stubble catching the light from the window. The light had a strange green cast. Tornado skies.

"You're mama will never know, little one."

"Mommy already does know." The Oreo started screaming. "Oh, it's an alarm clock..."

Candy sat bolt upright.

Her cell phone was ringing. She rubbed her face and looked at the caller ID. *Shit, it's Sam.* "Hello?"

"Hi."

"Hey..."

"I'm sorry. Did I wake you up?"

"Nah, I was awake."

"Good...can you meet me?"

"At The Palace?"

A sigh. "Nevermind. It's probably too late..."

No! "I can meet you. I'm so bored, why not?"

All she heard for several thundering heartbeats was her own pulsing blood and the clock ticking on the wall. Did he hang up?

"Alright, I'll see you there."

"Okay. Bye."

"See you soon, Candy."

She tapped the end button and sat on her bed, dazed. That dream. It had been so long since she dreamed about her Uncle Brian. Or her mom.

Sam.

She pinched her cheeks and scrubbed her hair.

Ugh. Wake up, Candy.

The clock read 10:23 p.m.

"At least it's not an Oreo clock." She tried to laugh to dissipate her unease. When it didn't work, she focused on a particularly yummy memory of Sam, and reminded herself she'd see a similar scene as soon as she got her ass out of bed and hauled it to The Palace. "That worked." She made for her bathroom to brush her teeth.

She saw less of Sam than she would have liked, since he worked a lot and lived way down south in the hollows, and she would meet him anytime, anywhere. She offered the impression that she was a night owl, and always up late, but she was just a light sleeper and she kept one ear tuned for his ring.

"Candy, dear. Look at you," she said to the mirror, smiling to think of Louis. It was exactly what he would have said, with a face to match his meaning: pathetic. She didn't care.

Not that much.

Never had she imagined her evening would've turned so fortuitous, but at least she'd fallen asleep with her clothes on. In less than ten minutes she was creeping down the stairs, listening for sounds of life from the den. All she heard was the television, but the last time she checked, her dad was already passed out watching The Discovery Channel.

"…the past 60 years, reports of a monster hammerhead, more than 20 feet long, have circulated through Florida. A team of scientists and anglers explore the waters of the world's largest hammerheads to see if these stories could be true…"

Shark Week.

And soft snoring.

Her sneakered feet padded through the patio door, the furthest exit from the den on the ground floor. She didn't risk getting her bike. It was in the garage and the wheels on the garage door were so rusty that screeching was inevitable.

Not worth the noise.

Candy lived on the ridge above The Palace, and though it was a steep climb down in places to get there, those woods had been her extended front yard since she learned to walk. She could reach The Palace from her house or Dad's shop in twenty minutes flat. Sam had to ride his mountain bike through the winding dirt trails around the face of the mountain. Sometimes she worried he might take a nasty tumble in the dark, less familiar with the terrain than she was, but Sam always seemed sure of himself. He said the views of the valley below were worth the ride. *He* was worth the hike, for her, though she was careful never to reveal that.

Her heart raced anytime she thought of him, it was both terrifying and thrilling to feel so out of control, even a stray thought of Sam made her burn from ears to toes. She had to remind herself to slow down, lest she arrive too early and have to wait around in The Palace by herself. Over the summer, Candy had begun to feel a weird sense of foreboding when she went there alone. Nothing she could identify, just a vague feeling of apprehension. She didn't know why.

She thought it was stupid, but repressed a shiver anyway.

She felt the weight of the night as she padded through the underbrush. The summer air was hot and thick and it felt heavier in the dark. She looked up and saw the moon was waxing, but not nearly full enough to explain the electricity in her palms. She tried to clear her head with the sense of the forest around her—the sharp tang of pine, the rich death in the loam under her feet, the smell of rain near—.

"Hoo-hoo. Ooooooooo....."

Candy jerked upright and loosed an avalanche of leaves over her head. The owl voiced more recriminations before taking flight. "Thanks a lot." She laughed at herself, her heart in her throat.

Why did owls sound so human? She could hear her mother talking in its call: "Oooo, oooo. Where do you think you're going, little one?"

If she had a mother.

She was getting close to the edge of the big bluff. Zebadiah's Bluff. She could smell sulfur in the Blue Spring and recognized the clot of lauryl bushes before the drop-off. Way before the cliff, she turned north. The path down to The Palace on that side was longer and more treacherous but she'd avoid that creepy cold spring at any cost. When she'd finally descended into the glen—grabbing branches in a slip or stumble more times than she was proud to admit—she squinted her eyes and noticed she could see light in the direction of the water.

Is it glowing?

She felt repulsed, but had to see, and strained towards it.

Is someone over there?

She stepped over a log and crept through fallen leaves, as gingerly as she could, clearing branches out of her line of vision. It felt like there was something happening over there—

"Thanks for coming."

"Jesus!" Candy sprang into the air like a startled bobcat. Panting, she clutched her chest to make sure her heart hadn't exploded.

A throaty chuckle sounded from the shadows, "Wow."

"Sam," she breathed. "You devil."

His teeth glinted in the darkness.

"So, you wanted to get some late-night painting done?" she asked, her voice not her own. Her heart was still thudding, threatening to jump into her throat. He moved closer without a word. And that didn't help her pulse. She took a step back.

"Something like that." He took a step closer. Sweat and fresh air, cigarettes and Dial soap underneath—Sam's smell. "You're the most beautiful thing I've seen all day."

"You can see me?" she tried to laugh. It was so dark.

He moved forward again, and rested his hands on her hips, so close that his hair tickled her face when a soft breeze ruffled by. "Yeah. I can see you." He ran his nose down hers. "Hi."

"Hi." She pressed her mouth to his and felt him wince. She put her fingers to her lips, tasting blood. "What happened?"

He was quiet when she tried to pull away for a better look.

"Did you get in a fight?"

His body enfolded hers, insistent. And not in the mood to talk. "Let's go inside, Candy. I'll light the lantern if you're scared."

chapter five

"Y'all have a good one now." Joe slammed the cash register drawer shut and wiped his meaty hands on his apron. But as he was turning to head back to the kitchens, he caught a glimpse of brown curls swing to a stop in hesitation, round expectant eyes fixed on his face.

"Oh, Shelby—your mama forget somethin' important?" he bellowed, and threw his head back into a thunderous laugh, the better to give his belly room to quake. "You come back over here and get you a pickle, sweet thang."

Joe lumbered over to the wooden pickle barrel and pulled open the plastic doors of the lid. The vinegary sweet dill spilling into the room made his mouth water every time: like he was one of Pavlov's dogs. He unhooked the tongs from the steal bands holding the worn oak cauldron together and fished around to bring the sleepers to the surface, chunks of garlic bobbing between them.

"Those are the best. You pick yourself one and I'll catch 'im for ya, honey."

The little girl teetered up the stepladder, steadying herself, with one of Joe's proffered hands. She went on tip-toe to look over the edge into the pickle barrel, "That one."

"That one, there?" Joe pointed to a different pickle than the one she had chosen.

"No, *that* one," Shelby insisted, jabbing her finger so close to her pickle that her choice could hardly be mistaken.

Joe, still teasing her, went to scoop up a different pickle, "Oh, I see now."

"No," she whined, her chin trembling just a bit, poised to grab her choice without his help.

Joe burst into another belly laugh, and ruffled her hair with a sweaty paw, then fished out the correct pickle. Still chuckling, he let the fat, salty cucumber drip a few seconds, licking his lips. Then he wrapped it in a napkin to soak up the extra juice, covered the bundle in a tight wax paper roll, and sealed the wrapper with a shiny gold "1st Place" foil from the bulk sticker roll next to the tub.

"There ya go, honey," rumbled his lilting baritone. Shelby stretched her chubby fingers around her well-earned gift. "That's your Shopper's Patient Assistant award."

"Thanks, Big Joe." The breathless whisper was barely out of her mouth before she was through the door in a flurry of sweaty curls and grubby feet, the tinny sound of the bell banging against the doorjamb. Her older brother was lurking close to the entrance as she made her escape, and he sneered, "Oooh, did you touch Big Joe's pickle?"

The lewd remark was vaguely audible inside the store; quiet enough for both of the remaining adults to pretend they hadn't heard. Shelby's mother blushed at the obvious reference to Joe Robinson's penis and busied herself digging for her keys in a deep purse.

"See you tonight then, Joe?"

"That's right. Friday night meeting."

She scooped up the bulging paper grocery bag in one hand, jingling her keys in the other, and gave Joe a wink over her shoulder as she hurried after her children.

"Make sure Paul comes, too, honey. Gonna be some good news tonight at the Rotary meeting. You don't want to miss a minute, I promise you," the big man hollered after them, then punched the keys on the cash register to open and shut the drawer; a bookkeeping formality for the free pickle.

He held his tongue as much as he could, a skill that decades of marriage had taught him, but it rankled that Sheila was planning to attend the Rotary Club event. The Reynolds owned the ruby mine in the hills up north of the valley—it was really just a tourist trap, but Joe didn't see any problem with bringing in more tourists. It was Paul who was the businessman, though, and damned if all the women in town weren't trying to turn the Rotary Club into a silly social party. It was meant for business, goddamnit. He shook his head in disgust and shuffled over to the window for a final wave good-bye to Sheila and the kids.

He grumbled at the stairway in front of the restaurant. "Hell's bells, that switchback."

He knew he had better survey the courtyard at the top of the hill before dinnertime. He wiped the sweat off his neck, in anticipation, before shoving outside and out of the blessed air-conditioning. He grabbed hold of the railing and hauled himself up, one step at a time, the wood groaning under his weight. Huffing and wheezing at the summit, he looked around for loose debris or trash: saw the hoses were coiled properly and examined the benches. He made a mental note to remind Frankie to wash the bird shit off the iron seat backing.

"Oh, I'll do it. Damn Mexican. He's probably already into the chicken."

He waddled over to the hoses to spray down the benches himself. As he worked, he sucked in the heavy aroma of lilies crowding over the rims of his flower urns. He reached behind the nearest one to finger a heavy rose, hanging listless from a thorny bush in the summer heat. He licked his lips and thought of how much the velvety inner cylinder reminded him of his second favorite thing in life, especially wet.

Maybe cut the girls and bring out the vases for tonight. He gave the roses one last gentle sprinkle, his thumb jammed into the mouth of the hose to rain a delicate mist over them. He let the flowers drink to their fill, his head lolled back in the heat, and he closed his eyes against the late afternoon sun. A bead of sweat rolled into the corner of his eye. He knuckled it away, hissing at the sting, and gazed across the square. Sunbaked bricks wafted a mirage upwards and he stepped into the shade of the maple trees that hung over the low courtyard wall.

Mmm. Mmm. Mmm—maple syrup. He patted one of the trunks thankfully and considered his first love—money. Those few maples wouldn't give out much, but he knew of a large stand of them a little north of Shirley, and wondered how viable a maple syrup endeavor might be. He leaned under their shelter from the blazing summer sun, but it wasn't nearly enough.

"So damned hot."

The old lodge across the way always seemed cooler, deeper in shade. He resented that, among other things.

Wouldn't mind a rest in the shade, though...

His shin banged into the concrete rim of the fountain before he realized he had wandered closer to the lodge, as if it were magnetic. He hissed and bent down to see if his leg was bleeding, his face over the still water.

"Beware the traveler..." The voice tickled behind his ear.

"Criminy!"

He stumbled away from the fountain, nearly tripping over his own feet. Reeling, he spun around, searching the shadows of the Buffalo Square courtyard.

"Where—" Joe clutched at his chest, gasping for air "Where are you?"

The dark woman whose face he had seen in the water, looming over his shoulder, her long black hair cascading around her face, was nowhere to be seen.

"Leave me alone, woman." Joe's plea was barely a whimper, before darkness closed in around him.

chapter six

"Oh, shit." Sam dodged behind the corner so fast his cigarette banged into the wood paneling, spraying ashes and sparks onto his forearm and T-shirt.

He brushed himself off, crushed out the fallen cherry in the dirt, then wedged between an overgrown azalea bush and the edge of the building. He peeked around the corner with one eye. He listened for the chatty female voices. One of them was his history teacher. He didn't hear anything more, but assumed the two women he had seen walking towards the premises were heading for the dining room, up and around the steep hill where he crouched.

Ms. Collins was a nice old lady, but Sam wasn't in the mood for polite conversation, so he skulked in the other direction along the back wall, towards the cellar entrance. It was almost dusk. The shadow of an enormous weeping willow hung over the Riverwalk and bled into the shadowy passage under the patio deck. Sam hunched down and hooked his finger into the pull chain of the cellar door. He winced at the loud screech as he pulled open the corrugated tin hatch and crept into the storage basement.

Hmph, wonder where he's going? Amanda watched him descend the cellar stairs as she and her mom turned onto Main Street from the state road, past the back of Big Joe's. She knew there was some big meeting there tonight, but never had she hoped to run into Castle. Sam had moved to Shirley the previous year as a junior. Amanda was a freshman and couldn't remember ever having talked to him—but who could deny he was attractive in such an, out-of-town, mysterious way? Once or twice she saw him glance back at her as she passed him in the hallway at school; his eyes glued to her ass. She had made sure to sashay a little more slowly, letting him drink her in like she was Marilyn Monroe in The Seven Year Itch. The thought made her twist a long strand of her hair around her finger and chew on it with a covetous smile.

Maybe that could be my new project for this year. Keep the boredom at bay…

"Oh good, there's Vanessa," her mom said, looking towards the parking lot, oblivious to the clandestine prowling going on right in front of her.

Typical. Amanda rolled her eyes before putting on a polite smile for the approaching Vanessa. *Mom always misses the interesting details. Case in point.*

"Hi, Steph," called the other middle-aged woman in a high-pitched squeal.

Mom rolled down the window and fluttered her fingers at her friend. "How have you been, girl?" She reached out to squeeze her friend's hand, "I heard Jasper already started training for this season, how's it going?"

"Oh, those boys. You know how they love getting sweaty." Vanessa giggled, as if she was still a schoolgirl herself. "I told Chris, 'You think I'm pickin' up stinky jock straps this early in the year, you're crazy. You and your sons pick up your own damn shit.' Whoops. Hey there, Mandy." Vanessa snorted, stifling her indiscretion with a fist when she saw Amanda sitting in the passenger seat.

Clearly already knocked back a few drinks in preparation for the meeting, huh, Mrs. Vanessa?

"I heard your new weight room is really coming along?" Steph said quickly, soothing her friend's embarrassment and fishing for an invitation.

That's my mom, Captain Obvious, like always.

"We should have coffee, you and me, and I'll give you the whole tour." Vanessa leaned in to whisper, with an I-don't-want-to-toot-my-own-horn confidentiality, "Remodeled the whole basement, you know, bathroom and everything."

"Oooh—You just tell me when, honey."

Both women squealed and pumped their fists. Vanessa cutely stamped her feet and Amanda's mom bounced in her seat. "See ya inside," they said in unison, dissolving in team laughter. Vanessa stumbled in her heels and caught herself against a parked car. Amanda smirked while her mom ignored her friend's early inebriation and steered them around to park.

"This is going to be a great meeting," she sang, and reached over to pat Amanda on the leg in merriment. "I'm sorry she called you 'Mandy,' honey. I told her a hundred times that you changed it to Amanda, but I guess she just forgot."

How can I 'change' a nickname to a real name? Amanda masked her irritation. "Good, Mom. I'm glad you're perking up, I thought you had seemed a little blue, lately."

The comment was a subtle dig; she knew how ashamed her mom was to have a glum mood or an un-pretty disposition detected. Turn that frown upside down. She herself was never allowed to display anything but cheerfulness, ugly moods not being what nice girls did. It was exhausting.

"Blue? Who's blue, Mandy-boo? Oh—sorry. I guess old habits die hard, sweetie," Steph laughed and patted Amanda's thigh again before jumping out of the jeep. "Let's hurry and get a good seat."

Amanda cringed, but accepted her mother's hand when she ran around to the passenger side to hurry her along. A good seat meant sitting next to Vanessa and, if possible, at least one more of her mom's old school friends still lingering in Shirley County. There were several who still grazed around there like cows instead of taking off and exploring the big wide world beyond the place where they were born.

They descended the stairs together in the last of the fading daylight. Her mom lost her footing and flailed for an instant. She pinched the bones of her daughter's fingers and clawed the air with her free hand before steadying herself on the railing. "Oh my! Good thing you had me, honey."

"You okay, Mom?"

"See, I always knew you were my little miracle."

Amanda considered the steepness of the stairs and wondered if the fall could actually have been fatal. *Maybe.*

"Steph, have you heard about what happened to Big Joe?" Vanessa said as she waved from the bottom of the stairs, frantic.

"No, what?"

"Mom, I'm going inside. It's hot out here." Amanda wrinkled her nose at Vanessa's stinky cigarette, pushed past the swarm of people milling outside, and pulled open the glass doors. The cool air-conditioning smelled faintly chlorinated, and she was surprised to find a new water fountain installed in the entranceway: a bronze toddler in overalls and a railroad engineer cap stood atop a tree stump and pissed into a mini bronze brook, while a mutt pulled a handkerchief from the boy's back pocket.

Am I supposed to be imagining the smell of urine, or charmed by the perkiness of his—

"Mandy, over here." Transfixed by the offbeat nostalgia, Amanda jumped when the sharp falsetto rang out to usher her into the dining area.

"Hey, sweetie," intoned her Aunt Meghan, also a high school buddy of her mom's. To both friends' delight, Mom had miraculously fallen in love with Meghan's older brother Mike, whom Amanda had the honor of calling her father, Sheriff Mike Jameson.

Around and around it goes.

"Hey, ladies." Her mom bustled in behind her, probably ecstatic to find that Aunt Megan had already begun to arrange a nest of familiar faces, all of them clustered around tables that someone had pulled together. Amanda looked past them to the back doors opening onto the deck, a dull glint reflecting off the river in the approaching twilight. Magic Hour.

Strings of white Christmas lights were strung from the wooden rafters, twinkling like stars against the violet sky beyond. She could see a bearded old man setting up to play an acoustic guitar.

Maybe a dulcimer?

Steph was bursting with news, "Oh y'all, lemme tell you what I just heard."

"We know," Aunt Meghan and their buddy Kerry said together.

Teehee!

"Mom, let's sit outside."

"What? We can't hear anything out there, sugar booger. Plus, it's so hot I think I'd melt."

Her mom was always afraid of melting make-up and wilting, sticky hair-dos, and lately Amanda had become attuned to her own friends' similar, nauseating anxieties. She made a point to ignore the hopeful summons of one of her contemporaries, her cousin and best friend Lindsay, nestled in the tables with another calf. Instead, she took a moment to appraise her surroundings; Amanda always liked to have something to occupy her hands and eyes during inevitable lulls in conversation with the herd.

The new Mrs. Walsh seemed to be setting up a presentation, against the wall farthest from the tables, where her mom's crowd had gathered. She looked so young that it was weird to think of her as a missus, but it was hard to tell the age of Asian people. Steph and company weren't front row seat kind of gals.

Mieke. Amanda spoke the strange name in her mind, jealous of the novelty.

Mieke had pulled two tables together, arranged some pamphlets in an official kind of way, and had a laptop sitting open and running, but she was flustered. She was searching for something and talking heatedly to the old Mexican woman who worked in the kitchens.

Amanda could just make out Mieke's hiss, "How could you not have a projector here? You did know we were holding a meeting tonight, didn't you?"

Mrs. Mendez put up both her hands, shrugged, and turned to walk back through the swinging doors. Mieke looked up at the ceiling, sighed, and seemed to plead for patience, before turning back to squat down and shuffle through a leather briefcase on the floor.

Amanda smirked and wandered in the direction of their saved tables. She idly read the framed newspaper clippings, circa 1960's and aged family portraits adorning the imitation log cabin walls, mentally gauging how much time she could waste before she started to look suspicious. Turning towards the group, she noticed Lindsay was wearing the same pleated plaid skirt that she was, her friend's long blonde hair cut in the same layered style to encourage soft curls as her own, and she groaned with resignation.

"Hi Lindsay," she said, sinking into the chair next to her. "Nice skirt. Hey, Molly."

Lindsay exploded into feigned trepidation about what big news was looming. Expressing sympathy for Joe Robinson's misfortune, Amanda nodded and murmured agreement. There was no menu to peruse, since there was only one family-style option for everyone, and either the normal fountain drink varieties or sweetened sun tea. All she needed to say was "yes, please," or "no, please," for both meal and dessert, so she busied her hands and eyes with grooming her fingernails, which was always acceptable in such a fastidious group. Lindsay chattered on and on about Big Joe's condition, and the trip to the hospital in a helicopter, and Amanda quickly deduced that the old man had had a stroke but was still alive.

Big surprise. Why do I care about this? Amanda finally had to shut her friend up or else risk choking on her own bile. She poked Lindsay's bare knee, "Know a lot about the medical world Lindsay?"

"Oh, you know, just what everyone has been saying."

"Hey, isn't Chad pre-med?" Amanda asked, knowing the first thing that would pop into Lindsay's mind about Chad Matthews: the blow-job incident, at a party earlier that summer, when he had come home from college. Right on cue, Lindsay's face turned beet-red. She snapped her mouth shut and glanced around for Chad's mom, Vanessa, mortified.

Bingo.

Suddenly, Mieke Walsh stood and called attention to her self-constructed front of the room by clinking her fork on her water glass.

"Excuse me, everyone. Let's bring this Rotary Club meeting to order," she called out over the milling crowd, clearing her throat and clapping her hands a few times for emphasis, "Excuse me, please. Whoo-hoo, up here. I have an announcement that I know you've all been waiting for…"

That was Amanda's best chance to be excused to the restroom without Lindsay and Molly following her, and she took it, "Mom, I have to pee."

"Okay, hurry back," her mom hushed her, with predictable embarrassment at the mention of a bodily function in public.

Amanda noted that the assembled townsfolk showed no sign of quieting for any announcement. She gave Mieke a pitied glance as she slipped past tables and chairs towards the bathrooms, and disappeared through the door to the basement instead.

§

"And, the town goes wild," Sam said in a normal voice, feeling no need to speak in hushed tones under the steady hum of the crowd upstairs. "What's going on up there?"

Ricky was bent over, replacing cardboard tubs of oats against the wall, under the steel shelving. He shoved the last barrel into place and straightened up, looking at the ceiling, in the general direction of the dining room. He shrugged, shook his head and tossed Sam a plastic baggie. Sam heard the clamor erupt through an open door as Mrs. Mendez popped her head in to holler from the top of the stairs. "Enrique, you got twenty!" And quiet, just as abruptly, as she slammed it closed.

"God, Mamá. I got it…"

"Isn't 'Enrique' actually 'Henry' in English?" asked Sam, pulling buds out of the bag to squeeze and smell for inspection. "Why does everyone call you Ricky?"

"Because no one speaks Spanish here, man. Bossman started calling me that when I was little, and it just stuck."

Sam raised his eyebrows and snorted. *Such power.*

"Sometimes he calls me Tito."

"Are you serious?" Sam chortled and accidentally sent some of the weed flying. "Shit," he bent to gather it. "What an asshole."

"Uh-huh."

"Doesn't that bother you, not being called by your own name?"

"Nah, who cares?" Ricky flicked his hand, but couldn't help laughing himself. "But, I'm so glad to know you care, bro." He opened his arms and walked toward Sam, who punched him in the chest to fend off the hug. Ricky slapped his face affectionately instead.

"Mind if I try a sample, before purchase?" Sam was already digging in his pockets for rolling paper. "Make sure your product isn't trash this time?" *Never can quite count on Ricky. Not quite.*

"Are you kidding, man? Didn't you hear Bossman keeled over this afternoon? Where you been? My Dad's on high alert, playing Big Joe himself tonight—no way."

Sam shrugged; not pretending to care about Big Joe's staffing problems.

"My dad probably saved his life today—you know that fat bastard fell onto his cell phone and ass-dialed my dad, because he calls him all day long. Do this, do that. That's the only reason that man is still alive. My dad practically runs the whole show every day. He should own this place, not that old crook."

"Running isn't the same thing as owning."

"Yeah, no kidding."

New place, old story. Same bullshit. "You're just another victim of circumstance…"

"The hell with that, I make my own fate," Ricky muttered, counting Sam's presented cash, and holding it up between them. "See? I'm an entrepreneur."

"Oh yeah, that's a real fortune. My fat bankroll there."

Ricky cocked his head to the side with mock concern. "Mommy short you on milk money again?"

Funny. Sam's friend knew how hard he'd worked for that money, but he couldn't have known that Sam was more likely to give his mother money than the other way around. So he put the joint that he had rolled, despite the warning, in his mouth and ignored the jibe.

"Seriously, man—you can't blaze up in here."

"Fine, fuck." Sam moved the weed behind his ear, his thick hair covering it easily.

"What was that?" They both froze when they heard a barely stifled giggle near the basement door. The two locked eyes and turned silently to see the stairway; gunmetal ballet slippers tip-toeing down the steps, and a plaid skirt floating well above soft pink knees.

"You guys aren't as sly as you think," whispered Amanda Jameson, closing the dining room door behind her. She pointed at the bag in Sam's hand. "What's that?"

"Nothing you could imagine in your wildest rainbow-unicorn dreams, precious." Ricky pocketed Sam's bag and met the girl's gaze straight on.

"I'm not as sheltered as you think. Just what do you think happens to the marijuana my dad confiscates?"

Ricky's eyes shifted to Sam's, incredulous. Sam wasn't fazed. *Big surprise, crooked cop in Shittown.*

Amanda used the pause to saunter closer, her flowery perfume overpowering in the tight space. She kept her eyes locked on Sam and plopped down on a nearby packing crate, daring him to refuse her.

"Forget it, jail bait," said Ricky, "go back upstairs to your mommy."

"I'm not jail bait—you're not 18 yet," Amanda told him, unperturbed, half smiling and raising an eyebrow at Sam. He remained silent and let insolent eyes roam over her body.

"I'll turn 18 long before you do, bobby-socks, and girls like you don't like to let go, once you sink your claws in," said Ricky.

"Whatever." Amanda flung her unbobby-socked bare legs off the wooden box in Ricky's direction and stomped up the stairs.

Ricky makes the girls cry. How ironic. "Hey," Sam called after her, "don't get your panties in a wad. Entrepreneurs like Ricky just get nervous around the sheriff's little princess."

Amanda stopped at the top of the stairs with her hand on the doorknob. "I'm not wearing any panties."

She waited just long enough for the shortness of her skirt to become apparent from Sam's vantage, and then grinned as a deep blush crept up his neck. She wheeled around, spinning her skirt to hint at the truth of her boast, before slipping out the door into the noisy restaurant.

"I hate chicks like that," muttered Ricky.

Sam rubbed his jaw and smiled. She actually had pretty nice legs.

§

Amanda's heart was hammering, her whole body zinging from the thrill. Rushing out of the hallway back to the dining room, she slammed into the swinging door to the kitchen as the old Mexican lady was pushing through. Her face burning, she muttered an apology and fumbled back through the tables to her seat.

She sat down with a smile, then looked around, trying to act normal. At a neighboring table, she noticed a couple of Sendalee Indian gentleman. That was weird. The older of the two was dressed in crisp clean blue jeans and a denim shirt, buttoned tight, and secured with an elaborate sliver bolo tie. He had a long silver ponytail gathered in a leather thong at his back. Some kind of chief probably. His younger companion wore a tailored, charcoal gray suit and had shiny, neatly styled, raven-black hair. Amanda had never seen the second man before, and she couldn't imagine him being a resident of Shirley.

He must have flown in especially. How could some dumb club that my mother belongs to actually be so important? Amanda realized that she had no idea what the meeting was actually about, and she tuned back in.

"…international acclaim," Mieke Walsh was saying, "in the long tradition of foreign exchange."

Several people shifted in chairs or crossed and uncrossed legs, leaning forward in anticipation, but most continued their private conversations, ignoring Mieke. But she had Amanda's attention.

"A foreign exchange student," she clarified, letting her arms drop heavily, her hands slapping her thighs, begging the room to share in her excitement.

"From another country?" asked someone, bewildered.

"Why, of course, another country. Oh—" She hurried over to her laptop and advanced the screen a few slides. When an image of the Leaning Tower of Pisa came into view, an auto-play accordion accompaniment of "That's Amore" began a static-filled rumble from the blown-out speakers. Mieke beamed, pleased with her artistry, and turned back to her recalcitrant audience to catch their applause—which never came.

"Hon, we're fixin' to leave. Vanessa wants to show us the new rooms they added."

Amanda's mom was already gathering her purse, and so were her friends. Lindsay was talking with Molly, oblivious to the Rotary Club developments.

"Mom. Aren't we even going to eat?"

"Vanessa has some stuff for grilling—less fattening anyway."

"But there's finally something interesting going on," said Amanda, incredulous. "What about the meeting?"

"Mandy," Vanessa took up her friend's reasoning, Steph nodding agreement in advance. "There can't be a Rotary Club meeting now that Joe's in the hospital. He's the President."

Molly pleaded with her mother, "Can we get Coke at the grocery?"

"I told you, you're already getting bagel-butt, honey. No carbs after seven o'clock."

"Well," someone spoke up from the table next to them. Amanda turned to see her History teacher, Mrs. Collins. She stood and addressed the front of the room, her brow furrowed in concern. "Foreign exchange is a wonderful program, and a perfect opportunity for educating our students, Mieke, provided we have time to consider this as a community. In order to offer a secure environment for a visiting child—"

Mieke pounced, "Oh, it's a done deal. We better be prepared, because the kid will be here before school starts." She said, and looked proudly from face to face, but most had lost interest in the meeting and were tucking into dinner or resuming previous conversations.

"Hey, is the student a boy or a girl?" Amanda piped up, desperate. She poked Lindsay, attempting to garner interest and slow the progress of their exodus.

"It's a boy," Mieke declared, like a triumphant obstetrician.

"Well, how old is he?" asked Lindsay, finally catching on to an adventure.

Aunt Meghan had slung her purse over her shoulder and motioned for her companions to do the same, but she paused when she recognized the teenage hormonal enthusiasm in her daughter. "Where is he going to live?"

"He'll live with a member of the club, of course," said Mieke.

"Well, I can't lodge a foreign boy in our house." Amanda's mom affected horror at the impropriety, "I have an under-age daughter."

"Mom…"

"I don't speak Italian, that boy can't live with us." Aunt Meghan narrowed her eyes at Lindsay's pout, "Forget it."

"Look, his name is Antonio, Antonio di Brigo, and he has to live somewhere." Mieke's face darkened a shade. "That's exactly what we're here to discuss tonight. Look, this is a really positive step for the club."

"I don't speak Italian either," another person lamented from a nearby table.

"He isn't supposed to speak Italian while he's here," Mieke explained, straining for patience, "That's the whole point of a language emersion program, to learn the host country's native language."

"So he doesn't speak English?"

"What was Joseph Robinson thinking, setting up a scheme like this, unbeknownst to the whole county, until now?" Ms. Collins said. "Mieke, do you have a specific plan to propose for the boy's lodging?"

"Yes," Mieke said, throwing up her hands, "How about Vanessa Matthews? They just renovated their entire basement, as we've all heard. They have plenty of room."

"If that's your plan, that's my exit strategy. Come on girls," Vanessa said, rising in unison with Steph, Kerry and Megan.

"You people are always going on about your kids, I thought you loved kids," Mieke fumed. "Now you can't stand the thought of hosting one?"

Vanessa shot her a look of contempt as the herd moved toward the door together.

Yeah, right. Amanda knew Vanessa had been waiting all summer for her kids, whom she so dearly loved, to go back to school and get out of her hair. She could picture her now, right after drop-off Monday morning, soaking in her bubble bath and sucking down chilled Chardonnay, with Shania Twain pumping on their new sound system: "Man—I feel like a woman!"

"Look, I'll take him first." Mieke stormed back to her table and snapped her laptop closed protectively. "We can figure out where he stays next later."

And I thought she had such potential. Amanda watched her shove papers back into her briefcase, avoiding eye contact. Lugging her briefcase in one hand, she shoved past a few mingling diners to the bathroom, covertly wiping a tear with her silk sleeve. *Someone needs a lesson or two in driving cattle.*

"What grade is he in? Do they even have grades in Italy?" Lindsay whispered, grabbing Amanda's hand so they had to squeeze through the doors together. Molly slowed down to join in, hooking her arm in Lindsay's elbow, her face alight with the titillation of a new young male on his way to Shirley County.

"Of course they have grades in Italy," Amanda said, "Oh no, I left my phone on the table. I'll catch up."

She had seen the Sendalee men stop at Ms. Collins table as they were leaving. They were talking in hushed tones and looking serious. Amanda found her phone immediately, but the neighboring conversation was too much to ignore, so she sat back down in her chair, leaned over and pretended to search for something under the table while she listened.

"...wishes to remind you, Madam Collins, of never-ending blood ties, and of promises made, but not kept," the sharply dressed young man was saying.

"Gentlemen, I cannot think of many promises that I have made, yet not kept, in my life. I have reached out to the Sendalee Nation many times."

The gnarled old man spoke gruffly into the other man's ear, who listened quietly, then responded to Ms. Collins. "Surely you understand the value of the treasure that your family has stolen from our people."

Treasure? Amanda risked a glance from behind her chair.

"If I only knew how to mend this, sir. I am but one person. I have requested private audience with your esteemed grandfather many times."

"We were disappointed not to have spoken with Joseph Robinson this evening."

"You are not alone in that regard, I assure you."

The elderly Indian stiffened and turned away, barking an unintelligible command, but the younger man gave Ms. Collins an apologetic smile. Moving to follow his grandfather, he seemed to reconsider, and returned, "I am an interpreter, but more than that. I would love to speak with you alone."

He stepped closer to whisper something in her ear and shake her hand. Ms. Collins sighed and nodded, offering a tentative smile. Resigned, but almost pleased.

"Thank you, Michael."

Michael returned the smile and hurried to open the door for his grandfather.

What was that about? Amanda thrilled secretly, sneaking through the door before Ms. Collins could suspect she had been listening. Outside, her mom and Aunt Meghan were fervently denying responsibility for the foreign exchange student and Lindsay was wondering, starry-eyed, about what part of Italy the kid came from. She and Molly were giggling about Antonio, saying his name with an imagined Italian accent and conspiring for who would talk to him first. *Missed all the good stuff again, poor calves. Man, was that Sendalee guy hot. Michael...*

chapter seven

Helen Collins gathered her things and left, to find that darkness had fallen. Passing a few Rotarians who stood around the cigarette urn, their faces darkened behind periodically blazing red embers, Helen wondered whether or not they were smoking Native American cigarettes—the Sendalee Nation's brand, in particular. She had often been told of their superior quality, apparently made with better tobacco, and lacking in the harmful chemicals common to most commercial brands. Never having tried cigarettes herself, she could only imagine.

"Hello, Aunt Helen."

"Oh, Charlotte dear." Helen was honestly surprised to see the girl. How long had it been? "I didn't see you inside."

"I know."

She wasn't actually Charlotte's aunt, but the girl's father had worked for Helen's family for so long that they felt like family. Charlotte must have been in her early twenties and she had become quite a woman since the last time Helen had seen her. Dressed entirely in black, she sank into the shadows—except for the buxom display of pale flesh tumbling over the top of her corset. A cruel streak of red lipstick was her only makeup.

"How have you been, dear? We haven't seen you at the house in years," Helen asked.

Charlotte's sullen lips puckered around a stream of cigarette smoke, the cloud billowing into Helen's face and stinging both her eyes and her pride. Not sure how to react, she nodded to her with patient generosity and kept moving. When she reached the summit of the steep stairway, and re-emerged into Buffalo Square, she was confronted with the backside of that ridiculous statue of the generic Brave. She wondered how Michael and his grandfather reacted when they met him that night. Embarrassed, she shook her head and resolved to put petty squabbles, ancient and modern, out of her mind for the rest of the night.

Helen inhaled deeply, winded from the steep climb out of the Big

Joe's compound, but instead of catching her breath, she nearly choked on the thick, humid air of the enclosed square. Cicadas droned inside the heavy ring of trees, their rhythmic strumming adding weight to the muggy darkness. Instead of plunging through that oppressive soup, she decided to take the Riverwalk home, and backtracked a little along the crest of the hill, towards the water. A well-worn footpath led through the trees, and down to an iron gate, opening onto the blessedly fresh air of the wide, quick running, Tenakho River. The river thundered down from a deep cleft between the Eastern and Western Mountain ridges to the north, spraying violent rapids over the rocky riverbed alongside Shirley's town center, before hurtling around the peninsular landmass on which Buffalo Square was built.

Helen's family estate sat atop the highest crag, overlooking a quick hairpin: the most violent part of the river's eastward turn before barreling back down through the south valley. In colonial times the towering structure provided the perfect vantage point for a warring clan to monitor both the lower valley and the opposite shoreline. The river itself had never threatened invaders. It was unnavigable to any but the most avid rafting fanatics in the modern day extreme whitewater rapids world, and even then, only during the calm season. When the Collins family had first settled there, centuries ago, attempts to run the river had always ended in tragedy. Every once in a while, Helen would see a rafting expedition rage past, but mostly the river simply provided a beautiful view from her upper rooms, which she employed as a library and shared with her daughter as a painting studio when she was in town. The Riverwalk provided a pleasant upwards stroll, through the rear family gardens, towards home. Helen chose that path, more and more in her advancing years, instead of the steep climb up endless stairs to the front entrance that faced Buffalo Square.

"A walk along the river is so much more refreshing," she said to herself, tilting her face into the moonlight and the crisp spray on the wind. She smiled, unsurprised to see another little ember glow brighter at the edge of the river, away from the light of the street lamps. "Good evening, Mr. Castle."

The disembodied cigarette flew upwards as he flicked it into the river and stood to greet her. He moved into the light and nodded respectfully as she passed. Sam Castle had a rough look about him but he had the best manners of any student Helen could remember in her long years of teaching. "Good evening, Ms. Collins."

"I trust you have adequate transportation home?" she asked without breaking her stride, knowing he would deny that he did not, yet she felt compelled to extend the offer.

"Yes, I do," he lied and cleared his throat.

"Take care of yourself, son."

"I will."

Helen continued towards home, hoping her butler Desmond would be there to greet her in that cavernous, empty place.

chapter eight

Sam watched her disappear and checked his watch. *Time to move.*

He headed away from the river and towards the foothills, where the train tracks snaked through the valley, hugging the bends and crags. Not for the tiny population of Shirley, but more for the erratic path it was forced to take right before the hillside opened up onto the wicked Wattahnga Gorge, the train ran more slowly as it passed the diminutive downtown. And it was always on time, one of the only dependable characters in Sam's life those days.

As he left Buffalo Square, he could still hear the clinking of silverware and the mumble of chattering diners on the outside deck of Big Joe's dining patio; a guitar gently strumming a meandering tune, in and out of the shushing of water over rocks.

"Crazy as it gets in Shirley." Even on a Friday night such a bustling crowd was rare.

The noise of the restaurant was swallowed by the steep hillside. As he moved closer to the foothills of the Eastern Mountain, the air became still. The sounds of the river were replaced by wary scuffling and an occasional hoot or chirp of some night creature. Walking quickly, he brushed against the side of a bush and caused a cacophony of squawking from a quail covey. Sam jumped back in reflex and clutched at his thundering heart.

"Damn birds," he muttered, ashamed of his own skittishness.

There was nothing Sam had seen in a dozen cities across the states that came close to the creepiness of Shirley Valley after nightfall. There was something tense, malevolent, in the air itself that he couldn't quite name. It felt alive—which seemed a ridiculous thought—but still, he could feel it. Something. He tried to shrug it off as silly, superstitious metaphysical crap that he sometimes recognized in other people he met, especially in small towns. But, it was hard to ignore how similar the damp, warm air of the valley felt to breath in the summertime. The hair on his neck stood up at that repulsive thought, as he tramped even further into the dark field.

A whistle shrieked in the distance, and Sam said a little prayer of thanks to no one in particular. *Why do I still pray, when there's no one to pray to?*

He picked up his pace, knowing the engine always sounded farther away than it was, echoing and ricocheting off rocky outcrops, thick stands of trees and receding passages. Jogging closer to the tracks, the train came into view, clamoring around a jut of stone cradling the valley of Shirley.

Sam gauged its speed. *Freight train.*

"Faithful as an old friend," he whispered in welcome, and ducked behind a stand of elm trees as the train's headlights whipped by.

Once the engineer's window was safely past him, Sam cleared the trees and ran at a steady clip along the tracks. Gradually, the boxcars slipped beside him, and he picked up his pace to match their speed. Looking backwards, he spotted a cattle car and couldn't believe his luck; the open wooden slats were perfect to hang on for a quick ride, and cows rarely bit, though sometimes licked with strong, sandpaper tongues. As the cattle car approached, he lunged and his callused hands found their grip. He hauled himself up to cling onto the side, his shoes finding purchase against a corrugated metal floor.

"Hi guys, how's it hangin'?"

The docile cows stood mesmerized by their gently swaying wood and steel prison. He peered into the dim car at the massive, rounded haunches and drooping udders. Dairy cows.

"Oh sorry. Ladies," he apologized, tipping an imaginary hat.

The breeze whistled through the slats, over the warm bodies and damp straw that covered the floor. Sam stretched his arms to hang away from the car, turning his face into the wind and closing his eyes to enjoy the ride. The wind whipped his hair into a tornado, a tunnel of sound enclosing him within the earthy smells of the cattle car. He felt disconnected, protected. He thought of the cavernous gorge that lay ahead, maybe sixty miles past his destination, and craved that clankety-clank of the rusty wheels over the skeleton trestle bridge; waterfall spray obscuring the river below. Crossing the abyss.

Sam had ridden the train past that abyss once, a few months ago, and landed just beyond it at a monstrous resort flanking the well-trailed, but still remote, Mount-Something–That-Allowed-Hunting. He had even convinced a bartender at the resort restaurant, eager to please visitors and make a good tip, to sell him a beer. It hadn't been a hard sell.

That unsettling feeling he often sensed in Shirley Valley was absent on the other side of the gorge, and the country gardens at the resort were quiet in a peaceful, charming way. It was almost like an historical fiction novel that let him forget who he was or where he came from. Maybe he would go out there again soon; maybe he would just keep going, one day.

Not tonight.

That night, his mom's vile boyfriend, Terry Finley might come over. Then again, since it had actually come to blows a couple nights before, maybe not. At seventeen, Sam was broad shouldered and muscular from hours of manual labor, and that helped discourage some of the creeps that wanted to hang around with his mom. Some guys got frustrated when he hung around, preferring to escape with her instead; but if Sam were home, guilt might keep her from disappearing for days. She wasn't usually hard to find in a place as small as Shirley, but still.

Still. Sam let a shiver run up his spine and opened his eyes to look for landmarks. Before long he saw Witch's Hat, the crag aptly named for its striking, villainous fairytale features, marking the entrance to a shadowy cleft in the mountainside. Set back from the road, hiding under ancient pines clinging to the precipitous slopes above, lie Southern Cove Mobile Home Village.

Home, sweet home—he'd have rather been anywhere else in the world. But that was where he got off.

Sam blew a kiss to the cows with a rueful smile. He landed with legs loose and springy to absorb the shock, jogging a few steps to avoid stumbling, and then tripped anyway. He rolled with his head tucked, then came to a huddled stop on two feet, with arms splayed for balance.

"Getting better," he chuckled as he dusted off his jeans and exposed knees, and headed toward the lighted windows sprinkling the shady, breezeless cove. Not wanting to arouse suspicion in his jumpy neighbors, with whom he had little in common, Sam kept his head down as he walked. What was the point in making friends when his mom would probably want to move on soon, anyway?

He was relieved to see that his house looked deserted—the porch light turned out. Searching for the right house key in the dim light, he could feel someone approaching from behind and tensed.

"What's up, man?" It was only his neighbor, Tyler, a scrawny kid maybe a year younger.

"Hey."

"You just come back from town? Pick up a shipment?"

"Maybe."

"I'll trade you for some 'shine," said Tyler.

"Eh." Sam had tried Tyler's moonshine once before and felt extremely sorry for that decision the next morning. *Where the hell does he find that shit?*

"I just got the new Resident Evil—you want to play some video games?"

"Maybe." Sam didn't mind hanging out with the guy, but his house sometimes reeked of cat piss. "I'm starving, let me get something to eat first."

"Okay, just come knockin', man."

He waited for Tyler to disappear before teasing his front door open. He listened, barely daring to breathe. He hadn't seen Terry's truck, but he couldn't be too careful. After a few seconds, his ears began to pick up the steady rumble of a news-broadcast and he recognized the blue, undulating glow of the television screen in the main room.

"Mom?"

Nothing.

He exhaled, switched on the kitchen light, and slid over to the refrigerator, hoping for something edible.

"Eureka."

A delivery pizza box sat in glorious surprise inside. But, when he flipped open the lid to find a completely uneaten pie, he became suspicious. He put the pizza on the counter and crept over to the opening of the living room. His eyes adjusted to the gloom. Mom was sprawled on the couch—alone, at least—with one leg thrown over the back and one arm trailing the carpeted floor. As Sam stepped closer, he saw that she had the cordless phone gripped in one hand, clutching it to her chest.

Waiting for Terry's call all night? Resentment washed over him.

He moved closer and listened to her breath, escaping in gentle snores, lips parted and eyebrows raised in dreaming wonderment. Sam kneeled next to the couch, slipped the phone from her hand and set it on the floor. That's when he saw it. Bending over to investigate, he picked up an empty vodka bottle. *So she was waiting for Terry.*

"Sorry Romeo had other plans," Sam whispered and dropped the bottle with a hollow thud. He plopped down next to her, not worried about waking her any longer, knocking her leg off the back of the couch to fall against his back.

"It's too bad you missed that Rotary Club meeting at Big Joe's you were so excited about." The sour tang of consumed vodka wafted up from her disturbed nest. "Don't worry, I took notes for you."

He searched around for the remote, found it lodged under her ass, and yanked it out. He switched off the television, wondering why in hell she had been watching the news. What did she care about current events? He glared hard at her undeniably pretty face, hardly the worse for all its wear, as if he could burn an answer from her. Her features were smooth and serene in a dream state and he had the urge to stab his fingers up both nostrils to wake her up. *Wake up, Mom. You spend your whole life in a fucking dream.*

"Oh hey, I know you were interested," he said, now feeling entitled and sorry for himself. "That PTA meeting you were looking forward to is next week. Start my senior year with a bang, right? Don't worry, I'll get the Bimmer all shined up for you, so you can roll in looking hot."

Sam glanced toward a window that he knew looked out over their corroded, beat-up car, permanently parked next to the trailer. He remembered how desperately she had wailed when the Oldsmobile died for good, only days after they had moved to Shirley County. She had talked about a new start, something about better disability laws here, and getting help for her Fibromyalgia. The memory of her perky, hopeful face, describing the 'quaint little mountain town' gave Sam's guts a twist. It had only taken him a few minutes upon arriving in Shirley to realize they wouldn't be living in the quaint section.

Whatever, who cares? He wasn't some rich little shit, who had to have crisp lacey linens on a damn porcelain washstand every morning and five-course fucking dinners every night. They were doing alright even if they couldn't afford a lot. He picked her fallen hand up off the carpet, and held it, watching her sleep.

Afford...

Suspicion flickered.

How the hell could she afford that bottle of—

He leaned over to read the factory label on the empty bottle.

"Grey Goose. Terry's favorite. If he never showed up, where did you get the money to pay for a bottle of Grey Goose vodka, Mom?"

Sam shot to his feet and stomped through the center room, blasting through his bedroom door in a fury. Scanning his shelves, he quickly confirmed that another of his mint condition Star Wars action figures—still in the box—was missing, and he knew exactly where it had disappeared to.

"Damn it, Mom."

The figures had been purchased by his maternal grandmother, right after the trouble with Sam's dad, the rare characters painstakingly sought out and bargained for. Grandma was an eccentric old lady, and had the crazy idea that the figures could be worth a fortune in years to come, and she had stored them away for Sam's college fund. Her will entrusted them to his care, and she made a last written request that they be saved for "his future." Sam doubted they could actually help pay for college, but they were from her, so they were precious to him.

Then, a couple years back, his mom cajoled him to take the boxes out of storage, saying how lovely they would look in his room, "You should care more about decorating, now that you're starting to have girlfriends."

He had been reluctant, annoyed with her for the "girlfriends" comment.

The figurines were probably worth plenty of money all together, if not really enough for college. She persisted and he relented. He didn't understand at first, but it wasn't long before he figured it out: not two weeks after Sam brought them home, and displayed them on do-it-yourself shelving from the home improvement store (what a joke), one of the figures had mysteriously disappeared. He railed until his mom admitted to selling it on eBay. Furious, Sam insisted on returning them to storage, but she cried for hours. She looked so pathetic he apologized and just tried to forget about it. Periodically, when cash got low though, he would find another figure missing and they would rehash the fight.

He never bothered to confront her anymore, dreading her tears and his guilt. Instead, he reproduced the lost characters on his walls: in marker, paint, pencil, crayon—whatever he had on hand. His new Shirley County girlfriend, Candy, was an art nut and was enraptured by his "ferocity" and encouraged him to "use it in his work."

He could be so enraged that the drawings would come out looking totally unreal. Sometimes, in the midst of recreating a dumb Storm Trooper or some alien's features, he would remember how important it had been to his grandmother. It was all so foolish. Then, he would scratch through his drawing, raking at the wall with his nails or his pocketknife, the pain too close and the memory to dear to relive it, again and again, in whatever shitty trailer park his home was currently camped.

Sam surveyed the boxes.

"Who's missing now?"

Admiral Akbar.

Trying to recall the alien's features, he plugged in his ear buds and scrolled to a good playlist for the occasion. He rifled through a box of broken oil sticks and worn chunks of pressed charcoal (a gift from Candy), found a blank spot on his grubby bedroom wall, and went to work. He attacked the wall for almost an hour, until he felt a modicum of relief, and stepped back a few paces to survey his work. His boot thumped against a box of paints Candy had recently urged him to take home from The Palace.

Why not?

He squirted paint directly on his hands and did whatever he felt like with the drawing for a while. It felt good. Finally finished, the drawing—technically a painting then, he guessed—wasn't bad.

"Thanks, Candy," he said out loud and actually laughed. He saw page after page in his mind of all the expressionist artists she had schooled him with; in support of Sam "finding his voice." He cocked his head sideways and regarded his recreation of the admiral. He shrugged and tossed the tubes and sticks back into the box, his hands stained with sooty charcoal and sticky with paint, then let out a long sigh, loosening his shoulders.

Sam decided Candy herself was what he needed. It was late but she was a night owl and might still be up. Fishing his cell phone out of his pocket—belatedly wishing he had washed his hands first—he pushed her speed dial key. She picked up on the second ring. He could hear her father gabbing in the background, "always rambling on about something," as Candy put it.

What does her dad get so jacked up about this late at night? He knew the man would often record old Masterpiece Theater re-runs or History Channel specials, and then make Candy watch them with him, talking over the television instead of watching it. *Sounds like you're ready for bed, Mr. Vale. I need your daughter to myself for a few hours.*

"I thought you'd never call, what took you so long?" Candy whispered into the receiver.

"Hi. Meet me?"

"Half an hour." She hung up without waiting for Sam's confirmation.

"Perfect," Sam agreed to the dead phone line.

He'd worked up a sweat drawing and he felt suffocated in his crowded little house on wheels in the musty, windless cove. He couldn't get to Candy fast enough. Not even glancing at his mother, who was still passed out and snoring on the couch, he strode through the trailer and out the front door. He let the spring snap the door shut behind him with a sharp, metallic slap.

chapter nine

Charlotte Finley massaged her temples, careful not to smear the long tails of black eyeliner, and tossed aside her dog-eared copy of Kerouac's "On the Road."

Where is that little Hershey squirt?

It had to be past nine by then; he must have had a rough night at After Dark, the little hidey hole in the hollows that passed for a night club. She spun her chair around and kicked her high-heels up to rest on a copper beer keg adapter. She thought about kicking it in an inconspicuous location.

Uncle Rottenbrain Twatts would never know a leak from his tight little asshole. That moonshine probably smells just as fresh.

Instead, she got up off her perch and pulled her long pencil skirt down tight over her round fanny, then appraised that endowment in the copper mirror of a nearby distilling tank. She stuck her cheeks out further to swell into the convex reflection, gave one a slap, then licked her finger and mimed a sizzle on her hip. Leaning down to correct a lipstick smear at the corner of her mouth, she saw her uncle stumble through the front door. She leaned down lower and squeezed her cleavage together for his viewing displeasure.

"Girl," he sighed. He shuffled past her, exasperated and already sweating in the muggy morning. "I can see clear down to your navel. Why you dress like that?"

"It's funny you should think of something shaped like a navel, when gazing into peaches, Uncle Boobie—I mean, Bobby." She followed him back into the man-cave they called an office, stepping around a collection of empty beer bottles. She kicked a stray cigarette butt. *Nasty monkeys.* "Where were you poking that gaze of yours last night, anyway?"

Robert Watts pinched the bridge of his nose and whined, "I don't have the head for that crap this morning, Charlotte; what are you doing here?" He was no match for Charlotte, whatever she had planned. He plopped some Alka-Seltzer into his Irish coffee and lumbered onto the closest Barcalounger, his eyes closed in a wince as the recliner careened backwards against his weight.

"I know; I should be at church," she vowed hollowly, in a cherry-red pout. Her uncle nodded in dazed, self-righteous agreement until she added, under her breath, "I have so many…sins to confess. Maybe I will, next time I see Father Ringold."

Robert's blood-shot eyes ratcheted open, his pudgy knuckles turning white on the armrests—she had his full attention.

Charlotte smirked. *Nothing wrong with a little threat and a diddle sweat.*

She rifled through desk drawers and paperclip holders that held random trash, wrappers, lost pen caps, and flicked a cockroach off the table lamp, wondering exactly how far she could push it. She was so tired of being a Finley Minion to the Squattin' Twatts. Looking over at the shivery mass of quaking blubber that was her uncle, she wondered how it had happened, not for the first time.

They were all equals in the beginning, both families moonshiners and both selling it fair and square; but somehow, in the salad days things got nasty, and—Charlotte still didn't really know how—the Wattses ended up cranking the gears while the Finleys ended up being the grease. *We kept making the product and they kept running the show; a case of hard work not paying off.* She thought of her honest, hardworking father, who, for all of his ethical convictions and moral codes, was now employed as a menial house servant. His hands were clean but his wife had died cleaning toilets. His brother Virgil hadn't minded slaving away for pennies on the dollar either, and now that the Wattses could smuggle in the fancy stuff, moonshine sold cheaper than ever. Virgil had built the very distillery that the Wattses now charged him to use, their own "bourbon" label produced and bottled in New York.

But that was the problem with hard work and ethics: they just didn't pay. Ideas did, and Charlotte had an idea. She had looked into the Di Brigo kid and, sure enough, he had connections to a winery back in Italy. Imagine if she, Charlotte Finley, could be the sole wine connection for a hundred miles in every direction. Those valley whores she saw at that joke of a Rotary Club meeting sucked up the Chardonnay by the bucket, and they had to drive across two counties to buy it. But they bought it by the case. Not only that, but now Joe Robinson was planning to open a "private" dining area that sold beer and wine to rich tourists. They'd all pay top dollar, and she knew how to bring it in cheap.

Thanks to connections of my own…

"You're a spunky little gal, Char," Joe had told her. All trussed up and swollen with need, he would've told her anything. "You find me the best buy, if you think you can, and I'll get it out the back door."

"Really? You trust me?"

He had accepted the handcuffs with a Cheshire cat grin, but that didn't necessarily indicate trust. With the pervs, they usually liked to get scared about what they *didn't* trust. It made powerful people feel controlled, and that got them off. *Whatever works, ain't no nevermind to me...*

"Let's see what you come up with, honey."

She made him pay for calling her "honey" and he thanked her more than usual afterwards.

"We'll work something out," is what he had said about her business proposal. Charlotte didn't really trust Joe either, but she could probably get him to do anything, especially with the promise of a whip or a riding crop. She smiled, thinking of the fun she had in store, then glanced at her poor, terrified uncle. He was no fun at all. She wished she was up against a little more testosterone; she had purposely come on a day that she knew he would be alone, unaided by his muscle crew. *This is boring, though. Poor little lamb.*

"Alright, I'll get straight to..." she swept one leg over his rotund midsection, her spiked heel narrowly missing his nose, "...the meat of it." Her ponytail swung around to whip him in the face, and she sat down with her crotch firmly placed over his own. *Never anything firm down there.*

"Oh, come on, now," he complained in a wretched strangle, and pulled his hands away from his lap like it was wildfire, raising his hands to shield his eyes. The split in her skirt ran the length of one thigh, reaching nearly to her waist. "My god, I can see straight through those lacey underwears. Jeezus, Charlotte—what do you want?"

If there was one thing that sent Uncle Robert into a panic, it was pussy. Charlotte rucked up her skirt a little further to make sure he had a good view, then she leaned forward for emphasis, pressing her pelvis into his limp groin and rolling it around in a smutty little dance. She almost laughed at his stifled whimper, and had to calm herself for a few seconds. She reached a hand up to cradle his ear and whispered, "I need a project."

"Whoo, girl. I figured there was something going on, for all the time off you been getting."

"Tyler Finley, you git." Robert bolted upright in a panic, tumbling the little vixen from his lap.

"Hey, Ty," she greeted her pimple-faced cousin, holding onto the arm of the chair to keep herself from falling to the sticky floor and ruining her favorite skirt. *What luck, a witness. You're in the palm of my hand now, fat boy.*

Charlotte wiped her palm off on her skirt with that thought. Sometimes you just had to get your hands dirty to get ahead.

Robert fumbled with his clothes: straightening his pants and stuffing his shirt in his waistband. He blustered past the sneering boy, his voice echoing in the cavernous warehouse, "Set to work or go home. We're talking business in here."

Charlotte stood in the doorway, making a show of readjusting her clothes like a frightened schoolgirl, while Robert came back with a warning look, a broom and a dust pan. He shoved the cleaning equipment in Tyler's hand, and slammed the door to the office in his face, the wooden blinds slapping against the window. A muffled curse came from the other side and a threat hissed underneath.

"You better fix that," Robert said shaking a finger in Charlotte's face, and walking an arm's length away from her to sit behind his desk. "Fix that misunderstanding."

"I'll fix him, when you talk business with me."

chapter ten

Big Joe slept peacefully, with cables attached to pressure points; IV's pumping, catheters draining and monitors beeping rhythmically. An old cathode-ray television, mounted high enough to discourage civilian fiddling, was mutely transmitting a "Price Is Right" re-run.

"I guess that's a re-run, do they still make that show?" Steph asked him. She tried to lounge back into the uncomfortable hospital chair and examine her nails. Nothing to pick, they were perfect. She smoothed her hair and sat quietly with her hands in her lap, looking at her shoes and thinking. Helen Collins had stopped by her house to talk about the new foreign exchange student. *Why is that my problem now?*

Steph was president of Andrew Jackson High's Parent Teacher Association, it was true. But she wasn't sure she wanted the hassle of anything to do with the Rotary Club anymore. It all seemed like fun at first—and a good excuse to get together with the girls—but a *foreigner* at Jackson? Steph's mouth puckered like she had just sucked on a lemon wedge.

She sighed and focused on Joe's slack face. "If only you'd wake up, big man. Take this off my hands and clear this Mieke Walsh slapdash up."

That woman thought she could just traipse into town, scoop up one of Shirley's most eligible bachelors, and start running the show. Not if Steph could help it. She folded her arms across her chest and shook her head. *No siree bob.*

Joe shifted in his sleep, his head rolling to just the right angle to produce a wet, guttural snore. Steph cocked her head to the side. *Just how well do Joe Robinson and Mieke Walsh know each other?*

"Time for Mr. Robinson's sponge bath." Steph jumped and turned to see a nurse, built like a fire-hydrant, bustle in sweeping aside screeching curtains. The nurse stopped short and grunted. "Oh. Thought you was the one with the black hair."

"Excuse me?"

"The one this man's always going on about? The black hair and the black eyes, on and on."

How often does Mieke visit? Steph sat up a little straighter in her chair. "An Asian woman?"

The nurse's eyes twinkled and she clamped her mouth shut—she'd said too much. She chortled and moved around the room checking monitor screens and rearranging cables. "I'll have to change his catheter, too, and you might see more than you bargained for. If you stick around."

Darn. Steph knew she had lost her chance for a little gossip by seeming too eager. "No, I should go. How long will he sleep?"

"Oh, all day, this one." The nurse belted out a humorless laugh. "And if he does come around, he'll probably just push his little button and go right back to dreamland."

Steph hadn't spoken to Big Joe since the collapse, so she had to rely on hearsay. His wife Pearl constantly retold the "fainting spell" story but Pearl had gotten that secondhand. All the reliable information Steph had was scraped together from the hospital staff's comments. Apparently, Big Joe suffered a couple of skull fractures when he fell and was in a lot of pain. His doctors had deemed it wise to keep him under observation for a couple days, especially on regular doses of morphine, with his unsurprising high blood pressure. That seemed pretty dramatic to Steph, and it had certainly been more than "just a couple days."

"Are you sure you should be doing that when he's unconscious? Seems a little unethical to me," Steph said, with a distasteful grimace at the way the nurse was moving body parts.

"Hospital schedule don't stop for nobody, honey. Monday morning sponge bath, first thing," the nurse said, unperturbed. She grunted at the considerable effort her task entailed. "You gon' let me do my job, or what, Ms…?"

The threat was clear: Steph wasn't family and could be barred from the intesive care floor. She had a mind to tell Ms. High-and-Mighty that Pearl Robinson herself had asked that she look in on him. Well, sort of. When Steph offered to help, Pearl was happy to accept; Steph had a feeling she needed a break from hospital duty.

Oh well, no reason to be ugly. She took her time rearranging the vase of roses she had brought that morning. They were just spectacular, and straight from her own garden. Glancing over, she got an unwelcome peek under the skimpy hospital gown, however. She made haste to the exit and didn't look back.

chapter eleven

"Hey, baby girl," George cooed and leaned in for a morning kiss on Candy's forehead. She clenched her shoulders and recoiled from the painful scrape of morning stubble on her father's chin. At least he had bothered to brush his teeth that day, even though he had once again forgotten how much she hated to have her hair ruffled, especially in the morning. Candy scowled at the back of his head, wrinkling her nose at the thinness of his embroidered silk robe.

She was in a sour mood. She hadn't slept well and she hadn't seen Sam in days. What was he doing all weekend? She still felt weird calling him, preferring to wait until he called her, even though she knew that was stupid. And she had that weird dream again, with her Uncle Brian. Why was she dreaming about that? She hadn't thought about it years. That night, her mom had also made an appearance, which was most upsetting. Back then was the last time she had seen her mom alive. Right before.

"Looks like rain today," her dad said with a yawn. He craned his head around the curtains that overhung the sink and fastened the tieback on the wooden cabinet next to it. He scrubbed his face and turned back to the kitchen table to smile at his disgruntled daughter, who hid her revulsion behind a peaceful smile. "Something's got to quench this heat."

"I better get going, then." Candy plunked her spoon into her empty cereal bowl. She had even drained the milk, a reminder lodged in her brain over a decade ago by Grandma Catherine; she could never pour cereal milk down the drain without some measure of guilt, warm and oaty-sweet as it became by the end of her Grape-Nuts. "I've got to stop by the shop and pick up those drawings from Ms. Willow to bring them to town."

"You'll never guess how this Rotary Club thing is turning out," George said, ignoring her plainly stated haste, as always, and speaking as though still in the middle of a conversation they had already begun in his head. He held her eyes and sat down, "So, it turns out Mieke and Joe have been cooking up this scheme for who knows how long, with this Italian foreign exchange boy. And he's not a kid at all, but a man."

Candy stifled a sigh, checked the time on the coo-coo clock out of the corner of her eye, and sat back down with feigned interest. Her dad had already told her about the exchange student several times.

"Oh, yeah? Some kind of prestigious thing to have one, right?"

"They had to apply and everything months ago, and never said a word to anyone. Can you believe that? Antonio di Brigo," George went on, rolling the r's with a flourish and raising his eyebrows. Candy knew he expected a laugh, so she delivered one dutifully. "Turns out, he's from Verona—which always reminds me of Zeffereli's Romeo and Juliet, I love that one."

"M-hm, me too."

"Well, it's interesting that his name is di Brigo, His family has lived in the Veneto region of Italy for generations. You see, common throughout Italy, but especially in the Veneto area, like Verona, they use the preposition 'di' to indicate parenthood. Many Italian names come from their professions or even nicknames, all the way back from the Middle Ages."

"Really? What does di Brigo mean?" asked Candy, actually interested.

"You know, I don't really know. We should look that up."

Typical. "So anyway, you said he was not a kid, but a man?"

"Oh, right. He's nineteen-years-old." He slapped his palms down on the table between them, rattling the teaspoon in the sugar bowl and leaning forward with anticipation.

That was new. "What? How can he be—"

"Well, I got this from Ian yesterday. Turns out, they have a dual enrollment program at his high school. A lot of schools in Europe do that. He'll be a year older than normal in his senior year. That's how this foreign exchange business that Mieke Walsh cooked up works." George raised his voice an octave and flipped imaginary hair when he said the woman's name. "You know how the Europeans are…"

Candy could tell he was on the verge of a political diatribe. Knowing she could be trapped in her seat indefinitely, she steered her father into a more manageable direction, fast. "Wait, wait—won't everyone freak out about him being nineteen?"

"Oh, you should have seen the reaction at the first hint of a foreigner here. They're gonna lose it when they find out his age," George predicted with glee, his eyes glinting. "Marge Tillman, that old cow—I thought she was gonna blow herself right out of her seat with that fart when she heard about the new Pakistani doctor—"

"Indian, Dad."

"Ejector seat," George exploded with laughter, wiping his eyes and turning to root in the cupboard for the coffee grinder. "Thank god I was on the other side of the room, so I didn't have to smell it. And then after Abe Waste-of-Good-Oxygen Becker found out about the Italian boy yesterday at the shop, he got all blustery and red-faced and said, 'We gonna have an eye-talian man living here for the whole dang year?' What an ignoramus. Then, the widower…" George shuffled around the kitchen, gradually retrieving his coffee supplies and gathering them around the grinder. Without stopping, he transitioned into a tangential topic. "But you know, I'll bet that we could work in some real-world experience at the shop for him. Part of the Andrew Jackson-Shirley County experience."

Amazing. He's trying to find a free labor angle with this poor foreign exchange student. Her dad was so cheap.

"Since this boy has work experience, and obviously a lot more work ethic than most kids around here…."

Great. She settled in for a long conversation. Didn't he hear her say she had to leave? Ms. Willow would be pissed. Candy always met her at Dad's shop on Monday mornings and brought the stuff she had worked on all weekend to Big Joe's; the poor old lady couldn't drive anymore and she depended on it. She would freak if Candy didn't get those drawings there before they opened; who knew why? She was old.

And, now I'll have to run all the way there and get sweaty.

She had let her dad's new assistant mechanic, Jo, borrow her dirt-bike the night before, but she had promised to have it back at the shop in the morning.

It had better be there—I can't run all the way into town for god's sake.

She hoped the ride down into the valley would dry her off after a jog to the shop. She looked wistfully out the glass doors in the next room that led onto their deck. The sunlight was blazing down, lighting up the plank floor as if it was on fire, the early dew long evaporated and the morning mist chased away.

Her dad was chattering on, not registering the stiffness of his daughter's back, her arm clutching the back of her chair, poised to go. "I always thought it would be cool to have real, die-cast replicas of the old classics. You know, like the '53 Chrysler—the New Yorker, maybe,"

"Yeah, that would be cool," Candy said absently.

"Well, it's good business to have more varied inventory."

"Uh huh…"

"You know, I always wanted to expand the shop into…"

She really hadn't wanted to arrive at Big Joe's sweaty that day. She was hoping to run into Sam—she had to. He usually had deliveries scheduled in Buffalo Square on Mondays. She pictured him hauling in bags from the supply truck, as she replayed each delicious second from the last time she saw him. She felt like she'd go crazy if she didn't at least talk to him for a minute. A blush started creeping into her cheeks as she thought and she started thrumming her fingers on the table.

"Oh, sorry," said George, "I know. You're going be late."

"It's okay. I'm good, Dad," she blurted stupidly, pushing thoughts of Sam out of her mind before they leaked out her ears. She stood and shoved in her chair, "I do have to go, though."

"Oh, and I saw Beth Robinson in town yesterday. I mean Beth Bennett. Guess she's married now. Has been for years—"

Candy froze. "Really? And?" *I know who "Aunt Beth" is—what?*

"She said John's coming with his dad next week."

"John?" Her heart seemed to have stopped.

"Yeah. I guess James is planning to take a sabbatical and run the family business for a few months, until his dad is himself again. Really, I think 'a few months' may be wishful thinking, a man Joe Robinson's age. Seems to me, James might need to think of a more permanent situation."

"Permanent? With John?" She almost choked on the words.

"Well I don't know about that," George corrected hurriedly, "But, I did hear that John will be attending Andrew Jackson High this fall."

What? Candy turned away from her dad's goofy, searching smile, and headed for the front door. "Wow...that's so awesome."

"It'll be nice for you two kids to be together again," George chuckled and turned his attention back to his coffee. "Have a good day, sweetheart."

Candy was already halfway across the house. "Thanks, be home late," she hollered, grabbing her backpack and shooting through the open doorway. She slammed the door shut just in time to muffle a surprised sob. She shuffled down the dirt driveway, her eyes blinded by sudden tears.

Prick. Now, I'm late. She knuckled her wet eyes with her fists. *Stop crying, you idiot.*

Instead of taking the path by the river that she usually preferred, which was rocky and winding, forcing a pedestrian to poke along, Candy took the longer, paved road to the shop to make some time. She slung her backpack over both shoulders and broke into a jog, willing herself to breathe more evenly and calm her racing heart into a comfortable, regular rhythm.

John.

She was overjoyed to hear that he was coming, and would likely stay for a while. Maybe even the entire school year? They had been close friends since childhood, when he had started spending summers with his grandma. Candy's Grandma Catherine lived on the property adjacent to the Robinsons' house, and since she spent most of the summer playing there, and in the surrounding countryside, it was natural for two kids of the same age to become summer buddies. John was a city boy, and he had been clueless about how to play outside in the country. The first time she brought him down to play in the creek that bordered her grandma's backyard, he walked right into the nettles growing along the bank, the stingy leaves and creepers tangled up and threaded through every toe.

He actually cried, Candy remembered, with a healthy measure of compassion. Those nettles stung like heck. He was embarrassed, but she showed him how to squeeze the juice out of jewelweed flowers and cool down the rash, making barfing noises, like the flowers were puking up the juice, so he'd laugh. They were best friends in an instant.

Candy reigned as queen of the countryside, with her superior knowledge of the flora and fauna, and John demurred to her leadership outdoors. She knew about the caves on the hillside where the foxes made their dens. She taught him how to climb the maple trees with a pocket full of hundreds of helicopter seeds, and then toss them into the branches to send them swirling down like pink snowflakes. She also knew how to creep up behind a horse named Popcorn, who lived on her uncle's ranch, and open up her umbrella so fast that the horse farted when it jumped and ran away, neighing with indignation.

John was the best at telling stories, especially scary campfire ones, and he was even better than she was at building a fire. He started attending Boy Scout meetings with his dad after he went home that first summer. Candy suspected he wanted to impress her, with his new knowledge about nature, when he returned to Shirley the following year. She let him build the first campfire of the summer, with his dad watching from afar. She was impressed. John didn't need any help at all. That was when Candy realized John was smarter than she thought, his brain filled with exact knowledge that he could always recall with ease. At the age of eight, he had methodically and precisely built a beautiful campfire, ringed by river-smoothed stones in a perfect circle. He placed neatly sawn logs for sitting safely beyond the spark zone. After the fire was well underway, he called to his dad to bring out the s'mores, and they all roasted marshmallows on hickory sticks gathered from the yard.

That was the first of many campfire nights over at the Robinsons', the summer air cool on their backs and their faces heated by the fire, melted chocolate running down their hands, filthy from a day of playing in the woods. John was an endless supply of long, drawn-out scary stories, embellishing them anew every telling. He always had surprise endings and loved to use sound effects.

And all that stuff with Uncle Brian. He never made me feel weird about it. Candy's thoughts turned sour, and she pushed her unsettling dreams of the past several nights away again. *Anyway, campfires were when we were kids. And we aren't kids anymore.*

About the time they were both entering their teens—and puberty—John had started spending the better part of his summers as a counselor at Camp Wekeima. The first summer he worked at the camp, he had bugged her for months and months beforehand, emailing her links to the website and writing tales of adventure awaiting. She had no intention of joining him there, and she told him so, but he wouldn't believe her until a couple weeks before school let out for the summer. She remembered the phone call vividly.

"You're kidding me. You haven't signed up yet? Candy, there might not be any spots left for counselors anymore. They have to do background checks and everything."

"I know, John. I'm not going." John hadn't spoken for several seconds, the silence on the other end making Candy's flesh crawl with guilt and impatience. "Hello…?"

"Why not?" He was still insistent. "We would have so much fun. I know so many other people that have done it and they go every year, it's such an awesome summer. We would have such an awesome summer—"

"Look, I just don't want to," Candy had snapped. "Why can't you get that through your thick skull?"

She instantly regretted saying it (and still did), but there was no way to take it back.

"Fine, I guess I'll see you around, then." John was obviously hurt, but he wasn't one to act brashly, and he held the line to say, "Bye, Candy."

It was Candy who hung up without saying good-bye. She didn't know what she got so pissed off about, but she remembered her blood was boiling. She felt oddly panicked by being forced to go that far away to do something that…well, actually sounded fun. But, anytime she tried to reason with herself to explain why she didn't want to go, she felt blank.

I just didn't want to. I just don't like to leave home. She was confused about it but there it was.

Even though John had come to Shirley for a quick visit before the camp started, the two had avoided each other. Candy blew off efforts to unite them, and she was sure John did, too. She wondered if his grandma was as embarrassing as hers was.

"Pearl said John's in town, honey. She invited us for lunch—don't you two want to play together?"

"Grandma, please. We're too old for playing."

"Oh, is that what it is?"

"What do you mean 'that'?"

"He's a good looking boy, isn't he?"

"What? Gross, Grandma."

"Well, what? You don't have to sleep over or anything."

"Forget it."

"If you want to, though, I'm sure Pearl could put you in separate rooms for the night."

"Ugh."

"I think it's sweet, and it would all be very proper."

Candy's face still went hot just thinking about it.

John had returned for a few days at the end of the summer, right before school started, and they saw each other briefly, each of them ready to forget the fight after a few months of cooling off. Things were awkward. They kept in touch over email during the next school year but John decided to make Camp Wekeima an annual event. He said he was saving money for a car and that the Wekeima job paid well. Candy doubted John's reason for keeping the job and jealously clicked through pictures online that were obviously his girlfriend, more often than she was proud to admit.

John and Clara, picnic at the lake.

John and Clara, fun at the derby with her family.

Clara with birthday cake on her nose, John laughing beside her.

That summer, he hadn't come for a visit to his grandma's at all, and hadn't bothered to supply a reason. Candy tried to shrug it off, but she was crushed. She had pushed him out of her head, until her dad sprang the news on her. She had no idea how to feel about the prospect of his actually living in Shirley and going to school at Andrew Jackson.

Does he already know? Did he email me about it already? Candy wasn't too big on email after she and John had lost contact. Who else would she get mail from besides him? All the people she knew lived in Shirley and email was usually all garbage and school stuff. She often received messages weeks after they were sent, so John might have already sent something. She couldn't wait to check.

Nearing the Eastern Mountain foothills, where her father's shop lay in view, the road started to level out and Candy picked up speed. She rounded the last turn at an all-out run, dashing off the pavement through the trees, the slick soles of her worn sneakers slipping in the dirt. She lost her balance and caught herself on an outstretched yellow buckeye limb, upsetting a couple of its low-hanging, overripe fruit. They bonked her in the forehead and almost tripped her, the smooth balls rolling between her feet down the last stretch of hillside. Steadying herself and wiping the sweat from under her hair, she winced at the smell on her hands. *Stinky sap. Whew.* Without thinking she wiped her hands on her cargo shorts. Too late, she remembered where today's errand would hopefully lead, and how badly she didn't want to be wearing stinky shorts.

"Nice," she panted and shook out her tank-top to let her armpits breathe in the breeze.

Slowing down to a walk, she glanced around the front of the gas station, expecting to see Ms. Willow. Luckily, there was no sign of her, only her father's mechanic, manning the counter inside. She spotted her dirt-bike leaning against the side of one of the mechanics bays in the garage.

Thank you, Jo.

Candy blew her damp bangs in relief and changed direction to wait under the shade of the sprawling Magnolia tree in a neighboring yard.

"Okay…email…"

She pulled her phone out of her backpack and swiped to the home screen. Concentrating on her phone, she stumbled on a creeping tree root and, realizing she was nearing the trunk, she dumped her backpack on the ground and leaned her hand against the ancient bark. Finally opening her inbox, she scrolled through the entries logged several days earlier.

"Robinson, John," was stamped like a beacon, twenty-something messages down. She exhaled in relief, and plopped down next to her bag to read.

"Candy. You'll never believe it, but I am transferring to Andrew Jackson this year. Weird, right? I'm sure you've already heard about my grandfather, and how my dad needs to come help run things for him. I decided to come with him, but mom's staying here. Will explain more when I get there, but I'm really looking forward to seeing you and experiencing that "quiet" country life this year. John."

Candy savored a long, cleansing sigh, settling back against the solid tree trunk and trying not to think too much about the joy rushing over her. She let her head fall back against the old tree, looking up into its interwoven branches, the wide, oval leaves filtering the harsh sunlight overhead. Oblong, delicately scaled, green fruit that gave the Cucumber Magnolia its name were visible here and there; most of them already split open in places to reveal the bright red seeds within. John always said those seeds looked like poison jelly beans. She patted the tree above her head in reverence, always feeling more comfortable in the surety of such an old, constant presence. She closed her eyes, breathed in the sharp scent of leaves, and felt the cool earth under her hands.

"Candace?" A jarring falsetto sounded around the corner of the shop. "Candace!"

Feeling like Alice in Wonderland, she shook herself out of her fog and stood, dusting herself off and waving lazily to the frantic crafter, Ms. Willow. "Hello, ma'am. I'm here."

At least half an hour later, after co-appraising each piece and listening to detailed instruction on how the artwork must be handled, Candy gingerly stowed Ms. Willow's handmade treasures for transport. She really did make nice stuff, and Candy was happy to help her get it sold. Big Joe's wasn't an art gallery, by any means, but a fair number of tourists wandered into the grocery and the coffee shop where Mr. Robinson let artisans display their wares, and they always loved local crafts. Candy had heard the instructions many times before, however, and her patience to get on the road was nearing an end.

Come on come on come on. She was desperate to get the morning errand over with. Her heart skipped a beat in anticipation of what hopefully awaited her at Big Joe's, beyond Ms. Willow's craft displays. She donned her backpack and hopped on her bike, assuring the good lady of her artwork's safety on the ride into town.

"Now, make sure to put them in the front window and in the case, Candace."

Yeah, yeah. Candy fired up the engine to speed the last of the conversation along. Ms. Willow was almost as long-winded as her father.

"And don't let Joe put pricing stickers on them—tell him to use the cards I made." Ms. Willow launched into another repetition of her instructions. Nodding and smiling widely under her sunglasses, Candy gave her bike some gas. "Alright, thank you, Candace. You're a dear…"

"No problem, Ma'am. Glad to help."

Glancing toward the back door of the mechanic shop, as Ms. Willow finally took her leave, Candy wished once again for the foresight of leaving a spare of clean, sweat-free clothes inside for just such an occasion. Knowing it was her last chance to primp, she rolled her bike over to duck down and view herself in a window. She polished her teeth with the wrist of her leather jacket and ran fingers through her short hair, knowing it would just get crazy again on the ride. Looking around to make sure she was alone, she reached in her shirt and adjusted her breasts, smooshing them closer together in her sports bra to enhance her cleavage.

As she rolled away from the garage, she glanced down and saw remnants of a mud splatter on the inside of her Suzuki's front fender and smiled. It hadn't rained the previous night; Jo must have gone looking for trouble. At least she had attempted to wipe the bike clean after "muddin'" and Candy saw the gas gauge registered at full.

Think I might like this Jo. Maybe I should go thank her for the gas. Candy shook her head and blew her breath out through her lips in a raspberry. Why was she so nervous? First, she was anxious to get there, and then she was stalling. *He'll be working all day. Probably just say hi and good-bye, anyway.*

She ran her fingers through her hair again.

Well, Sam likes me messy.

She pulled away from the gas station in a roar of determination. Speeding away from the mountain, along the valley road, she hoped that at least she would smell like fresh air when she showed up.

chapter twelve

"You roar in like a parade," Sam said, hooking a finger into Candy's belt loop and reeling her in.

It was hard to keep her thoughts together when his face was so close to hers. "A parade?"

"Dirt bike echoing off the water, red hair screaming in the wind." He smiled, but he was watching her mouth, not her eyes. "That yellow jacket, where'd you get that?"

"This old thing?" Her lemon yellow leather jacket was her favorite vintage eBay find. "I don't remember. You like it?"

"Yeah. I do."

How does he make three simple words sound so naughty? When his voice was husky like that, Candy felt it in her thighs.

"Comin' up!" Ricky Mendez's voice sounded the alarm on the stairs leading from the cellar, and Sam moved away from Candy with a scowl. He turned back to the pushcart he was supposed to be manning and Candy spun away to go finish setting out Ms. Willow's display.

"Wait…" Sam stood the cart up and, keeping a grip on the handle, twisted around towards Candy to stop her hasty retreat. "Hey, if you have a minute after you're finished, you want to come over to the Buffalo Lodge with me to drop off their shipment?"

"The Buffalo Lodge?" she stopped, surprised.

"Yeah, Ms. Collins gave me the key a while back." Sam gave her a gleaming, heart-stopping smile. He had her complete attention and he knew it. "She got tired of meeting the supply truck when her brother couldn't drag his hung-over ass out of bed. There's nobody there, we could hang out for a while."

"You're done working?"

"Well, we don't have much of a delivery today. Since the 'bossman' is in the hospital."

"Bossman?" She couldn't imagine Sam thinking of anyone as a bossman.

"That's what Ricky calls Joe Robinson," he said with obvious distaste. "Guess Shirley's at a standstill."

"Oh yeah, I know." Candy grasped at her chest and made a hysterical face. Parents were so easy to ridicule out of earshot. "Everybody's in a dither, can't run the town without him."

"Anyway…" Sam said, finding her hand. "Larry told me they need to overhaul the whole ordering system. I think we may have a minute."

Candy's pulse was racing. She tried not to squeak in astonishment when she said, "Really?"

"When you're done with your stuff, come around to the back and we'll walk over together."

"Okay."

He leaned in with warm, soft lips. His hand reached for her and she felt him touch the fringes of damp hair that still clung to the back of her neck. "Sorry," she whispered into his mouth. "I'm a little sweaty."

He pulled back, his eyes holding hers for several heartbeats. "I like it." One side of his lips rose in a crooked smile; he winked, then released her and turned back to his work.

Whew. Candy gathered her wits enough to go back to hers. She finished in record time, though she tried to slow down and pretend her little charity gig was more important than it was. She was rounding the corner at the top of the stairs, casing the scene below, when she heard Mrs. Mendez call Sam's name and held back.

"Samuél!" She was waving a small parcel wrapped in brown wax paper over her head. Moving slowly, on joints still morning-stiff, she sent her authority ahead of her in a commanding voice and with the promise of motherly devotion.

"Yes, Mrs. Mendez?" Sam appeared from the cellar instantly. It was odd how polite he was when he wanted to be.

"You take this with you, in case I don't see you before you leave." She pressed a freshly assembled, fully loaded sandwich from the deli, without an identifying price label. Candy knew the wrapping well; Big Joe's deli made killer subs and Mrs. Mendez always piled on the extras.

"You must eat—you are so skinny, Samuél," she admonished him, shaking her head sternly when he reached in his pocket to retrieve his wallet. "No need to pay."

"Oh. Mr. Robinson always charges me—"

"Mr. Robinson isn't here, my boy." Rosa Mendez pinched his cheek, and then opened her palm towards Sam's face to thwart any further protests. She barreled away, shouting loving recriminations as she limped back toward the kitchens. "You boys work too hard. Work, work, work. You got to take care of yourselves. But since you won't, I will."

Sam smiled and nodded in silent agreement, letting her protective tirade wash over him.

Well, now. She must know more about Sam's home life than I do. Feeling like an eavesdropper, Candy pushed away from the railing and started towards him. Sam's boss Larry was on his way out of the restaurant, and he paused to give Mrs. Mendez a kiss on the cheek. Ricky was right behind him, and he did the same, before she waddled back inside.

"We're done, Sam. Get outta here." Larry gestured towards the Buffalo Lodge just as Candy came trotting down the steps. "I really need you to get into the buff—I mean get this stuff into the Buffalo fast. It's sensitive inventory."

Sam glanced over and saw Candy, then shot Ricky a desperate look. Ricky steered Larry toward the cellar stairs, saying, "Sensitive and *private*, man."

Candy was only a few feet away from them; she couldn't pretend she hadn't heard. She pursed her lips, and felt her blood quicken, but she thought she could let it slide. Whatever "it" was. She looked at Sam and was startled to find him shifting his weight awkwardly. *Awkward Sam— that's a first.* "Ready?"

Sam waited until the guys were out of sight, then he finally ran a hand through his hair, and smiled. "Yeah, let's go."

They eased the heavy cart around Big Joe's, and up a dozen or more brick steps, finally cresting the hill on the riverside and were hit with a warm Southern breeze. The Riverwalk was well-made with sand and earth filling in cracks or shifting cement. Moss filled in the details. It was a gentle uphill slope, effortless and open, with a perfect view of the mountains. Fresh air rushed through the ravine, bringing with it the earthy smell of muddy shoreline. Their fingers rubbed together around the handle of the cart, their shoulders bumping companionably.

Candy broke the silence, "So, Ms. Collins gave you her key?"

"Yeah, I think she likes me."

She rolled her eyes; all the ladies loved the mysterious dark visitor, Sam Castle, no matter what their age.

"She calls you Candace. Do you prefer that?"

"Do you? I mean, it *is* my name, but hardly anybody calls me that. My dad does sometimes. Old people do." It was a subtle dig. Immature, but she didn't care. She watched the Western Mountains until Sam found her eyes. "What? My mom used to call me Candy. I was her first daughter, after three boys and a husband—even four male dogs. She said I was like candy when she kissed me."

Sam moved one finger over on top of hers. "I agree. Your mom was right."

Candy pulled her hand back and Sam's eyes were wary. Intelligent. She wasn't ready to talk about her mom, and she was wondering how long before he asked about it. He watched her, waiting or wondering. She never asked him about his own mother. Should she say that?

He seemed to read her mind, though, and finally said, "I can't believe you've never been inside the Buffalo Lodge. It's a pretty imposing building in such a small town."

"I guess it is." She could see the lodge, just ahead, at the end of the Riverwalk. The familiar sight of the wind-worn stone, topped by a green copper roof, was comforting, though always remote and forbidding. "I don't know. The families don't get along."

"I thought your family's been here forever."

"My mom's family. Yeah, they have. But not until the 1840s or '50s, after the Great Potato Famine."

"Potato Famine?"

"McBride?" Candy pointed to her red hair. "Irish?"

Sam shrugged.

"You know, a lot of Irish immigrants came here back then. But the earliest frontiersmen got here first, like in the 1700s. It took a while for colonies to spread this far—hard to get over the mountains from the east and all. It was rough travel, with rough people already here. Few and far between, sure, but always ready for a fight."

"Indians."

"Yeah. The Sendalee's still have a nation here, you know?"

Sam shook his head.

"Well, anyway..." There was so much to the story. So much she couldn't remember.

"The Sendalee Nation..." he prompted.

"What? You're bored, aren't you? All the history."

"I love history."

"Yeah, right." How did she get onto history lessons with Sam? Candy was mortified. "I don't remember much of the history. Ms. Collins would be disgusted, tucked away in her castle on the hill—reading about Indian war ornaments or sacrificial rituals or something." She gestured to their history teacher's grand domicile, on the other side of the lodge, its tallest towers reaching high into the sky.

"Don't like the old lady, huh?"

"I do. I guess, just … the point is, those first settlers had to band together, and they formed a tight bond. Unbreakable. And impenetrable to some."

"Not that impenetrable," Sam said, dangling the keys at his hip. "We'll be inside in two minutes."

"Bet they wouldn't be too happy, either," Candy mumbled. She was almost to the back gates of the Buffalo Lodge. It was surreal.

"'They'. You mean the Collinses? They didn't want to help the McBrides when they settled here?"

"The McBrides were farmers—starving, immigrant farmers—and the Wattses were horse thieves."

"Watts? I thought we were talking about Ms. Collins."

"We were, but the Wattses have always been Lodge members. Big time."

"Ah, of course." Sam made a face, to pretend he had just been gifted with vital information, and Candy shoved him on the shoulder.

She could see him thinking, "Small towns and their family squabbles," and her face was aflame. He gave her a curious look, taken aback by her demeanor, then smiled and opened the rusted iron gate to the lodge's side courtyard. He motioned for her to walk through first, then followed on a cobblestone path, balancing the boxes behind him. When she looked back, he had his head cocked to one side, watching her. "So, who were the bootlegger's? You said the McBrides were Irish, right?"

"Hmph. I wish they were bootleggers."

"We're going in the back, over there," Sam jutted his chin toward a second wooden gate covered with clinging vines. A rotting trestle arched overhead, with tangled jasmine fighting for sunlight, the vines twisted together in tight coils around the diminishing support. Candy breathed in their heavenly aroma as she walked underneath, fighting the urge to flinch—the whole structure looked like it was ready to collapse. It was hard to tell if the wood was supporting the vines or the other way around. Sam brought the cart to a stop next to a steel door and Candy's gaze bore into the grimy frosted windows of the Buffalo Lodge's backside.

She felt so wrong being there. So uninvited. "Are you sure this is okay?"

"Why not?" Sam muttered, casually sorting through a clot of keys on the end of a chain attached to his belt. When she didn't reply, he turned to look at her with the obvious question in his eyes. "Hey." He ran a finger up her arms. "Goose bumps? It's got to be a hundred degrees out here."

She shrugged and looked back at the rotting trestle.

"It's just an old building."

"Yeah, sure." She met his gaze. He just didn't get it. The Buffalo Lodge was nothing to him.

"Come on, it's just us. I've done this a million times." He held the right key up with a triumphant smirk, fit it into the lock, and turned the doorknob. The door swung open with a creek, cold, musty air spilling into their faces. Candy stepped back a pace.

"Okay, so the door creeks, don't panic." He reached in and flipped the light switch to reveal…an ordinary office space.

What did I expect, coffins?

Sam pulled the cart over the doormat and produced a smile that she was helpless not to follow. "See? Boring desk, ugly carpet, sappy kitten wall calendar. Oh, look—there's even the cliché water cooler."

"I'm fine." Besides feeling a little childish, she actually was. There was nothing like seeing under somebody's skirts for regaining self-possession. She looked past Sam and the mundane office room to the doorway that led deeper into the lodge. "What's through there?"

Sam parked the pushcart next to a desk. "In there? That's a little more interesting, I have to admit."

"Are you just gonna leave those boxes?" She wasn't a fool—the "shipment" was obviously booze. "Doesn't that go in the bar?"

"I have no idea what those are."

"Yeah, right."

"None of my business, Candy Vale."

Sam headed towards the inner hall and beckoned her to follow with an outstretched hand. She accepted it, and sidled up close; still a little nervous she had to admit. Her breasts bumped against his back and she tripped over his heel. "Sorry."

"That's okay," he chuckled. He squeezed her fingers and led her out into a wide marble entryway; their steps echoing against a thirty-foot ceiling.

"Wow," Candy breathed.

The central staircase plunged past them. It lead to a sumptuous foyer: the handrail curled around ornately carved dancing women that stood guard at the top of each stair rail. A dusty crystal chandelier hung inert over a threadbare Persian rug. Candy stepped onto the richly patterned carpet. She spun, slowly, taking in the details of the Baroque balustrade. A circular gallery ringed the room overhead before reaching back into shadows.

"I never imagined it would be so beautiful. From the outside it's so old and crumbling. All mildewey."

"I think there's plenty of mildew inside, too," Sam said. He pulled her towards the mezzanine, dark in the recesses, around the outskirts of the main hall. "Look at these." He flicked a light switch as if he owned the place. The track-lighting ran under the entire upper gallery and the effect was instantaneous and brilliant—the bulbs shone down on half-a-dozen stoic paintings. Serious faces regarded her in disinterested surveillance.

Candy's sneakers squeaked on the checkerboard marble floor. "The

Collinses sure musta poured plenty of their money into this place over the years," she said reverently. Whatever she felt about the history, Candy loved art. Sam flipped the lights on the other side of the expansive hallway, introducing her to the other half of the dainties. He watched her reaction, as she spun around, her eyebrows shooting up in surprise.

"That's exactly the way I felt," he said.

Candy nodded, speechless, the faces were so realistic it was like she had an audience. Gilded paintings hung across the wall: a parade of Collins dignitaries. She looked from one intelligent face to the next and their eyes following her as she moved past.

"Those must be the oldest, by the way they're dressed," she whispered, pointing to the other side of the hall. She walked over to inspect them up close. The first few in line seemed to have been painted during a much earlier time; though there weren't dates on most of them. They were more refined—richer than what one would expect from painting in early Colonial America. "Shipped over from Europe? I don't know who could've painted them here."

"Probably."

After those few gauzy, pastel likenesses, there was a much more crudely painted portrait. Candy strolled over to stand in front of an image of a bearded man with generic features. He was wearing a leather jerkin with some kind of animal skin draped over one knee and a rifle resting on his lap.

"The legend, himself. Fredrick Jessup Collins. I remember him from History class," she laughed. "In my freshman year. He founded the first settlement here."

"He could be Daniel Boone. You think these Collins people might have been trying to prove something?"

Candy smiled and let out a steadying breath. What had she been so scared about? The paintings revealed the truth of the present: the people that had founded the town were once powerful but had faded into history. She thought Ms. Collins and her brother were probably the last of the line; neither of them ever married, and neither produced heirs.

Another painting that was quite different from the rest caught her eye. "Look. A Sendalee woman, right next to Daniel Boone. She looks important, like a princess or something. What was that thing about the 'Beloved Woman'?" She tapped her finger against her lips, searching her memory. "They were almost like female chiefs or princesses or something."

Sam looked from Candy's eyes to those of the Native American woman in the portrait; his face went slack with revelation. "You have the same eyes," he blurted.

"Huh?"

Sam pointed at the face in the portrait, "You got any Indian blood? I always wondered about your eyes."

She cocked her head to consider the painted woman's face more closely, and the hair stood up on the back of her neck.

"Eyes so dark in someone so fair. Almost black," said Sam. "Fathomless."

Candy chortled. She had always heard people say that her eyes were unnerving. "Those aren't my eyes. It's just a painting. How exact could the likeness of that woman really be...to me?"

"You can't see it?" asked Sam, incredulous.

"Not really."

But she could.

Candy stood in front of the painting and took it in. The Indian woman's portrait lovingly captured the unique and intimate details of a real woman's face and person—it was in no way a caricature, like the Danielle Boone painting. Her shiny black hair was parted in the middle and flowed like silk over squared shoulders. Her face was angular, but soft at the edges, and she wore a simple feather headdress with an elaborate brocade gown. Wisps of gossamer undergarments both covered and revealed her breasts. The hem of her gown stopped just above jeweled wooden sandals, and her ringed fingers rested demurely in her lap. The woman's smile was alluring but her posture was erect; the combination lent an air of aggression, and challenge, mixed with seduction. Her eyes twinkled with wit and private speculation, one eyebrow half-cocked, not with a need to please. A tiny plaque underneath read, "Ahnaanvwodi." No date.

"Turbulent waters," Sam mumbled. "I know that look."

"What?"

He looked at her pointedly and smiled.

"Me?" *That woman in the painting reminds him of me? How? She's gorgeous.*

He moved away from the painting, towards the vast marble staircase, holding out his hand to her. "Join me."

"What's upstairs?" Candy asked, ready to change the subject. She knew she had a temper on her and Sam hadn't seen anything yet. He knew nothing about turbulent waters. "We can explore?"

He looked back, his dark hair falling over his eyes so that she could only see his lips, one corner raised in a smile. "I think you'll like the upstairs."

Halfway up, she stopped, sniffing the air suspiciously and crumpling her nose. Ode de bar: stale cigarette smoke and the strange, sweet sourness of old liquor spillage. With realization dawning, Candy's face split into a wide grin. "Really?"

"Really."

When they reached the top of the stairs, Sam strutted over towards an expansive oak and brass bar with an astonishing array of liquor twinkling behind it.

"This is illegal in so many ways," Candy said, thrilled.

He reached up to the nearest hanging stained glass lamp. Feeling along the chain, to find the wire twisted within, he rolled his thumb along a power switch. A warm glow lit the countertop and bounced off the mirrored wall behind endless bottles of booze. "Trust me, no one ever sets foot in this place until after noon. What's your poison?"

"How, without them catching on?"

"They'll never know." He walked behind the bar, stretching his arms wide in illustration of the mass quantity of alcohol lining the shelves behind him. "They never do."

"What do you mean?"

"Rickie's been nipping the stock for years. Sample randomly, only half a shot from this one, half from that one. Gets lost in the shuffle."

"Yeah, I guess it would." Candy read some of the labels aloud. "Maker's Mark, Jameson, Jack Daniels, in the whiskey department. Absolut, Chopin, Grey Goose vodkas; Bacardi, Meyers, Captain Morgan rums." There was even more of the cheap stuff; the bottles went on and on in a rainbow of colors and a surprising variety of shapes, many of them not even labeled. Moonshine. "How do they get all this booze in a dry county?"

Sam shrugged.

"The unmarked boxes we brought—Larry's in tight with the Wattses, huh?" She had to ask.

Sam shook his head, his smile saying something about girls' big mouths. "How about Bacardi Limón?"

"Mm-hm, one of the boys, I get it. Girls talk too much?"

His eyes twinkled, but he kept silent on that score. Candy dismissed the unanswered question and swiveled around on her stool. "Limón sounds great, I've never tried it."

"Have you tried many rums, Candy?"

She shrugged, watching him pour. She could be tight-lipped, too, if that was the game.

"I guess not much would surprise me, coming from you."

"Really? Well, lemme show ya." She threw the drink back in one gulp and slammed the shot glass down on the counter with a defiant look, then wiped her mouth to cover her cough. She laughed, caught in her lie. She had actually never tasted rum.

His eyes gleamed, never leaving hers for a second. "Dimples."

"Mine? You like 'em?"

"Yes."

Goodness. She was trying to be flirty, but Sam was always so serious. "Well anyway, everyone's parents have liquor cabinets, right?" She kicked her feet against her chair as she swiveled back and forth. "Though, my dad is more of a Scotch man. I think his grandma's name was Mac-something."

"Family lines galore," Sam said. "I'll try the Scotch then, in your dad's honor."

He regarded the amber liquid in his glass, tinkling the ice thoughtfully. Candy suddenly realized that she had been talking about her family tree all afternoon, and the only family Sam had ever mentioned was his mother. And sometimes one of her boyfriends gave him a bloody lip. "Don't be jealous of family ties, they tie you down."

He shot her a piercing gaze that she couldn't read for anything in the world. Two more bottles came down from the shelves for sampling, plunked on the counter in front of her. Candy couldn't help but think of it as a challenge. She watched Sam saunter around to her side of the bar with a hooded gaze. He sat down on the stool next to her and swiveled her way with a smile. The alcohol was already buzzing through her brain and melting her knees. Hers were pressed against his like so much soft wax.

"So, have you ever heard old-time mountain music?" he asked.

"Have *I* heard old-time? Uh, yeah…," she giggled. *Bacardi Limón sure gets things rolling.*

"I mean, I haven't. Sorry. There's a concert at the campgrounds, is what I meant to ask. This weekend."

"Ask? Are you asking me out on a date?" She shoved his thigh away playfully, scooting her butt closer to his at the same time. "Yeah, I love that show. I'd love to go with you."

"Ricky offered us a ride. His brothers are all going, too."

"Oh—" She halted mid-squeeze and pulled her hand off of his thigh. "Like, a group thing."

He looked down at his boots. "Candy, I'm not gonna lie to you."

"What?" Her pulse raced. What was he about to tell her? Another girl? *I was so stupid to think—hope—we were exclusive. Neither one of us said so.*

"I don't think we could make it there on my bike." His face split into a grin. "Or even yours."

"Oh." She let out her breath and her shoulders fell in relief. "Right."

Sam smiled and fingered the ends of her tank-top, leaning closer.

Crap, I don't want to ride with a bunch of guys. Candy wanted Sam to herself. She had a thought. "Well, the campgrounds are right at the edge of my Uncle Ray's property. We could take the horses. If it's just you and me…"

"Horses? Are you kidding me?"

"Do I look like I'm joking? Well, I probably do," she laughed, trying to work the grin out of her cheeks.

He brushed his thumbs back and forth under her shirt, tickling her belly. "Only in Shirley County…"

"Have you ever ridden a horse, city boy?" She goosed his inner leg and he jerked in reflex. "I love to ride."

"Oh, yeah?" He grabbed her arm before she could pull it back and wrapped it around his waist, but she squirmed away.

Forget it, pal. Group thing my ass. Candy decided she did want to be asked out on a date. Officially. She slid off her barstool and wandered around. "So…the Buffalo Lodge…"

The bar was almost an island in the large ballroom, the room circling around it in clusters of squatty leather armchairs and baize-topped card tables, with brass floor lamps and cigarette urns sprinkled throughout. Walls were decked with flat screen televisions, dartboards and chalky scoreboards, or racks of cues for the half-dozen pool tables that lay just outside the inner seating area. Towards the rear of the building, Candy was surprised to find a small dance floor with a shining grand piano at the far end.

"Wow, look at this." She waved him over and skipped behind the piano to sit. "Who woulda thunk it—in here? I wonder if it's in tune." Picking out "Ode to Joy," she looked up, her face bright, "I think it is."

Sam followed her halfway across the dance floor and stopped to watch, with his hands in his pockets.

"Come play with me. Do you know how long it's been since I played a piano? Grandma Catherine got rid of hers." She carefully began the duet that any child of a large family with a piano would know, "Heart & Soul," and once re-familiarized with the keys, she bounded through the chords with confidence. "Come on, it's a duet. Don't you know this one?"

"Sorry." Sam held up his hands, fingers still taped for moving heavy merchandise. "Still gotta work later."

"Oh, come on." He was so weird about his hands, she had noticed. Fastidious. He watched her bang away, joyfully humming the tune in harmony as she played. She felt like she was glowing she was so happy. "I love it!"

"Beautiful," he agreed. "The piano, too."

Whoa, okay. She tried to stymie her surprise. Sam thinks I'm beautiful. "I'll just play both parts then, Mr. No."

He shrugged, then stuffed his hands back into his pockets and began to wander the other way, toward the pool tables. Candy jumped up from the piano bench to join him, plucking a cue from the wall on her way over. She tossed it from one hand to another, challenging.

"You play pool, Sam?"

"Do *I* play pool?" He crossed his arms over his chest, flexing the knuckles of one hand. "You don't want to know."

"Oh, but I do. I'd love to know more about you, Sam Castle."

He leaned against the table behind him and followed her with his eyes as she flitted around the room looking for chalk. He was so intense, fixing her like a predator. Candy swallowed hard, chalking the tip of her cue. "You've got to play something with me, Sam. Afraid of a girl beating you?"

"No." He grinned, those green, beast of prey eyes lighting as he moved through the maze of tables to get closer to her.

"My dad has a pool table in the basement. I warn you, I'm pretty good." She rapped the cue against her palm and changed direction to put another table squarely between them. Her foot got caught up in a fallen magazine and she glanced down to catch herself. When she looked up, he had already stalked her around the other side.

"I bet you are."

Placating me. But she loved when he looked at her like that. "You might be surprised," she sang, leaning across the table to gather the balls together for a game.

"Nothing would surprise me about you."

"You never know..."

She made to feint once again, but his hands shot out and grabbed her hips. He spun her around and pinned her against the table, his grip as hard as iron. His body engulfed hers, measured breaths blowing against the back of her neck.

"Got ya," he whispered, barely audible. His lips brushed behind her ear in a gentle kiss.

Candy tried to slow her own breathing, but it was only speeding up, the heat of him bleeding into her. He was holding back, unsure. *Oh, come on.* She reached behind and hooked her fingers into his belt loops, pulling his hips against her and pushing back into him. Sam buried his face against her shoulder with a groan. She felt a boot shoved between her sneakers and one knee rammed between her thighs. Sam pressed her forward over the table, his breath rasping, as she dug between them to fumble his belt buckle loose.

The cool ivory pool balls scattered in front of her, rebounded, and rolled back against her arms in sweet rhythm.

chapter thirteen

"Yo man, let's roll." Larry hollered down into the cellar, banging his fist on the door. "Finish up your whore's bath, we gotta move out." He mounted the stairs two at a time and hopped into the cab of the truck, already idling at the summit. Sam Castle's wet head popped up through the ground. As he jogged up the steps, Amanda caught an exciting glimpse of his naked, tattooed chest before he pulled a T-shirt over his head.

A nipple ring. He's even dirtier than I hoped. "Hi, Sam," she called across the yard from the door of Big Joe's grocery. He looked around with a smile, searching for the origin of the female voice. When he recognized Amanda, he jerked his head back around and returned a perfunctory wave without breaking stride. He jumped into the passenger seat of the waiting truck and slammed the door.

Lindsay watched the truck pull away in a swirl of dust. "He seemed nervous."

"I told you—we had a moment," said Amanda. "He was bewildered. You should have seen him blush."

They both sniggered and clasped hands, heading back to Lindsay's family Land Rover.

"What are you gonna do? Do you think you guys will be together this year?"

"Please, my dad would freak if he found out. I feel sorry for poor Sam already, don't you dare mention a word to anybody."

"Oh, sorry…"

"Well, I mean, you can talk about it with *me*."

"He's totally hot, Amanda," Lindsay restarted on cue. "Did you kiss or anything?"

"I am not saying. I don't kiss and tell. But, I will tell you that he is one dirty boy." They burst into a fit of whispered giggling together, waving their hands like little birds to quell the uproar. The charade reminded Amanda of her mother enough to almost make her puke, but she needed to play the part Lindsay loved best. *Like a tasty salt-lick to grab a little calf's attention. Moo.*

"Have you ever seen him with Candy Vale? I saw the two of them together at the river's edge earlier this summer. You don't think they're a couple, do you? What if he's the unfaithful type?"

"Unfaithful? He's what—seventeen, eighteen? I doubt he's said any vows."

"You know what I mean, don't mess with a guy that cheats."

It didn't matter who Sam Castle was currently dating. Amanda would make sure he wasn't for long. "They're not together. Candace Vale is a total lesbian, Lindsay. Can't you tell?"

"What? Are you serious? How do you know?"

"Please." Amanda held up her hand for patience. "Don't you know a lesbian when you see one? Look at her hair, look at her clothes. She rides a dirt-bike? She even races in motocross, I heard. That's code for 'I'm a dike.'"

"I guess I never thought about it like that."

"How do you think one lesbo meets another?"

"Right."

"Well, anyway," Amanda reassured her, "trust me, I know. I've…heard things."

"Like what? You mean—"

"You girls, what are you gossiping about?" Lindsay's mom was heading towards the parking lot with two arms full of groceries.

"Sssshhhhh," Amanda hissed, drawing a finger across her neck. "Aunt Meghan, that looks so heavy. Lindsay, come on, let's help your mom."

Amanda passed the proffered grocery bag to Lindsay and took her aunt's purse off her shoulder. "Here, it's so hard finding your keys sometimes," she lectured, digging through the woman's purse. "You should make it easier on yourself and get them out beforehand. Hook them on your belt loop, like this." She pulled the largest key fob through a loop on her aunt's jeans and pushed the unlock button. *Beep beep.*

"Oh, good idea." Aunt Meghan sounded annoyed, familiar with her niece's condescension. "Thank you, little darlin'," she shot back, but Amanda didn't care. Her aunt loved her unconditionally and the show was for Lindsay.

"Aunt Meghan, don't you think you can spot a lesbian about a mile off?"

"Hhhmmm, I don't know that I've met many lesbians, Mandy."

"We know, don't we, Lindsay?" Amanda ignored the nickname taunt.

"Yeah, Mom. We can spot them a mile away."

Amanda knew Lindsay always felt bonded by a shared secret. She rolled her eyes at Aunt Meghan's back as she headed to the front of the car, then smiled conspiratorially at Lindsay, who nodded and stifled her humor behind her hand.

"All buckled in, girls?" Meghan pointed the air conditioner back towards them, adjusting her side mirrors and checking her reflection in her visor.

"Yeah."

"Yes, ma'am," Amanda corrected her cousin, catching her aunt's eye in the rearview mirror.

The Land Rover pulled out of the town center, tires squealing, and headed for the state highway leading southwards down the valley along the river. The small collection of buildings clinging to the peninsular hillside gave way to wide-open fields, with only a single country house nestled here and there. They sped over the bridge across the Tenakho River, and followed the road into the foothills of Western Mountain, where the houses were more densely packed, with smaller, manicured lawns and gardens. The Land Rover pulled into the driveway of a spacious stucco house, sitting between mirror-image dwellings that differed only slightly in tint and architectural details.

"They certainly are large and bright, though," Aunt Meghan muttered, as though in the middle of a thought. "And brand new. No old pipes or drafty corners like we have, I'll bet."

"Excuse me, Aunt Meghan?"

"You're always listening, aren't you, honey? So girls, Mrs. Ryan will be bringing you girls back here after your shopping trip, okay?" Meghan brought the car to an idle in the driveway. "Amanda, you're spending the night with us, so I'll take you to get your toothbrush and everything on the way to our place."

"Only if that's okay with you, ma'am."

"Of course, it is. Right, mom?" Lindsay whined.

"Yeah, honey," said her aunt, obviously straining for patience. Amanda narrowed her eyes at the back of her head as the two teenagers tumbled out of the car, in a continuous stream of gossip, grabbing purses and primping. Aunt Meghan already had the car in reverse before they reached the cobblestone pathway leading to the front door.

What is her problem? Amanda wondered where she had slipped up and resolved to pour on the sugar later that night to make up for it.

"Lindsay, make sure you get sensible shoes this time. And new panties, and a bra. I think you need the next size up, honey."

"Mom," Lindsay screeched, going almost purple. "I can handle it."

"Well, it's my money—don't waste it," her mom hollered from the street, then raised the window and drove off with a wave from inside.

"Yeah, Lindsay. I think you might be in store for a new *bra*."

"Whatever, wishful thinking." Lindsay, who was slight of frame and rather small chested, folded her arms over her chest and sulked. Amanda bounded up the stairs to the heavy oak door, coming to an abrupt stop at the summit that made her own large breasts bounce in her clinging blouse. Lindsay trudged up behind her, her mood considerably soured. Amanda looked back just in time to see her cousin eyeing her rear-end with a look of satisfaction; she knew she had been growing wider in that region over the last year. Lindsay brushed her hands over her own perky ass in her skinny jeans, and prepared her face for the opening of the door.

"Hi!" Gracie screamed, ripping the door open and scooping Amanda into a hug.

"Easy there, tiger." Amanda readjusted her clothes as Gracie enveloped Lindsay next.

"I am so happy to see you guys." Their friend had spent most of the summer away on a European vacation with her extended French family.

"We've missed you, so much. Tell us about Europe." Lindsay had been eager for dish all summer, Shirley County fun having fizzled out early, after the Chad Matthews tryst.

How long do we need to wait here on the stoop? Rich people with absolutely no manners are disgusting. "Is Jessica here, yet? It's so hot out here, Gracie."

"Sorry—come in, of course. Yeah, she's online, in my room." The chilly air inside was a gift from heaven. Or from Mr. Ryan's deep pockets. Whatever worked. "You guys thirsty or hungry? My mom won't be ready for a few minutes. Mom, Lindsay and Amanda are here."

Lindsay shook her head, "Thanks, we just ate at Big Joe's."

Is all you ever think about eating, Gracie? "I'm good, what are you guys doing online?"

The three trouped through the house, shoes clicking against the Mexican tiles. Their voices echoed through the cavernous front room and Amanda gazed through the panoramic windows at the manicured back yard. Even with all the expensive art and furniture from their travels, and the plants filling ceramic pots or hanging from artful baskets everywhere, the entryway seemed monstrous. The ceiling soared to almost thirty feet above their heads, with two higher stories jutting into the main room in lofts and alcoves, climaxing with a sunroof at the apex that filtered natural light.

Overcompensating. Mr. R probably has a tiny little peter.

"Hey, y'all." Jessica peeked her head over the railing of an upstairs loft. "I was just telling Gracie about the Italian foreign exchange student—I found him online."

"No way."

"What's he look like?"

The girls rushed up the carpeted steps, their bags and purses thudding against the walls, and their shoes suddenly muffled in the tight stairwell. They tumbled into Jessica sitting at the desk in front of a large flat-screen display.

"Is he cute?" asked Lindsay.

"What about Mark, Lindsay? Save some for the rest of us—you've been with the hottest guy on the football team since day one of freshman year."

"He's leaving for Florida State in two weeks, Gracie. That's so unfair. I need to get my mind off of him, don't I?"

Jessica began, as if on cue, "Tristan's the hottest anyway—"

"Gross!" Amanda hated that all her friends creamed their panties over her brother. It did give her some clout, but she hadn't found a way to use it to her advantage yet.

"Gracie, what do you care, anyway?" Jessica went on. "Martin would never let his precious little sister date someone in his grade. Your parents would freak, too."

"I know." Gracie loved to defer to that excuse, rather than admit that no guy would date her anyway. "Well, what does Antonio look like? What's his profile say?"

"It's not really his profile, it's his band's page. Band looks cool, though. They have lots of fans," Jessica said, scrolling down the page in illustration.

Amanda plopped down on the bed, no longer interested. "Band guys are so self-involved. He'll probably be missing his boys and playing air guitar the whole time he's here."

"No, he's the drummer."

"Mmm, that's a little better…"

"Drummers are so sexy," Lindsay agreed. "So masculine and powerful."

"Yeah, but that's why you never get a good look at his face." Jessica clicked through chaotic photos in dark bars; most of the clear shots were of the lead singer, who was not really handsome but definitely attractive. He was always clutching the microphone, his features frozen in a wailing grimace. "Antonio's so far in the back, and like banging his head and thrashing his drum sticks all the time. He's always a little blurry."

Amanda pooh-poohed. "Banging his head?"

"Well, I mean, not in a head-banger kind of way, but just getting into it, you know? Looks like a glam band. They're kind of cool."

"Sounds cool to me," said Gracie. Everything sounded cool to Gracie. "What's the name of the band?"

"Il Vagabondo. I already Googled it—that's Italian for 'The Tramp'," Jessica replied, raising her eyebrows mischievously.

"What's that mean?"

"You need Dictionary.com, Gracie?" Amanda laughed.

"No, I mean, like a slut? I know what 'tramp' means."

"'Tramp,'" Jessica read aloud, clicking over to the reference page she had already searched, 'A firm, heavy, resounding tread. The sound made by such a tread. A long, steady walk; trudge. A hike.' It doesn't mean slut."

Lindsay frowned. "Weird, that's kind of ominous."

"It means 'slut' in my book."

"Oh, Gracie." Amanda pinched her friend's plump tummy. "What's that book, the Bible? You're such a prude. Don't worry, Martin won't ever find out Antonio's your new shower nozzle masturbation material."

"What? My gosh, Amanda."

"Oh, come on, we all do it."

"My brother probably thinks I don't even have one," Gracie stammered, going pink.

"Trust me, Martin knows about girl parts," said Amanda. "Even though I doubt he's ever seen one. In the flesh, if you will."

"I don't want to hear about it." Gracie plugged her ears as the other girls howled. It was no secret that her brother wasn't a lady's man.

"I think it's romantic," Jessica said in her deep, husky, Southern drawl that Amanda would have killed for. "I mean, he's in this band named after basically the need to roam, and here he is, traveling to Shirley County. What are we in for, girls?"

Their laughter died, and the silence loomed, as Jessica clicked through snapshots. The girls closed in around the magnetic screen.

chapter fourteen

Candy looked at her watch again. She pulled her phone out of her pocket and scrolled to Sam's last text: *"if not there by 7 probably won't get there today"*. It was 7:30.

She slapped a mosquito on her shoulder. There wasn't much going on in Buffalo Square on a Thursday night. *Shoulda gone over to Ender's Village to see if they're doing anything there.* But she really didn't want company. Not from anyone but Sam.

The air was muggy in the courtyard in summertime, but she wandered in that direction all the same. She had been thinking about that painting of the Sendalee woman. Sam was so sure that Candy was somehow related to her.

Do my eyes really look like that? She was so exotic.

Not the hair, obviously. She ran her fingers through her own. Candy's thick red shag was still damp from her shower, even after the ride into town on her bike. And she was so fair. She looked down at her arms, pale as milk, in the gloaming.

But my eyes? He called them fathomless. That was exactly how she felt staring into Sam's eyes. Though she tried not to stare (difficult as that was), she often felt lost in them. *Fathomless...*

Without warning, the front door to the Buffalo Lodge opened.

Crap!

She was jolted out her reverie and she cast about to find something that would explain her loitering in front of the lodge. She couldn't run away. Too obvious and childish. There was nothing close-by but the bronze buffalo, so she busied herself looking at its plaque.

Ms. Collins closed the door behind her. The tinkling of a grand piano and throaty masculine dialogue bellowing over some televised sports game tumbled outside, an echo of the hubbub within filtering through the stained glass paneling of the front entrance. She picked her way down the old stone steps, watching her feet while Candy's color skyrocketed in embarrassment.

"Why, Candace Vale. Hello there."

"Er. Hello, ma'am."

"Can I help you with something?"

The entrance to the lodge was far enough away from anything else in Buffalo Square that Candy's presence there would obviously seem strange. "Oh, just…you know. Doing some research." She studied the plaque harder hoping for the look of taking mental notes.

"Research? That's nice to hear."

"Well, my hometown and all."

"You won't find much history there, I'm afraid. The buffalo is simply an icon borrowed from the organization. No buffalos ever roamed here."

"Yeah, of course," Candy guffawed, feeling examined under the woman's searching gaze, even though classes hadn't even started yet.

"What were you looking for, exactly, dear?"

Oh, no. How could she have been so stupid as to talk about research with the resident history teacher? Now she'd have to come up with something that made sense. After all, she'd have to see Ms. Collins every day for the rest of the school year. Such a champion for education was sure to follow up. "I guess, just the early stuff. Like the Native American history."

"How wonderful. You'll hear plenty about that in History III, I assure you."

"Oh? Cool."

"Not much in the library over there," she motioned to the used bookstore. The top floor of the converted Victorian house was a tiny library. "But, my own library is quite extensive."

A birdcall sounded from Candy's pocket. New text. "Excuse me," she said as she fumbled for her phone.

"meet me there" was the message, from Sam.

Her heart skipped a beat and she punched in, *"ok"*. Send.

"A summons?"

"Oh." Candy looked up to see a knowing smile. "I'm sorry. I forgot I promised to be somewhere."

"I understand. Until next Monday, Candace."

"Sure. Bye, Ms. Collins," she called over her shoulder as she raced towards her bike.

chapter fifteen

Steph balanced the stacked Pyrex containers against her hip with one hand, hauling grocery bags onto her shoulder with the other, then slammed the trunk shut with all the force she could muster. She had already hooked her key fob into a belt loop, and she fumbled blindly to find the lock button. "Beep, beep," said her shiny silver Honda and flashed its headlights.

"Oh—thank you, Henry." She turned around to see the kindly old janitor walking up to her with a rolling dolly. Steph had called ahead, like she always did, to confirm that she would be arriving early to set up for the PTA meeting that evening, and Henry had agreed to meet her there to unlock the school library doors. She squinted into the persistent summer sun, still blazing hot doggonit, but with shadows lengthening faster into twilight than they did the week before. The meeting started at seven but, she knew from experience, everyone would arrive early with new-school-year-fever. "You are so sweet to help me get everything inside."

"My pleasure, ma'am." Henry plucked the Pyrex stack out from under her arm, and set it on the dolly in one fluid motion, then deftly lifted the grocery bags without touching her person. Steph sighed at the sudden lightness in her shoulders.

"You have a nice summer?" she asked, her hands now free to fluff up her hair and straighten her shirt to flatter her considerable bosom.

"Aw, you know Martha always loves to have the grandkids runnin' around to tickle and fuss over."

Steph smiled up at him; she liked to encourage the storyteller inside every old gentleman. "That's so nice they can come stay with y'all in the summers."

"I tell you, that Sammy..." he began, launching into a tale as he pushed her refreshments up the sidewalk to the open library doors. He eased the wheels over the threshold, and Steph nodded and murmured appropriate exclamations at his grandfatherly revelations about mischievous little boys. She appraised the library, unused for months, for signs of dust or stale trash leftover from the previous school year, and she realized that Henry had arrived much earlier. He had already cleaned the floors, wiped down the tables, opened the windows to let some fresh air in, and probably even vacuumed the upholstery.

My mama was right; sugar really does attract more flies than vinegar. Steph laughed at Henry's finishing joke and he returned a deep chuckle. "You have made this place sparkle like new, and you've done half my work for me, Henry."

"Y'all have a good meetin', you hear?" Henry placed her supplies carefully on a table and took his leave. Steph approved. He was accommodating, but it was best not to socialize too much with the help. She noticed that Henry had placed fresh garbage bags in all of the trash cans throughout the room and also left a pointed box of new bags on the counter for replacing. The message was clear: *I did my share, now you grown adults do yours.* "We'll clean up after ourselves, don't worry," she called through the door.

"I thank you, kindly," Henry answered, his voice already receding into the parking lot.

Humming a random tune, Steph peeled the tops off of her containers and placed paper doilies on serving plates. She breathed in deeply, smelling the homemade cookies and muffins she had spent the past few days preparing. She thought fondly of her youngest son, Tristan, as she arranged the food. He loved everything she baked and never forgot to tell her so.

"Mom, your cookies are almost as sweet as you are," he always said.

If you can't find a perfect man, make one of your own. She chuckled as she sorted through the deserts, inspecting for perfection as she pulled them out. Each of the four platters got a little of everything—chocolate chip and peanut butter cookies, cinnamon apple and blueberry muffins, and of course, brownies.

As she distributed the platters through the room, she thought again of her mother, and as her role as a mother to her own children. Steph could feel her youngest daughter becoming distant. "Mandy—*Amanda*," she corrected herself with a little stomp of her foot, "...that girl is so easily annoyed lately."

A lot of love went a little way sometimes. She supposed she had been the same with her own mother when she was a teenager, but things had certainly turned around when Brandon was born. At only twenty, with one unruly toddler running rampant, a tiny newborn to care for (and that had been only the first two), and her husband always out working, Steph sure appreciated her mother then. Friends hadn't been so easy to come by, suddenly, but the real ones had stuck with her. And she with them.

Vanessa and Meghan. Kerry, too. Reminiscing on group picnics turned awry and buckets of dirty diapers at afternoon house parties, she looked towards the windows, hoping to catch a glimpse of one of them, bouncing up to the door, their familiar voices asking how to help.

"Whatever happens tonight, I will have my friends with me," she soothed herself, her stomach turning over in anticipation. The foreign exchange debacle would be brought up that night, she was sure of it. "Bestfriends."

She pinched her cheeks to make them rosy, knowing one of them would show up soon. Feeling buoyed, Steph divided the plastic cups into four neat towers and positioned them in a semicircle around her Tupperware pitchers—one of iced tea, one of lemonade, and both of them fresh. "Everyone is more pleasant with a full belly and a wet whistle." She fluffed armchair pillows and pushed chairs under tables. "I'm ready for anything."

Footsteps echoed behind the adjoining door leading into the main corridor of the school. She paused to listen and heard the unmistakable sound of someone fiddling with the locked doorknob. Wondering why in the world someone would try to enter the library that way, she walked over to investigate. The only person with keys to the school was the headmaster, who was still out of town. Tracing the stranger's obvious path to that particular door, she realized that someone would have had to break in through a side door to get there.

She heard a muffled exclamation, then a woman's voice behind the door, "Why is this door locked?"

"Who is that?"

"This is Mieke Walsh. Who is *that*?"

"What?" She could hear Mieke jiggling the handle with increasing insistence. "Hold on a minute, it wouldn't be locked from this side. It's probably just stuck or something."

Mieke pounded the door with what sounded like a fist. "Well, unstick it."

"It won't unstick that way, Mieke." Steph heard a dull thud towards the floor. "Don't kick the door—just hold on a minute."

What in tarnation is she doing here? Steph turned the handle to make sure it was, in fact, unlocked and stepped back to check for a deadbolt or latch that might be keeping it from opening. Not seeing any other obstruction, and knowing the wood was probably just warped in a building so old, she grabbed the doorknob, straightened her elbows and hefted up with her back. She leaned all her weight in towards the library and the door came open with a creek.

Mieke stood on the other side, frazzled and offended. "Well, sheesh. Why is everything so complicated in this town?"

"We don't like to go through the main school building without an authorized school official—it's actually against the law. How did you get in there?" She locked the door from the other side before wrestling it closed again. "We're supposed to use the library's front door."

"Sure, next time," Mieke said, ignoring her question.

"Next time?"

"Well, now that I'm the parent of our newest teenage resident, you know. I mean, Antonio will be here in a few days."

Steph was so caught off-guard by the other woman's imagined status of motherhood that she couldn't think of a better response than, "Oh. Well."

"So, where should I set up?" asked Mieke.

"Set up?" Her eyes scanned Mieke from immaculate bob to expensive shoes. *A pants suit at a PTA meeting. Jeez Louise.*

"Yes." Mieke threw up her hands in exasperation. "I'm sure all the other parents will want to know about Antonio. They'll have plenty of questions, of course."

Do you really think you're going to run my PTA meeting, with your laptop and pamphlets? Not gonna happen, honey. Steph would not allow her meeting to be high-jacked—certainly not by someone who was practically a stranger in Shirley County. As head of the PTA, she had plenty of important subjects to discuss before the start of the year. They would discuss them and be home for supper. "Oh, darlin'." Steph employed her most solicitous tone, "You are our guest this evening, and I want you to relax. You don't have to worry about a thing. I'll let you know when it's time for that subject and we'll just have a simple question and answer session."

"Well, I don't mind at all, if you need help organizing the meeting."

"Already done. You just sit yourself here where I've got the pillows all fluffed for you." Steph knew that people like Mieke needed to feel important and special. "I heard you loved my brownies at the July Fourth barbeque, so I made them just for you. I'll just get you some."

"Oh, people are starting to show up. I'll go welcome them," Mieke said, breathless, as she rushed to meet parents walking up the path from the parking lot.

Steph kept her smile in place until she was hidden behind the door in the library office. If there was one good thing about being married to the town sheriff it was taking people like Mieke Walsh down a notch. She pulled out her cellphone to text Mike, who was probably already on his way. She typed in a quick message and hit send, muttering, "Break into my school? Oh no, Mrs. Insta-Mother…"

§

"This is going to be the best Homecoming week yet, I just know it, y'all." Steph said into the microphone. She glanced toward the front door of the library, and was again disappointed to see it standing open, empty. She saw her husband walk out with Mieke over an hour previously, and the two—maddeningly—had never reappeared. "And I think that just about sums up tonight's meeting…"

"I have a question, Stephanie," Nurse Meyers asked, standing, her hand waving in the air, "about this foreign exchange student?"

Alright, here we go. "Yes, Ms. Meyers, I think we've reached the final Q & A segment of the evening. I know everyone is pretty tired and ready to turn in for the night…"

Another hand shot up from the middle row of folding chairs. "Actually, I have a question about that, too."

"Please, Ms. Meyers is first. What is your question, ma'am?"

"I've heard that this boy is not a boy at all, but a man!" Nurse Meyers burst out. "We'll need all different forms filled out for the clinic, if he's an adult."

Someone spoke up from the back of the room, "What do you mean? He's an adult?"

Steph shielded her eyes from the spotlight to discern the identity of the speaker. "Um, hold on a minute. I am not sure that information is correct."

"He's actually nineteen-years-old," George Vale supplied with an expectant grin. "I heard it from Ian a few days ago."

Steph fumed inwardly. "Ian Walsh? Is he sure about that?"

"Very sure. Antonio took a year off his school studies for a dual-enrollment program. You know, to work for a year. So, now his senior year is a year after it would normally be; hence, he's nineteen, not eighteen," George finished triumphantly and sat back to watch the circus.

"But, Sharon's a senior this year, and she's only seventeen," a confused mother said somewhere.

A helpful response from the back: "That Italian boy must have an early birthday, Pam."

"Okay, if everyone would wait to be called upon, so we can all hear both questions and answers."

A woman stood amidst the chairs, with her hands on her hips. "I'm not going to sit here with my hand raised like a child, Stephanie. This is important. Why didn't we *begin* the meeting with this information? How long did you think you could keep this secret?"

"Becky, please. I would never withhold something like that, I assure you."

"Oh my god. You didn't even know, did you?" Becky shook her head in disbelief.

"This isn't a joke? He really is nineteen-years-old? Can he still play football legally, then?"

"So, you're saying that we're going to have an Italian man in class with our kids—with *my daughter*?" Steph squinted her eyes and saw Barry Donahue standing on the top step of the control booth, and he was enraged beyond reason. He had been so helpful manning the controls up until that point; his anger felt like a slap. "I thought you were supposed to be in control of these things as the darn PTA president."

"Excuse me, but being the president of the PTA gives me quite limited power, Barry," Steph retorted.

"Well, maybe someone else should take over, if you can't handle the job," muttered an anonymous audience member.

"The foreign exchange program is not part of my job," Steph pressed her hands together in prayer to the group of angry parents, begging for decorum. "This was something that the Rotary Club set up." She casted around for help—Mike was only supposed to threaten Mieke about the break in, not gosh darn leave with her. *This is the one time Mieke could help out a little and where is she now?*

"But, you're supposed to be our liaison, Stephanie. How could you do this to us?" Margie Tillman's frantic wail was a stark contrast to her soft, bulging form. She jumped to her feet and shook her fist towards the podium. Steph felt like crouching down and hiding behind it.

"Don't scream at her, Margie." Vanessa moved to stand in front of the stage, shielding her friend.

"Don't tell her what to do—Margie has a right to be upset," someone whined. "I'm upset."

Where the heck is Mieke? Where the fudge is Mike? Steph seethed, understanding finally how violently her plan had backfired. She wiped the sweat from her forehead and stomped off-stage, plugging her ears with her fingers, as her PTA meeting erupted into chaos.

part two:

old friends & new enemies

chapter sixteen

"Here, take this." Vanessa ran after Meghan, holding a small white garbage bag in front of her. "It's just one we missed, that's the last," and then she added, with a pinch on her friend's behind, "from the bathroom."

"Gross." Meghan wrinkled her nose and took the bag between two pinched fingers, raising her other hand to cup it around her mouth, "That floor is spic 'n span, Kerry."

"Okay, I'm done." Kerry dumped the remnants from her dustbin into a toilet in the girl's bathroom and flushed it down, then skipped over to the checkout counter to pour four lemonades. "And I'm thirsty."

"Alrighty then," Meghan sang, reappearing from outside with a grocery bag over her shoulder. She grabbed Steph, who was lingering in the foyer checking that everything looked as perfect as old Henry had left it. They pulled their seats around an educational coffee-table with a scuffed, world-map finish. Meghan dropped her bag on the map, "Gimme your lemonades, girls, cuz I'm fixin' to make them hard lemonades. Not yours, Kerry, I know."

Kerry was the accepted teetotaler of the gang, as the wife of Greg Davis, a devoutly religious member of Shirley County who campaigned to keep the county dry. But she always kept a "don't ask, don't tell" policy when it came to her best friends' illegal habits.

"Watts' Sportsman Store; you get more than you bargained for," chanted Vanessa, accepting her plastic cup from Meghan.

"Especially the morning after," joined in Meghan and Steph, tipping their cups to their foreheads with affected frowns. Kerry kept her lemonade pure, while Steph handed hers back for extra vodka.

"Meghan, make mine a tad stronger, will ya?"

"Wish those Watts hillbillies would sell my chardonnay," said Vanessa. "I'd probably drink less if I didn't have to buy it by the box in Tenakho Falls. Wait, wait. We have to toast."

Everyone spiked and seated in their frumpy circle of lived-in chairs around the map of the world, the women raised their cups with gleeful eyes and burdened hearts. But they were buoyed to the storm by being linked together. "To us," was their simple toast.

Vanessa slammed hers down first. "I'm gettin' a re-fill."

"Just bring the whole pitcher back to the table, honey."

"Where did Mike disappear to? He get a call or something?" asked Kerry.

Steph steeled herself and sorted through the automatic replies she always kept in her back pocket; replies learned from being married to a man for twenty-four years who had been called away constantly, no matter what the occasion. First birthdays, a family with the flu, spring recital, Christmas Eve, dead father—nothing was sacred. And she was left behind to do the explaining. Even closer still did she hold her gut-wrenching suspicions about where Mike 'disappeared' to; she would not show that kind of weakness, even to the girls. "You know how duty calls."

"Well, hope it's not anything dangerous."

"You know what I say is dangerous, is that Margie Tillman," said Vanessa. "I mean, she would have ruined the whole night if we'd had to call an ambulance for her. Lady that size..." She put her fist to her forehead and let it explode. They were all sensitive to the possibility of stroke since Big Joe's collapse.

"But what about this Italian kid being nineteen, Steph? What are we going to do about that?"

They had talked of little else from the time the library cleared out and Steph was about to become very unpretty about it. "Please, Meghan. I thought I'm supposed to be relaxing now, done with the cleaning and with all the kids away for the night..."

"I'm sorry, honey. You're right." Meghan prayed to the cracked and moldering ceiling, "Thank you, Annie Ryan, for taking the monsters off our hands. We'll figure it out." She patted Steph's knee.

"There's not much to figure out. I mean, why worry?" Vanessa reiterated. "It's illegal for the guy to mess with a minor. Statutory rape."

"But, Vanessa," Kerry wailed. "Who wants her daughter involved in a 'statutory rape' case? You only have boys, you wouldn't understand."

"Excuse me, but your girls are like my own daughters, thank you very much. Anyway, I thought Greg doesn't allow Missy to date. And Ashley and Tristan are practically married..."

Steph let them argue about protecting the 'weaker sex' while she mused over her own daughter. An older Italian boy would be exactly the kind of thing that would excite Amanda, if only to make her mother squirm. The boy being legally an adult was the best thing Steph had heard in weeks. Mike would forbid Amanda from dating a legal adult, and use the law to reason with her when she let loose the inevitable 'Please, Daddy' routine.

"Did you see how upset Nick Richards was, that the foreign kid—"

"Antonio."

"Yeah, Antonio, might not be able to play football?"

"What—are we short a player? That's not going to mess up Homecoming, is it?"

"Did you hear that John Robinson will be here for the whole fall semester this year?" Steph pretended to suddenly remember. "I bet he would be into it, if we're short of players. His daddy played real well."

"Jamie Robinson, back in Shirley!" Vanessa hooted. "I wondered when you were going to mention it, girl."

"Steph's high school sweetheart, so sweet."

"Oh, please." Steph, red-faced, hastily mixed herself another glass of their makeshift brew. "That was centuries ago, y'all."

"So very, very sweet," said Vanessa. "Some flames are never snuffed out."

"Well, that one *was*." Steph fired over a warning look. John Robinson's father Jamie had been her steady boyfriend all through her first two years at Andrew Jackson. To most of the oblivious audience of Shirley County, they had carried on the perfect, respectable courtship. Vanessa knew differently, since she was the sole confidant to whom Steph poured out her lustful, adolescent heart. She and Jamie had shared most of which two young rural kids could imagine physically sharing. When he graduated two years ahead of her and took off, it was devastating. She started dating Mike in solace.

"John sure is a cutie-pie, though. Blonde curls galore," Meghan said. "I don't know if he plays football or not."

"I like it when Nick Richards gets all passionate like that. Did you see how upset he was?" Vanessa said, not caring a lick about football, though Steph knew she had her eye on the coach. She swirled the ice around in her cup, "He's usually just a little too…stodgy or something."

"Yeah, Nick is pretty good-looking. But, you're right—too serious. Maybe if he just popped a few of those buttons loose up top." Kerry mimed tearing open her shirt collar and sweeping an arm across her brow to illustrate the possible release.

"It's all that finance brain having to deal with his loony artist wife," said Meghan. "You should hear that woman sometimes. She's got some lungs on her, I swear."

"What, you mean like they fight?"

"So loud you can hear from your place?"

"Well, no. But you know I walk Trudy all up and down Forest Lane, and then into the brush to hunt. It's not like I'm eavesdropping or anything—they keep their windows open most of the time." Meghan sat back and twirled her straw, but Steph could tell she was brimming with a story and so could the other girls.

"Spill it, Meghan," said Vanessa, affecting boredom in her tone, but not her eyes.

Meghan didn't need much bait. "I hear a lot more than that, when I take Trudy down into the woods south of our place, let me tell you."

"Like what?" breathed Kerry.

Everyone leaned in at once.

"Well, one morning last week, when Trudy and I were out early—like break of dawn, when the mist was still heavy and the light was just starting to filter through the trees," she primed them, lowering her voice. "There's a place where you can walk out over a big outcrop. You know, Zebadiah's Bluff? It's actually the top to an old cave, and you can look down into the forest below. About a hundred feet down."

"Why is it called Zebadiah's Bluff again?"

"Shhhh. Don't you remember from history?"

"No."

"I don't know, it's just always been called that," Meghan dismissed the confusion and continued her story. "Anyway, way down below, there's an old wooden shack that's been there since as long as I can remember. It's rickety and falling apart, sort of growing back into the forest, but still a weird little house, you know? I know the boys have hung out there before—Chad and Preston, for sure."

"Why would Chad and Preston have gone there?"

"Uh, to smoke pot."

"No way, Chad?" Vanessa chuckled. "Well, boys will be boys, especially in the woods."

Steph wondered why Mike had never mentioned anything about the boys smoking pot up in the mountains. She was sure her oldest son Brandon would have known about such a secret hide out; all the kids had been fast friends since babyhood. She couldn't imagine Mike not having caught wind of such a clandestine affair. Apparently her husband had more secrets than she realized. "Marijuana—that's terrible. How do you know it was marijuana?"

"Because I smelled it," Meghan answered, ignoring the real question. "So, one morning right at the break of dawn, like I said, I see Candy Vale coming out of the old shack with none other than that new boy Sam Castle."

The other women looked at her, stunned and puzzled by the unexpected revelation.

"Like, you know...they had been there during the night? Like, *been together*?"

Kerry was aghast. "Sam Castle, that boy who moved here at the end of last year? He's in Ashley's class."

Steph kept quiet. She had seen the way Amanda looked at that boy.

Kerry tried to reason through it, always a little slow on the uptake, "Well, her dad owns the gas station just down the way from there. She lives right up the road..."

"The next house north of ours, correct," Meghan narrowed her eyes and nodded slyly. "So why would she be sleeping in that shack?"

"Only one reason," Vanessa said simply, "and no surprise. That Sam Castle, whew. You gotta admit."

"What a little..." Kerry spluttered.

"Please, they're just kids, guys," Steph admonished. "That's dangerous, though. That area has weird stuff going on there. Why would you go out there at night, Meghan?"

"It was dawn, and I had a pit-bull with me." Meghan collapsed back into her chair, her story over, ready to settle in with her second lemonade.

"Candy Vale did, too, I guess," Vanessa tittered, and then stuck her tongue out when Steph narrowed her eyes over her plastic cup.

"What do you mean, 'dangerous'?" Kerry, who had always been valley-folk and decidedly more vanilla, wanted to know.

"Well, not dangerous." Steph relented some, never really knowing how serious Kerry was about her possibly self-imposed ignorance of worldly (and maybe otherworldly) affairs. "Of course, you better watch your step over by the bluff's edge; it's definitely a steep drop. You've been there, right?"

Kerry looked bewildered. "No."

"There's a sort of mystery or legend about the spring and the cave," Meghan helped. "I mean, a cave is always kind of creepy, right?"

Vanessa always grew tired of Kerry's Pollyanna routine faster than the others. "This is something that we all know about from history classes. There were several Indian tribes that lived in this area, before European settlers moved in and there was some kind of strife or breaking of the peace between them a long time ago. Some say that it happened in that cave under Zebadiah's Bluff. There used to be cave drawings in there, but some scientists up at the University found a way to take them off the walls a couple years ago and move them to their laboratories."

"My dad has an original piece," Meghan proclaimed.

"Yes, people started *defacing* the anthropological treasure, and so the town council decided to have the cave paintings preserved."

"That doesn't sound so creepy," said Kerry.

"The creepy part is the spring," Meghan blurted, and then amended in lieu of Vanessa's withering look, "I mean, not terribly creepy, no big deal. Just sort of strange, is all."

"So, in front of the cave, probably not too far from this shack thing?" Vanessa waited for Meghan's affirmation before moving on, "There's a natural spring that is…"

"Blue," Meghan continued, nodding in agreement at Vanessa's sudden loss of words. "And icy cold, even in the hottest months of the summer. The blue comes from the source of the spring deep in the ground, you can tell by looking at it. It's dark and murky down there—but the water is crystal clear—and it gradually becomes lighter like a sapphire catching the sun, then glowing in aquamarine, until finally fading out completely at the edge of the spring."

Kerry was confused. "We learned that in History? About the spring?"

"Kinda…"

"It's a natural phenomenon," said Vanessa.

"Natural what?" asked Meghan. "Look, I don't know why it's blue. But Trudy won't go near it. They say it's poisoned."

"Poisoned with what? Come on." Steph didn't see any reason to freak Kerry out more than necessary.

Vanessa sighed. "Environmentalist scare. They just don't want people diving in it. Some kind of rare algae they're trying to protect."

"Who would dive in there? It's so cold and deep." Steph tried to stop the shiver rolling over her.

"No, it's more than that," insisted Meghan. "I dipped my toe in once—Trudy was barking and freaking out, so I took her home and came back." She looked at the ceiling, then her hands, as if unsure where to find the right words. "I have never felt so cold. So alone and desperate. So scared and angry. I never want to feel like that again. That spring is so frightening because it is somehow alive and…"

Kerry looked like she didn't want to know, but couldn't help herself, "What?"

"Vengeful."

chapter seventeen

It was well past midnight when John turned into his grandparents' driveway. The Mustang's headlights swung around the bend and flashed into the massive oak tree that shaded most of the front lawn. The convertible top was down and he savored the sweet aroma as he passed the gardenia bushes, sucking in the perfume of his childhood summers. Where was the old magnolia tree?

Poison berries.

He glanced reflexively toward the neighboring McBride house and wondered if Candy was at her grandma's that night. Probably not, and he was beat anyway from the long drive.

He turned his attention back to the long gravel drive approaching the familiar old Robinson homestead, a sprawling two-story country house with a wrap-around porch on both levels, their white slatted railings like a set of smiling teeth, and tiny twin attic windows peering like a nearsighted granny above them. All entrances were shut tight, too early in the season for cool, bug-free nights, and only the bay windows downstairs were lighted. He told Grandma Pearl that he would be arriving alone, his dad staying on one more day in the city to finish up some last minute paperwork. He had hoped the welcome party would be saved for the weekend.

Looks pretty quiet. Good.

John wanted nothing more than to pass out in a cozy upstairs bed. His grandma always kept the bedrooms immaculate, with fresh white linens and a well-worn, incredibly soft, down comforter rolled up at the foot of each four-poster. He loved to get tucked in, toasty up to his chin, and let the ceiling fan overhead freeze his face on high speed. He didn't really hope for dinner (his grandma wasn't really that into cooking anymore, after years of feeding everyone everyday for most of her life, she said), but that was fine with him.

She was no chef anyway. He smiled when his stomach growled despite memories of her less than enthusiastic cooking. Over-cooked meat, plain potatoes, and iceberg lettuce side-salads. Left-overs, stretched to their limits. Store-bought lasagne for Christmas dinner. *Sure I'll find something.*

He parked in front of the garage door, never used anymore since they had turned the space into an entertainment room that was half television room and half bar. His grandma's sewing room was off to one side and Grandpa Joe's workshop was in another corner. The family simply called the compound room 'the den.' There used to be a need for increasing space, with grandkids around all the time, but the den was silent that night. With a nostalgic twinge, he shut off the engine and swung up out of his seat to have a look around.

There's nobody here. How eerie.

Thinking he'd just get his bags later, he headed for the front door, brushing his fingertips over the rosemary bushes and clusters of overflowing potted oregano. He knew the door would be unlocked, and it was. He rapped on it, turning the handle at the same time, and pushed it open.

"Hello? Gram?"

"Hello, dear," Grandma Pearl's voice echoed from the kitchen. He was surprised to see her come walking out, wiping her hands on an apron. "I thought I heard you pull up." John walked towards her through the dimly lighted, and rarely used, formal sitting room with his arms held out to her. She hugged him and kissed his cheek, "So good to see you, sweetie." He felt a prickle and guessed Grandma was getting a little whiskery in her old age.

How long have I been gone? "You cookin' for me?" he asked, pulling back with a shocked expression.

"Oh, hell no." She turned back to the kitchen, motioning for him to follow. "You know the whole clan will be here tomorrow ready for a feeding, and I'm not about to slave away in the kitchen with everyone running underfoot."

Passing through the doorframe, John was welcomed into the heart of the house—a cavernous, stone walled kitchen with wide marble countertops surrounding an enormous wooden butcher's block. A simple chandelier blazed overhead, gleaming off the brushed metal refrigerator and massive gas oven. Copper pots glinted over the spotless enameled sink. The ultra-modern kitchen was Grampa Joe's brainchild, since his restaurant was the crowning glory of Buffalo Square and the main source of his wealth, though he rarely cooked for the family at home.

Grandma had been chopping carrots and onions, their decapitated tops piled in a heap on one corner of the chopping block. Potatoes awaited dismemberment in a mesh sack hanging from one of the hooks under the wooden platform, and a cauldron of a crockpot crouched on the countertop.

"Pot roast?"

Easy guess. It was one of her signature dishes for a house full of family, made with plenty of potatoes, and as little actual roast as she could get away with. Though she was quite wealthy in present times, as a small child his grandma had lived through abject poverty on a failing farm in northern Iowa. She had stinginess etched into her at an impressionable age.

John looked toward the pantry. *Probably has a couple dozen brown-and-serve rolls ready in there, for soaking up juices and filling up bellies.*

"Those kids are ravenous, I tell you. They devour absolutely everything you put in front of them—or anybody else, for that matter," she said, referring to John's five cousins, The Bennetts, begot by his Aunt Beth and her ultra-religious husband, Uncle Dan. John could never figure out to what religion they actually conformed, and they had switched from one warehouse church to another over the years, but at least one of them seemed to be born again at all times. "I just give them plenty of potatoes." Pearl ticked off her fingers like a memorized grocery list, walking back to the butcher's block to resume chopping. "Lots of bread, got some rolls. Plenty of onions—they're cheap, have Vitamin C, and they're good for flavoring. Not that they care, they eat anything. Anything and everything."

John could tell she was getting tired and crankier by the second just thinking about the welcome party the next day. "Grandma, let me?" he asked, motioning to the formidable chef's knife and the sack of potatoes.

"Oh, honey, thank you." She surrendered the knife instantly, handle first. "You're a dear."

"No problem, Gram. You already wash these potatoes?"

"Of course, I did," she said, throwing up her hands and plopping onto a nearby stool. "One of them is always sick every time I see them. Beth says, oh, it's because there are so many of them that by the time everyone catches the bug, it's already mutated again. That's ridiculous. I had five children of my own and was raised in a family of nine during the war, mind you…"

"Yeah, you guys didn't have much," John supplied, knowing where this story led and playing his role in the script like a gentleman.

"Well, we didn't. And I don't have a problem with large families, provided you can afford to—honey, cube those a little smaller, they'll cook faster—provided you can afford to feed them adequately."

"Of course." John nodded, his brows threaded in theatrical concern. He used the wide blade to help shovel a handful of potatoes, and walked over to dump them in the crockpot, keeping his attention trained on Grandma Pearl.

"I mean, I love all my grandchildren, and I love my daughter, Beth..."

She went on and on without a break (he didn't even know how she breathed with so much talking), and John was happy to supply the necessary dialogue conjunctions.

Wow. He felt the steady rhythm of the knife in his hands and the clicking swoosh of the blade cutting through raw potatoes. Lulling him like a dream. *It's like I've never even left.*

He glanced around the room as his grandmother ranted, companionable in her way. The house was just like he remembered it; only small improvements here and there. He noticed the new coo-coo clock hanging next to the entryway to the den, and he knew Grandma Pearl had a story on deck. The nook to the left of the clock was still filled with the old-fashioned diner table and wooden benches whose seat cushions were embroidered by Grandma Pearl's own hand thirty years before. She was reticent to speak of love or show overt affection, but the love she had for her family was threaded into those cushions. He hoped they would be able to get a card game together sometime soon, like they had done in years past. Pearl played a mean canasta, just like all her sisters from up North.

It was oddly peaceful for John to listen to her familiar complaints, and he could tell that she didn't have many people that just listened those days. He waited for an appropriate pause to ask the obvious next question.

"So, how's Grandpa?"

"Well ... he's not so good, John."

John concentrated on the potato cubing; her sympathetic expression and gentle tone was out of place from a woman who loathed showing her soft side. She was thoughtful while they both watched the steady roll of the chef knife.

"I'm sure you've heard about the stroke, and all that went with that," she said, in a tone more like the one he remembered.

John nodded encouragement and turned calm features towards her to show that he was ready for whatever she needed to say.

"Well, I think we were all lucky for that minor stroke, because he had no lasting harm from it. He regained his ability to speak within a couple hours. And you know he hadn't been in for even a check-up in so long."

"Grandpa..."

"I know. You have to force the man to do anything out of his regular daily routine," Pearl said, exasperated. They both laughed, lightening the mood. "I mean, if 'Dr. Visit' was on his daily schedule, then he'd have no problem going to the doctor."

"Yeah, Mr. Two-Eggs-And-Spam."

"Spam and eggs is part of the main problem, of course. You've probably heard that while in the hospital for the stroke, the doctors decided that your grandpa will need bypass surgery on his heart, as soon as possible."

"Yeah…"

"So, we're planning on *that*," she said using her hands for emphasis. "At least when that's done, he won't be on the verge of a surprise heart attack. Not that a heart attack would have been a surprise, in the shape he's in…"

A little kick when he's down probably means that she's defending herself against something worse. John knew Grandma Pearl's usual defense mechanism was meanness. "But?"

She paused a beat. "Well, he's having a hard time with the recovery. You must be famished after that drive. Can I make you a sandwich or something? Salami? Bologna?"

"Sure, whatever you've got sounds great, Grandma." John's stomach had actually begun to cramp.

"I'm sure we have bologna, always do—ugh." She yanked open the heavy refrigerator door and her small frame was jerked towards the icy interior. The old nursery rhyme, 'Jack Sprat could eat no fat, his wife could eat no lean,' had worked in reverse on his grandparents. John remembered remarks by aunts and uncles, whispered under a hand, about how quickly a shrew mouse burned calories, as she sorted through the meat and cheese drawer mumbling about how kids ate her out of house and home. "Of course, it gets more troubling, the longer your grandpa stays in the hospital," she resumed her story without missing a beat, emerging from the fridge with bologna, sliced cheese, and Miracle Whip. "More people die in hospitals from infections they get there, than from the problem they actually went in for."

"Why can't he come home, then?" *Did she actually just say 'die,' in reference to her husband of almost fifty years, without flinching?*

"He's still too weak, dear." She opened the breadbox and John recognized the familiar smell of spearmint gum and licorice candy that his grandma had stashed in there for decades. "And he's been having…"

John stopped slicing and turned to look at her after a few moments, and he found her studying her hands, pensive. Trying to decide whether or not to say more. *Am I the first to hear what comes next?*

"He's been having hallucinations, John. He sustained quite a concussion from the fall, but there's no evidence of any further brain bleeding.

Could be they're just nightmares. He sleeps a lot and sometimes it's hard for me to tell if he's awake or asleep."

"Well, that would be pretty normal, on pain medication—the sleeping, I mean. I read that morphine can cause hallucinations, too. Is he still on that stuff?"

"Oh, plenty, I'm sure. He is still in a lot of pain, he says. I guess some people can handle pain better than others." She slathered two slices of Wonderbread with Miracle Whip.

"What is he hallucinating—or dreaming—about?"

"Masks, if you can imagine."

"Like, gas masks? Grandpa was never in a war, was he?"

"Too young for Korea and too old for Vietnam. No. More primitive, more like African or maybe American Indian masks. He made some drawings of them after he woke up. The nurse tells me he wakes up wailing in the most dreadful way, saying all sorts of incoherent things, and he won't calm down until she gets him a pen and paper."

"Shouldn't someone be with him during the night?" John knew his grandma could be pragmatic to the extreme, and expect toughness when most wouldn't consider it necessary.

"He's in the intensive care, honey. No visitors at night." She walked over and began rifling through some papers on top of the phone stand, then opened the little drawer underneath, where they usually kept pens and markers for taking messages or keeping score in a card game. "Here's one, look."

She flicked on the wall sconce and John set down his knife. His grandfather wasn't one to sketch or draw. John imagined the scene of Grandpa Joe waking in a fever and frantically needing drawing utensils, and felt embarrassed for him. He sat down to take a look at the evidence his grandma offered him, her reading glasses perched on the end of her nose.

"They look like … animal faces. There's a bear. This one looks like a snake?"

Crude faces were scattered randomly on the page, without thought to illusory space or narrative, but with an urgency to record as much as possible. The drawings reminded John of times when he had had a particularly vivid dream and he would grab a notebook to write it all down before it faded into memory. Candy was big on dream journals and she always liked for him to turn the best dreams into campfire stories. Some of them became famous epics between them, like their own personal folktales. *That was a long time ago, though.*

And their stories were light compared to the darkness of his grandfather's drawings; they had sharp, hard lines and fractured edges. He had been so savage with the pen that the page was torn in places. Fangs, pointed feathers, a ragged mane, screaming mouths.

"Grandpa's eyes were as wide and hollow as those drawings, the last time I saw him," Pearl said.

John sensed that his grandfather being held in intensive care was not the only reason that she wasn't visiting him at night. She was scared. "This one is a vulture—the long neck and hooked beak."

"But, they're masks, you see?" she insisted, pointing to the empty eye sockets and lack of neck or body. "And see this one," she pulled the first page out of his hands and laid it on the table, to reveal the paper beneath. "See, this one has a human body, and his hands are holding the mask to his face."

John placed the second page next to the other so they could look at the drawings side by side. There was another human figure on the first drawing that he could discern, since his grandma had pointed out the form. That one seemed to be dancing, with feathered, clawed, stomping feet, and calling up to the sky. Were they depictions of some sort of ritual? The drawings laid bare a man's intimate fears, and suddenly John felt the lamp was shining too brightly on them.

"They look like dreams to me. Nightmares," he said, hoping his grand-father was not actually seeing that stuff in his waking moments.

"They do, don't they?"

"Dreams are pieces of our memories knitted together in creative ways." John tried to remember what he had learned about the phenomenon of the dream state in a recent psych class at school. It was all vague theory rather than provable fact, though. "These could be scenes from a movie that he's seen or a book that he's read."

"Why would a movie or book have been so important to him?" she asked, tracing the lines of a particularly fierce mask with a sharp tongue darting through the howling jaws of what looked like a jaguar. "The nurse said he's also been talking about someone. A..."

John looked up when he realized she hadn't finished her last comment, about to prod her to continue. But when he saw the expression on her face, he thought better of it. Jealousy. She rearranged her features and forced a smile.

"Does he talk about the drawings, Gram? You know, later? When he's more with it."

"Honey. He's never really very 'with it' anymore."

Something in her voice brought the edges of his awareness into sharp focus, and the hollows under her eyes matched the late-night cooking. When he first walked in the front door, he had noticed two empty slots in the bookcase. Over his grandma's shoulder, he saw two books stacked there. They spoke volumes as to how she had been spending lonely nights: a *Book of Common Prayer* and *The Bible*.

"We'll figure it out, Grandma."

"We always do," she agreed and willfully snapped herself out of the moment. "Anyway, I'll finish these potatoes, honey. You eat your sandwich. God knows you'll have to fight for your food tomorrow…"

She resumed her harangue of the Bennett brood and finished stocking the crockpot with vegetables while he ate his snack. Finally, the only job left to be done was to add the meat and plug in the power in the morning, and though John was ready to collapse with exhaustion, he knew Grandma Pearl would probably stay up watching Carey Grant movies until the wee hours.

At least that would be more cheerful than bible study, for a woman who doesn't believe in God. He gave her a gentle kiss goodnight and headed up the stairs without bothering to fetch his luggage. He felt bad about leaving her alone but he was going to pass out in t-minus-sixty seconds.

As John collapsed onto the bed upstairs, splaying his arms and legs over the sides, he let out a groan of pleasure. It didn't take much will to chase thoughts of Grandpa's nightmares out of his mind. He ran his hands over his scalp, erasing the tortured drawings from his memory, and then kicked off his shoes with a delicious stretch. He considered letting himself fall asleep right there on top of the covers.

"Ow," he grimaced as he rolled onto his side and the starched lace duvet scratched his face.

He decided getting underneath was worth the effort and pulled off the itchy duvet, folding it neatly over the end of the bed. Getting up to flip on the ceiling fan, he glanced out the window across the field separating them from the McBride house and thought again about Candy. He turned off the bedroom light, and his reflection disappeared to reveal darkened windows next door. He stripped off his jeans and left them in a heap on the floor, then snuggled under the down comforter in his underwear, the fan roaring overhead.

He didn't dream of howling masks and dancing shamans. He dreamt of dark eyes and soft lips, and he slept more soundly than he had in years.

chapter eighteen

"Somethin' wrong, hon?" Mike asked, not bothering to close the bedroom door, since all the kids were blessedly out of the house that night. Their golden retriever bounded in against his leg and jumped onto the bed. "Hey, Copper. Good girl."

Steph was standing in the master bedroom in her nightgown, her slippered feet firmly planted and her hands on her hips, frowning at her husband in dismay. "What happened to you tonight, Mike?"

"I had a call. I had to leave." He pulled off his gun holster in one fluid sweep and dumped it on the mule chest. "Look, I'm sorry I missed the end of your meeting, but you know I can't ignore a call."

"I saw you walk out with Mieke Walsh, and neither one of you came back." Steph could hear the panic in her voice and she cringed at the sound.

"Yeah, you told me to ask her about the security breach and I did. She showed me where it was." Mike stopped undressing, mid-button, and turned to face her squarely. "Why she didn't go back to the meeting, I have no idea."

"Oh." Steph gulped, feeling ridiculous and forcing her tears back with an effort. "What was it, a broken window, or something?"

"An unlocked door." Mike resumed disrobing. Steph knew how much paperwork an unlocked door at the school meant for him in the morning. He scrubbed his hands over his face and waved it away for the night, "I'll talk to Henry about it tomorrow."

"Good, okay," Steph said, her voice breaking with relief.

Mike twisted around, startled. Seconds passed between them in silence, before he rose from the bed and approached her with his arms spread wide and his voice a caress. "What's goin' on, now?"

She choked on a sob, turning it into a laugh, as he pulled her into a bear hug. "You guys just left, and I didn't know…"

"Oh, you're somethin' else, Pussycat. I get a call and suddenly I'm— what?—diddlin' Mieke Walsh in the janitor's closet?"

"I'm sorry. That woman just really gets my goat, is all."

"Oh, come on." He released her and fell onto their king-sized bed, pulling off his shoes with a groan. "She seems like a nice enough gal to me, why don't you like her?"

She pretended she hadn't heard his question. "Well, what was the call? Where'd you have to go?"

"Oh, way down south by the gorge."

"Really? Why?"

"The Derringtons."

"Who?"

"You remember that tourist that got lost about a week ago? Husband went missing; wife didn't have the car keys, so she had to hike out of the canyons with her two kids?"

"Yeah, you said the poor little girl had to be hospitalized."

"Uh huh. Well, we found the husband."

"Was he alright?"

"No." Mike put his head in his hands and rubbed his eyes, as if to erase an unwelcome image. "Trust me, you don't want to know."

"Ew. Don't tell me, then."

"But, I brought you a present." He stood up and dug into a pocket hanging loose from his already unzipped fly. He brought out a rolled-up plastic bag and waved it in the air, grinning wickedly. "Had to stop in Finley Cove, too. Seems like you need to relax a little."

"I see." Steph folded her arms across her chest in a pout, her disgruntled mistrust reawakened; Mike knew how much she loved screwing when she was stoned. He kicked his pants down the rest of the way to the floor, and plopped on the bed in his underwear. Giving her time to cool off a little more, he went to work raised up on his elbows, silently sorting through the pot and ready to listen to her complaints.

Steph was ready to voice them. "I don't know, I just don't trust her."

"You know you're my queen." Mike looked up and fixed her gaze, before looking back to his hands to continue his work.

"I trust *you*, I just don't trust *her*. You should have seen what a mess she saddled me with tonight."

"You don't trust anyone you haven't known your whole life," Mike chuckled, separating the sticks and seeds into a little pile on the bedspread, brushing Copper's nose away when she tried to sniff it.

"Well, that's right," Steph agreed, throwing up her hands. "I'm not going to apologize for that. What's wrong with knowing who your friends are? Knowing where you come from?"

"Nothin' at all, Pussycat."

Steph rounded on him, thinking she heard sarcasm in his reply, but when she saw his eyebrows knitted and his toes laced together in complete concentration on his task, she stopped pacing to watch; it was one of his most endearing habits, those interlocked toes.

He noticed the quiet, looked up and smiled. "What?"

"I love you."

"Come 'ere, beautiful." He held out a hand in invitation.

Steph dug into the drawer of her nightstand and brought out her favorite glass tobacco pipe, designed to look like a cute little caterpillar. She bought it at the old-time music festival, more than twenty years before, right after the birth of their first baby. When their daughter, Liza, was a toddler she used to think it was the funniest little puppet. Steph would make it talk with a silly voice, often to *Alice in Wonderland* playing for background entertainment. "Spark it up then, honey. I guess I wouldn't mind relaxing with you for a while."

chapter nineteen

The sun was barely up, the morning still cool, when Sam hiked up the dirt pathway around the edge of Shirley County's town center. Candy had told him to meet her early, so that they might have a pleasant ride up to the campgrounds before the heat of the day was upon them. Her uncle's horses were calmer in the morning, still a little sleepy and not yet harassed by tourist brats. She warned that there would be plenty of 'out-of-towners' that day, in lieu of the music festival and at the close of summer, and she had asked her uncle to save them a gentle gelding on the Shirley side of the ranch. She knew that Sam had never ridden a horse before, and was delighted to offer her expertise. Thinking of a day with Sam would normally have made her nervous, but she was never nervous around a horse.

"Looking pretty charged already," he said when he spotted her sitting atop the enclosure wall, kicking her dangling feet in anticipation.

"Hey, you made it." She hopped off the wall and bounded over to him for a hug.

His voice was still husky with sleep, "Whoa, tiger."

"Still not awake yet, even after a shower?" Candy mussed his wet hair and planted a loud kiss on his freshly shaven cheek. "Ooh, baby soft. I like it."

"Are you on drugs, or just part Chihuahua?"

"Sorry, I've always been a morning person. Not you, though, huh?"

"Nope." He plunged his hands deep into the pockets of his hoodie, but flashed her a wolfish grin.

Her belly did a backflip in response. "Well, day's not gettin' any younger." Looping her arm in his, she steered towards the footpath leading northwards up the valley. Their shoulders bumped as they loped along together, so Sam pulled his hand free of its cozy pocket and grabbed hers. Candy swung their clasped fists between them and chattered happily about the ranch, her uncle who owned the ranch, his kids, and how easy the horses were to handle. Her uncle was already working the stables closest to the campgrounds at the top of the valley when they arrived, so one of her cousins greeted them and showed them to their mounts. One was a shiny chestnut mare and the other a dappled grey and white gelding, both munching oats serenely, already brushed and saddled.

Her cousin had recently ascended to assistant manager, and she eyed him warily, cringing against the moment he realized she was on a date. Thankfully, Sean was a little slow in the mornings, especially that one. "These are trail horses, so they're used to unfamiliar people that don't really know how to ride. One'll follow the other. Candy, you know how to lead."

"Yep, I got it," she said, nodding briskly and checking the saddles and reins on both horses. She selected the mare for herself and leaned down to adjust the length of the stirrups a little higher, since she was about a half-foot shorter than Sam.

"Here's your pack." Her cousin patted the zippered canvas backpack attached to one of the horses. "Water, map, and long range walkie-talkie."

"Sean, I don't need that," Candy started, annoyed, but he cut her off, all business.

"Hey, it's a big ranch and insurance says the pack's required."

She whined, "Do I have to stick to the trail?"

"With these horses, you do," Sean said in his big boy voice. Candy thought he might be feeling the aftereffects of partying with the carnies the night before, but at least he hadn't embarrassed her. Then, when he turned to walk back to the stable office, he added under his breath, "… fire crotch."

"You butthole!" Candy grumbled in a strained hiss, not wanting to upset the horses, but slapping his broad shoulder so hard it stung.

He jogged away, snickering. "Have fun, kids."

"Nice." Pissed off and embarrassed, she turned back to the horses with a red face.

The family squabble had put Sam at ease, though; he seemed loose and relaxed, letting Candy direct him with authority and regain her dignity. His assigned horse for the day, the comely grey and white named Popcorn, loomed enormous next to Candy, but she had no trouble leading the gentle giant to where she needed him. She moved him around the paddock to demonstrate how to use the reins while Sam watched, his hands in his pockets. Though he seemed aloof, she had the feeling he was taking meticulous mental notes.

"Popcorn's a little round in the belly, and likes to move slow," she apologized. She wouldn't have minded a rowdy stallion for herself, and it was hard to get a feel for how a guy like Sam would want to ride. Every move he made impressed her and every word he said she savored. She wasn't sure how to handle being in charge.

But, Sam was acting as pliable as Popcorn, "Sounds good to me."

Whoa, this is weird. Note to self: take Sam riding more often.

They started out on the trail together, Popcorn following Candy's horse, Brownie. Candy would have liked to let her horse run free in the fields, but it was probably best they were forced stick to the trail. The trail had been designed especially for tourists and flowed through the prettiest stands of trees (to hide any unsightly commercial buildings or stinky trash dumps), and regularly opened onto sundrenched meadows speckled with wildflowers. As the going became steep and rockier along the river, the horses slowed down to pick their way along. The ranchers had routed them through an area with the best view of the rapids and the cliffs, and the trail narrowed and dropped about twenty feet to the water below.

After plodding along for about fifteen minutes, Sam called over the roar of the river, "How far is it like this?"

"We're almost past this part," she hollered back, twisting around in her seat casually. "Isn't the view beautiful?" They were at her favorite section of the trail—mountains on one side and steep drop-off on the other. Spectacular.

"Alright, alright." He waved at her, urging her to face straight ahead.

She pushed her sunglasses to her forehead and saw that Sam face was blanched, his knuckles white on the reins. *Oh shit, he hates it.* "We can ride side by side in a sec." After several hundred feet, their path took a sharp turn into a line of elm trees and then they were in open, rolling hills. Candy glanced back and was relieved to see Sam's color returning.

She remembered the reason for the detour: an old wooden mill backed into the clearing and jutted out into the river on the other side. *Oh, he'll like that.* Feeling like a tour guide, she motioned towards a peek at the backside of the mill and he peered through the trees at the impressive relic from the 19th Century. "Now the valley will narrow, and then we'll come to the top of it and head up into the foothills of Western Mountain."

"Western Mountain? So, we'll have to cross a bridge?"

"Yeah, we're due north of Shirley, the campgrounds are straight ahead, but the river curves around in front of us along the ridge." She pretended nonchalance, but she knew that bridge, and consoled herself. *Rickety, but still safe.* Nothing for it but to soldier on and prattle on, "The festival is always held at the entrance to the grounds, right in the foothills. See, we're headed out of the valley and coming into Balick County, which runs along the ridge of the Western Mountain. *Bealach* is Scottish Gaelic for 'mountain pass;' I think Balick is sort of a bastardization of the term. There were a lot of Scottish settlers here in the early days. They still have a Highlands Festival, it's really cool."

Sam seemed to have regained his swagger, as if the horse were connected with his own swaying hips. "I always wondered about the name 'Shirley' for a town. Is it Gaelic, too?"

"You know, I never thought about that. 'Shirley' isn't strange to me, since I've lived here all my life. I guess it is, kinda. But, I don't think it's Gaelic. We learned about the origin in a history class a long time ago, but I can't—"

"Shit, what's he doing?" Popcorn dropped low and prepared to roll. Sam sprang off his mount in a flash.

Candy jerked the slipknot tethering the two horses and launched herself to the earth.

"Stand clear, Sam." She pushed him behind her and stepped them both back to a safe distance.

The horse neighed and thrashed his head, thrusting the saddle against the ground and scrambling his legs in the air. Brownie sidestepped several paces with a nervous whinny.

What the hell, it's like he's possessed.

Candy handed Sam her own reins and reached out to take a hold of Popcorn's, then cinched them tight. "I think he wants his saddle off, maybe it's hurting him." All hell was breaking loose but she kept her mind on the mundane. She snuck a finger into the saddle buckle and unhooked the latch with a flick, murmuring lovingly, like she was manipulating a naughty child, "There, there. We can fix that, boy." The strap loosened, Popcorn calmed down enough for her to pull it free. The heavy saddle fell away with a thud.

The horse wiggled and flailed before he found his feet, then tried to trot away with an angry snuffle. Candy still had ahold of his reins, and she led him into the shade of the trees.

"It's okay, sssshhhhh…"

Popcorn reared up on his hind legs, his eyes still wild.

It wasn't the saddle, then.

She gave the reins some slack and let him lead the way.

"Alright, quiet now. Shush, boy."

They moved away from the meadow, the sound of the river building and the shade deepening under the trees, and Popcorn finally relaxed.

Thank god. Candy let out a tense breath and mentally retraced her steps. She hoped they hadn't gone too far; the thought of Sam alone in that meadow, probably shaken and disgruntled himself, filled her with shame. *What a fun horseback riding adventure.*

She tied Popcorn to a stout trunk, catalogued surrounding landmarks, and told herself she'd text Sean later. The important next step was finding Sam and—somehow—trying to make things right after…after that… whatever.

What the heck was that? That saddle wasn't too tight. Was there a hitchhiker under the blanket, sticking him? She knew there was no way. Sean could be total A-hole to his cousins, but he was never careless with a horse. Possibilities and justifications for the unsettling occurrence dwindled as she made her way back to Sam. The thought occurred to her that Popcorn had grown calmer going in the other direction, but she put it out of her mind.

She emerged from the trees, dusting her hands off on her jeans. "Man, you sure move fast."

Sam was standing with his thumbs in the pockets of his jeans, watching the woods on the other side of the clearing. He turned back to her, his expression guarded. "Good thing, too."

"No kidding, right? If Popcorn had rolled over on you—which was exactly what he seemed to have in mind—you could've broken a leg at best."

Sam shrugged, "Not the first time I've felt like that here."

"What do you mean? Like what?"

"Ousted," he laughed, low and soft in his chest. "Like maybe I shouldn't be here. Don't belong here."

"Don't belong?" The thought of Sam leaving Shirley County sent Candy into a panic she would be loathe admitting to a locked diary. "People make you feel like that?"

His smile was bitter, enigmatic. "No. Not people."

"I don't know what happened, maybe he had a sticker in his saddle blanket—he's never done anything like that before. I am so sorry. Have I ruined the day?"

Sam read the hysteria she was trying to hold back; the tautness left his shoulders and his whole demeanor softened. "Don't worry, Candy. I don't belong anywhere. It was a shock, but let's not make too much out of it."

"Darn horse was chomping on wildflowers all morning. He's getting so fat, he must need to keep his saddle on the next buckle hole now—I better tell Uncle Robin," Candy babbled, casting around for a foothold back into normalcy.

"What did you do, put him down?"

"I tied him in a nice shady spot, right next to a patch of *wildflowers.*" Candy kicked at the retired saddle, still lying on the ground. "Good thing we're right by the old mill, I can tell Sean where he can find him."

"Poor Sean."

"Whatever, I'm glad he'll have to work a little harder today." Candy was still bristling at her cousin's earlier remark on the probable color of her pubic hair. "Serves him right."

"So…." Sam blew out a long breath, snapped his fingers, and clapped a hand on one fist. "What now? Should we walk the rest of the way?"

"Uh, no. It's still pretty far. We can ride together, if you don't mind sitting that close to me."

"With that soft, fat arse between my thighs? Heaven." Sam dodged a punch and slung the backpack from Popcorn's saddle over his shoulder.

They left their remaining horse at the Balick County end of Colemann Ranch, and walked the last quarter mile to the campground entrance on foot, hand in hand.

"Is that the train?" Sam cocked his ear as a hand-painted banner came into view: Mountain Sound Festival 2014. After a few more steps, an old log cabin with a deep porch emerged from behind the trees, and they saw that what had sounded like a steam engine's whistle was actually a song produced by the gnarly old man sitting in a rocking chair. He had one boot propped up on the porch railing, trundling himself back and forth in a bentwood rocker, a harmonica barely visible between his fluttering fingers. The tune changed from the chugging train to a slow, mournful wolf call, before picking up the melody of "Angeline the Baker."

"He's good," Sam said under his breath as they neared the porch.

"Yeah, he's like ninety-something years old. He's had almost a century of practice."

"That's a relief. Then he won't pass out in a second."

It was true. The old man was huffing and puffing on his instrument at an amazing rate, impressive at any age. Candy hated that old bastard, though. "No, but he probably won't remember who I am, either. Hello, Mr. Lowry, sir. My, that is a fine tune."

"Eh?" The old man came out of his trance and the music stopped abruptly. "Why'd you shut it down, then?"

"I am sorry, sir," Candy said, smiling widely. "I didn't want to startle you. Are you accepting the festival entrance fee?"

The old coot spat affirmation and walked away without explanation.

"He's such a grumpy…" She held her tongue. Talking trash about old people wasn't attractive, even on Pluto. "If we had walked past without interrupting his music, he would have chased after us, accusing us of stealing. There's no winning, I swear."

Candy grabbed Sam's hand—almost protectively—and waited. Mr. Lowry came back outside, still cursing and spitting, but he pulled a money pouch out of his voluminous overalls. At least things were moving forward.

"That's $10 for two, son." He thrust an open palm towards Sam, with no recognition of the girl standing next to him, who had lived in the sparsely populated neighboring county all her life.

"Thank you, sir," Sam said, handing over the cash. The man snatched it into his claw and stuffed it into the zippered bag, then turned his back on them.

"Tickets, please, sir," Candy said sweetly, undaunted.

Mr. Lowry wheeled around with a scowl, chewing his cud and peering at her under thick, wiry eyebrows. She held the gaze serenely for a couple of seconds, and he growled something incomprehensible about stupid tourists, plunging his knobby knuckles into another pocket. He withdrew two numbered raffle tickets and tossed them towards Sam, who was quick enough to catch them midair before they fluttered to the ground, foiling the old codger's attempt at making him grovel. The man cursed them again and hobbled back to his rocking chair, his harmonica already on his lips. Within seconds he was piping out beautiful music, once more.

"Shit," Sam whispered, chuckling under his breath, as Candy hauled him through the entrance under the banner.

"He's always like that, forget it." She was using most of her will to smooth down her hackles. That bastard. "But you don't want to get on the Lowry clan's bad side. It's pretty backwoods in these parts, and they're sort of...."

"Hillbilly gangsters?"

"Yeah," she said, catapulted out of her funk. "How'd you know that?"

Sam caught her gaze and held it for a heartbeat. His smile was easy, a lifetime of experience behind it, somehow. "Something about the eyes."

"Know a lot of gangsters?" She wasn't sure she wanted to know.

Sam shrugged and glanced back at the skinny, partially senile sack of bones, whose eyes were murderous behind his jubilant tune.

Candy felt a primal urge to be gone. "Well anyway, I wouldn't stare."

chapter twenty

The old man's song grew fainter as they strolled up a tree-lined path. Birdsong joined in with the fading harmonica, high in the canopy above them. Before long, the din of a bustling crowd started to rise in between the fluttering notes of a fiddle. They rounded one last turn around a granite outcrop and were greeted by a raucous party, the mountain pass widening into full-scale country jamboree. People of all shapes, colors and sizes were meandering around tables and tents full of hand-woven clothing, jewelry with local gemstones, Civil War paraphernalia, old Appalachian replicas of all sorts and any other oddity that made the grade that year. A stilt walker was handing out fliers, probably for the late-night show that was reportedly pretty bawdy. Candy had never attended the show, but one of her cousins told her it was the closest Shirley got to cabaret. Makeshift stalls lined the avenue to serve a hungry, bustling crowd. Her stomach clenched when the smell of roasting meat hit her nostrils.

"Whoa, what a party." Right on cue, orange flame shot up in a diagonal next to the stilt walker. The crowd oohed and aahed. "Jesus, there's a firebreather."

"Unexpected?" Candy smiled; it was rare to see Sam caught off guard.

For Candy, after months of the wide-open fields and lonely mountain roads, such a throng was an admitted novelty She imagined a bird's eye view of the festival grounds, like there were tiny ant lines trickling through the countryside, draining into the cauldron of people before her. Festival time was easy to love. The crowd was mostly tourists, snapping pictures and pointing and generally behaving badly, though. She pulled Sam off to the side to wander in between the tents and tables from the inner alleyway between vendors.

Right away, she spotted a tall, gangly girl in overalls sporting two long braids on either side of her neck. Candy didn't know many people she'd call a best friend, especially at school, but Erica Norman was a close buddy. "Hey, Erica," she called, going in for a hug.

"Hey, guys." Erica pushed her horn-rimmed glasses higher on her nose and regarded the new guy warily. Of course she would've recognized him from the previous school year, but up close was a different story, of which Candy was well aware. "Whatcha been up to?"

"You've met Sam?" Candy beamed.

"Uh…no. I mean, I remember you started at Andrew Jackson halfway through last year, right?"

Sam held out his hand, those impeccable manners surfacing again. "Yes. It's nice to finally meet you, Erica."

The three chatted for a few minutes about how they had spent the summer, school starting, and Erica's dad's new line of mountain dulcimers. They were gorgeous instruments, all hand-made, with intricate inlay work, hanging from the roof of a tent and lying in row upon row on display tables. Candy hoped they sold well at the festival; Erica had often described how much hard work and expert craftsmanship went into them.

"Hey, let me get a picture for Dad's scrapbook," Erica said, producing a cellphone from her pocket.

Sam ducked out of shooting range, and held out his hand to accept the phone instead, "Let me take it, you two get together."

"Oh, okay. Come 'ere, Candy."

Sam snapped several shots with Candy dwarfed under Erica's armpit. Under his direction, Erica leaned down and Candy went on tiptoe so they could grin into the lens on a level. His oh-you're-so-precious-little-Candy look made her want to smother him with kisses and kick him in the balls, simultaneously. He captured a few with Erica holding one of the beautiful dulcimers and asked her to demonstrate how they were played. She was happy to oblige but Candy ushered them on, assuring her they would come back soon.

"You do not want to set Erica Norman on that course right now, trust me," she said, holding onto an elbow and weaving them through the crowd to reach the other side of the avenue. "We could be stuck there for hours."

"Is she good?"

"She *is*, but I'm starving." She pointed to the line of food stalls across the way. "Let's eat."

Candy's stomach had been growling since before Popcorn tried to kill Sam, and the smell wafting from the food carts was heavenly. There were several smokers chuffing out wonderful incense, and Sam headed for the pulled pork lines. But, smell could be deceiving, especially with barbecue. "You want my advice; you should go for the kebabs." Candy redirected him towards a shorter line to the left, where the locals were milling and gesticulating about something either important or gossip-worthy. Several were holding her favorite variety of gyro sandwich. "The Williams' goats herd right in Shirley Valley. The meat is fresh, organic, and for sure cruelty free—you can meet them, if you want to be sure."

"Are they friendly goats I'd be eating, then? Good personalities?"

"I meant the *Williams'* are good people, smarty pants. They treat their animals well," she said. "Hey, better to know they frolic in the fields, rather than stand around in their own poop."

"Yes, of course."

She got in line, and didn't care for once if he followed. Not that much. "And the cucumber mint sauce is to die for, trust me."

"Locals always know best." Sam sidled over next to her and slid his arm around her waist.

"Darn right." She rose up to give him a quick peck on the lips, but he held onto her and made it a kiss to set her body aflame.

"Next!" Sam let her go and she spun around, forgetting where she was for a second. A pimple-faced boy was working the register. "Oh hey, Candy."

"Hey, Jimmy," she said, returning the lukewarm attitude. Not a friend, but not an enemy. "I'll have the veggie, and he'll have the regular."

"Twelve bucks."

She frowned at the little thief. "Tourist prices," she said flatly, while Sam handed over the money.

"We ain't givin' local discounts today, sorry." The boy craned around her to see the next customer. "Next."

They moved to the side to await their meal, and Sam regarded her curiously. "I didn't know you were a vegetarian. I guess I never have seen you eat meat."

"I'm not a 'vegetarian.' I don't like rules."

"Hmm, I noticed that."

"No, but I do know those goats," she laughed, embarrassed. "They're next-door neighbors to my grandma."

Another teenage boy that Candy nodded to, but didn't greet, pushed two steaming pita sandwich cones wrapped in paper into their hands, and they both went silent devouring their lunch.

"God, that *is* good sauce," Sam said between bites. Juice from the rare meat mixed with cucumber sauce and ran down his wrist. "And the goats are definitely friendly."

"Mmm-hmm," Candy managed with her mouth full. She snatched several napkins to take with them and they sauntered through the throng towards the sound of a fiddle, devouring their messy gyros. The avenue opened onto a large, circular clearing, and they hung at the edge while they finished their feast and watched the stage on the far side.

"Think this is the fiddle competition," Candy offered between bites.

A makeshift stage had been erected on risers, about two feet off the ground, and a young girl was planted right in the center of it, sawing away at a fiddle for all she was worth. She was probably only eight years old, and though her execution was not perfect, in terms of exactness in tone, the notes flowed naturally and there was no denying her passion. When she was finished, she held her bow on one side and her fiddle on the other, giving a petite curtsy in her flowered dress, to modest applause. Sam looked at Candy, with raised eyebrows.

She shrugged. "Pretty good."

The atmosphere quieted, while a middle-aged man dressed in most of a three-piece suit (he'd already removed the jacket in respect for the rising afternoon heat) claimed the stage, next to the emcee. A smattering of applause erupted in pockets around the clearing, and several older couples moved to the center of a loose crowd, taking up position and establishing the dance floor as others graciously moved aside.

"Y'all, now we'll have a listen to our own Albert Young, while the judges make their decision," the emcee, a portly man in overalls and a baseball cap, said into the microphone. He backed off the stage, then amended, "Thank you, Harriett Woods," clapped awkwardly with the microphone pinned under his arm.

The gentleman on center stage brought his fiddle to his chin and straightened his back, breathing in deeply and loosening his shoulders. He brought his bow up to the strings and pulled a long, cool, high note before erupting into song. The dancers flowed with him; it was a song they all knew well.

"Oooh, Mountain Waltz," Candy said, dreamily. Her impromptu clapping ended in cherished fists clasped to her chest.

"Fuck it," she heard Sam mutter next to her.

"Huh?"

He grabbed both of her hands in his and pulled her towards the center of the clearing.

She pulled him backwards in a panic, "No, I can't waltz!" She had always wanted to learn, watching the adults covetously since she was a kid. But no one ever taught her. She looked around, wild-eyed; Sam was so strong, he had moved them to the dance floor with little effort, even with her protestations.

"Well, I can." He held her still with his eyes and positioned their hands for the dance, squaring his shoulders in a solid frame. "Just follow me."

He pushed forward, his body a driving force, and she fell back into his momentum, their bodies locked together, spilling into the rhythm of the dance floor. The fiddler turned the love song into a bittersweet lament; his high notes masterfully off tune, hopeful and desperate, and his low notes lengthening into mournful regret. As Sam and Candy whirled in a slow, sweeping rhythm, the strings wailed against the circle of enclosing trees and the noise of the crowd escaped into waves of afternoon heat drifting into the open sky above. He spun her around in a perfect twirl, and pulled her back into a strong embrace, reclaiming her eyes with a sure, steady gaze.

"I... I didn't know you could dance," she spluttered. "How do you know how to dance?"

"How does anyone know how to dance?"

He spun her out and pulled her back in. Artful. She smiled up at him, entranced and tongue-tied.

"Someone taught me, Candy."

"But..."

"Never would have thought?"

"No—I mean, who?" Sam hadn't told her much about his family beyond snippets. "Your mom taught you?" she asked doubtfully. When he remained quiet, her face darkened, "Some girlfriend?"

He laughed, "My grandmother taught me how to dance."

"You have a grandmother?"

"Candy." He dipped her with a flourish. "Just dance with me." He held her inches from the ground. His face was silhouetted in shadow, but the sunlight behind him lent a halo to the edges of a dark, tousled mantle.

Well that's a sight to keep from your mama, if ever there was one. If she had a mama. She blinked hard. *Oh, screw it.* Her surrender was complete. She heard the music and felt Sam's body, reacting to every nuance, as he moved them around the floor. He watched her face and let her lose herself, his eyes glinting when she opened hers and focused. She smiled and melted into him, feeling herself glide along with his steps. Effortless. *What is happening? Is this really Sam?*

The song was over before it had begun, and Candy felt empty as the crying fiddle went silent. When would she ever feel so strange and lovely again?

The cloddish emcee was back, barking into her consciousness. "Okay, y'all. The results are in."

In silent accord, Sam and Candy slipped away from the announcements to the shade of the trees. They sat together on the limb of an old oak; Candy snuggled into the nook of Sam's arm. Four fiddle contestants returned to the stage and formed a line, awaiting the results.

"Oh, it's Carol," said Candy, pointing to a red-haired thirteen-year-old who was waiting close by, fiddle and bow in hand, for her placement to be announced. "I wasn't sure if they were coming."

"Who?"

"My Uncle Pat and fam—Pat is Carol's dad. They're my favorite cousins, that's cool you'll get to meet them. If Pat is here, everybody's in for a celebration, family style. He just doesn't know any other way to be, and neither do his kids."

They watched the results from their hiding spot and Candy cheered inwardly, not ready to be found just yet. But, it was only a matter of time if Pat were there. She bounced up and down and grinned ear to ear as each musician was given some kind of award. Her cousin took third place and the eight-year-old girl in the flowered dress won first prize. "Huh, you never know," she whispered. "Cuteness tempers the sound of the music, I guess."

Sam looked offended. "I thought she was great."

"Nah, now you're gonna see the good stuff," Candy murmured and pointed to a musical troupe too large for the stage. They were setting up around it, in haphazard arrangement.

The unnamed band was always changing, but that day Candy counted three fiddlers, two guitarists, and a woman dragging over a chair and pulling out what looked like one of the mountain dulcimers that Erica Norman's father made. A bearded man pulled up a chair next to her, with no apparent instrument, and another lady wheeled over a cello case. Before all the others were even set up, a beautiful Asian girl in a sundress, her long hair tied to one side in a leather thong, hopped up to sit on the stage with her fiddle. Her boots dangling over the edge, she began playing casually. The bearded man pulled out two spoons from his back pocket and, after listening to the fiddler for a few beats, joined in. He used not only his spoons and hands, but also his legs, chair and even his shoes for percussion. His rhythm was simple at first, then gained in complexity, as he found his groove and others joined in. Before long, the whole ensemble was rolling along together, meandering in and out of a basic melody, each player randomly assuming the lead and taking up a complicated solo. A banjo player from the crowd sauntered over and took up the song, the cellist nodding and smiling at him in encouragement.

Most of the band was tapping their feet already, and then the first fiddler hopped from the stage while taking a solo. She began to shuffle her feet in time, almost as if beyond her own will. Sam seemed to understand the inclination; his thumbs were tapping out the beat of the joyful music on Candy's thighs. The audience seemed to agree, and several old men began a shuffling dance, similar to the fiddler's.

"Is that clogging?" asked Sam.

"Buck dancing."

A large woman in the center of the clearing was directing people to stand in formation, and others to move back. She assumed her own place next to a man in a cowboy hat who clapped in time, standing alone in the configuration. "Two, three, four." The whole group of dancers sprang into motion, keeping time with the band and passing partners between themselves, spinning and whirling.

"Square dance." Sam said. "I don't believe it. They all just started square dancing."

Candy shifted around to look at him, bemused. "Well, yeah. You act like you've never been to an Old-time Musical Festival."

He grinned. "I haven't."

"Want to dance?"

Sam's smile disappeared and his eyes flicked to the dance floor. "I've taken the odd square dance class in gym…"

Candy winked, taunting him.

"I can't square dance, sorry," he admitted.

"Well, I can," Candy said, raising an eyebrow in challenge to his earlier boast.

Sam looked towards the group of well-acquainted dancers looping arms and swinging each other around at an increasingly rapid pace, obviously willing to try it rather than back down.

"I'm not serious, Sam!" She broke into a fit of laughter at the very thought. He buried his face in her hair and she felt him shaking with mirth against her back. "I'm not really in the club either," she said, when the giggles finally subsided. "I can buck dance, though. Used to take lessons with my cousin when I was little. Want to see?"

He released her and leaned back on their tree limb to watch. "Definitely," he said, his voice still uneven and his eyes still alight.

She stood up and waved her hands around to make sure she had elbowroom in their snug clearing. "Have you ever done any clogging at all? That's where it comes from."

Sam shook his head and smiled in anticipation.

"Well, you start with a rock step, like this. Step, step, rock step. Step, step, rock step." She watched her feet, each clomping down next to the other, then one stepping back, like a swing step. She was a little rusty, but she warmed up as she gained the rhythm. "And you can add a scuff, like you're trying to get gum off the bottom of your shoe," she said, kicking her foot forward in a low slide and pulling it back hard.

"I like it."

"Let's see. You can do a knee lift like this." She raised her knee up level with her hips on one shove-and-pull. "Or a dip," and she clicked her heels, bringing her knees in together for quick bop to each side.

"Never with a partner?"

"Well, people can dance off of each other, but it's pretty much a solo dance. Of course, it gets harder when you speed it up to the music."

She quickened her pace in time with the band playing in the clearing. Picking up the quick banjo and lilting fiddle, her feet got away from her and she spun around out of control. Unable to help herself, she bobbed her head and clapped her hands, laughing with glee, and grinning up at Sam. He grabbed her arm on her next spin and pulled her in for a kiss, but she was too electrified and spun back out again, cackling. By the end of the jam, though, she was out of breath and was ready to collapse against him for relief.

"I love it," said Sam, her breath blowing his hair in wisps.

She clamped her mouth shut, remembering that cucumber mint sauce. "Whew! I forgot what a workout that is."

Feedback from the stage made them both wince, then the emcee announced, "Alright, y'all. Next up is the buck dance competition."

Candy and Sam burst out laughing. "Hey, you should have entered."

"Me? Oh no, I'm not very good," she said. Out of the corner of her eye, she noticed one of the dancers waiting by the stage. "Oh my god, that's my cousin Reagan up there. She was who I took lessons with when I was little. You'll see the difference—she's incredible. Way better than me."

"Such a talented family."

"I wish I had gotten some of that talent. Or, maybe I just haven't found mine yet."

"Are you kidding me?" Sam regarded her, confused. "What about all the painting?"

"I'm okay," she allowed. "Not as good as you."

He frowned at her like she was crazy.

"I'm not trying to be modest—trust me. I mean..." How could she explain? "Don't you ever feel like there's something just around the corner? Something you're waiting for. Like, that you're *really* meant for?"

Sam's face changed. Darkened. "Yeah," he said, his eyes shifting away from hers.

Candy had the feeling they were talking about two different things entirely. "But, when me and Reagan used to dance together..." She began prattling away about her childhood lessons, desperate to take the coldness out of Sam's eyes. She snuggled back under his arm and he hugged her in closer, asking polite questions to move her story along, content to keep moving away from whatever had spoiled his mood. The band resumed playing, gradually rolling into a discernible melody. A tune close to "Oh Susanna" emerged and one of the waiting contestants, with a nod to the emcee, climbed the rickety stairs to take center stage. The dancer picked up the rhythm in a more methodical way than the impromptu audience members had, stamping his shoes loudly. The boisterous audience clapped along, cheering the contestants. Candy joined in atop a tree stump with hoots and catcalls when Reagan took the spotlight. The girl recognized her and made a bee-line for their hideout as soon as she was finished with her performance.

"Hey, you," Reagan bellowed, grabbing Candy in a fierce bear hug. "I wondered where you went, after *the waltz*."

"Oh yeah, you saw us dancing?" Candy stuttered, looking to Sam. He had regained full composure and was smiling serenely. "This is Sam. Sam, Reagan."

Reagan's eye went wide, and Candy knew exactly what she was thinking. *Please don't say boyfriend or anything, please, please.* Sam would be her first. If he even was her boyfriend.

"So nice to meet you, Sam. You're quite the dancer, aren't you?" Reagan insisted on hugging him like he was already family.

Sam's voice was muffled by the embrace, "Pretty good yourself."

"Should be, after twelve years of lessons every weekend. Too bad Candy dropped out. Spoil sport."

"Oh come on, it was just a kid thing," Candy muttered. *Please don't embarrass me, Reagan.*

"Yeah, and you're a bad girl," Reagan said, her eyes narrowing. A hand darted out to tickle her cousin's ribs and Candy jerked away with a sour chuckle.

Here it comes…

"Sam, you should give your girlfriend a spanking."

chapter twenty-one

After a few minutes of small talk and promises to reconnect later with more of the McBride clan, Sam decided to let the two girls catch up and left them gossiping about the day's juried events. He wandered back down the broad lane of booths and tents, meandering through the crafts for sale and munching a pulled pork sandwich. Candy was right, of course; the barbeque wasn't the best—sort of like dry meat soaked in ketchup. A flash of light caught his eye and he looked toward it; there was a tent larger than most, shadowy inside, with bright flecks glinting off of what seemed to be gems hanging from the roof. He trashed the rest of his mediocre meal and went inside.

The space was more of an environment than a simple craft tent, like the others. He smelled Nag Champa incense burning and heard ambient music tickling his eardrums. Sam smirked in response; he'd met more than a few earth children in his travels across the States. The gems he had seen were actually glass beads, sparkling with iridescent spiraling wisps within, and there were many more hanging about in a myriad shapes and sizes. Larger, more intricate glass sculptures stood on pedestals draped in velvet around the space, each piece enhanced by individual track lights. Mesmerized by the atmosphere, so quiet and cool, with most of the festival attendees gathered for the show on the dance floor, Sam jumped when a woman's voice broke the spell.

"You must be Sam." She was holding out her hand to him. "I'm sorry. I didn't mean to startle you."

He let out his breath in a chuckle, "That's okay."

"I'm Rachel."

Sam shook her hand, his eyebrows knitted in question. "Hello."

"I saw you dancing with Candy earlier."

"News travels fast?" asked Sam, still not understanding how the strange woman knew his name.

"She hasn't mentioned me? She's told me a lot about you…your build particularly." She walked around him to appraise all sides, boldly sizing up his physique. "But she never mentioned those cheekbones. Who needs a diamond wheel for cutting when you've got those? Black hair and olive skin—Russian descent?" Sam's eyes followed her as she came back around to face him. "Candy has shown me your work. It's fascinating, Sam. I'd love to talk with you about a particular drawing. Such passion," she hissed, holding his gaze.

Sam let the silence stretch between them. She was attractive, though much older, and her frankness was refreshing in a small town full of guarded looks and whispers behind hands.

"I know too much about you for your comfort, don't I?" she finally asked, though Sam was sure she already knew the answer. "And you know nothing at all of me. I have an apprentice position open that your friend Candy thought you might be interested in."

Oh. He relaxed his shoulders, no longer wary. "A glass apprentice? I was actually admiring your sculptures, before you came in."

She waved a dismissive hand at the sculptures. "Bongs."

Sam took a closer look at the nearest; a green glass smoke chamber, encrusted with a golden patina, twisted up into an inhale hole at the top, with a delicate stem jutting out at the bottom. The bowl was a tiny, pink flower bud. *Huh. Sure as shit are.*

"They're a lot of damn work, and I'm tired of doing it." Rachel threw her arms overhead and whirled around, motioning to the jewels hanging around their heads. "Honestly, this stuff is my bread and butter, though. Anyone loves pretty beads and tabacco bongs, especially at a festival like this—my real work would never sell here. I've got to churn this stuff out, and Rudolfo quit on me last week. I need to get back to my *work*, Sam. Are you interested?"

"In…the apprentice position?"

"Well, what other positions should we be talking about?"

Oh, you're a handful, aren't you? Sam watched the aging hippie with mirth.

"It's hard, sweaty work, Sam. I'm not going to lie to you," she said, gripping his shoulders. Her face was close enough for him to smell her Patchouli cologne. "You have to want it. There could be blood. Do you want it?"

Sam had absolutely no idea what a glass apprentice position entailed, but this Rachel creature was already easier to take than Larry.

"You'll be my slave at first, until you can handle the torch. But, you'll be learning every minute, and you will never be bored. Grinding, blasting, painting, firing, and at last...the flames—molten glass over two-thousand degrees. What do you think, Sam?"

She had started pacing around patting her pockets, looking for something important. She found her object of desire, and breathed a sigh of relief. She lit her cigarette with a monogrammed butane lighter and inhaled deeply. Superficially calmed, with her arms crossed over her chest, she awaited his response

"When—"

"I know you're still in school, I wouldn't dream of interfering with your studies," she waved the unasked question away with a flutter and tapped the slender fingers of her other hand against an elbow, watching him intently.

"When can I start?"

"Marvelous," Rachel intoned from deep within her chest.

§

Candy sidled past Mr. Norman's tent on the far side of the alley. She could see Erica through the throng, demonstrating how to hold a dulcimer to some tourists. She caught Candy's eye and waved, then turned her hand into a secret thumbs-up before moving it behind her ear to adjust her glasses. Candy smiled back and nodded, then continued on her way. There was an amazing array of tents, much more varied than she remembered from the previous year. She moseyed along, the summer sun beating down on her back, stopping to investigate the more interesting vendors and keeping an eye out for Sam.

"Tell your fortune, pretty girl?" an oily voice asked, close to her ear. She spun toward the offender and saw a slight man, standing at least ten feet from her.

Whoa, that was weird. It was like he was so close he was inside my head. She walked closer and he offered her a business card between two fingers. "Tarot Cards?" Candy pocketed the card and read the hand-sewn sign hanging over the man's head. She had always been curious about tarot reading. "How much?"

"For you, pretty girl? Ten dollars," he said, grasping an edge of the tent flap with one hand and holding out the other for her to take.

"What do I get for ten dollars?"

"Your complete reading, as you like it. Three card spread, five card horseshoe, Celtic cross. As you like it."

Candy had no idea what he was talking about, and she had a feeling he knew that. "Okay. Do I pay you?"

"Please," the man shook his head, as if money were an impropriety. He motioned her inside, tucking his hand behind his back when Candy refused to take it. After the blazing summer sun of the avenue, the darkness inside the tent was almost complete. She blinked, trying to adjust her eyes to the gloom.

"Hello, my dear." A woman was seated behind a table draped in shimmery fabric. When Candy inched forward, her eyes more accustomed to the light, she saw the cloth was midnight blue velvet sprinkled with silvery thread. Like moonlight. A round orb glowed next to the woman's face. Candy had seen the same light in an Ikea catalogue, but the way it lit up the seer's features in the gloom was disarming. Not quite a crystal ball, but close. "Sit, pl—"

Candy walked closer to the chair that the woman had indicated, but halted when her expression changed from solicitous to guarded. "Should I sit here?"

"Yes…" the woman said, with less authority.

Candy lowered herself into what she could tell was a folding chair under the same glittery fabric, then settled her hands in her lap. She had no idea of what to expect from a tarot reading. The woman was shuffling a deck of cards, watching her with eyes rimmed in charcoal black. The shuffling went on. Candy cleared her throat and looked around, beginning to feel uncomfortable.

"My dear, I cannot read your cards," the woman finally said. Her voice had changed. Candy could no longer detect the Eastern European accent she had heard only minutes before.

"Oh. Why not?"

The woman smiled. She looked down at her hands, finally still. She folded them on top of the deck of cards. "It's not often that I meet such a one."

What the heck is that supposed to mean? "Such a one…like me?"

A throaty chuckle.

"I have the money. I tried to give it to the guy outside but he wouldn't take it." Candy stood to dig in the pocket of her jeans. She pulled out a few bills and rifled through them. "Here."

"Darling, sit. Please."

Candy crumpled the money in her hands, feeling like an idiot.

The woman watched her for a beat, but then seemed to make a decision.

"Have you ever brought a strong magnet too close to a television? To a speaker? No, that's not right. You have satellite radio?"

"My dad does, in his car."

"And sometimes the connection is lost? Something blocks the signal."

"Well, yeah I guess. The reception isn't that great in Shirley."

"Oh, there is nothing wrong with my reception, my dear." Her eyes were intense and reproachful.

Candy sat, twiddling her fingers. She shoved her bills back into her pocket, unsure of how to proceed. "So, what's wrong with me?"

The woman watched her across the table, covetous. "There is nothing wrong with you. I would give anything to be as you are."

"Okay… well, if you don't want to read my cards…" Feeling partly alarmed, partly embarrassed, but most of all irritated, Candy made to get up. A hand shot out to stop her.

"You want me to read your cards?" The woman flipped one over. "Judgement. Ruled by fire. Big surprise." She laughed, but it sounded more like a crow squawking. "Here's another. The Magician—Mercury, the fiery planet. And you haven't even touched the deck. Oh look, the Ace of Cups. Summer. Heat."

Candy felt less fiery than she ever had, the slithery coolness of trepidation seeping over her skin. "I don't understand what you're saying."

The seer leaned back in her chair and pulled her black wig off of her head. "Neither do I, sweetheart."

She produced a cigarette from a hidden pocket and lit it. Candy watched her inhale deeply, closing her eyes as if calming herself.

Was she supposed to pay her after that? She hadn't really done a reading. "Fine. I guess I'll just go." She rose from her seat and moved toward the bright line of sunshine that marked the tent's exit. A last glance at the woman showed her apparently deep in thought. *Meditating? Bizarre. Should I tell that guy outside she's on a break?*

"You're mother's the same?" the croaking voice asked, just as she reached the edge of the tent. "So full of fire?"

Candy turned back. "My mother?"

"The gift is usually passed down, mother to daughter."

"Full of fire"—my bad temper? Candy was completely confused. How was being prone to explosive outbursts a gift? Everyone her whole life had chastised her about her temper. *Like I'm a freak.*

"She never talks about it?"

"My mother killed herself when I was seven," Candy spat. *None of your damn business.*

The seer's face registered neither surprise nor sympathy. "You better be careful with it, then."

Candy wanted to slap her. "Well, thanks for nothing." She ducked through the flapping curtains, dazed by the blinding sunlight, and pushed past the little man outside. He had been listening; his features were wary and he moved aside, his eyes cast away from her.

"Nice scam," she said over her shoulder, stalking down the alley. For once, she was happy to blend in with the tourists—she didn't feel the prickles on her neck subside until the "Tarot Cards" sign was out of view behind the bend.

"What a load of horse shit," she muttered as she walked. What had she been expecting? Everyone knew fortune telling was a hoax. She felt ridiculous for going in that tent, but at least she hadn't let them take her money. *Definitely won't mention that to Sam. He would laugh his butt off, I bet.*

Where was Sam? Candy resolved to find her boyfriend (if he was her boyfriend) and put the seer's cryptic remarks out of her mind. She roamed through the tents with more purpose until she finally saw his distinctive outline; he was standing with his arms crossed over his chest, his weight resting on one foot, with the posture of listening intently to—

"Rachel!" Sam glanced back and smiled as Candy approached. "There you are. Good, you guys have met." She pushed her sunglasses onto her head and entered Rachel's quiet tent, bringing carnival smells and sounds with her.

"Candy, my dear," Rachel growled, accepting a hug and giving her an air kiss. "I must thank you for the lead, Sam is exactly what I need."

"Oh, cool," Candy said, inspecting the displays. "I thought it might be a good match up." She walked along the perimeter, appraising the pedestaled sculptures and trying to keep her grin from spreading. She knew Sam would make a good apprentice at Rachel's glass studio.

"I'm holding a workshop soon, my dear."

"In Shirley?" Candy chirped, surprised. "Love the new iridescent stuff."

"Oh, honey. I'll show you what it's really capable of. You can't imagine. I'm still playing with it in these, but I'm perfecting a technique that is simply fabulous."

"I can't wait to see it." Candy moved closer to Sam and grabbed his hand.

Thank you, he mouthed.

He had accepted the job, then. Maybe he could work more regular hours with Rachel, instead of being at that creep Larry's beck and call. That was Candy's plan anyway. She was always welcome at Rachel's place, too, and her mind exploded with the possibilities of better Sam access.

"Wonderful. I need to get back to the studio. I'm ready to start packing up for the day—Sam, come with me." Rachel disappeared through velvet drapery, her muffled commands continuing through the fabric. Candy looked at Sam, who was clearly taken aback, and she stifled the humor bubbling up inside. Though she loved her, Rachel was a caricature of the nutty, eccentric artist. Did she really expect him to start working immediately? When she realized Sam was not following, Rachel popped her head back into the showroom. "Well, come on, do you want the job or not?"

"Yes, I do," Sam assured her, but motioning to the extensive display environment around them, added, "How long will it take to dismantle this?"

"I have a team to do that, darling. We're just taking the major pieces in the truck. I'll take you both home, after we drop everything off at the studio and I show you around. You game?"

At mention of how they would be getting home, the memory of rolling Popcorn sprang to mind, and Candy was relieved to have better transportation than the horses. She nodded eagerly, accepting for them both, "Yes, please."

"I'm game," Sam agreed.

The three of them packed the more expensive glass artwork and arranged the boxes in the bed of Rachel's F-150, Sam and Candy exchanging secret smiles and quick kisses every time they passed each other. Though their afternoon had been unexpectedly cut short, Candy figured they would have more time together after Rachel dropped them in Buffalo Square. By the time the truck was ready to leave, the festival seemed to be dying down, the wail of cicadas picking up. Candy had already slapped several mosquitoes on her neck, and was glad to be getting clear of the thick woods and into the air-conditioned cab. She couldn't wait to get Sam alone, maybe ask him to waltz her around in private somewhere.

Rachel had a way of bending plans to her own needs, however. When she heard that Sam lived far to the south of town, she decided that Candy should be deposited at her grandmother's house in the valley, before she and Sam drove to the glass studio over the river, in Western Mountain. Candy wished she could change her mind and ask to be taken home (closer to Sam's house), but—*drat*—she had already promised her cousin that she would spend the night at Grandma Catherine's with her. On a map, the new transportation plan seemed logical beyond argument, her grandma's upper-valley neighborhood the obvious first stop. Arguing would seem foolish. And desperate. Candy felt cheated and disappointed, though, as they drove down the state road from the festival.

"But Rachel, I wanted to see that new work you were talking about," she tried.

"Oh, we're having an open studio in a couple weeks, love—First Thursdays are starting up again now that autumn is almost upon us. You'll see plenty of work then, mine and everyone else's. It will be fabulous, don't miss it."

Candy felt lame disagreeing, and not even sure what she had wanted to happen at the end of the day, except for that she had wanted Sam. She listened to the glass-blower shoptalk, sullenly. She thought Sam felt the same, but watching him with Rachel, she had to wonder.

When they pulled onto Riverbend Road, Candy was picking at her nails, despondent, while Sam and Rachel chatted away on either side of her. Looking up to watch her grandma's house approach, she saw her uncle Pat's SUV and two other visiting cars in Grandma Catherine's driveway. Beyond, there looked to be a party developing at the Robinson house. She caught her breath. *The bonfire's smoking. Is he already here?*

She offered abrupt good-byes, annoyed with Rachel and aware she had already lost Sam's attention; he didn't even register that there was a party starting right under his nose, couldn't even smell the campfire. Something about that gave her evil pleasure, seeing him so absorbed in tech-speak with Rachel. She felt guilty when he leaned over for a familiar, boyfriendly peck on the lips, though.

He murmured, "See you, baby," watching her lips as he slouched back onto his seat.

Her insides fluttered at the endearment. *Baby. Holy crap.* "I'll call you later," she said and delivered one last kiss.

chapter twenty-two

Rachel put the truck in gear. She was already driving towards the bridge, when Candy burst through her grandma's door to get the scoop. "Grandma?" She dumped her bag on the floor and kicked off her sneakers, noting the already large accumulation of shoes by the front door.

"We're in here," several voices shouted at once from the direction of the living room; a deep masculine voice mixed with a young female one and her grandma's familiar melodious greeting. She bounded into the room to find John and Reagan sitting on either side of Grandma Catherine, who held a large, leather-bound photo album on her lap. John pulled himself out of the snug sectional sofa and spread his arms out, white teeth shining from ear to ear.

"Oh my god—John!" Candy took in his new physique before crashing into him. She couldn't help blushing against his chest; she had rarely seen him in the last few years, during such a rapid growth stage for adolescent boys, and it was hard to keep up with the changes via photographs. A single glance showed her that John had grown attractive in a way she hadn't noticed before. Over six feet tall, he was still slender, yet much more filled-out in his shoulders and chest. Manly. The cute cleft chin that he'd had since he was little was more defined, his jaw line more angled.

He squeezed her tight and raised her up off the floor with a comic growl, and the strangeness that had been lingering between them for years was gone in an instant. "Hey, Candy-cane. It's good to see you."

"Jaw-breaker." She knitted her brows and rubbed his velvety blonde head, bleached against his summer tan. "Your hair is so short—where's the curls?"

"Oh, sorry," he said, the timber in his voice hinting at genuine concern. He knew how much she always loved to boing his curls; they were a novelty, since her own hair was as straight as a board. "I have to keep it short while I'm life-guarding or it'll turn green."

"Well, grow it out."

"I will," he promised.

"So, what are you guys looking at?" Her grandma had the photo album opened to a page where Candy had just gotten a pair of purple terrycloth training pants, her favorite Christmas gift that year.

Reagan quoted the famous song Candy had sung, while dancing around waving the present in the air, "Purple panties, purple panties." It had become something of a family anthem for Candy.

"You were so thrilled to have something a little less boyish. All those older brothers, who can blame you, sweet thing?" Grandma Catherine recalled, gazing at her granddaughter with kind eyes. "Fit for a princess."

Who could be embarrassed, after the thousandth re-telling? Candy indulged them with her next scripted line, "Purple was just my favorite color, is all."

"Your Aunt Maeve had to dye those purple—nobody could find real purple panties."

"Oh, there they are in action." Reagan pointed out a photo on the opposite page in which Candy stood with her feet planted on a makeshift first base, holding a huge baseball bat over her shoulders. She had a lop-sided, gamine grin plastered on her proud face, still baby-fat. She wasn't wearing anything but the panties and a ponytail pulled through an over-sized Bobcatts cap. "Yeah, you were a real princess, Candy."

"Alright then, let's find some Reagan gems." Candy knew just where to start.

They flipped through the album, trading jibes and telling old stories, welcoming Reagan's little sister Carol and then the eldest, Ursula. Ursula's baby slept in a sling around her shoulder, not waking even at Carol's periodic shrill of dismay. She was still too young to accept embarrassing jokes, Candy knew, but still her reaction was a little ridiculous. She glanced at John, guessing she wasn't the only girl in the room to have noticed he'd become so good-looking.

After finishing the first album, they grabbed another. Then another. "Oh look, there's John—that must have been when you started staying summers here. Oh my god, the Boy Scouts uniform."

"Yep. There I am. Look at all those badges," he laughed, a deep rumble in his chest.

Reagan tittered, "Candy was so impressed with those."

"What? No I wasn't."

"Oh come on, Candy," Ursula said, lowering her voice when the baby started to squirm. "That's all you could talk about the next school year—how unfair it is that the Boy Scouts don't accept girls."

John regarded her, wonderment in his expression. "I didn't know that."

Candy shrugged, suddenly feeling examined. Then, in blessed distraction, Uncle Pat burst onto the scene, insisting that everyone get their butts outside to eat. "The fire's a-blazin' next door, grab a hotdog on the way outside."

"Dad, where'd you put my fiddle?"

"Eat first, Carol; then playtime," Uncle Pat admonished, trying to sound tough.

Grandma Catherine eyed the baby, "I'll take Micah, sweetie."

"Awesome, I'm starving." Ursula plunked the baby into her grandma's waiting arms. "I'm sorry, Gramma—he needs a change."

"I think I can handle it, honey. You get some food in you, before he wakes up starving himself and howling for Mama again." She set the baby over her shoulder, shushing and bouncing when he mewled in dissent of the transfer.

"You even had those sultry eyes back then, Candy," Reagan said, halting in the act of closing an album. A picture of Candy had caught her attention. Candy leaned over and saw her nine-year-old face, gazing forlornly at one of her cousins, who was opening birthday presents during a party.

"Selkie eyes," her grandma whispered over Micah's shoulder.

Candy's ears pricked at the description, "What do you mean?"

Reagan frowned at her. "You've never heard the legend of the selkies? My dad used to tell it at bedtime, it's an old Irish folktale,"

"Come on, even I've heard of selkies," said John. "The Secret of Roan Inish is one of my mom's favorite movies."

Candy looked from face to face. "Never heard of it. Come on, tell me the story."

"Selkies are mythical creatures who are seals in the water, and humans on land."

"And they're beautiful, with deep black eyes." John nudged her ribs.

"The story my dad always told was of a selkie woman who shed her seal skin to come ashore, because she had fallen in love with a human. She hid her skin, so that she could return to the sea after seeing him—my dad never said 'making love' but that's the way I think of it now—but the man found the skin first and stole it, so that she would be forced to stay with him forever and be his wife. Apparently, selkies make great wives."

"How cruel."

"No, she was happy with him, and they had several children together, whom she loved very much. But she was often seen gazing longingly at the sea, kind of like you were gazing at those birthday presents." Reagan held the album closer, so Candy could see it better. "Anyway, one day while their father was away, the children were playing in their toy boxes and costumes, and they found the seal skin. They showed it to their mother, thinking nothing of it. She took it and immediately returned to the sea, never to be seen again by her husband. Although, the father did see the children playing with a seal and splashing in the water by the seashore."

"That's the basic story in my mom's movie, too."

"Wow, that's really sad," said Candy. She wondered if her uncle thought of how young she and her brothers were when their own mother died, 'never to be seen again.' "Your dad told you that story when you were how old?"

"But, look your mom had selkie eyes, too." Reagan flipped to an earlier page, which showed a picture of Candy's mom, flashing those haunting eyes at the camera in a close-up. The word "impish" came to mind. "They say the children of a selkie sometimes carries the gene, and that's why you have Irish folks with black hair and black eyes in a family of green-eyed red-heads."

"Well, who had the eyes before my mom?" Candy asked, trying not to feel ruffled at Reagan's light-hearted manner; she obviously didn't understand the sudden importance for her cousin. But Candy couldn't help but imagine that Uncle Pat had been thinking of his dead little sister, with her black selkie eyes, when he told his kids that story.

"Suzanna was the first in our family, as far as I know," their grandma answered. Her sympathetic look said that she regretted having brought the melancholy story to Candy's attention. "It's just a story, sweetie."

Candy watched her grandma disappear up the stairs. "Well, the dark eyes had to come from somewhere."

"Oh, Candy." Reagan snapped the album shut. "There aren't really any selkies."

"Of course not," John interjected. "But, genetically speaking, there would have to be a precursor somewhere."

Candy smiled at him. He understood.

"Yeah, in the mailman. Maybe that's why Grandma doesn't want to talk about it." Reagan laughed, springing out of her seat and grabbing Candy's hand to pull her up, too. "Come on, let's eat."

Candy let herself be towed along, looking back and making a crazy screaming face at John. "I'm gonna find those eyes."

"I have no doubt," he said. "When your mind is set..." He went to give her a teasing slap on the rump, but apparently realizing that would be inappropriate, turned it into a brotherly pat on the back.

Candy felt her cheeks flush and she shook her head at him, "You weirdo."

"Too bad you missed the festival today, John." Reagan's voice echoed as she entered the kitchen. "It was awesome; you should've seen *the waltz*. Candy was dancing with—"

"Everyone. And Reagan was in the buck dancing competition and kicked butt," Candy broke in, cutting Reagan off. She pinched the back of her arm in warning.

"Ow. What?"

Sshh, Candy mimed under her hand. She didn't know why, but she wanted to keep that memory close. Cherish it for a while longer. She secreted a look at John, certain that he hadn't missed the exchange; John never missed anything.

"Really? Did you place, Reagan?" He grabbed a paper plate and helped himself to heaping portions of potato salad, macaroni and cheese, baked beans and two hotdogs. He congratulated Reagan when she held up two fingers, for second place.

Seems to be letting it slide. For now. Candy wondered when John would bring it up again. She had no doubt that he would.

"Are we grilling these over the fire?" he asked, feigning ignorance and innocence.

"Probably, I think the grill is still out of commission from Fourth of July, right Reagan?" She fixed her buns up with dill relish, onions, ketchup and mayonnaise, but left an empty space for a veggie dog. She smiled, thinking about what Sam would say of her faux-vegetarianism, as she searched for one in the fridge.

"What happened on the Fourth of July?"

"My dad was experimenting with a new recipe again," said Reagan, rolling her eyes.

"I thought it was really good," called Candy from deep within the fridge. Nobody else in the family ate veggie dogs; she usually brought them over herself and stocked them away, where they remained undisturbed by anyone but her. *Grandma better not have thrown away the last ones I bought.* Finally unearthing a package of Tofurkey in the back of a drawer, she tossed one onto her bun and followed Reagan and John outside.

Then she stopped short. "Simon?"

Candy shoved her plate at Reagan. Her cousin fumbled dangerously for a few seconds before John helped her steady the extra load, then finally took it from her once it was balanced. Candy, meanwhile, vaulted onto a backlit shadow of the young man who had been walking across the field between the McBride and Robinson houses. She knocked him down like a professional wrestler, demanding, "Why didn't Dad tell me you were coming? Is that your new car? Is David with you?"

"I don't know. Yes—pretty sweet, huh? And yes," her brother answered her string of questions with a string of answers, his shoulders pinned to the ground and his little sister straddling his chest. He grabbed her waist and easily removed her. He got his feet back under him again and crouched down to offer her a ride. "I was just coming to get you, wondering what was taking y'all so goshdarn long."

With Candy riding piggyback on Simon, drilling him about college and when he had to be back for the final year, the group finally reached the bonfire. The party had definitely already started. Uncle Pat was entrenched in a story with Candy's dad, Simon's twin brother David, Uncle Garrett, all of them sitting on folding chairs next to the beer cooler. Carol, who had probably inhaled dinner, was rehashing her performance at the festival for their pre-teenage cousin, Zoë, punctuating with her fiddle. Zoë was one year Carol's junior, and she listened and nodded and congratulated, clutching her own preferred instrument, a classical guitar, at her side. Joshua and Alex, in their terrible two's, were shrieking, giggling and crying intermittently. They raced dangerously close to the fire and then sprinted away into darkness, keeping Aunt Cammy on her toes. Ursula stopped wolfing her hotdog for a second to strongly suggest that her husband run after his own son, so she could eat in peace. Candy's cousin, Peter, mired in the middle at the lost age of eight, sat at the edge of the fire looking bored and watching his hotdog turn black on its stick.

"Someone better give Peter something to do, before he starts burning live things," Candy surmised aloud, then saw that John already had the same thought. He squatted next to Peter and asked him about the proper method for grilling hotdogs, then offered his uncooked dogs for inspection.

"Candy, hi."

She turned to find John's dad on his way down the front steps, lugging a heavy cooler behind him with one hand. She ran over to take the handle on the other side. "Hi, Mr. Robinson, let me help you."

"Thanks. It's good to see you, honey." He straightened his back, his tailored khakis and neat polo unwrinkling like magic (so much like John, Candy had to stifle her smile), to carry the considerable load in a more dignified manner. James Robinson was not the kind of country macho who never accepted help from a little lady, and Candy loved that about him. "My sister's kids might come out to the fire, if the soda is out here. As it is, Beth has them all inside playing board games, quarantined from everyone else. I don't get it."

"Hmm, that's funny," Candy shrugged, wiser than she let on. Of course Aunt Beth would keep her brood tucked away from the licentious horde, with all the beer and secular conversation amidst. Heck, she even kept them from watching Disney cartoons, because of some church boycott about Disney's Gay Days or something. Candy knew that was the reason John's cousins were playing board games instead of watching the dangerous television set. John's Grandma Pearl had showcased all of her Disney movies and artifacts prominently in the den, where the television was located. Pearl had even found a way to make the Disney Channel the home station when you turned on the set, claiming it was some "auto-glitch" in the programming.

No sooner had they thumped the sodas down next to the beer cooler, than Pearl Robinson herself appeared out of the shadows to plant a kiss on James's cheek. "Thank you, Jamie. Candy. Don't worry—they'll swarm like locusts when we bring out the s'mores."

S'mores always reminded Candy of John, and she looked around to find him again. Somehow, she found herself in front of the high school principal, Mr. Warren, instead. A much less pleasant outcome.

"Well now, Candace Vale. Ready for school to start tomorrow?"

"Oh, you mean Monday—day after tomorrow, sir," Candy replied. Big surprise: Mr. Warren was already in his cups.

"Blessed news about Joe, isn't it?" he said, slurring without apology.

"Oh, is there good news about Mr. Robinson?"

Mr. Warren found someone more interesting to talk to and wandered off.

"Yes, there is good news," Candy heard from behind her. She turned around to find John sitting with his back close to the fire, letting the blaze roast his behind so that his front side felt unnaturally cool. Like he always loved to do. "This is sort of a triple celebration—the after-party to the music festival, me and Dad's homecoming, and the surprise information this morning that my grandfather made a turn for the better."

"Really?" Candy felt ashamed that she hadn't even wondered about the health of John's grandfather. Though she arranged her face to look concerned and relieved, she had the feeling that John was well aware of her self-centered preoccupation. *I wonder if he's already connecting it with the waltz comment.*

"Yeah, me and Dad went to see him at the hospital this afternoon. They say he might be able to come home in a couple days. He was having a hard time I guess, but late last night things just sort of… 'turned' as his nurse said." John smiled in a way that said he cared, but it was okay that Candy didn't, and then he motioned to the empty log seat next to him. "I don't want to bore you with the details. Come on sit down, there's plenty more to talk about."

"Is there?" she asked, plopping down next to him. "Like what?"

"Me living here."

Oh, that. She had been feeling mounting anxiety about that impending situation. John going to school with her meant he would see all the sides of herself she wasn't sure he would understand. Candy searched her mind for something to deflect the conversation away from herself. "Isn't your girlfriend going to miss you. What's-her-name?"

John looked at his hands and chuckled. Candy knew her name, and John knew she did. "Clara."

"Yeah, Clara?"

"Saw pictures online, huh?"

"Didn't everyone. So, aren't you two going to be broken-hearted?"

John's smile faded. "That wasn't anything serious, Candy. No. I'm not."

Sure looked serious. Candy's jealousy piqued, hearing him talk about her. Clara was very pretty.

John was good at deflecting, too. "Come on, Candy-cane, you're the expert on Shirley County. Tell me what I need to know about Andrew Jackson High."

"Somehow…" Candy leaned back, appraising his athletic build and all-American face. And the beauty wasn't skin deep; she was well acquainted with John's confident spirit and friendly disposition. She shook her head and had to admit (with a sprinkling of shame and a pinch of pride), "I think you'll probably do a lot better than I ever have here, John."

He let her comment sink in, acceptance and understanding in his features. He already knew. "Don't do well with rules, huh, Red Hot? Square peg in a round hole?"

He was so perceptive Candy felt naked. Not ugly, but not beautiful. Just her. How could he have such unfettered access to her heart and mind, after all the time he'd been away? It was like they'd never been apart, and she knew with the certainty of death that John didn't give a crap about how anyone else judged her. Candy was ecstatic to have her best friend with her, once again. Finally. "I don't want to talk about school. I want you to tell me a campfire story."

John's face split into the grin that Candy had known and loved most of her life. "Funny you should mention that, because I have one ready for you, Candy Vale."

"Really? For me?"

"Just for you. Wait—let's get something to drink first, this is a long one."

"Ooooh, good." Candy thrilled, clapping her hands with glee. "Need to wet your whistle, I know."

When they arrived at the coolers, Candy reached in for a Coke just as her brother Simon reached in at the same time. He pretended to search for a drink for himself, but he grabbed her hand and pulled it out of the ice. The image of stealth, he shoved two beers into her hand instead, blocking the adults' view with his body.

"Thanks, Bro," she whispered.

Simon gave her a benevolent nod.

She and John rotated their seating arrangement so that the bonfire shielded them from the adults and the rest of the party. Between the blaze and the deep, black woods, they enjoyed their own private space. Uncle Pat had brought out his guitar, strumming chords and tuning, while Zoë gingerly picked through a melody and Carol tested her strings. But they sounded far away and so did the constant murmur of conversation on the other side of the fire—like the rumble of a dog pack, interspersed with the occasional quacking duck. The muted sounds made the real world sound like a dream, the perfect ambiance for a campfire story. Candy hoped it was a spooky one. She sipped her stolen beer and leaned in closer.

John cleared his throat.

"Once, a very long time ago, there lived a beautiful Indian princess—"

"What was her name?" Candy interrupted, thinking what a strange coincidence it was that John had chosen an Indian princess for his heroine. She had been thinking of that Indian woman in the painting at the Buffalo Lodge almost nonstop. "Bet she had black eyes."

"Yes, as a matter of fact. Black as yours. Let's call her Beloved. It would be a perfect name for her, because not only was she young and lovely, with flowing selkie hair and fathomless dark eyes, but she was also a great treasure to her people. Her mother was the matriarchal ruler before she died, and Beloved inherited her mother's charisma and natural leadership. We come upon Beloved's story at a most important event in her life—her wedding night."

"Wow, that's so romantic of you, John."

"I try to please the ladies when I can. So, Beloved's tribe decided to join forces with another, more powerful, neighboring tribe. The other tribe chose a man suitable for the princess—"

"She was actually a princess?"

"Sure. The other tribe chose a fierce warrior, the son of their chief. We'll call him Champion. The Indian tribes in the region had a tradition, that when a warrior lost a battle, he had to cut his hair, to the scalp. Champion's hair had never been cut, since birth, and it hung far below his waist. He won the princess' heart, and even though the marriage was arranged, Beloved and Champion were in love."

"Nice touch."

John winked and took a sip of his illegal Budweiser. "On the night of their wedding, both tribes came together in celebration—the party of the century. There was a grand feast, with dancing and music…"

As if fated, Pat, Zoë, and Carol brought their tentative notes together into a real song. Carol's fiddle rose joyously above the fire. Pat's wife, Aunt Mickey, joined the song with a high, trilling soprano. John and Candy froze, fixing each other in surprise. They erupted in stifled laughter, snuffing out their snorts on each other's shoulders, not ready to be discovered in their hidden seats.

"…with dignitaries and medicine men." John continued, catching his breath and clutching his side. "People came from all around to give their blessing. The joining of the hands was presided over with religious chants and incantations. Even the sky above blessed the union," John mimed a heavenly explosion, "with an unexpected meteor shower."

Candy gasped. "Ouch, that could be a bad omen."

"Don't be so superstitious. It was like ancient fireworks."

"Uh-huh…"

John sent her a sly look over his beer. "So, the feasting lasted from early in the morning until late at night, long after the newlyweds retired for the evening to their wedding tent, to consummate the union." John lifted his eyebrows once or twice suggestively. "Champion's long, uncut hair hung around his chiseled abdomen." Candy snorted and almost blew her drink out through her nose. "You like that? But before our hero could make his move, thunk! He was taken out cold, with a heavy wooden club from behind."

"Oh, no. Was he killed?"

"No, not dead, just knocked out. A villain emerged from the shadows behind Beloved, shoved a gag in her mouth, and pulled a bag over her head. Another burglar grabbed her feet, and the group of thieves silently made away with our poor princess. Not that they needed to be too quiet, remember the raucous party going on all around?"

"Of course. No one would hear." Candy bit her knuckle. "But who would do such a thing? Everybody loved Champion and Beloved."

"Yes, and a warring tribe that hadn't been invited to the party knew that. They didn't love Beloved and they sure as hell didn't love Champion."

"Why?"

"Champion was a fierce warrior."

"Right. And, Beloved?"

"Who can really love someone so beautiful—so perfect—yet, so beyond reach?"

"But did they hate her for that? Seems unfair." The beer had numbed the edges, but she still felt the injustice of the ages. Maybe more so because of the beer.

John dismissed the question with a mock frown: she wasn't derailing his story. "They were a band of fierce, raiding nomads, and they wore terrifying animal masks to frighten their prey when they attacked. They named themselves things like Pouncing Cougar…"

"Only the aging widows looking for new young husbands, though, right?" Candy couldn't help interjecting the obvious.

"Okay, Pouncing *Leopard*, then. Slashing Bear, Stinging Viper—stuff like that. We'll just call them the Animals, because their tribe was a lawless pack, with no real leader. They had been waiting for the right weapon to use against Beloved's and Champion's peaceful tribes. Because, though the Animals were cruel and fierce, they were a smaller band."

"The peaceful tribes put all their eggs in one basket. Stupid," said Candy, taking a swig.

"Exactly." John fixed her with one long finger, pointing so close it almost touched her nose. She stretched out her neck and kissed the tip, and John's face crumpled into confusion and hilarity at once. "Okay. Anyway… don't worry, the Animals didn't want to harm Beloved. Not really. They tied her up and hid her away as a hostage. The next morning they made their demands known."

"What were their demands?"

"That's not important." John waved those details away, apparently not having polished that part of the story yet in his mind. "You know, Indian stuff—land disputes, territory, hunting zones, trading rights. What is important is that the debates went on and on for weeks, while Beloved was held captive. She was held for so long, in fact, that the lowly slave the Animals had assigned to her began to fall in love."

"Oh, no."

"His name was Chewing Spider. Or, that's what the Animals named him when they captured him during a raid years before. He was considered the lowest of the low, and was regularly beaten and ordered to do all of the dirtiest work, like picking up horse manure in the campsite or cleaning carcasses after a hunt or…"

"Tending to a woman's womanly needs."

"Right. He was ready to escape his horrible life of slavery. And when he found out that the deliberations between all three tribes might finally be coming to a close, with Beloved poised to be returned home…well, he decided it was time to try. With her."

"But, Beloved was about to be rescued."

"Yeah. She wanted to go back home, not escape with the slave guy, right? So, naturally, when Chewing Spider forced her to leave with him, she started screaming and going crazy. He covered her mouth, trying desperately to silence her before she alerted his torturers."

"Torturers?"

"Of course, torturers. The Animals were cruel, marauding beasts, remember? Anyway, he only meant to silence her. He didn't mean to push so hard, for so long. He was just scared…" John looked down at his hands, affecting desperation.

"He suffocated her."

"He did. When the Animals found out that they lost their bargaining tool, they were furious," John nodded at Candy's gasp. "They made quick work of Chewing Spider. They returned Beloved's body to her people, as a paltry peace offering. She was buried facing the rising sun, to encourage a happier future in the afterlife. Champion refused to ever marry again, and he became a warmonger, taking out his sadness on his rivals with great savagery for the rest of his days. And Chewing Spider? Well, his soul haunts the land, still. He pines for his darling Beloved, tormented by the knowledge that it was his own hand that extinguished her beautiful flame."

"Poor Chewing Spider…"

John sat up straight and stared at her, dumbfounded. "What? What about poor Beloved, or poor Champion?"

"It's a sad story all around." Candy sighed and looked at the sky. Somehow the stars helped her regain normality. That story was so weird, but somehow so familiar. She loved it and hated it at the same time. "That was a love story?"

"Don't be so sure. They say that when you hear the wind whistling through the high mountain passes in Shirley County, that's Chewing Spider crying for Beloved. And when you feel the hair stand up on the back of your neck and you catch your breath in the dark, that's Chewing Spider trying to take your breath away, just like he did Beloved's."

"Oh—a real ghost story, then," Candy sighed with relief, the unsettling tale suddenly making sense to her. "Good one. I think I'll have a hard time turning out the light tonight."

John tweaked her nose in an avuncular way, like he was ten years older than she was. "Glad you liked it."

The odd spell over their side of the campfire was dispelled like a soap bubble popping against a cashmere sweater, delicate and evanescent no matter how gently handled. Hard to remember the point of blowing soap bubbles once you're older, but you can call up an image of one like a physical thing in your brain. Something about that seemed important to

Candy just then. *So fleeting, but there's always a wet soap mark on your clothes after a soap bubble dies. Like a dream you can't quite remember, but casts a weird mood over your whole day.* A shiver ran up her spine, but she shook it off and smiled. "Loved it. That was one of your best yet."

"Thank you."

Candy tried to replay all the details of John's story in her head, figuring she would have to hear it a couple more times before she knew it by heart. She sat next him trying to get her thoughts together, like osmosis was possible between humans, until she realized John was unnaturally quiet. "Are you okay, John?"

He remained still for a moment, before he looked up at the sky. His eyes focused on clusters of stars, a planet, the moon—just as hers had—before he confessed, "That story actually came from a dream I had last night."

"Really? Tell me about it—"

"Hey, there you are," Reagan popped around to their side of the fire. "I thought I saw you guys talking all serious over here. We're doing s'mores, come on."

John took her hand and they followed Reagan around the fire. As predicted, the Bennett kids did brave the party for their share of the gooey, melted chocolate desert sandwiches, a bonfire requirement at the Robinsons's. They trouped out as a group, but Candy noticed one was missing.

"Where's Gage?"

John shrugged. "Sulking upstairs. Grandma thinks he stole one of her china dolls."

"One she made?" Grandma Pearl's baby dolls were beautiful, every meticulous detail handmade, from the delicate porcelain faces to the crocheted eyelet collars on their dresses. "Whoa, she must be pissed."

John nodded; his expression dire. His grandma was known to be strict. Candy wondered if she still kept a paddle and couldn't help but feel sorry for Gage. Fourteen was a little old for paddling, but she wouldn't have put it past Grandma Pearl.

"Did he really steal it? That's weird," she lowered her voice. "The Bennett's are usually so...disciplined."

"And weird," John whispered, pulling her to a seat at the fire opposite his cousins after they got their marshmallow sticks.

Uncle Pat was strumming some acoustic spirituals on his guitar. After several refrains of "Awesome God," and "How Great Thou Art," which everyone knew or at least hummed, he closed with "Amazing Grace." But, when John's Aunt Beth started singing just a little too fervently, raising her hands to the sky and closing her eyes in exultation, the rest of the crowd fell silent. By that time, Carol and Zoë had already licked their fingers clean enough to pick up their instruments, and the three launched into "Oh Susanna" again, a tune which Candy knew the girls were attempting to perfect.

"Just one more, Zoë, and time to get into your jammies," Aunt Cammy reminded her daughter, just as her husband began picking along on his banjo next to her. "Garrett—when did you bring that out?"

"I just got it from the car," he shrugged, and then composed a hopeful question on his face.

"Okay, two more times." Cammy relented, knowing how the two brothers, Pat and Garrett, loved to play together. "Don't make it too long of a jam…until after the girls go to bed, anyway."

Grinning widely, Garrett blended into the rhythm with gusto. Even the Bennett kids stayed huddled together by the fire watching the musicians for a while.

"Hey, John." The little boy Peter tapped on John's stomach. "Are you going to stay at our grandma's tonight?"

"Oh. I don't know, buddy."

"We're all sleeping in the bunk bed room. And we have sleeping bags, too," Peter said, clearly not thrilled to be the only boy bunking together with a bunch of girls. The babies, Joshua and Alex, didn't count. They would probably sleep with their mothers anyway.

"Yeah, John. You don't want to sleep alone after that ghost story, do you?" Candy chimed in. "I'm staying here, too."

"Wonder how long Grandma Pearl's will be overrun with Bennetts," John said under his breath, watching his Aunt Beth hustle her kids inside to get ready for bed. Secular time was over. Their dad was kicked back by the beer cooler, absorbed in discussion with Candy's dad, and a discussion with George Vale could last until everyone passed out. "Easy decision. Let me just get a few things."

§

Candy padded through the living room, bleary-eyed. If she was so tired, why couldn't she just sleep? Maybe staying out late with Sam was catching up to her. She didn't care.

"Sleep's over-rated anyway," she yawned, plopping down on the cozy sectional. "Ow." Something hard poked her in the rump as she sat, and she turned to investigate. It was one of the photo albums they had been looking at, sticking out from under a pillow.

Selkie eyes... Candy opened the book to the page of her mother that Reagan had turned to earlier.

"Where *do* we get them?" Candy searched her memory, trying to think of any other family members that had the same dark eyes she shared with her mom. No one she could recall. She scanned the top of the bookshelf, wondering how far back the pictures went. Her grandma had once shown her the faded black and white photographs from her own babyhood, from the 1930s. There weren't many.

"Can't sleep, Miss Candy?"

"Candy, Candy, Candy."

Her Uncle Tommy and his nurse were descending the carpeted stairs, he holding onto her arm with a goofy grin plastered on his kind face. Tommy usually stayed in an assisted living facility, ever since Grandma Catherine had gotten too old to care for him properly. Grandma liked to have him spend the night whenever there was a large family gathering, though.

"Oh, yeah. You, neither Uncle Tommy, huh?" Tommy didn't answer, but walked over to look at the photo album Candy held in her lap. He craned his neck to see the picture of her mother.

"Suzy." He smiled and began petting her hair in the picture. Candy wondered whether he understood that his sister was dead.

"Suzy touch my head," Tommy said and brought his hand to his forehead. He started petting his own hair.

"She touched your head, Tommy?" his nurse asked, looking at the photo of Candy's mother. "When you had a headache?"

Tommy nodded. "Suzy touch my head." Candy looked at the nurse, her brows knitted together in question.

"Tommy gets headaches a lot," she supplied with a shrug.

Candy sort of remembered that from when she was little and Tommy still lived at home. Sometimes he would cry at night because of it. "Oh yeah..."

"Suzy touch my head," Tommy confirmed, then began to wander toward the kitchen.

"Looks like someone wants a midnight snack," his nurse said, catching up to him and taking his arm. "You hungry, Tommy?"

Candy could hear her uncle repeating "Suzy," his voice echoing as they entered the kitchen. She looked down at her mother's face. The photograph was beginning to fade. She ran her finger down her face, petting her hair as Tommy had done.

"Suzy touch my head," she heard him say from the other room.

"Weird," Candy murmured. But there was a thought, nagging at the edge of her consciousness. What was that thing Grandma Catherine said about Candy's mother?

"Suzanna was always a little touched, I'm afraid." "Touched" was Grandma's euphemism for crazy. Still, what a coincidence.

"The gift is usually passed down, mother to daughter," that fortune teller lady said. I wonder if the crazy was passed down, too. If she was crazy.

After Candy's mom had thrown herself in the Tenakho River, that was most of the family's estimation—Suzanna McBride was crazy. That was how everyone explained her mom's death to Candy when she was little. It always seemed a rather flimsy explanation. Suddenly deciding she wanted to be gone before Uncle Tommy reemerged from the kitchen, Candy snapped the photo album closed and shelved it next to a book that looked much older.

Hhhmmm…

She plucked out the older book and flipped it open to find her grandma's careful scrawl inside the front cover, "McBride, 1900-1930." Candy tucked it under her arm and glanced around to make sure she was alone, then stashed it in her backpack by the door before heading back upstairs.

chapter twenty-three

"Amanda, wait up," Gracie bleated, then tripped over a tree root. "Shoot! Your flashlight is better than mine."

Amanda also already knew the way to the Blue Spring; she scouted the path earlier by herself, before the daylight faded, to make sure the ritual went off without a hitch after midnight. The Witching Hour. Her mom had picked up the group of friends from Gracie's house that morning and took the girls to the Jameson residence to hang out, while some of the other parents went to the festival. Amanda and her friends had no interest in attending what they called the Hippie Hillbilly Show, and her mom hadn't minded missing it that year either, for some reason.

They had planned to each go their separate ways that evening, but then Amanda heard her mom and dad arguing about some shack in the mountains where kids—including Sam Castle—went to smoke pot. After hearing them mention the famous Blue Spring, she knew that shack must be close to Lindsay's house and quickly cooked up a scheme for a night-time adventure. She could tell Lindsay's mom was annoyed to have them over, but they all begged that it was the last Saturday of the summer. Aunt Meghan really couldn't refuse gracefully after Amanda's mom had watched the girls all day. The only missing piece was Jessica, who was never allowed to spend the night anywhere but home on Saturdays. She always had to attend the sunrise Catholic mass the next morning. She was welcome to invite friends to her own house, but any guest would also be required to rise and shine early (a mistake Amanda had only made once).

"You'll just have to miss out, Jess," Amanda had taunted her friend, while she begrudgingly helped them compile the clearest pictures of Antonio from Il Vagabondo's fan page. "I'll put in a good word to the gods for you."

"How much farther is the spring?" Gracie whined.

"Here's where the path goes down around the bluff and then the spring's right over there." Lindsay shone her flashlight down a steep path through some sparse trees. "Be careful guys, it's kind of slippery."

Amanda peered over the edge of the bluff in the opposite direction and saw the shack, but she decided to keep that knowledge to herself.

For now...

She had investigated the musty hideout when she came alone earlier. There wasn't much inside but a few barely homey touches, like a kerosene lamp, an old loveseat and a folding chair. Really ugly drawings all over the walls. A wooden spool had been made into a table, with an ashtray and some magazines lying on top. It all looked very masculine and sort of dirty.

Nothing wrong with a dirty boy, though, Mr. Castle.

"It's smaller than I imagined it, from the reading Ms. Collins gave us," Gracie said when they finally reached their watery destination. Amanda knew she was attempting to calm her nerves by making light of their errand. There was nothing small or inconsequential about the Blue Spring.

Amanda glanced beyond the tallest pines overhead, at the glowing orb dancing in and out of billowy clouds. "Good, the moon is full tonight," she remarked with satisfaction. "That will make our spells even more powerful, ladies."

"Can't we call them 'wishes,' please? It sounds so much less evil."

"Gracie, there is nothing evil about working with the natural forces of our universe," said Amanda. "Come on, it's just a lark."

Lindsay crouched down by the water. "It's kind of glowing, you guys."

"The moon?"

"No, the spring," Gracie pointed out in a quavering voice.

"Whatever, Nervous Ninny." Amanda squatted down by a boulder to pull their occult items out of her backpack, placing each one on the rock with care.

"Isn't that cool?" Lindsay grew up near the queer body of water and had played in the surrounding woods with her two older brothers all her life, so she didn't seem nervous in the slightest. "There's some kind of bioluminescence that happens in the algae. Or maybe it's the bugs that eat the algae, I can't remember."

"It's haunted, that's why it's like that."

"What? Gracie, don't be silly."

"No, I'm serious. My mom said this is where the Indians met right before they were forced to walk the Trail of Tears."

"Your mom is full of it," Lindsay chuckled.

"Hey..."

"I bet a full moon makes the spring glow even brighter." Amanda handed the others each a candle taper, a photo print-out of Antonio, and an index card with the moon chant she had found on her Wicca website. "We read this by the light of the moon."

Gracie tried to hand the index card back. "It's too dark, I can't see it."

"Hold on a minute." Amanda pulled a lighter out of her pocket and lit each of their candles in turn. "We need fire to bind the incantation."

"The *wish*," insisted Gracie.

"Abundant Mother, moon so bright," Amanda began, and the other girls followed along with her, reading their cards. "Hear my plea upon this night. Your fertile power lend this spell," she shot Gracie a warning look for substituting 'wish' for 'spell' and finished, "Make it potent, strong, and well."

Each of the girls stated their plea for what the new school year should bring them, while lighting the picture of Antonio and letting it burn as far as they dared, before tossing the blazing paper into the spring. Each was extinguished with a loud hiss. Amanda held onto hers the longest and finally threw her wish into the spring. She watched the blue water glow brighter around the flame before the fire went out, and added, "With this wandering soul, the tramp Antonio di Brigo, let arrive also our dreams."

chapter twenty-four

Candy bounded from her front porch to John's waiting car. The passenger door was already ajar and she ducked inside under the ragtop. "Good, you put the top up."

"Yeah, looks like rain," he murmured, still sleepy-eyed and sedate. He watched Candy bounce in her seat with a bemused look.

"I'll finally arrive somewhere without being a crazy, wind-blasted mess."

"I thought you did that on purpose." John smiled and eyed her artfully tousled hair. "Fine line between careless and tangled, I guess."

"Yeah, there is, Mr. Un-tucked Yet Miraculously Un-wrinkled Oxford Boy."

"Mmmm." He looked down at his wardrobe and lifted a shoulder in assent. "Grandma Pearl frowns on wrinkles."

"I bet she does, is that where you learned it? So, first day of school—are you ready? Did you get all your books? Of course you did."

"Forgot how electrified you are in the morning." He caught his empty thermos off the passenger seat, under her butt-cheeks and in between bounces, and tossed it into the back.

She frowned at the flying metal cup. "Coffee? You don't drink coffee, do you?"

He glanced at the discarded drink container absently. "Protein shake. Ready?"

"Ready as I'll ever be. I mean, I'm excited to see some people again that I haven't seen all summer. And people I'd just like to see more often, you know?"

"Oh yeah, like who?" John swiveled around in his seat, put the car in neutral, and let it roll down the driveway into the street.

"Just some friends." Candy's mind settled on one friend in particular, but she decided not to mention Sam yet. John would meet him soon enough and the thought sent the butterflies in her stomach into conniptions. "I guess, the first day back I just dread all the polite small talk, the cagey remarks, the searching questions. Especially at lunch—the lunches are broken into two sessions, and you never know who you'll get or who you'll miss."

"Can't be that bad?" John turned to face forward again and caught sight of the worry in her face. She was wringing her hands in her lap. "Didn't forget anything inside, did you?"

She shook her hands out and laughed. *I'm being ridiculous.* "Nope, let's go."

Candy's house was a little out of the way for John, but she needed moral support on the first day of school and he said he didn't mind picking her up. He turned off Forest Lane and onto Hemlock Drive, easing down the winding trail, listening to Candy chat about her class schedule. His dad must have taught him to downshift into the lowering grade of the road instead of burning up the brake pads, and he concentrated intently, still unused to the terrain. Finally, they reached the intersection with the state road, which leveled out into the valley. John came to a full stop and turned to Candy, who had grown pensive and quiet. "What are you thinking about?"

"Hm? Oh, just ticking off lists in my head. You know, school supplies and stuff," she lied. All she could think about was Sam and how strange it would be to see him at school. Who did he hang out with? She had no idea who his friends were, besides Ricky Mendez. Would they sit together at lunch? The thought of food made her want to vomit. Did Sam have girlfriends at Jackson the previous year? She searched her mind for Sam Castle gossip memories and came up with nothing concrete.

John wasn't fooled. He watched the side of her face, scanning for clues. "You sure?"

"Yeah." She started bouncing in her seat again, urging him on. "Let's go."

John put on his sunglasses and put the car in gear. "Alright. Andrew Jackson, here we come."

The pair lapsed into silence for the last thirty minutes of the drive, the countryside zooming by in the pale morning. The only sound inside the car was a low purr from the engine and the wind whistling against the glass. Candy could feel him monitoring her out of the corner of his eye and she tried to act normal. She flipped on the satellite radio and searched for something good to pass the time, surprised to find that John had several of her favorite channels already programmed into his speed menu.

Shirley Valley was narrow, but long, and Candy lived at the extreme north end. Andrew Jackson High School sprawled in the last wide bulge of the southern valley, before both Eastern and Western Mountain closed together and strangled the land in a bottleneck. Farther south past the school, there was hardly more than a hundred yards straddling either side of the train tracks and the river for miles. Then, the two ridges became one: Red Ridge Mountain. The train was forced into a tunnel and the river spilled down Hell's Gate waterfall. It was a hike for Candy to get to school, but plenty of kids had it worse; Jackson was a tri-county public school and serviced all the little towns south and west of the waterfall. There was no way across it close to the school, so students would have to circle around north or east and backtrack down to the school.

Pain in the butt. Candy felt sorry for all the backwoods mountain kids.

As they neared the bottom of the valley, a billboard flanking the road screamed in garish orange and white (with blue details to further set off the orange, just in case one missed it): "Go Bobcatts! Let me hear you ROAR!" The lettering was set to appear shouted straight from the pictured quarterback's mouth. Tristan Jameson had his hand cocked back, holding a football, ready to throw a winning pass. Candy watched his face as it slid by outside her window. She had to admit, he was as hot as everyone said. *What a cheesy smile, though.*

The first building they saw as they neared the school was the old library and John sat up straighter in his seat. "Gorgeous," he said, pulling off the main road.

"What?"

"That library. It used to be a communal school house. I looked it up last night—it's from the Victorian Era. Donated by Esther DeWinter Collins in 1878."

"You and your research." Candy was well acquainted with John's insatiable thirst for details. His nerd side was so sweet.

"Look—Gothic windows, exposed trusses, brackets, spindles, scrollwork. It's stunning."

"Yeah, I guess."

As they passed the main school building and turned into the student parking lot, passersby rubbernecked to see who was driving John's unfamiliar car. Candy braced herself for an overly familiar assault. As soon as he turned off the engine, she grabbed her book bag and set her jaw, steeling herself for the fray. John got out of the car and enjoyed a stretch and a groan after the long drive, looking around with an easy, open face.

"Did you say they split the homerooms into two?" he asked; finally awake enough to concentrate on Candy's earlier details about class schedules.

"Yes. Freshmen and sophomores in one homeroom, juniors and seniors in the other."

"Good, so we should be with Antonio, that new foreign exchange student. Grandma Pearl told me to 'befriend the poor boy, and make sure he gets along well.'" John reproduced a commendable Grandma Pearl voice. "He'll be in our first class—awesome."

"We better get over to homeroom then, make sure he's not sitting there by himself," Candy said; ready to plow through the parking lot as quickly as possible. Sam would be in their homeroom, too.

"Hey, Robinson."

They both turned to see a beefy boy, with the build of a linebacker, grinning in their direction. He crossed the parking lot in two strides and held a fiver up high. Not one to leave a person hanging, John supplied the other side.

"Word on the street is you're coming out to play this year, Robinson."

"Play?"

"Football, dude. Come on, Candy, introduce us for Pete's sake."

"Oh, sorry. Will Bartlett, John Rob—"

"Robinson, I know who you are, man. Eat at Big Joe's once a week, at least." Will draped a lead arm over John's shoulders. "So, can we count on ya?"

"Sure, love football."

Candy appraised him anew. "So, that's why the protein shake this morning. Always so prepared."

John gave her a wink.

"Awesome, man. We already started pre-season, but you haven't missed too much. Come to the field for an info session after school, alright?" Will slapped his new recruit on the back and abruptly changed direction, walking backwards towards another car that had just pulled in on the other end of the lot. He pointed at John with one outstretched hand, fist-pumping the other. "This season's gonna rock, dude. Yo, Chambers…"

"Shouldn't he be heading the other way?" John watched the friendly giant lumber over to strong-arm another able-bodied Bobcatt onto the team.

"I'm sure Mr. Warren won't mind if he's late. The football team is much more important to any honest Bobcatt than an education."

Candy turned toward the new voice and grabbed her friend in a hug. Erica bent her knees to shorten her gangly frame a few inches and returned the embrace. "Hey, Erica. This is my friend John. John, this is Erica Norman. I think you guys met years ago."

"Yeah, of course. I remember Erica." John hugged Candy's friend like he would one of his own. He never forgot a face, even after three or four years of pubescent changes. "Good to see you again."

"You, too." Erica's face was beet-red when she pulled away from him.

Candy looked at John. *Jeez...her, too.* "So, we're headed to homeroom to befriend the foreign exchange student, as per John's Grandma Pearl's request."

"Yeah, since my grandfather set up the exchange, she wants me to help ward off Shirley County embarrassment on an international scale," John said. "I'm sure you've heard that there's been a little confusion."

"Melodrama, you mean," Erica corrected. "What's the big deal, anyway? Oh—there he is over there, I bet. I don't think that lustrous, gelled mane is from around here."

Candy saw a slender guy dressed in tailored, fashionably grungy jeans, cowboy boots, and an antiqued Guns N' Roses T-shirt. He was looking around with his shoulders thrown back, taking in his surroundings with the air of an explorer. He nodded and murmured to the woman in a pantsuit and heels standing next to him, accepting the expensive leather backpack she handed him. Mieke Walsh. Candy had seen her jogging along Forest Lane the last few days, and of course she had to listen to Dad's sexist comments about that. Mrs. Walsh looked furtively at her watch, then to the boy, then back at the front doors of the school. She had double-parked right at the front of the library, unsure where to head next. Antonio looked content to wander but Mrs. Walsh gripped his shoulders in anxious claws, like a nervous mother eagle shielding the helpless chick she had yet to realize was actually a mountain goat.

"Let's rescue the new guy," John chuckled.

"Aren't you the new guy, John?" Candy asked, shaking her head at Erica.

"Not as new as him." John walked over with the girls in tow, holding out a welcoming hand. "Hi there. You must be Antonio di Brigo. And Mrs. Walsh?"

"Hello," Mrs. Walsh accepted the handshake first, pulling Antonio closer with her other arm and giving him a squeeze. "A welcome party, how wonderful."

"I'm John Robinson. My grandfather has told me a lot about you, ma'am, and it's a pleasure to make your acquaintance."

"Joe's grandson? Well, that's great—Antonio, you're in good hands, then." Mrs. Walsh's features smoothed into a more natural softness and her shoulders visibly loosened.

"Is nice to meet you." Antonio cranked John's hand, while looking past him, at Candy. "This is Erica Norman. Oh, and Candace Vale. I call her Candy." John gave Candy an evil smile, as Antonio zeroed in on her.

"Candace Vale?" The name seemed to ring a bell for Mrs. Walsh. "I met your father George at our PTA meeting recently. Parent Teacher Association."

"Oh, sure." Candy glanced around the grounds, distracted. Was Sam already inside? It wasn't like him to be early.

"We live on Forest Lane, so I guess we're neighbors. Maybe you kids can come over to our place and hang out after school or something. Antonio and I would love to have you."

"Sure, that sounds great. Thank you," said John.

"Thanks, Mrs. Walsh," said Erica, beaming at John.

"Uh…" Candy attempted to pry her hand out of Antonio's, but he pulled it to his lips and gave it a quick kiss. John stifled his amusement badly and she served him a scalding glare. As the group parted ways with Mrs. Walsh, Antonio sidled in close to Candy's side. Candy jumped around John, shielding herself from Antonio with no attempt at subtlety.

"Awesome, we can check out his digs at the Walsh place for Grandma Pearl," John whispered.

"*You* can. Great—the notorious, womanizing Italian male."

"Aw come on, Candy." John said under his breath, slowing down to put more space between himself and Antonio. "You're playing your part, too: the delicate—yet fiery—redhead, immediately rejecting his advances. His macho hunter instinct is engaged."

"Nice. I'll just stop, then."

John shook his head, with a sympathetic smile. "The game is already underfoot, after two minutes on campus."

Antonio reached the doors first and held one open. "Please, Candy."

Candy's smile was a grimace as she stepped past him and into the main vestibule. John watched her elbow into a crowd that lingered by the front doors, and then he lost sight of her. He wrinkled his nose at the smell of Lysol and musty air-conditioning, the aging units still filtering stale air that hadn't been circulated since spring.

"Morning, Bobcatts," a shrill voice greeted them.

Wow. John fought the urge to recoil. He recognized Stephanie Jameson from his dad's photograph albums, dressed in an orange T-shirt emblazoned with the pouncing, growling-Bobcatt mascot. Her big blue eyes and bouffant hair looked out of sync with the dangerous animal—at first. He changed his mind as the woman advanced, with a pink smile full of shining white teeth, giving orders with fiercely sweet insistence.

"No dilly-dallying, y'all. Straight to homeroom. You'll find your names here on this chart, so you can see which room is yours."

It's too early, read Erica's expression. John nodded agreement and looked at the flier Mrs. Jameson had shoved into his hand. Peppy promises of a fantastic new school year. A hand-painted paper banner was strung across the wide entryway claiming similar predictions and eliciting Bobcatt enthusiasm. More flyers littered the table supporting the homeroom assignment chart, with encouraging reminders to join various school clubs. Debate Team. Drama Club. Future Farmers of America. John picked up one or two and Antonio followed suit. Uniformed cheerleaders were manually supplying their own incentive handouts—full-colored postcards picturing the squad in a pyramid formation, with an attached Tootsie Pop. They were shoving them into student hands with coquettish smiles and masked aggressiveness.

"Come out and support the supporters, everyone. Guys are welcome, too." One of the cheerleaders smiled sideways at John and gave his body a once-over with her painted eyes.

Yeah, maybe in Memphis, but a male cheerleader in Shirley County? John entertained a brief picture of himself in a boy-cheerleader uniform (maybe an orange polo shirt and white sweater-vest with matching short shorts), being tied to the back of a pick-up truck and dragged the length of the valley.

"Where'd Candy go?" John scanned the small crowd milling around the club tables.

Erica shrugged. "Guess she took off. That's so Candy."

"Well, she's got to be in homeroom, then. Antonio, I'm sure you're with us," he said, glancing perfunctorily at the homeroom chart. "How hard could it be, with only two groups?"

"Well, in recent years, people have claimed confusion just to annoy the faculty and cause first period to be set back," Erica explained. "Like, sitting in the empty rooms, pretending to wait for roll call or heading over to the cafeteria and getting lost in the kitchens."

"That's kind of funny," John conceded. Grandma Pearl would call it "tomfoolery."

When he saw Antonio's uncomprehending smile, he launched into a carefully worded explanation, with Erica supplying theatrical clues. John caught sight of Candy down the hallway, peering through doorways off the main corridor. He could hear muffled voices in a constant hum, with intermittent bursts of laughter or shouts of friendly recrimination, coming from two rooms located on opposite sides of the hall. As she neared one of the doors, she stopped and investigated the interior.

"Since Andrew Jackson lacks a school-wide intercom, students go to homeroom every Monday morning for fifteen minutes before classes, to hear important weekly info and stuff. Another classic example of Shirley County's outstanding tech-savvy," Erica explained, flipping the locks on the lockers as they walked along. "The teachers don't actually take roll, but with a total student body of only about six-hundred kids, if you miss often it becomes obvious."

They used the two largest classrooms, the music room, and the art studio, to split the student body in half. Candy had assumed a sentry position close to the art studio door. She looked past John as he entered.

"Who are you looking for?"

"No one," she muttered, clearly annoyed.

What the hell is her problem? With an effort, he returned his full attention to Erica.

Erica went on, bringing in the rear, unburdened by her friend's moodiness. "Yeah, they use the smaller of the two room for us, because by junior and senior year lots of kids have dropped out."

John wandered around checking out the studio. There were several large drying racks set against the wall, with about a dozen easels stacked close by, and slop sinks in the back of the room. Farther on, he could see several pottery wheels and kilns, and a doorway with heavy velvet drapes that probably concealed a photography darkroom. The place was huge. "How big is the music room, then?"

"Well, that's where the band practices, so pretty big," said Erica, pulling her shoulders back with pride.

"I hear the marching band is pretty good here." John remembered that the girl was an accomplished musician, in a family of musicians. "Don't they win lots of competitions?"

"State Champs four years in a row, and last year we were National Finalists. I should know, I'm the best trumpet player they've got."

"I'd love to hear you play—"

"Robinson, you hiding a secret arsenal or what?" Will Bartlett boomed through the doorway, his voice echoing off the polished concrete floor and metal lockers in the hall. "You already grabbed the Italian Stallion, huh?"

Wondering if Antonio had any idea what was in store; John looked around for him to deliver a quick warning. He found the Italian Stallion was already seated next to Candy, flirting with the back of her head. She was still watching the door, looking through the massive football player like he was so much air.

§

Sam checked his watch with a groan, then jangled his bike lock to make sure it was secure. Rachel had kept him late at the studio, gabbing until after two o'clock in the morning. He overslept, vaulted out of bed, and rushed to school without even showering.

The campus was quiet.

"Already into second period, great."

He combed his fingers through his messy hair and eased in through the front doors. He would've thankfully crept in a side door, but Andrew Jackson kept all doors but the main entrance locked from the outside.

For security, right.

Sam believed the practice had been enacted to catch late students sneaking in, and to discourage clandestine smoke breaks or lunchtime jolly rides. He wasn't surprised to see Mr. Davis emerging from his office, as soon as the doors closed behind him.

"Sam Castle," the guidance counselor said in a reserved tone, at odds with the subtle menace in his narrowed eyes. "Late on the first day."

"I'm sorry, Mr. Davis." Sam straightened his shoulders and turned to face the man. "I'm late. Is that a crime?"

"Not at all, not at all, son." He warmed his tone and widened his smile. "I understand."

Mr. Davis had been after Sam's ass ever since his precious daughter, Ashley Davis, was caught trying to pass Sam a note the year before. The bastard had taken Sam into his office for over an hour of lecturing about the merits of education and the pitfalls of squandering it, sitting under an ominous display of wooden paddles on the wall behind his desk. Sam hadn't even seen the girl's note before it was intercepted and had technically not done anything to warrant punishment, especially of the corporal variety. Nothing happened beyond the lecture. He didn't think Ashley was so lucky, though. He saw her tear-stained face when she left school early that day, and she hadn't given Sam anything more than furtive glances since. Claiming concern for Sam's welfare (the health of just another troubled Andrew Jackson student) Mr. Davis had persisted in his eagle eye approach all last year.

And it just keeps gettin' better. Sam narrowed his eyes at the man. The counselor's arms were folded over a lumpy sweater-vest. He leaned against the door to his office with one mushy, khaki-covered leg crossed over the other in supreme arrogance. The truth was, Mr. Davis could give Sam much more trouble than he had any wish for, whether anything had happened with his pretty daughter or not.

Your daughter's too tight-assed for me, buddy.

"I'm concerned about you, Sam."

Here it comes. God, I hate Shirley County.

"How about you spend lunch in my office, and we have a little talk about starting the school year off right."

chapter twenty-five

"Get on your feet and give 'em a clap! GOOOOOOOO, BOBCATTS!"

Ashley Davis performed a perfect pike jump; both her legs locked in a ninety-degree position above the ground for a split second before coming back down to earth. She transitioned into hoots and cheers, rolling her fists and pumping them overhead. John had a perfect view of her backside from his position on the field and he didn't see a hint of jiggle in her muscular legs as she jogged in place and bopped up and down. Her back-up squad of about a dozen uniformed girls followed along, while a handful of hopeful freshmen watched covetously, holding their paperwork and shifting from one foot to the other. One of the new girls joined in, hooting with one hand cupped around her mouth and shaking her mini pom-pom on a stick (a welcome gift from Ashley).

John willed patience to Candy. She was perched on her haunches in the stands, reading a book propped on her knees. She shaded her eyes and looked across the field to where the football players had been huddled together with seven or eight new recruits for the last half-hour. The gathering was supposed to be a quick "info session," but it wasn't shaping up that way and John knew Candy was probably royally pissed off by then. First, there was a big welcome pep talk, then they handed out paperwork. Next was a tour of the locker room and weight room, followed by a field demonstration. And probably summing things up: this huddle thing.

Candy had already been approached several times by some cheerleaders trying to cajole her into listening to *their* "info session." He could imagine her reply, "Hard not to hear it," and he couldn't help but grin.

A chant brought his attention back to the huddle. There was a final communal shout, and the guys were slapping each other's shoulders, backs and buttocks, and starting to disperse to the locker room or parking lot. John breathed a sigh of relief and motioned for Antonio to follow him to the bleachers. He hailed Candy as they approached—

"Come on girls; let's give a cheer for our newest Bobcatt boys." Ashley led the others in an impromptu chorus, "J-O-H-N! Rack -em, stack 'em, pack 'em in! T-O-N-Y! Hit 'em, hit 'em, hit 'em high!"

John waved politely (Antonio mimicked him), as the cheerleaders clapped and jumped. Ashley vaulted into a backflip and several others cartwheeled and bounced into round-offs, their bloomers flashing bright white under the sun. Whether their display was an attempt to impress the guys or their new recruits, John couldn't say, but they obviously held top scores with Antonio. He watched their flailing limbs and exposed bloomers with open admiration.

Candy stuffed her book and hopped down the bleachers to meet them. "Are you okay with 'Tony'?"

"Mieke said expect nickname." Antonio was clearly not thrilled with the idea, but willing to accept the American penchant for shortening names. "I like 'Tonio.' Is more correct."

"Ah, it's a sign of affection, man," John reassured him. "Look at the essence of sweetness, Candy-cane, here."

She aimed a kick at his rump, but missed as he dodged out of range. "I'll call you whatever you prefer to be called, *Antonio*."

"Hey, Tony! Hey, John!" A cute blonde sang as she skipped over, hauling along one of Candy's more distant cousins, Jessica McBride. "I'm so happy you're going out for the team, you guys."

The group exchanged introductions and John noticed the blonde, Lindsay, elbow her friend in the ribs. Jessica gave her a frown. John had met Jessica once or twice; she and Candy were related by their grandfathers, who were brothers. The two girls were not enemies, yet not exactly friends. Candy was a tomboy, raised by a less conventional branch of the family, while Jessica was a princess. She wore her own red hair in long, soft curls, usually tied with a bow. Candy called her a cookie-cut, and ridiculed, "Her bright green Irish eyes are always smiling."

"Candy," Jessica said. "Lindsay here has been dying to meet both Antonio and John, so I guess you're the woman of the hour, cuz."

"Happy to oblige," said Candy dryly.

"So, what are you guys doing now?" asked Lindsay. "We were thinking of heading over to Big Joe's for a smoothie or something. We could find a ride, but if you guys are going, too—I absolutely love your Mustang, John."

"Oh…thanks," John had actually been thinking of heading over there to see how his dad was doing. "Yeah, I might go too. I don't know what everyone else had planned…"

He looked to Antonio. His face said he was up for anything, especially with beautiful girls.

John looked to Candy.

"Why not?" She shrugged, and then added in an undertone, "As long as I'm finally allowed to leave the Andrew Jackson campus."

"Cool, I just love convertibles." Lindsay grabbed Jessica's arm and looked up at John through her eyelashes, as they all walked towards the parking lot.

"It's kinda tight in the back seat for three." John noticed Candy falling back and he slowed down to match her pace. "Candy already called shotgun earlier."

His best friend's face brightened considerably, and she looped her arm in his.

§

"Thanks, man." Sam performed the necessary hand maneuvers—shakes, claps, clicks, and bumps—in the correct order to signal, "we're chums." He almost flubbed at the last, remembering some other town, some other time.

He handed Ricky the inventory log to sign. "She ever sell much stuff here?"

"Rachel? Yeah, bro. They're perfect souvenirs—little bobbles like the sunset over green mountains to hang from your rearview mirror, with a Shirley Valley tag. She's got some that look like the rapids and shit, they're nice. Of course," Ricky admitted, "we don't get that many tourists, but those that we do get almost always buy her stuff."

"Hmph."

Sam had only been working at Rachel's glass studio for two days, and he hadn't been given much to do yet besides grind glass—a tedious, dirty, mildly dangerous job that he felt he had mastered about twenty minutes into his four-hour long project—but he knew there was a lot going on that he hadn't seen, and he was interested to learn more. As an added bonus, Rachel hated to leave her house or studio at night (the two were connected by a gated atrium), and she told Sam to just keep her truck overnight after he dropped off her work at the post office and Big Joe's. Then, her assistant Caleb wouldn't have to pick Sam up from school—right after school, rushing to get back to Rachel's so Caleb could get his shit done and leave early.

Sam would have a truck to drive, two or three nights a week and the following mornings, thanks to Rachel. She sold most of her work online, and that meant regular mailings for her, with much less bike riding and train hitch-hiking for Sam. Maybe he could show up at Candy's house in relative style.

"I gotta get out of here if I can make it to Candy's tonight," Sam said. God, the first day of school had sucked. He was exhausted and he could use some Candy.

"She's here, yo."

"She is?"

"Yeah over in the restaurant, bunch of kids from school. Bossman's grandson. Catch ya later." Ricky yawned and punched Sam on the shoulder, before disappearing back inside the grocery.

Bossman's grandson? Sam watched his friend disappear, hoping Ricky didn't suspect the way his comment had just slapped him in the face. He dug his phone out of his pocket, checking to make sure he hadn't missed her call. He hadn't. *I guess I never called her either…*

He heard boisterous laughter erupt from the front of the restaurant and turned in that direction. Putting his phone back in his pocket, he prowled along the side of the grocery, listening and alert to the noise of the grounds. Nearing the entrance to the dining room, he ducked under hanging flowerpots and hung back at the edge of a window to peer inside.

It was well past the dinner hour and the place was mostly empty. Guests who remained were picking at their food, kicked back and relaxed. Candy was seated between two guys, across from a couple of girls in cheerleading uniforms. They all were watching a hulking giant of a football player (still wearing his jersey) pantomiming some hilarious story, according to the raucous laughter of the girls. Candy wasn't laughing, but she seemed content, leaning over to listen when the guy next to her whispered in her ear.

The new foreign exchange student. Sam smirked. He had been introduced in English class. *Seems alright. But the other guy…*

The other guy sat with his chair at an angle to Candy's. He kept one eye on her and one shoulder possessively behind her, corralling her into the group like she was an errant lamb.

Who the hell is that?

Sam fought with the urge to walk in, introduce himself, and sit down next to her. Claim her for himself. Or maybe he'd offer her his hand and tell her it was time to take off.

What the fuck… Sam flexed his fits, knuckles cracking. What if she wouldn't leave with him? He turned from the window and jogged up the stairs to Buffalo Square, passing by the Brave without a word and heading for the river.

Amanda Jameson held her hand to her mouth, unseen as Sam passed by. She was crouched behind a flower urn at the top of the stairs, waiting for her mom to do "some Rotary Club business" with Jamie Robinson.

"Can you believe it? Jamie's the new head of Big Joe's and maybe the Rotary, too," her mom had said, trembling with excitement.

Amanda agreed to accompany her to the restaurant, but declined going inside at the last minute, pretending to have menstrual cramps. That gave her mom an instant sour puss, but Amanda was richly rewarded for her transgression when she saw Sam Castle pull into the parking lot in a big manly truck. He got out and gathered an armload of boxes from the back. She followed his progress through Big Joe's and considered changing her mind on socializing for a bit. But she stopped in her tracks at the sight of Sam watching a party through the window, at the bottom of the stairs in front of the restauraunt. There was no doubt who he had been looking at. His heartache was palpable, even from her vantage point.

"What a bitch," she muttered, after Sam disappeared through the trees. Who did Candy Vale think she was?

"What are you doing? Did you decide to come in after all?" Amanda's mom's shrill voice preceded her, as always. She rolled her eyes and stopped watching trees, then turned around with a plaster smile to watch her mom mounting the stairs, with Lindsay in tow. "Amanda, Lindsay was here! Did you know? Anyway, I said I'd take her home, so John didn't have to drive all over dropping people off."

"She lives right by Candy, mom."

"Well, you know. Lindsay's family. How'd you know Candy was here?"

Whoops. "She isn't?" It was easy to disarm fools with insight.

"Hey, Amanda." Lindsay bounced up the stairs, full of pride at hanging with Antonio and John first. "You should have come in, but your mom said you had a stomach ache."

"Yeah, cramps." Amanda grabbed her tummy, just above her crotch. She enjoyed seeing her mom turn green.

"Oh, is that what it was?" Lindsay looked at her aunt, confused.

That was good; confused Lindsay was more pliable. Amanda needed information and she knew Lindsay would spill all possible beans just to impress her. "You can fill me in on the ride home."

"Oh my gosh, you have no idea…"

chapter twenty-six

John dumped his book bag on the floor. The same chair he had chosen the day before had Candy's yellow leather jacket draped over the back. She pulled her seat saver into her lap with a welcoming nod, and he tossed his keys into his bag as he slid into the chair.

What page? he mimed to her, opening his book.

She shook her head and motioned to her open notebook, "Lecture first."

Ms. Collins had her back to the class and was already writing an outline for the day on the whiteboard at the front of the room:

Mississippian Culture
1. Mound Builders
2. Widespread Trade
3. Maize-based Agriculture
4. Southeastern Ceremonial Complex (SECC)

She said she started class promptly and she wasn't kidding. John could tell that she was irritated having Monday's homeroom steal at least 20 minutes from her first period class, so she made up for it by extra homework and heightened efficiency during the rest of the week.

I'm what, one minute past the bell? Even though he should have made time by not picking up Candy that morning, he seemed to have lost time. He glanced sideways at her, a portrait of concentration, under violently windblown hair. *Her hair looks better a little wild, actually. More her.*

"Alright, class." Ms. Collins finished her outline and turned to face the room. "Mr. Robinson, so glad you were able to join us. Our focus for the year is on regional culture—who is able to recall yesterday's homework assignment? Start us off today. Yes, Miss Douglas."

"Well, you asked us to think of what makes our culture our own, like in Shirley?"

"And have you brought in an example for us?"

"Yes…" The girl seemed to hesitate, proud of her show-and-tell, yet not sure she was on the right track. She pulled a pair of well-worn, mud-caked, hiking boots out of a paper grocery sack. "I've hiked on every trail through Eastern and Western Mountain, and along the highest ridges—as high as you can go, to 6,319 feet up on Aurora's Dome. Four times."

"That's an impressive feat, Julia." Ms. Collins congratulated her, with a reproachful look around the room at the origin of groans and snickers. Dried mud flaked from Julia's boots, sprinkling the floor with Eastern and Western Mountain. "And tell us how your story fits into an examination of our culture."

"Well, the mountains close us in, don't they? It's a pretty remote place because of that, and I just feel like the mountains have made us what we are in a lot of ways." Shoving her boots back into her bag and stuffing them under her seat, she collapsed back into her chair. Her part in the morning lecture was finished.

"What a wonderful beginning to our conversation; thank you for being our first brave contributor, Julia." Ms. Collins moved amongst their desks, examining faces, wardrobes, postures. "You are quite right about our geological surroundings being an integral force in shaping culture—ours and others. We will revisit this concept again and again this year, class, so remember it well. Let's have another example."

Julia looked around smugly, waiting for someone to best the very mountains themselves.

"Miss Norman?" Candy's friend Erica stood, and held aloft one of her father's mountain dulcimers.

A girl behind John murmured, "Predictable." A guy next to her snorted.

"I guess most of you probably know my dad builds these, but I thought it was the perfect example right in my house, of both regional music and craftsmanship. Definitely a part of our culture, past and present."

"Hey, that's not fair. She took two examples: music and crafts," a girl that John recognized from the cheerleading squad complained, springing to her feet.

"We will all have our turn. Sit down, Abigail."

"But, *my* example was music." The girl sat down and folded her arms across her bright pink polo shirt, her ponytail swinging.

"I'm sure examples will intertwine and overlap, everyone. That's the beauty of cultural fabric. A fine example, Miss Norman. Mr. Bartlett?"

The friendly linebacker stood, nodding hello to John when they met eyes. "My example is sports. Football."

Someone reproached him in a lazy drawl from the back of the room, "You can't be your own visual aid, man." John turned to see the famed quarterback, Tristan Jameson, lounging back in his chair with a lopsided smile on his handsome face. Ms. Collins quieted giggles from a few female classmates with a look.

Isn't this third-level history? I thought that guy's a senior. John shrugged. Good looks don't always pair up with good brains.

"I'm not," Will argued, his cheeks showing more color than usual. "I brought pictures, too." He opened his notebook and brought out a thin stack of photographs, positioning himself closer to the front of his aisle for better viewing. "See, my family's been playing football so long—even before photographs were invented. But I don't have visual aids for those, of course." Tristan laughed and several girls followed suit. "See how the uniforms change? Seems like bodies change, too. Everyone looks so skinny in the old ones. Even the rules of the game change, my grandpa told me."

"And why would 'bodies changing' be of cultural significance, William?" Ms. Collins prodded. The whole classroom leaned in to admire Shirley County's most glaringly significant cultural phenomenon, football.

John had to admit the photographs were enthralling; the oldest were faded and torn at the edges, youthful faces like smiling ghosts: the proud heroes of their day, probably dead for more than a generation. And there holding the pictures was the essence of youth, wearing the newest version of the Bobcatt-jersey, just as his father had and his father before him. He nodded at Will with respect. *Good one, man.*

"Bodies change, because food changes, I guess," Will shrugged. "When we got good roads, and the train, more food could come into the valley. Plus, people didn't have to work so hard on the farms or hunting no more."

"It wasn't just that, though," Candy's friend, Louis, spoke up. "In the modern age, there are magazines, TV's, movies. Now, players want to look like Hollywood football stars. All beefed up."

"Thanks." Will collapsed his photos into one hand and headed back to his seat. "I never thought of myself as a Hollywood star type, but that'll work for me."

Louis scowled at the general amusement. "You know what I mean, cultural ideals shift," he insisted.

One by one, students offered their own examples of cultural determinants. John brought a shadowbox that he filched from the restaurant; an old photograph of his grandfather as a child, helping some long-dead relative at a barbeque grill, grouped with a yellowed, handwritten recipe and an obsolete Fourth of July firework that was probably banned by the ETA. "Tradition."

The musical cheerleader jumped up and waved her hand in the air when he said that word and proceeded to sing from her church choir's program. Afterward, she explained it was *traditional* Sacred Harp music, a cappella.

Candy showed some handmade paper greeting cards and talked about the Fine Craft movement in the Appalachian Mountains. When Ms. Collins recognized one of the painted designs as derived from a Native American motif, she transitioned into the lecture and instructed the class to begin taking notes. Sighs of relief sounded around the room, from students who hadn't participated in the show-and-tell, until Ms. Collins told them she'd expect a one-page, written explanation on her desk by the end of the day.

Candy leaned over and whispered to John, "We'll be tested on the lecture stuff."

He held his pen poised over his loose-leaf paper, and made a studious face. "Ready."

"Our current culture is not only knitted together by the food we eat, the language we speak, the art we produce, and the land on which we live and work today, but by the myriad of peoples who have travelled here, migrated here, and those who once lived here. Many ages past. Remnants from our cultural past, in all its stages and transformations, survive today. They are not simply in history books or in museums, but also in our newest art like Miss Vale's example, in our favorite foods or past times, in our ideas about ourselves, and in our very genes. So, this is where we will begin our formal investigation into our culture, class; in the furthest reaches to our past, with the first peoples whom we know inhabited our land."

She moved to the whiteboard, extended her metal pointer, and tapped under the title of her outline.

"The Mississippian Culture, lasting from about 800 to 1500 CE, was the most complex, far reaching, and most culturally homogenized ancient society that we recognize from this region. Many modern Native American tribes you should be familiar with arose from this culture: Sendalee, Cherokee, Seminole, Masapiti, and Timohukhs, among others. We'll go over them in detail later. Important to note, however...David, please turn off the front lights."

The lights flickered off and the whiteboard dimmed. Ms. Collins let down the window blinds and headed to the back of the room. "You'll have more time to copy my outline later, if you haven't already finished. It's important that you listen, as well as copy."

The hum of a projector motor whirred behind them and the screen showed a green expanse of grassy fields, and a large earthen mound in the center, surrounded by sparse trees.

"Note that archeological records point to a much earlier civilization, of whom we know very little, except that they were capable of organizing to build massive earthworks. You are seeing one here that was built nearly a thousand years before the pyramids were constructed in Egypt."

She advanced the slides to an illustrated collection of several mounds, which together formed an elliptical pattern.

"This is a map of the oldest one we know of, Watson Brake in Louisiana, circa 3400 BCE."

She slowly clicked through several slides of different aged, grassy, flat-topped pyramids, cones or elongated ridges. Many were bird's-eye view, to capture the vastness of their total area.

"These are here, in the United States?" a girl from the middle of the room asked dubiously. "How come I've never seen one?"

"I've never seen one, either," Candy whispered and pinched John's arm. He shook his head in agreement; he had never even heard of them. "Sort of creepy, all lurking in the hinterlands, almost invisible."

John nodded. *Yes, it is.*

"This one is called Monks Mound, near Collinsville, Illinois." The projector showed a double-tiered, flat-topped pyramid, covered in green grass, with a stone stairway climbing to its summit.

"At over one hundred feet tall, this is the largest Pre-Colombian earthwork in America, north of Mesoamerica."

"What were they for?"

"We can't be sure since these are Pre-Historic sites. Remember, there is no written record. Some evidence suggests they were part of complex villages. Yet some were known to be built by hunter-gatherer cultures, who would have only visited them seasonally. They speak to a cross-cultural belief in cosmology. The Mississippian Culture that came later recognized a religious triad: a spiritual underworld, a celestial realm above, and our middle-earth between."

"So, the mounds are like a bubbling up of the Underworld?" Abby Miller's sweet singing voice trembled.

"No, they *built* them, she said," Louis supplied, pretending to comfort her, but then added, "They might have buried dead people in them, though."

Abby gasped and Louis chuckled.

Ms. Collins clicked to an undulating earthen serpent. "Some were effigy mounds of culturally significant animals. This is Serpent Mound, in Southern Ohio. It's over thirteen-hundred feet in length."

The eerie glow of the gigantic snake, a skulking predator carpeted in weeds, was mesmerizing. When the automatic cooling fan on the projector made a loud noise, several students jumped.

"This old machine won't last much longer, but just a few more images here..." and they were greeted with watercolor renditions of bustling ancient cities. They were full of mounds, with working smokestacks in between and people carrying goods or conversing along neatly delineated streets. "Some of the first Europeans to encounter indigenous communities here in the 1500s recorded what they saw. So, here you see the building of mounds still in practice, some five thousand years later. During the United States' westward expansion, the mounds had faded into pre-history and the Native Americans encountered didn't know about the earlier civilizations that produced them."

The next slide showed a modern collection of buildings decorating a steep hillside—

Will Bartlett was the first to ask, "Is that what I think it is?"

It took a few moments for John to recognize what he was looking at. Candy and elbowed him, "Oh my gosh."

Louis supplied the obvious, "That's Buffalo Square."

"Well, you didn't think such a landmass was natural, did you? A hill that large and steep jutting into the river, in the midst of a flat valley," Ms. Collins said simply, enjoying the reaction.

"There aren't dead Indians buried there, are there?" Abby wanted to know.

So did John, come to that.

Ms. Collins gazed at the image of Buffalo Square for a moment before answering, "The mound has never been completely excavated." The classroom had fallen silent and she let that thought sink in.

"David—if you please, the lights?" Ms. Collins pushed the projector back into a corner and cranked open the blinds, continuing her lecture in her more habitual, brusque manner. "The mound-builders were earlier, as I said. The Mississippian Culture that probably derived from them is more clearly understood and better recorded. So, that will be our primary focus this week."

She reached up and selected a pull-ring from a dozen or so spring-loaded, rolled display charts, and stretched out a map of the United States. "Similar artifacts, including highly stylized clay pots and carved medallions made by the same artist, have been found throughout what is now," she used her metal pointer to tap regions on the map, "the Midwestern, Eastern, and Southern United States…"

Her voice faded out, John's mind swimming with implications. Did Grandpa Joe know his property sat on an ancient mound? Ms. Collins said it hadn't been "completely" excavated. Had it been *partially* excavated, then? John looked around at his classmates; everyone else seemed to be recovering from the shock of such new, important information much better than John was. He felt Candy watching him and when he turned to her, she offered a sympathetic smile.

"Creepy, huh?"

He nodded. It was a lot more than creepy, though. Maybe it was different for John, since his family owned a large part of that mound. How could he not have known anything about it?

Does Grandpa Joe have more secrets than I thought? Grandma Pearl, too?

Ms. Collins crossed to her desk and picked up her copy of their assigned textbook. She began thumbing through pages marked with florescent tabs. "Turn in your text to page…154."

John lingered before reaching for his bag. *Yes, they must know about it.*

Most of the class had not yet unearthed the heavy books, so there was a general clatter of scraping chair legs and rummaging in backpacks. Ms. Collins waited and watched, while books were thumped on desks and pages were flipped through. One by one, students opened to pictures of intricately carved stone sculptures and finely painted shell gorgets.

"What do you see? Look at the craftsmanship, notice how skilled the artists were." Ms. Collins nodded at begrudging murmurs of assent from her students. "Now, turn to page 158."

John flipped through the next few pages, mildly interested, but he froze in consternation when his eyes focused on the next illustrations, in a table explaining the meaning behind a list of artistic motifs. His eyes went immediately to the "tri-lobed" symbol, which looked like three circles joined, melded into one at the center. He had seen it scratched all over his grandfather's drawings, running through some of the animal faces like tattoos. John figured they were just random doodles at the time, but he had wondered about a decorative motif within such otherwise hideous drawings. Now that he saw the design in another context, he was chilled to the bone. The description read, "The Tri-lobed Motif functioned as a serpent marking and may have symbolized a supernatural ability to travel from the Underworld to the Celestial World."

John ran his finger down the list and found another familiar symbol. The Swastika. Also prominently featured in Grandpa Joe's nightmares. John had tried to ignore the Swastika when he saw it in the drawings, feeling ashamed that his grandfather used the Nazi symbol. But, next to a depiction of the Swastika, the caption in his book read, "Symbolizes the creative, generative power of the Underworld."

Where would Grandpa Joe have even seen this stuff? And why would he be drawing it? John recalled the grisly, screaming masks, the primitive, sharp claws and teeth, and the savage tears through the paper. He felt his head start to swim and his blood go cold. *He does know about the mound. He has to.*

He flipped to the next page in the text, and was confronted with a cave drawing of a winged beast. It had the horns of a stag, the face of a mountain lion, and a writhing serpent for a tail. In a flash, the same creature that John had seen in his own dream came back to him—but in fleshy, snarling realism.

The room seemed to tilt.

John muttered a quick, "Excuse me," his hand over his mouth. He moved slowly and calmly towards the exit, though *calm* was no emotion he could hold onto.

The closest men's room was blessedly empty. He gripped both sides of the porcelain sink and stared into the basin, willing the nausea to ebb. When his hands steadied, he turned on the faucet and splashed his face with cold water. He let the water trickle off his chin and watched it swirl down the drain, trying to regain his grip on reality. The forgotten creature—from the dream he had shared with Candy, the night he arrived in Shirley—was bright in his mind. The campfire ghost story. He didn't embellish the ghost story with the winged monster that pounced on him right before he woke up—trying to tear out his throat—because he hadn't remembered it before.

How did I forget that part? I must have fallen back to sleep and...

A bell announced the end of the period. John grabbed a paper towel to dry off his face and raced back to class.

§

Candy wondered if she should grab John's backpack for him, since he hadn't come back from the bathroom yet. She looked back towards the door. Everyone else was rushing out, ready to quit the classroom and enjoy the scant eight minutes and thirty seconds of freedom before the next bell rang for third period. She stuffed her book and notebook into her bag, then leaned over to gather John's things.

Class over and the room mostly empty, Ms. Collins fiddled behind her desk.

Now's the time. Candy took a deep breath.

She had to know more about that painting of the Sendalee woman in the lodge. The photo album she snagged from Grandma Catherine's turned out to be a gold mine; Grandpa Raymond's mother had the black eyes, just like Candy's. Grandpa had died before Candy was born and she'd never seen pictures of his mother. But there in the photo album, only two pages from the back, was Maeve McBride, holding her little baby boy

Raymond, in 1936. Her eyes were deep and dark as night, even though she was fair. Flipping to the front of the book, one childhood picture stood out. It was one of Maeve on her mother's lap. Black eyes again.

After so much amazing info from the first stolen album, Candy had been tingling with knowledge and trepidation. She raced back over to Grandma Catherine's and found an even older album, yellowed and waxy and falling apart. Most of the pictures proved fruitless. But one was of a woman who was much darker than the other McBrides—black eyes and black hair. And more like the Sendalee woman from that painting. A daguerreotype. Candy carefully removed the picture from its black corner tabs and turned it over, her heart racing. There, written on the back was, "Ahnaanvwodi, 1861."

Candy's heart almost stopped.

When she asked her grandma about it, she confirmed the album was from Grandpa Raymond's family. Grandma Catherine said she had never known much about the early McBrides in America. Candy could tell by the uninterested way her eyes skimmed over the photos that she was telling the truth. She went back to her crocheting without another thought to her granddaughter's new secret obsession.

But, Ms. Collins knows everything about Shirley County history. She had to know something about this Ahnaanvwodi person. Candy slung her bag over one shoulder, John's over the other. Determined. "Um. Ms. Collins?"

"Yes, Candace," her teacher said without looking up. She was stooped against the window, searching for something in a bottom drawer of flat files.

"I was just wondering. When would painting—like oil painting..." Candy shifted both backpacks. "When would that have come to the colonies...back in the early days? The first settlements?" Ms. Collins straightened up and cocked her head in question. "I mean, the Indians didn't paint on canvases, obviously..."

Ms. Collins smiled. "You've seen the painting of the Ahnaanvwodi."

Candy's blood thickened with sudden chill. *How the heck does she know? Oh shit.* She wasn't sure what she could admit to without getting Sam in trouble, since he was the one with the keys to the Buffalo Lodge that day. "Er...what painting?"

"Your secret is safe with me, dear. In my opinion the lodge is a museum that should be enjoyed by all citizens of Shirley County, not the select few."

"Oh. Well." Candy cleared her throat. She still felt silly asking, but. "You said the Ahnaanvwodi. It wasn't her name?"

"It's the title of a woman who is considered to be a healer. In the Sendalee dialect, the word 'ahnaanvwodi' translates roughly to 'the touch.' In a feminine context."

Holy crap. "What does that mean? She could heal with a touch or something?"

Ms. Collins shrugged. "That's the legend. I highly doubt there's any truth to that. More likely an Ahnaanvwodi simply had more knowledge of the best healing herbs in the region. But of course, I've never met one, so how would I know?"

Candy could've sworn she saw a twinkle in the old educator's eye before she bent down to open a lower desk drawer. When she straightened up, she had a nondescript brown book in her hand. It looked like a small text book.

Candy accepted the book from her with reverence. "Are there accounts of…how an Ahnaanvwodi would have healed someone?"

"Written accounts?" Ms. Collins frowned, disappointed. "The Sendalee relied on oral history, Candace. You should remember from last night's homework—if you read it—that written language was only introduced by the colonists who arrived here in 1793."

Heat bloomed up Candy's neck. "Oh, right."

"However, I am certainly glad that you've developed an interest in our town's history." Ms. Collins looked past her. "Glad you decided to return, Mr. Robinson."

"Sorry." John jogged through the classroom, breathless. "Thanks for picking up my stuff, Candy."

"There you are, what happened?" She crammed Ms. Collins mystery book into her bag before John could ask about it.

"I'm sorry I had to leave like that." John took his backpack off Candy's shoulder. "I don't know, I…felt sick all of a sudden."

Ms. Collins set a practiced eye on John. "Do you need to see the nurse, son? You do look pale."

"No. Really, I'm fine now."

"It's those morning protein shakes, John. Do you know how much artificial crap those things have in them?" Candy was happy to nag; she wasn't thrilled about his new role as a Bobcatt football player.

"Yeah, you're probably right. It won't happen again, Ms. Collins."

"Well, should you feel the urge to vomit in the future, I would always prefer that happen in the bathroom instead of the classroom, Mr. Robinson."

"Right. Of course." John laughed, steering Candy towards the door.

"Miss Vale can catch you up on your homework assignment." She turned her back and began erasing the whiteboard in preparation for her next class, dismissing them.

"Well, anyway," said Candy, leading out into the hallway. "You didn't miss much, except some ignorant remarks about the quality of Native American art."

She and John merged with the stream of students making their way to third period.

"Stayed behind to chat with Ms. Collins, huh? I didn't think you liked her."

"Oh, she's okay—" Candy stopped in her tracks so abruptly that a kid close behind nearly slammed into her.

"Watch out," he grumbled, elbowing past.

Candy paid no attention to the kid, focused as she was on her favorite pair of green eyes. "Sam. Hi."

Sam had his thumbs hooked into his backpack straps, about to stroll past without stopping. Insolent eyes were locked on hers; curious if Candy would notice him, but determined not to speak first. When she called out his name, he tipped his chin almost imperceptibly and moved next to the lockers, out of the flow of traffic. "Hello."

"Hey...uh. I've been looking for you. I...I didn't see you all day yesterday," Candy rambled, caught off guard and tongue-tied. She'd been wondering why she hadn't seen him around, worried that he hadn't texted or called or anything.

His face was expressionless. "Really? You should have called me."

"Oh, yeah. I guess I could have." She turned to John, forced a smile and awkwardly shoved him in Sam's direction. "So. This is my friend John. He just got into town a couple days ago. We've known each other since we were little."

"Haven't mentioned me? I'm hurt." John stuck out his hand. "Hi, nice to meet you..." He looked from Candy to Sam, waiting for a name.

"I'm Sam." Sam took John's hand with a firm grip, peering into his face and scrutinizing every curve. Sizing him up. John narrowed his eyes.

"Oh, sorry," Candy said. She slapped her forehead and made a dopey face; introductions were not going as planned. *What plan? I should've had a plan!* "And this is Sam."

"Nice to finally meet you. John."

That tone. Candy's nerves zinged with adrenaline. Sam looked pissed. *Why? What did I do?*

John looked back and forth between the two of them; surely noticing her deep embarrassment and Sam's challenging expression. She watched realization dawn on John's face. Then jealousy. "Yeah, you too. Sam."

*Should I have introduced him as my boyfriend? Is he? He never said...*Candy's face was aflame; the right moment seemed to have passed.

After a few seconds had ticked by in uncomfortable silence, Sam decisively said, "Well, then." He hooked his thumbs back under the straps of his backpack and continued down the hall. He gave a curt nod over his shoulder, "See you around."

Candy watched him walk away from her, her mind oscillating between hurt and fury and sorrow.

"Oh, *the waltz*," she heard John say.

She turned to him and saw jealousy change to curiosity.

Candy blew her bangs out of her eyes, hoping John couldn't see the pulse in her neck, the red in her face. "Whatever. What class do you have next?"

"Creative Writing." John's face was impassive, as if he hadn't noticed anything odd about that obviously strained exchange. He jerked a thumb over his shoulder, "That way."

"I'm that way." She motioned in the opposite direction. "Ceramics. See you at lunch?"

His brows knitted, John suddenly seemed on the verge of laughing. "Yeah, sure. See you there."

Screw you. Candy waved, affecting perkiness, "Bye."

When she turned around to trudge to class, she let her head droop to one side and she heaved her shoulders in a frustrated sigh. What had she done? She glanced behind and saw John watching her, but when she caught his eye, he smiled and headed the other way.

chapter twenty-seven

Driving into Shirley from the east always shocked Aaron Walsh after he had been away for a while. He'd be driving through the gentle rise and fall of the highway, traversing mostly highlands between the taller peaks, for miles. Then, he'd round the last summit, Widow-maker Point, and then *bang!*—the valley plunged, a deep crevice in the countryside below the granite cliffs. The transition was breath-taking. He usually felt contented by the vision, flooded with memories of a happy childhood spent rampaging through the forests with friends, siblings and cousins. But not that day.

That day, the scene made him feel homesick and sorry for himself. He wanted nothing more than to curl up in a cozy lounger and watch a Mystery Science Theater marathon under blankets. He turned up the volume on a melancholy country song and let his mood settle in. Aaron reached up to squeeze Henri's collar; he hung it from his rearview mirror after the vet had returned the collar, empty, along with other personal items. The grain of the fabric was worn and soft, slightly oily from years of use.

Henri had started out as his wife Chloë's, dog years before, but the dog had taken to Aaron. Aaron loved to give Henri bacon treats and dinner handouts under the table. Chloë bought him for a show dog. He was a Bichon Frise with Champion lineage—his sire was actually named Champion, no kidding—but Aaron had spoiled his wife's chances in a matter of months. He smiled, thinking about how mad she was when Henri got too fat to fit the standard. He remembered that glorious, flowing-white tail that Henri would wrap around his wrist while he petted him. Aaron had grown up with hounds and mutts, and he never would've imagined a fluffy white dog would or could steal his heart, but he had.

Then, Henri started showing signs of mysterious health problems. A pure bred dog after all, Aaron had tried to reason that inbreeding often caused strange issues. He took him to dozens of specialists and spent thousands of dollars on testing and treatments. Finally, he had to accept it. Henri was dying. Once Aaron decided to have him put to sleep, he made the commitment to be there with him when he passed away. He cried like a baby for days leading up to it and for days after it was done, but he was able to stroke his fur and whisper thanks in his ear, for being such a good dog. As difficult as it was, he was grateful to have been able to tell him good-bye.

Chloë was sympathetic and patient at first. But after several days of Aaron's prolonged mourning, moping around the house uselessly, she started to lose patience. He lashed out at her for not seeing Henri's worth as a show dog (which was ridiculous; Henri would have hated that prissy crap), and Chloë suggested a week in the mountains might help.

She was right, of course. Camping always helped heal the soul. Aaron couldn't wait to get out there, among the elements. He'd spent too much time indoors the last few years. City life did that to you. He figured he'd stop in and say hello to Dad before he headed south, into the most secluded wilderness along Red Ridge.

"Oh, shit." When he neared the house, he saw his dad's car was not in the driveway. Mieke's was. The idea of a solo conversation with that woman made his skin crawl. He couldn't imagine her understanding his pain, remembering how she never seemed to like their family dogs and refused to take any responsibility in caring for them. He always resented that.

Aaron parked next to Mieke's SUV and got out of the car, then approached the back door with dread. He felt around the top of the doorjamb for the key, considering sneaking in without announcing himself and falling asleep in the den before anyone noticed he was there. But, even if he could get away with that, he knew it would make things awkward later. So, he rapped on the door as he entered and called, "Hello?"

The kitchen was empty but all the lights were on. There was an opened bag of chips and half-empty glasses of soda on the breakfast table. He could hear the television in the front room and the muffled voices of a woman and man talking. Leaving his suitcase by the back stairs, he walked down the hallway to the front of the house and leaned his shoulder against the entryway, taking in the scene.

"'Sumpin lack at'—did you hear that?" Mieke pointed to the television screen and then enunciated clearly, "Something like that."

It wasn't a man, Aaron was surprised to find. "Yes, yes." The boy next to her nodded and scribbled on a pad of paper.

"See? 'Uppin awr.' That should be pronounced 'up in there,' but that's not really correct grammar anyway."

"Yes."

Mieke and the boy whom Aaron assumed to be their new foreign exchange student, were sitting with their backs to him on the sofa, watching some reality show that apparently took place in a pretty backwoods southern community. The characters' hillbilly accents were so thick that there were English subtitles at the bottom of the screen.

"Having trouble with the accent here?" Aaron asked.

Mieke jumped, grasping her chest and turning around with terror in her face. Something told Aaron she wouldn't have been showing the kid that show if his dad had been home. Recognizing Aaron in the doorway, she broke into a smile, flicked off the television and rose to greet him.

"Aaron. Hi. I didn't hear you come in."

"Hi, Mieke." He gave her a perfunctory hug, looking over her shoulder. The kid was waiting with his hands in his pockets, his gaze averted to allow them privacy while they embraced. "You must be the new foreign exchange student. I'm sorry—Dad told me, but I forgot your name."

"Oh, this is Antonio di Brigo. Antonio, please meet my step-son, Aaron." Mieke held out her hand to welcome Antonio over, and he came around the couch to hug Aaron just as she had.

"Hi, Aaron. It's nice to meet you," Antonio said clearly, looking to Mieke for approval.

"Yes, that's much more natural now," she assured him. "I'm just helping him work out some quirks, you know. Learning to speak the language fluently is a big part of the program. He's already fluent, just a little rough around the edges."

Antonio raised his eyebrows in question, and Aaron supplied in the clearest American English, as accent-free as he could make it, "Rough around the edges means unrefined."

"It could be smoother." Mieke made a smoothing gesture with her hands. She flicked her shiny black bob away from her eyes and chuckled. "But, like I told you, American girls will love your Italian accent."

Antonio nodded with a revelatory smile, and though Aaron wasn't sure that he had understood every word, he certainly got the gist.

"Look, but don't touch, though, right Antonio?" she laughed, and shoved him on the shoulder with manicured fingertips.

"What do you mean?" asked Aaron.

"Oh, that stupid Stephanie Jameson brought over a written declaration yesterday, stating that Antonio would refrain from dating any under-aged girls. She insisted he sign it. Because he's nineteen, you know? Isn't that ridiculous?"

"Seems like that could be difficult to monitor," Aaron guessed. When he was in high school, most parents were pretty clueless about the sexual diversions of youth.

"Anyway, I told Antonio that being forbidden would only make the girls want him more, right?"

The two snickered companionably, clearly having shared more than a couple private jokes between themselves already.

"Um, actually Aaron…" Mieke turned to him and cocked her head in solicitation, then touched his forearm. Aaron flinched—she wasn't much older than he was himself and physical contact with her was always a little creepy when Dad wasn't around. "I'm glad you're here. I need to get to the pharmacy before it closes and I can't take Antonio with me. He has some friends coming to pick him up for football practice in a little while. Will you watch him, while I slip out?"

"Sure," Aaron shrugged, not sure why a nineteen-year-old needed watching, but always happy to see the backside of Mieke. As soon as she left, he plopped down on the sofa and flipped the television back on in hopes of catching more of the show they had been watching.

I don't have an accent, do I?

The show had already ended. He searched his mind for something to talk about with the kid while flipping through channels.

"So, school lets out early, huh?"

"The last for me is house school, with Mieke."

"Oh, homeschool? Cool."

He flipped past a dog show and his stomach lurched. There was no way this foreign kid would see him cry. "Want a beer?" he ventured, but they were interrupted by the doorbell. "Hold on, lemme get that."

Cursing Mieke for her insistence on keeping the house on lock-down, Aaron searched for the key to the deadbolt and found it in a brass box next to the coat hooks.

"Just a minute," he hollered.

He finally fit the key into the lock and lugged the heavy oak door open to find a pretty, black-haired young woman on the stoop. He thought she wore a little too much make-up for a high school girl, but what did he know? It looked like a style, with thick '60s eyeliner, red lipstick and bangs trimmed short.

"Hey there, you here for Antonio?"

One plucked, penciled eyebrow shot up in surprise. "Why, yes I am. Were you expecting me?"

"Yeah, Mieke said friends were coming to get him."

"How interesting." She leaned in to give Aaron a better view of her cleavage and he backed away, embarrassed to feel things coming to life down below his belt. "Hey, Antonio! Your friend is here."

Thankfully, the two kids went straight to the guesthouse, where Antonio probably kept his football gear. Aaron waved good-bye and forced a fatherly smile. *Her lipstick is the same color as her heels. Fire-engine red.*

He shook the idiocy from his brain, shut the front door, and leaned his back against it. He savored a long sigh of relief. Things were going better than he had dared to hope; only fifteen minutes after arriving, he was blissfully alone. No Mieke, no foreign stranger. Leaving his suitcase where it was, he fetched himself that beer from the fridge and headed down to the basement den. He left the lights off, turned the television on, and kicked his feet up in the lounger. He pulled a fleece throw over his legs, aching with the absence of a warm, fat dog on his lap.

"Oh, Henri."

Fresh tears rolled down his cheeks as he flipped through channels.

chapter twenty-eight

Candy sped up the mountain road on her bike, worried she might not catch Sam before he had to leave for work, and she desperately needed to talk to him. She didn't know why she froze up when she saw him in the hallway with John on Tuesday, but she walked away feeling like someone kicked her in the stomach. The feeling had stayed with her all day. Sam ignored her texts all day, too.

Maybe I should have introduced him to John as my boyfriend. But, it felt stupid even saying it in her mind. She felt like she should have called him something, though she was kind of glad she hadn't when he blew her off, right in front of John. Sam had seemed pissed off; surely he didn't think she was anything more than friends with John?

Maybe she should have called him after the music festival. *But then, he didn't call me. Not even to tell me how it went with Rachel. What was that about? After I got him the job.*

Maybe Sam didn't care as much for her as she hoped he did, but she wouldn't know until she could get him alone. Candy hadn't seen him at school at all and she was starting to feel frantic. She squeezed her eyes shut when she sent her last text, *"please meet me at the palace"*

She was so relieved to see his reply that her stomach had unknotted for the first time in days.

"ok"

She spotted Rachel's truck parked just off the road, where the trail to The Palace could be found if you knew where to look. She parked in a hurry and jumped off her bike, left her book bag in the dirt, and breezed in through the door. "Guess the gig with Rachel is paying off royally—"

She halted in her tracks when she saw Amanda Jameson sitting on the edge of the loveseat, her hands clasped primly on her knees. Sam was leaned against the wall with his arms folded across his chest, his face unreadable.

"Oh hey, Candy." Amanda made a pretense at surprise, but Candy could tell by the calmness in her tone that she had been expecting her. "What are you doing here?"

"Um," Candy looked at Sam. He watched the ceiling and sighed in exasperation. "That's actually a good question all around."

"Oh, us? My brother Tristan dropped me off to see Lindsay. She wasn't home yet, so I just took a walk and who did I run into but Sam, on his way here? We're just hangin' out. Cool place."

Sam was shaking his head, "No," and making a slicing motion across his throat. Remaining irritatingly silent.

"You know what?" Candy heard her voice shake with rage. She reached over and grabbed the box of art stuff she had given Sam, then flipped the lid shut, her eyes embers of defiance. "I'm just picking something up."

"Don't worry, you're not interrupting us. You can stay…"

Amanda's voice trailed away as Candy stormed out, her heart thudding in her ears and her skin prickling all over. She raced to the road and was on her bike in a flash, ripping her keys out of her pocket and stuffing the art box into her backpack. She slung her bag over her shoulders and started the engine.

Sam was right behind her. "Candy, wait." He grabbed her arm, clutching it so hard that it hurt. "It's not what you think."

"Yeah, right."

"It's not!"

"Why did you just stand there and not say anything then?" She felt the tears springing and her throat swelling.

"I didn't think you'd want someone like that girl knowing your private business, Candy."

"I don't."

"What about you and that blonde guy?"

"John?"

"Yeah. John."

"John and I grew up together—he's been my best friend since we were little."

"So, why didn't you ever mention him?"

Candy was at a loss for words. Why hadn't she? Because all she ever thought about when she was with Sam, was Sam. "Please back away. I don't want to run you over."

"Don't leave like this."

"And what—stay here, with the two of you 'hangin' out'? Forget it."

"Come on. I'll tell her to leave."

"No, you know what? I think I'll bring a friend next time, too." She gunned the engine. Suddenly, she didn't care whether she ran over his foot or not. She tore through the woods and made it to the road before Sam could see her stinging tears.

"Stop crying, you baby," she choked to herself. The engine sputtered. The gas gauge was on empty. *Perfect.*

She was so amped up to see Sam that she hadn't even noticed she was almost out of gas. She made a U-turn, shut off the bike, and coasted towards her dad's gas station at the bottom of Hemlock Drive.

"Amanda Jameson, that little twit," she muttered to herself. Her possessive attitude made Candy's blood boil. *How dare she act possessive over my Sam?*

The wind blew her hair back and she sucked in a few cleansing breaths. Sam was right, of course. She didn't want Amanda Jameson to know her business and then blab it to the world. What had she wanted Sam to do, exactly? She wasn't sure, but she knew she hated the way it all went down. She just saw red sometimes, like her blood was raging in her skull, and once it started it was hard to stop.

Now, Sam's seen the real me—just a touch of my temper. What's he gonna think?

She swallowed hard and wished more than anything that she could back up and erase the last few minutes. She rounded the last curve and spotted her dad in the parking lot of the station. He was chatting with John. *Crap!*

Candy struggled to rearrange her face and thought she painted on a pretty good mask of nonchalance, before her tires crunched in the gravel parking lot and her dad spotted her.

"What happened, Sugar Booger? Forget you need gas to run that thing?"

John turned towards her and waved, "Hey Candy."

John leaned against the side of his car in a jersey tank and sweat pants, his long legs stretched out in front of him and crossed at the ankles. He had just filled up, by the look of it, and her dad was in the middle of one of his monologues. They had taken the top of the "new" Mustang down and popped the hood. She could hear her dad's expert suggestions on how to spiff up an old classic. Dad rocked back on his heels and took a last gander at John's car. "Well, I'll let you get back to business, but think about that tune-up. I'm sure she needs it, and I'd love to really check her out."

"Tomorrow after school is good—we've got nighttime practice on Thursdays. I'll drop by." John shook his hand to seal the deal.

"Good to see you again, son."

"Good to be back, sir. Oh, and you'll be at the party Saturday?"

"Wouldn't miss it. Candy, you staying?" her dad asked, hesitating in the doorway to the store. "Or just fillin' up and firing out?"

She wished he'd stop peering at her face, terrified another tear would roll from under her sunglasses any second. *Why does his nice-guy voice always send me over the edge?* "I've got lots of stuff to do, Dad."

"Alright, see you kids later."

He waved and headed inside, and Candy started breathing again. "Wow, I can't believe he let us off the hook so fast." She could usually expect her dad to linger, talking well past the point that everyone else was fidgeting. Her dad never heard finishing clues like, "Okay, well I'll let you go, then," or "Well, it was good talking with you." She often thought maybe he never heard much of what anyone else said.

"He kept mentioning some lady he had waiting inside that was in the middle of a transaction," John kept his voice low, and raised his hands, palms up, in helplessness. "I was wondering how long she would wait, until she just took off."

"You gotta admire my dad for being in ownership of all the time in the world. What party?"

"They're having a welcome dinner for Antonio at the restaurant. An Italian theme, if you can believe it."

"Whoa, exotic. Real Eye-talian?"

"Yeah, I know. Hey, what are you doing now? I'm picking up Antonio for practice, but we don't have to be there until 3:00. Got some time."

"Yeah, early release on Wednesdays is nice, huh?"

"Want to hang out for a while?"

I guess everyone's "hangin' out" today, she thought, her anger simmering just below the surface. "Sure, why not?"

"Hop in. I'll drop you back by here to get your bike, on our way out," John said, moving around the car to open her door.

"He's living at the Walsh's right?"

"Yeah, and apparently he has the whole guesthouse to himself. I guess they weren't prepared for hosting him, so he has the bed and breakfast suite until his room in the big house is ready. Sounds like it's pretty nice." He closed her door and slammed the hood shut on his way around to the driver side. Without bothering to open his own door, he slid over and in with a practiced slide.

"So Dukes of Hazzard."

"You like that?" The car roared to life. He gave it some gas and raised his eyebrows in time to the engine.

"Very nice," she laughed. Laughter was exactly what she needed; she felt her heart rate normalize and her breathing slow almost instantly.

Just before leaving the parking lot, though, John pulled his sunglasses down and frowned.

Oh great. Tear tracks, right?

"You okay?"

"Ugh. Fine," she said, sniffing and pulling off her sunglasses to wipe at her eyes. He let the car idle, and waited for her to say more. She met his gaze, steady and silent.

"Uh-huh." He put the car in first gear, pulled out of the station, and started climbing into the mountains. After a few minutes, he asked, "It's that Sam guy, right? He's your boyfriend?"

"Yes, it is Sam. And no, he's not my boyfriend."

"Okay…" Doubtful.

"I don't want to talk about it."

"Alright." John let the wind fill in, as they drove past increasingly taller trees in the thickening forest of beech, maple, oak and hemlock. They turned onto Forest Lane, and the shade deepened, the air cooler with a faint smell of mossy undergrowth. The trees cleared for a small waterfall and the mist kissed their faces as they passed. "Well, if you do want to talk, I'm a good listener."

"I know." *Too good.* Candy squeezed his hand on the gear shifter. "Thanks."

Before long, they neared the turn-off for the Walsh's place, which sat back from the road amidst a spacious woodland property. Candy was surprised to see an emerald-green Thunderbird convertible coming toward them down the driveway. To pass, both cars were forced to leave the drive for the relative safety of the grass on either side. Candy peered at the woman in the other car, who raised her gloved hand in a Jackie-O wave. Her hair was protected by a white kerchief, and most of her face was covered by oversized black sunglasses. Candy turned around and watched her disappear around a bend in the driveway. "Was that Charlotte Finley?"

"Who's Charlotte Finley?"

"Well…I only know her slightly. She's a cousin from Grandma Catherine's family—extended family. But, she's weird. Well, I mean really into that whole Moonshine Mafia thing."

"Is there a 'Moonshine Mafia' in Shirley County?" John parked in front of the guesthouse and pulled the emergency brake. "I've been away for too long."

"I assure you, it's been going on since way before we were born." The Finley-Watts story was one she had grown up with, and though it was scandalous and highly gossip-friendly, she enjoyed holding John's ignorance over his head. John ignorant about anything was such a novelty. "I guess Grandma Pearl never told you that particular bit of town history."

"No, she didn't."

"She isn't much of a drinker, true. Well, it's kind of adult information and you haven't really been back since we were twelve or thirteen. Not for more than a week anyway."

"Please. Acquaint me." John was spellbound. He turned off the car and faced her, life's other trifles forgotten. He leaned forward like a lion ready to pounce.

"I can't tell you the whole story right now," Candy bent closer, glancing toward the guesthouse to make sure they were speaking privately. "But, suffice it to say, there are dirty bloodlines galore, crossed and uncrossed by more ties and treacheries than you can imagine. Whiskey has always bought plenty of profit for the backwoods boys, and now there's much more than whiskey involved."

John waited for more, but Candy just smiled and opened her door. He sat back against his seat. "Hmph."

She didn't miss the light in his eyes, the clinking of the keys John twiddled in his lap. She loved it. *The game is afoot, isn't it, Sherlock?* "Come on, let's go in."

"Yeah, okay." He narrowed his eyes at the empty rearview mirror—oh, how Candy loved investigative John. He'd probably be scouring the internet later, but for the time being, he shook himself out of it. "Let's go."

The door of the guesthouse was painted a deep forest green and set into a wooden log frame, recently stained and lacquered. John rapped on the door and waited. After several moments, Antonio's muffled voice sounded from inside and he pulled open the door. His friendly smile spread when he realized John wasn't alone. Before Candy could react, he leaned over and gave her a kiss on each cheek, then a body squeeze. She saw John stifle a laugh at her discomfort over Antonio's shoulder and she helped stymie it with a glacial scowl.

He gave John a high-five. "Welcome to my house."

"Uh, could you put a shirt on?" Candy asked, averting her eyes. Antonio was shirtless and barefooted, with jeans that were unbuttoned at the top. He was slim but muscular, and Candy was annoyed to feel a blush blooming up her neck at the sight of the happy trail creeping up his abdomen.

"Sorry, honey," he said, flirtation personified. "I was not expecting a lady."

Candy snorted, hoping to sound as unladylike as possible. "Oh, really? Who was that lady we just saw leaving?"

"From Rotary Club," his voice trailed away, as he went to retrieve his shirt from the bathroom.

John and Candy followed him inside, wandering and snooping. The guesthouse was well-appointed, with a small seating area, a flat screen television and a kitchenette. Looking through the French doors leading to the back deck, Candy could see a wicker table and chair set, with an umbrella, a surrounding garden, and a lovely view of a meadow and the woods beyond. "Boy, did he luck out with this host family. The Walsh place is nice," she whispered to John.

Antonio reemerged from the bathroom in a T-shirt and soccer shorts, ready for practice. "She wanted to check and see I am fine."

"Isn't Mieke Walsh the Rotary Club's vice president?" asked John.

Antonio shrugged and made a face that showed how little he cared about the Rotary Club. He picked up a guitar before plopping down on his unmade bed, and began strumming it.

Candy picked up knick-knacks, and switched table lamps on and off. "I love this place." The bathroom was all bright white porcelain and shiny golden brass. There was even an antique bathtub.

Antonio shook his head when she came out of the bathroom, "Is femminile—too much for me."

"Feminine?" offered John.

"Yes, thank you. Feminine." He played a few chords and fiddled with the tuning knobs.

"Yeah, it is a little girlie, with all the lace and flowers," agreed Candy, sitting down on a tufted sofa and examining a throw pillow embroidered with roses. "Too much maybe."

"I think Mrs. Walsh is appealing to antique-trolling tourists," allowed John. "Still, too bad you'll have to move to the big house. This looks cozy. And private."

"Why can't you stay out here, anyway?" Candy headed over to a miniature refrigerator to investigate. *Empty. Must not be eating out here.*

"I am too young." Antonio smiled at the irony.

"To stay alone out here?" John was incredulous; everyone heard of the PTA uproar about his age. "All the panic about you being nineteen, I don't get it."

"Yeah, 'a grown man.' My dad said all the parents freaked out when they heard you were of age."

"Mieke says, 'you are just boy,'" Antonio scoffed, always eager to prove his manhood to Candy.

"Hey, what did you do for your year of work-study, anyway?" asked John. "Something in music? I heard you're in a band."

"No, that is just hobby. I love, but not for career. I work at… veterinario?"

"Veterinarian? An assistant or something?"

"Yes."

"Cool," Candy piped up. She came back into the bedroom area and plopped down on a spindly Windsor chair next to the bed. The chair creaked and she knocked another embroidered pillow onto the floor, but she didn't care. She was finally interested in Antonio di Brigo; Candy loved animals. "So, that's what you want to be—a vet?"

"Yes," Antonio cocked his head and leered at her close proximity to the bed.

Ugh! Just when you were coming up in my esteem. She shook her head at him and narrowed her eyes, but he *was* sort of funny.

"Hangin' round, downtown by myself," Antonio began to sing, his thick accent lost entirely, the American English rolling off his tongue. "And I've had too much caffeine, and I was thinkin' 'bout myself. And then there she was…"

"Ha, I know this song." Candy chortled; she knew exactly what was coming as Antonio strummed louder and zeroed in on her with his large brown eyes. "Retro—like I've never heard it before…"

"Like double cherry pie, and there she was…" John joined in the song and plopped down next to Antonio to serenade her from the bed. "Like disco Superfly."

"I smell sex and candy here," the guys sang together. Candy plugged her ears. They brought up the volume, so she could hear anyway, "Who that loungin' in my chair? Who's that castin' deviant stares in my direction?"

"Okay, okay." She grabbed the guitar, "I know, 'I surely am a dream.' Nice guitar, though. Did you bring it from Italy?"

"No, is Mr. Walsh's. Do you play?"

"A little. Not as well as you."

"Aw, come on, Candy." John fell backwards on the bed, his hands knitted behind his head. "You're too modest. She's from a whole family of musicians, Antonio. She can play."

"Really?"

"Play us something, Red Hot."

Antonio crossed his legs in listening fashion and nodded like a grade-schooler. "Yes, please."

"Okay…" Candy squinted up towards the ceiling, searching her head for a simple song she could play well, without warming up. John was being way too kind, she thought. She really wasn't very good. Uncle Pat had shown her to play a couple of songs with simple chord changes, and usually a modified, easy version at that. She chose one that she had always loved and had practiced the most, a short segment since she couldn't remember all the words. John and Antonio leaned in. She screwed up once or twice, and felt shy when she finished.

"Your voice is like angel," Antonio breathed. She handed him back the guitar with a warning look, but he shook his head, vehement. "Is true, honey."

"Don't call me honey," Candy said. But she smiled anyway.

chapter twenty-nine

John dragged his feet up the porch stairs. He groaned at the ache in his quads, his glutes, his calves.

God, am I gonna be sore tomorrow.

After conditioning drills on the field and then stadiums, they hit the weight room for another grueling hour. And that was after going through plays for the first hour of practice. Shirley County was serious about football. His duffel bag thudded to the floor. He looked down at it with a grimace; the mess would piss off Grandma Pearl, so he lugged it into the hall closet, his biceps whining in objection.

"That you, John?" Grandma called from the kitchen.

He found her sorting through mail in the dining nook, with her reading glasses perched on the end of her nose. He slid onto the bench across from her and laid his head on his sore forearms, wincing at the draft from the direction of his armpits. He reeked, too.

"Rough day, dear?"

"Long practice, is all," John mumbled, his face nestled into his arms. "I could probably fall asleep right here."

"Oh, no you don't. We only sleep in beds in this house, John Robinson."

"I was only kidding, Gram." He raised his head and beamed a smile up at her, his eyes still closed, then flopped his head back down.

She had been snippy ever since he approached her the previous night, wanting to know about Big Joe's and ancient Native American mounds. She denied any knowledge of the relationship and strictly forbade John mentioning such a "preposterous" idea to his grandfather. "Helen Collins is a nutcase. That is simply ridiculous. Imagine her. And your grandfather in the state he's in…" She had ranted for at least twenty minutes before John finally excused himself, claiming he had a mountain of homework to get to.

John rolled his head to the side to watch her ripping open envelops with her fingernail. He wondered how unpleasant the evening would be. "Do you need help with dinner?"

"Now, I'm not going to make everyone dinner every night of the week." She rose from the table and began filing the opened mail into proper slots and bins, tossing the junk mail into the trash. She bustled around the kitchen cleaning things randomly and griping about there being three grown adults living in the house, and how there was no reason that she had to tend to everyone's needs. John tuned her out and thought he should probably call the restaurant and warn his dad that Grandma Pearl was in one of her moods. Her voice was still ringing through the house when he quietly made his escape from the kitchen and climbed the stairs.

"John," she shouted up the stairwell after him. "See if your grandfather wants food with his evening medication. Whenever he is *finished* with his *meeting*."

"Okay, Grandma," he answered, sure that he was about to glean a better understanding about the nature of the bee up Grandma Pearl's skirts. He didn't realize his grandfather was scheduled to arrive home from the hospital already, but there was no one on earth who could send his wife into frenzy faster than Joe Robinson. Wondering what kind of meeting he could possibly be having in his bedroom, John hobbled down the hallway, quads screaming after the climb upstairs. Muffled giggling and a lower baritone rumble emanated from his grandfather's room as he approached. He stood outside with an ear to the door for a few seconds, uncertain of what he would be interrupting should he knock.

"Oh Joe, you're terrible."

"You have no idea, darlin'. Come over here and I'll show you."

"Oh, I have no doubt." *Tee hee…*

"You don't need to doubt—"

What the hell? John rapped sharply. When he tried the knob, it was locked. "Grandpa?"

"Yes, who is it?" was the reply, in a woman's voice.

"This is John."

A soft, scrambling sound, then a quiet click as the door was unlocked, and Mieke Walsh pulled the door open. A rush of air blew her hair back from her plastered smile. There was annoyance under the mask.

"John, you come over here and give me a hug," Grandpa Joe bellowed, holding his arms out from a half-seated position, cranked up in a mobile hospital bed. "Damned if it ain't good to see you, boy."

His grandfather's face was ruddy, but his sheets were still tucked, John noticed. "Hey, Grandpa."

His reply was almost lost, as Grandpa Joe bear-rolled John in a painful squeeze. At least he was feeling more himself. When John righted himself and stood again, though, he could see the man had lost quite a bit of weight. His breathing was labored from the exertion.

Mieke checked her watch, feigning surprise at the time, "Oh my. Antonio must be home already then, too, if football practice is over."

"I dropped him home." John repressed his pique; he hadn't realized how taxing being the guy with the car would be until he'd driven the length of Shirley Valley several times in one day and made side trips into the mountains, as well. He was going to have to come up with a better plan, and fast.

"Thank you, John." Mieke's demeanor softened towards him, and she wrung her hands with a thread of guilt. "I should have picked him up, I just didn't think about that. Motherhood is a lot of work."

"Motherhood. Girl…" Joe reached out for a tickle, and Mieke jumped back, slapping his hand away and giggling.

"Oh, Joe!"

"It's no problem, Mrs. Walsh," John lied, yawning and plopping into the armchair next to the hospital bed. It was still warm. *At least she was sitting here, instead of in there with him.*

Mieke petted the top of his head. "I'll bet you're tired, huh? You're such a dear, John." John took the opportunity to breathe her in, noting her perfume, her hairspray, her body lotion and her probable laundry detergent. He hadn't smelled the same on his grandfather. "I really must go. Ian will probably be wondering where I am. Aaron's visiting, too, and I bet they're waiting on me for dinner."

"Somebody's in trouble," Joe chuckled. "Better get outta here."

Mieke fluttered her fingers with a mock-frazzled look, already punching in numbers on her cell phone as she ducked out. "Bye, boys."

John turned back to Grandpa Joe and caught his lecherous gaze, barely disguised, right before his face slid into a benevolent smile more suitable for a grandchild. The old man's philandering had never been much of a secret. Not to John anyway. Sometimes he thought his grandfather would purposely leave sly clues to the males in his life, to prove his virility. A wink after certain women parted company. An evil look behind Pearl's back after announcing he'd be home late.

"Grandma wants to know if you want anything to eat with your pills."

"Now, what do you think, boy?" He patted his still ample belly. "Got to regain m'strength, before the next round."

Grandpa roared with laughter and John tried to join in. He hoped he was sticking to the special diet the doctors prescribed to help control cholesterol and high blood pressure. The "next round" would be heart surgery. John suspected Grandma Pearl would be only too happy to enforce the joyless diet, and for once her meanness was a comfort.

"I'll tell her." He rose to go, but hesitated at the door, "But Grandpa, while I've got you alone…"

"What's up, son?"

"I was just wondering if you were still having those nightmares."

"Nightmares?" Grandpa Joe's eyebrows spiked, like he was in shock. But his color bloomed, like he was embarrassed.

John cleared his throat; he was more than embarrassed, but he had to know. "Well, Grandma told me you were having nightmares, or maybe hallucinations, while you were in the hospital. Pretty scary, I guess." Grandma Pearl warned him not to speak of the drawings, and technically he hadn't mentioned *them*.

The old man burst into a belly laugh so loud it rattled the metal railings on his bed. He slapped his thighs, his considerable abdomen shaking with mirth. A bowl full of jelly. "The only thing scary about that hospital was the food. The food, and that awful Nurse Ratched—though I did love those sponge baths. Hooey!"

The theatrics carried on for several minutes. Grandpa Joe finally ended in a mute smile, gazing at John and shaking his head with pretended confusion. He wiped his eyes and thanked the Good Lord. It was such a ridiculous subterfuge that John felt prickles on the back of his neck. And he thought the drawings were unsettling. But after such a reaction, he realized the experience must have been worse than he suspected.

And now I'm seeing half-animal creatures in my own dreams and the family enterprise is sitting on top of dead Indians. All manner of interrogation techniques and their probable success rates raced through John's brain. He pushed them aside with an effort. *Well, Grandpa's a dead end. Time to branch out on my own.*

"Nevermind, I must have misunderstood. I'll tell Grandma you're hungry."

chapter thirty

Candy saw John's yellow Mustang through the open hangar doors of her dad's shop. She parked out back and jumped off her bike, heading into the garage with a smile. "There you are, I was hoping to find you here."

"Hey, Candy," came his muffled greeting. One arm was deep under the hood of his elevated car and the other was covered with grease almost up to his elbow. He leaned his head out and smiled from ear to ear, knowing how funny she would think it was to see him working on an engine.

"I have it, man." Antonio rolled out from under the car and took over whatever John was assisting with under the hood. His gaze roamed over Candy's body as he strode past, before he went back to what was clearly not women's work.

No more sweet Veterinarian music lover, and back to the macho dickwad. I could show that little Italian boy a thing or two about American cars. Candy was unperturbed in her security of over a decade helping her dad in the shop.

"Not really my thing, to be honest," admitted John. He wiped his blackened hands on an old T-shirt-turned-rag. No use. The oily smudges were like glue. John frowned at his hands and Candy hid her smile behind hers.

"You'll need some mineral spirits to get that off," she said. "Maybe some Lava soap. What happened, did it break down?"

"No. Tune-up, remember? Your dad's loving it," and waving a hand towards Antonio, he added, "and his new assistant, apparently. Antonio's quite the *Renaissance* man."

"You must have been talking with Dad, if you think working on an engine is like making art."

"A '65 Ford Mustang *is* art, honey," Antonio said, smacking her rear as he strolled by. He banged through the door to the shop like he owned the place.

"Never heard that one before, Michelangelo," she hollered after him, bristling over the unwanted contact. "Anyway," Candy grabbed John's arm as soon as they were alone. "I know where the eyes come from."

"The eyes?"

"My eyes. Remember? 'Selkie' eyes?"

"Oh, right."

"Well, I found the line through the McBrides—on my grandpa's side. It was his mother. That's why I never saw them. She died way young."

"Oh, that's too bad," said John, noncommittal. He looked past her through the door to the shop.

"No, you're not listening. One of the women in the oldest pictures looked totally Sendalee—you know, like there's an Indian line running through. But where, right?"

"I don't know, where?"

"Well, Ms. Collins gave me a book on the history of the families here—"

"There's a book on that?"

"Her daughter wrote her graduate dissertation on it."

"Ms. Collins has a daughter?"

"Yeah, adopted."

"Really?"

"Pay attention, why are you so distracted?" Candy couldn't get the story out fast enough, and John wasn't keeping up. "There's this painting of a Sendalee woman—really old, from like the 1700s—the book has a picture of it and snippets of Faith Fairbrother's diary. You know, Fairbrother Field, right by school?"

"Yeah, sure."

"I guess this Sendalee woman was some kind of mistress. Apparently Faith Fairbrother was okay with it, because she was the artist who painted her. Anyway, the mistress—the Ahnaanvwodi—died in childbirth and the Fairbrother's raised her daughter as one of their own."

"Was she?"

"Yeah, I think so. She took the Fairbrother name. But anyway, guess who her great-great granddaughter was?"

"The Collins's keep tabs that far back?"

Candy nodded. "I know, mildly disturbing. But, guess who she was?"

John had started pacing, and he kept looking back through the shop like he was anxious they would be disturbed. "I don't know, who?"

"She was Maeve Boyd, who married to become Maeve McBride. My great-grandmother!"

"So, mystery solved."

Candy's valorous shoulders crumpled into a slump. It was a big deal to her and she thought he'd be as ecstatic as she was. "Aren't you proud of me?"

"We should call you Fair Feather," John mumbled.

"What? Why are you acting so weird, John?"

His eyes snapped to hers.

"What's going on?" Candy demanded. Butterflies were swirling in her stomach—John was waiting to tell a story of his own.

"Alright, look." John sat down on an abandoned mechanics creeper. He rolled back and forth with his heels, hesitant and anxious at the same time. "I found out something, too."

"What?"

"I dug up some troubling information about another one of," he waved a hand towards the door where Antonio had disappeared, "your guys."

"Well, Antonio isn't 'my guy,' John" she said, with air quotes. "As you know very well. Get to the point."

"Fine. I'm talking about Sam Castle. Or whatever he calls himself these days." John stopped rolling, came to stillness with his eyes locked on hers, as if needing her full attention before he went on.

"I imagine he calls himself by his name." There was enough question in her tone to tell him he had her attention. All of it.

John cocked his head to the side, considering how much to reveal. "I noticed the irony in his expression, when he introduced himself to me in the hall the other day."

"Irony?"

"As if he were saying another name in his head. Mentally correcting himself when he said 'Sam.'"

"That's ridiculous."

"What's ridiculous is not being able to find one shred of information on a person—anywhere—in the information age."

"Some people are more private than others—"

"So, I decided to check out that tattoo on the inside of his wrist."

"The mermaid?"

"Not just a generic mermaid. Stylized and detailed, encircled in type. And so small, it's more like a crest. A stamp."

"Yeah…so?"

"And why would a person put a stamp like that on the inside of his right hand wrist?" John stood up and extended his right hand to Candy in the gesture of offering a handshake. When she didn't accept, he seized her hand and turned it over, exposing her wrist. "So certain people know who you are. And you know them. The stamp is the crest of an old neighborhood up north. A rough neighborhood. It's a gang crest."

Her heart was hammering, her mind buzzing with Sam's half-understood idiosyncrasies. She had no idea where he came from. Candy waited, ready to listen.

John was ready to tell; he dropped her hand and crossed his arms over his chest. "Why is the neighborhood important? Because, when I found 'Sam' there, he finally appeared on the grid. Only, his name isn't really Sam Castle."

"What is it?"

"That depends on how far you want to trace it. Which city. In that one he was Stan King."

"He told me his mom has moved them around a lot, and he's from nowhere. That's not his fault."

"No. He grew up in New York City," John challenged, daring her to disagree.

Sam wouldn't just out and out lie, would he? Candy was starting to realize that she didn't know the answer to that question. "Well…I know he's had an unconventional upbringing."

"He's done some time in juvenile detention centers, too. But that was when he was Shawn Kent. Luckily, they take mug shots for juvie."

Candy tried to swallow, but her throat felt dry. What could she say?

John went on, "Once I had a few points on the map—to triangulate the data, if you will—all sorts of interesting information came into focus. The guy sure tries to keep a low profile, but his girlfriends don't. And he's had a lot of those. They sure like taking pictures with him, too. Whatever his name is."

Candy remembered how Sam dodged Erica's request for a picture at the music show. "Well, that's not so unusual."

John rounded on her. "The name swapping, or the girl swapping?"

"Now you're just being mean, John. I'm sure he's met plenty of chicka-dees throughout his life. Like I don't know that." She didn't know if she was defending Sam, or herself, but she knew her hands were shaking. "Look, I'm not his girlfriend."

"Yeah? Good, because he's dangerous, Candy."

"Dangerous—don't be so dramatic."

"He's got a rap sheet that you can check yourself." John shrugged, moving away from her as Antonio returned, chatting with her father about hoses and belts. Candy looked at them, stricken, and John finally registered the anguish in her eyes. He sighed and grabbed her hand to pull her outside into privacy. "I'm only telling you this because I care about you."

"I *will* ask him," she said, yanking her hand out of his. She didn't believe a word.

"Do. Just be sure to use his real name. You know, the one he was born with?"

John was baiting her, and he knew she couldn't resist. She tried to, she really did. "Okay. What is it?"

part three:

hello & good-bye

chapter thirty-one

Candy said the name to herself as she walked up the dirt path to Rachel's studio. Sam had his back to her, cupping his hands around his lighter to shield the flame as he lit a cigarette.

Please don't turn around. Please let this all be John's imagination. "Sasha."

Sam turned his head—a knee-jerk reaction, as if he'd heard the name since infancy. Candy's stomach turned over.

"Hi." He closed the door on the sound of Mazzy Star's "Fade Into You," lilting out of the cavernous workroom, and collapsed on a timber and cinderblock bench. He brushed his hair out of his eyes, calm and clear.

So green and perfect, with coal-black lashes—stop it! Get your head together, Candy. "Your name isn't Sam, is it?"

"Sasha's a girl's name in the States; do you expect me to go by that?" He raised his palms in supplication. "My father is—"

"Russian."

He pursed his lips in a rueful smile and nodded.

"Some kind of Russian gangster, Sam? And you're from New York?" Her whisper turned into a shrill hiss. "Who are you?"

"I'm exactly who you think I am, Candy." He looked at her, unflinching. As if he had always known the confrontation was near.

"Not Castle either, or King," Candy challenged. "What was the other? Kent?"

Sam raised his eyebrows in surprise. "Guess I'll have to be more careful about who posts on goddamn BroadcastMyPicture.com."

"I can't believe that all this time I haven't even known your name."

"Hey, they're just names. My mom isn't that creative with them. We keep our own castle, king and queen. We had to take care of ourselves alone. We wouldn't be controlled by—" He stopped, like he'd said too much. But Candy didn't understand a word he said. "People. And, stupid shit…" He let his voice taper off, defeated. "Don't judge me by my family. Family ties tie you down, remember?"

She was instantly chastened, slapped by her own words. His humbled expression made it worse. She almost felt a tinge of remorse for him before, believing him to be fatherless, but the truth seemed even worse. What did she know about his life before she met him? She slumped down next to him on the bench. "I thought you said you were from nowhere— everywhere? I don't understand."

"I am. Ever since my father went to prison when I was a kid, my mom's kept us on the move. Vegas, New Orleans, Phoenix, Houston, wherever she could make a buck when I was little. Lately, wherever she thinks she can get the best state help." He fell quiet again. Always editing. "Small towns are easier to hide in; with all you disconnected country bumpkins."

They both laughed at the obvious error; even Shirley County was connected enough for his life story to come tumbling out in a matter of months after moving there.

"You never told me your dad was in prison." She strained for encouraging; she desperately needed to know the full story and she needed Sam—Sasha?—to talk.

"Well, it's not really something I like to spread around," he said, lighting a new cigarette. They watched the trees across the clearing together, in silence, as the breeze picked up and shivered through the branches. Rachel's studio backed up to a sharp decline in the landscape, with a spectacular view. A million shades of green mixed with splotches of gold, blood and rust so shocking it was almost indecent. Candy watched the forest dance from top to bottom in the shimmying wind. When the air finally met them on their sunny perch, it was cooler than she expected, and goose flesh stood up along her arms. Autumn was on its way, screaming in the leaves but lurking in the lengthening shadows. She remembered that same tingle up her arms, tickled by Sam's breath.

She cast around for some way to help instead of criticize, "Are you guys in danger or something?" She thought she already knew the answer, though; why else would Sam's mother be trying to hide him?

"We'd rather not be around when my dad gets out. Let's put it like that." Sam regarded her with a face of steel: and that's all you get.

"Well…" Candy looked up at the sky and sighed hard.

"I understand you need to know more, but I don't really know much, myself. I was just a kid the last time I saw my dad."

"Well, when does he get out?" Candy persisted. Sam put up his hands again and shrugged. Candy cocked her head, bewildered, "Doesn't that freak you out? Having some vague, possible peril looming sometime in the future?"

"Well, yeah," he laughed bitterly. "What am I supposed to do about it, though?"

"Something." She shook her head, puzzled. Looking around, she saw Ender's Village preparing for a party. Folding tables were stacked alongside buildings. Doors that were usually shut tight were open, the lights and smells and sounds of activity within trickling outside. *Oh, right. First Thursdays.* She was unable to feel excited about one of her favorite events in Shirley.

She kicked a couple pebbles away from her flip-flops. Sam blew impressive smoke rings that floated over their heads like a Walt Disney dream sequence. After smiling graciously at the show for several minutes, she frowned at him, ugly and hard. She needed something more. Surely he understood that.

"Look. My name is Alexander Volkovski Koselov. But, I'd appreciate if we kept that between us."

The blood drained from Candy's face. Another name? "Alexander? I thought it was *Sasha*." She sang the girly name in a taunt, suddenly furious and needing to injure. She jumped up with her hands on her hips, her black eyes smoldering.

"Candy…"

She hated being lied to. It made her feel like such a fool, her head completely twisted and jumbled. "You have so many names I can't keep track of them all. Why don't you get your stories straight if you're gonna bother lying in the first place?"

"I can't take this anymore," Sam said, sounding tired. He stood and turned away. Avoiding her eyes, he stalked down the side of the corrugated metal building to retrieve a broom. "I've got to get back to work."

"So, that's it? I get nothing else? Nothing?" Candy balled her fists at her sides.

"Sasha's a nickname for Alexander," he said, narrowing his eyes in a resentful green gaze as he brushed past her. "Thought you did your research." He winked and clicked his tongue on the side of his teeth, before disappearing back inside.

chapter thirty-two

The heavenly aroma of garlic sautéed in butter greeted John as soon as he snuck into the kitchen. People were already arriving around the other side of the restaurant. When he walked up, he heard doors slamming in the parking lot and people hollering to friends that loitered around the front entrance, so John went in the back. He had been studying in the café and would've rather kept doing that, but there was no way he could miss "Italian Night." James Robinson's first event as restaurateur, Antonio's welcome party, was a big deal on many levels.

More than anything, he was hoping for a sample. He found Rosa brushing fresh loaves of sliced Italian bread with one hand, and sprinkling minced oregano with the other, with all the finesse of wrapping a present.

She saw John inching nearer with shoulders scrunched and hands poised for picking. "Don't even think about it," she warned him with a throaty giggle. Rosa was a sweetie; she slapped his head, but then tweaked his cheek. "You see how perfect these are laid out?"

"You're killin' me, Rosa."

She brandished the little brush in his face. "Get outta here, go on and help your papa."

"Alright, alright." John pushed through the swinging kitchen doors. His dad had just opened the front doors by the look of it, and he was already having trouble.

"For heaven sakes, I'm starving," he heard someone whine.

"It's about time you opened up, Jamie. I was wondering if we bought tickets for nothing."

"I'm glad I waited to take my pill, my stomach can't handle it without some food…"

"Don't worry, everyone—there's plenty of food. Good food." Dad held the door open, and bowed to the elderly Shirleynarians wandering in. Their faces were screwed up and their eyes were strained, as if they had never been to Big Joe's in their long lives. "The early birds can be harder to stomach than the worms," was Grandpa's sage advice. "The old farts always arrive early and ravenous, hoverin' by the door like vultures." Dad thought the idea he found online of making two separate buffet lines, to split up the crowd and keep people moving, was expert. He had lectured, "Serving the cold meats, fruits, cheeses first is more in keeping with the Italian diet." John wasn't so sure that authenticity mattered so much.

A senior patron looked at the first buffet table and then at Dad, aghast. "This is all there is—salad?"

"This is the antipasti, ma'am—the main course is on the patio," Dad assured her.

"What's *anti*-pasta?" someone else asked. A younger woman (though at least sixty herself) took her by the elbow leaned close to her ear, "Mom, you like this stuff. Look: salami, cheese, tomatoes, melon. That's just olives and peppers; you don't have to try those."

Dad kept his calm, but John heard the edge in his voice. "Folks, you can either start here at the antipasti buffet—which is really just Italian-style appetizers—or you can head out to the patio and dig right into the main course. Theresa, would you mind."

"Welcome to The Kitchen's Italian Night, everyone." The new hostess, dressed in traditional black, took over. She started shunting people gently yet forcibly into proper corrals as soon as they walked in. The pretty smile and long blonde hair helped. More dubious older folks were sent straight to the patio buffet, assured they would find familiar dishes there (bread and meat).

Escape to the patio sounded good to John, so he wandered in that direction before his dad could enlist him. As he turned away, he heard a shaky, confused voice ask, "We're eating in the kitchen, not the dining room?" John kept walking. *Poor Dad.* Probably shouldn't have introduced the new name tonight, although he had to admit "The Kitchen" was far superior to "Big Joe's."

The band was already setting up their gear outside. The spot his father had chosen would set the musicians' backs to the cool breeze and rushing river below. It was a beautiful night and they would be comfortable there. Also, anyone milling around the immediate area of Shirley's downtown would be able to hear the music. If they hadn't already planned to attend the party, the sound of music or the smell of roasting meat would reel them onto the deck. That was the idea, but John didn't think Shirleynarians needed reeling in for an event at the only restaurant in town, whatever the name. People were already hiking up the stairs to the patio, bypassing the clogged bottleneck at the front. He wondered if the hostess stationed at the entrance had sold them a ticket first.

"Better make sure they know about the rogues," John mumbled to himself, then headed back inside.

He found his dad talking with Mrs. Jameson, the PTA president John had started thinking of as The Bobkitten. That nickname was the height of irony; there was nothing kitten-like about Mrs. Jameson, though she played the role and wore the costume and thought she had everyone fooled. The two parents were so absorbed in conversation that they didn't notice John's approach. He tuned his ears in their direction.

"…and you could have waited for me, before traipsing off across the world," she was saying.

James Robinson ran a hand through his hair, always his first gesture of discomfort. "You would have wanted to join me across the world?"

"Maybe."

"Why did you start screwing Mike Jameson the minute I left, then?"

She put her hand on her hip. "Why did you leave the minute after graduation?"

Dad mumbled something John couldn't quite hear.

"Don't be silly. You're all I ever wanted, Jamie."

"Mike Jameson, of all people. After that time when I passed out." He was pissed.

"Oh, come on," she said. Her knuckles grazed his chin like they were just old buddies, but her smile said the opposite. The Bobkitten was practiced at coy; John had seen her use a similar tactic on half-a-dozen male faculty members. "You know that was just an evil rumor."

Dad finally caught sight of John, and his expression went from confused to relieved in an instant. "Well there he is."

John put an arm around him. "Hey, Dad." He offered his hand, "Hello, Mrs. Jameson."

"Hey there, John."

Shoulders went rigid under John's arm. "You two have already met?"

"Of course. Mrs. Jameson practically runs Andrew Jackson."

"Oh, John. I'm just the PTA President." She grinned, clearly pleased with the honorable mention. "I always have a lot to do around the school, especially in the first few weeks of classes."

"Well, I have to do the formal introductions," James broke in, not willing to let the moment pass so unremarkably for some reason. "Stephanie Sherman—Jameson, sorry—I would like for you to meet my beloved son, John Robinson. He's my pride and joy."

"Aw shucks."

"It is lovely to meet you formally, John." She patted his cheek and broadened her smile, Vaselined teeth gleaming.

"And you, as well, ma'am."

The Bobkitten looked from John to his dad, all innocence. "So, where is Amy, anyway?"

"Uh…" John searched his dad's face. Snippets of his parents' hushed arguing over the phone trickled through his thoughts. "Mom'll probably be in for a visit next weekend, I think. Right?"

"That's what she said."

"She's not coming to stay, Jamie?"

"Well," James began awkwardly. Most people in Shirley would view the fact that his wife was not attached to him as strange in the extreme. The supposition that the couple might be living apart for some time raised questions.

John rescued him, "Mom, leave Memphis? You've gotta be kidding me." Imagining his mom there in the country, especially at the 'Italian Night,' gave John the willies. He actually enjoyed meeting all the strange civilians, teasing out their shady histories and discerning their twisted connections, but he knew his mother would have lost patience days after arriving. She had only visited sporadically through the years, putting in an appearance every other holiday or so, to keep face.

The Bobkitten pouted her sparkly pink lips. "Well, that's too bad. I'd love to get to know her."

By the way she was twirling her hair around her finger and bumping her elbow against Dad's, John was sure the woman would have loved almost anything more. Right on cue, someone pushed past in a hurry and she fell into him, touching his chest in apology.

"Whoops," his dad said, all awkward and goofy, helping to steady her without touching anywhere inappropriate.

John cleared his throat in embarrassment, but not for his father.

A teenage girl appeared with an equally well made-up frown. "Mom, I'm not going to wait forever. I'm not even hungry."

"Oh, okay honey. Whatever…"

"You must be John. I'm Amanda. Let's get out of here and let the old folks make goo-goo eyes at each other in private." She grabbed John's arm and steered him to the back patio. "Wow, there's even a band playing. Nice touch."

John looked for her face again, but cascading deep brown locks ob-scured it. "Uh, thanks. My dad found them last night in Ender's Village, at the 'First Thursday' event."

They were buffeted with a surprising crowd just outside the doors. Amanda held onto his arm as they watched the band from afar and said, "They're pretty good. Kudos to Jamie."

John agreed. He nailed it, in more ways than one. Rusty Pick-ups on Dusty Roads was playing a quiet jam, moving in and out of a basic melody. They weren't blaring, but their music was endowed with enough of a perky bounce that the people loitering around talking were tapping their feet, feeling upbeat. A lady excused herself from her group to find the restroom, then twirled and clapped in admiration as she made her way across the central space. The space was perfect for a dance floor. John eyed the extra drums stashed behind the band. At Ender's Village, Rusty Pick-ups hosted a drum circle, audience invited. Everyone in town knew that Antonio was a drummer. *Nice thought, Dad.*

"Ender's Village, huh?" asked Amanda, over the music, jerking her head to one side to indicate they might find a quieter spot. They settled in a corner away from the crowd, along the railing overlooking the river. John admired the view of the rapids, while Amanda kept her eyes on the people. "Good party. Your dad did an admirable job."

John detected a hint of condescension. "Have you been to the First Thursday art opening? I didn't go, had too much homework, but my dad is all about getting the feel for the real Shirley County."

"Sure, they have them every month." John waited for her to say more; when she didn't, he knew she had never attended the event. Candy went all the time and couldn't stop gushing about it for days afterwards. "But John, if you want to know the *real* Shirley County, you need to know its secrets. Where's Candy?"

"I don't know." John looked around for show, not really expecting to see her. He didn't regret warning her about Sam Castle's dubious past, but he could have been more delicate. Candy had been snubbing him ever since. Not really angry. She was morose and he felt like shit about it. When he got on a research kick, though, it was hard to turn his mind away. Coming up empty about the stuff with his grandfather's drawings and the possible ancient burial ground under Big Joe's was frustrating in the extreme. The Sam mystery wasn't as hard to solve and it helped let off some steam. Maybe he shouldn't have thrown it in Candy's face.

"Miss your girlfriend?" asked Amanda.

"Candy?" John kept his face steady, because the chick was digging for something. "She's my best friend, not my girlfriend."

"Are you wondering where she is tonight?"

"No." John zeroed in. He got it—Amanda was more interested in Candy than she was in him. He hadn't missed the "secrets" comment, and she was about to go in for the kill. *Hmm, what's the game?*

"Ever been to The Shack, where she likes to meet up with Sam Castle? Late."

Oh, I see. She wants to destroy Candy's reputation. "No, I haven't. Of course, you've been there yourself?"

"As a matter of fact, I have. Would you like for me to show you where it is?"

"What do you think?"

"John, my man!" John glanced back to see Antonio cutting through the crowd towards them, his adopted parent, Mrs. Walsh, trying to keep up.

"Hey there," Amanda said, tossing her hair. "This is your coming out party, so now you need to let us get to know you, Tonio."

John was shocked to watch her actually tickle his chin with one curled finger. He could tell she was trying to set him off balance, and John smirked as he watched Antonio grab her hand and kiss it. "You want to leave now, honey?" Antonio's English always improved in such situations and John wondered how many American pornos he'd watched back in Italy.

Amanda was the one caught off guard. "Oh, heh. You sure live up to the Italian stereotype."

"Stereo type?"

Candy's nemesis is flustered, so she has to resort to insulting the poor guy. John gave his friend a reassuring pat, "It just means the standard image of an Italian man is one who is aggressively flirtatious and sexually virile."

"Oh, I am, Signorina…?"

Amanda looked at him, then at John.

"He wants to know your name."

"Yeah, I get it. I'm Amanda." She leaned in for a kiss on each cheek, regaining her composure and ready to play her part with gusto. As Antonio openly appraised the sizable breasts she had just pushed into his chest, she gave John a triumphant smile. "I didn't think we need an introduction. Everyone knows who you are."

"I'm sorry to interrupt, but your presence is required over here, Antonio." Mrs. Walsh finally pushed her way into their circle and grabbed her charge's elbow. "Hi, kids. I'll give him right back, but there are so many people who want to meet him tonight."

"No problem, Mrs. Walsh. He's an important guy."

"You're a dear, John."

As soon as Antonio was out of earshot, Amanda resumed her earlier persona. "What a cliché. Every girl in town wants to do the Italian Stallion."

"So, you just threw yourself at him, not because you want him—you just want to keep him away from your friends."

Amanda jutted her chin and squared her shoulders, arrogance flooding her smile. "Actually, I'm not really sure what I want with him yet."

Always plotting, with no plan? John narrowed his eyes and tried to read beyond the veil. There was something she wanted, he just had to figure it out.

"Oh, not the dumb football player after all? Good. I hoped you might be more exciting than the other Robinsons. Your dad was a black sheep, too. Maybe the seed didn't fall too far from the tree?"

Black sheep. John remembered bits of the story he pieced together about his dad and Amanda's mom dating in high school. He guessed it had been quite an upset when Jamie Robinson left town after graduation and never returned. Bruised pride had traveled through at least one generation. "Of course, you know that I was adopted and I don't derive from my father's 'seed.'" Everyone in the small town would be privy to that particular information.

"Don't worry, lamb chop. We all accept you."

"I'm not worried."

"It's okay to feel out of place, John."

John clenched his fists with the effort it took to hold his tongue. Out of place was exactly the way he had always felt in Shirley. His family's home, but not his.

Amanda didn't miss the fists. She smiled sweetly and touched his chest. "Anyway, I hear you're just as good a running back as your dad was."

Pouring on the sugar, now—you've got to be kidding me. Once she established herself as the champion of wits for the time being, she could relax. John felt like slapping her, but he decided to let it go. The image of Amanda sharpening her claws on his shirt, like her aged Bobcatt mother had done to Dad, was ridiculous enough to help him return the smile. "You coming out for the game next weekend?"

"Probably. My cousin Lindsay's a cheerleader and I like to show my support. Those poor girls jumping around and shouting all night—somebody has to answer the whole, 'We got spirit, how 'bout you' thing."

John chuckled, "Such a kind soul."

"I do what I can. Oh, our boy's coming back."

"Antonio, we'll need to give a short speech in just a few minutes." Mieke Walsh was breathless with the activity of the party, as she deposited the boy back among his friends.

"Okay, Mom," he said agreeably, with such an angelic smile that it made Mieke's heart melt. A slender blonde girl was happy to jump into Mieke's spot as she moved away, and Antonio greeted the girl like a gentleman, "Hello, Lindsay. It is nice to see you."

"Hi, Tonio."

Mieke thought his English was improving. *Polite, but still a little stiff.* She worked on his accent with him every night. *That Lindsay doesn't seem to mind his accent at all, that's for sure.*

As soon as she turned away, she saw another person waving to her from across the room, wanting a word. Mieke made her way over to them, her head buzzing with it all. She knew her instincts were right when she and Joe arranged the foreign exchange. Perfect to distinguish their chapter within Rotary International; and an opportunity to have Shirley County emerge as the beautiful destination it could be. *Now, the whole town is here to recognize my achievement.*

Yet, she never hoped to add a son to her life in the bargain. In just a few short weeks, she had learned so much about what it really meant to be a parent and parenting gave her so many new connections. *Now, I can count myself as both a PTA member and a Bobcatt football mom.*

"Hello Mr. and Mrs. Campbell. Are you enjoying the party?" The old couple had been pointed out to her, and by the look of their elegant, moldering vestments, Mieke guessed them to be one of the wealthier families in Shirley County. Worth a chat.

"Oh, please call me Laverne," the old blue-hair croaked, grasping Mieke's hand with a trembling fist. She wore a glittering ring on each finger. "Yes, what fun this is. Howard had never tried spaghetti and I always told him he'd like it. He never tries anything new."

The portly man next to Laverne was wearing a seersucker suit and prim bowtie. He offered his hand, with a distinguished nod in Mieke's direction, "Howie."

"Well, he had one bite of mine and then stuck to the meat and potatoes, but it was a big moment. Right, dear?"

"Certainly, dear."

"Of course, we rarely have a chance to get out anymore. The roads are so dangerous, you know. We only drive in for the monthly lodge function."

Mieke's ears pricked at that. "The Buffalo Lodge? I wasn't aware they had…functions."

Laverne focused on her with intelligent eyes, surprisingly bright in such a wrinkled, faded face. She laid a hand on Mieke's shoulder and leaned in, her grip strong. "You think you understand what you see. You assume that what seems, is."

"Me?" Mieke put her hand against her chest in surprise. Was she about to receive inside information? She had always wondered about that old lodge, but it was strictly forbidden to anyone who wasn't a member—something she resented. "I wouldn't dare to assume anything. I'd love to hear the truth from you, Laverne."

The woman smiled and drifted backwards, her eyes dulling. Mieke worried that she had seemed too eager.

"You wouldn't know it now, but the balls we used to hold there…"

"Balls?"

"But we couldn't miss this Italian Night, with all the buzz going around, even up where we are. Well, you know the maids always talk." Laverne became the frail, helpless senior once again. "We have yet to meet this boy we've heard so much about. But of course we don't speak Italian anyway, do we dear?"

"No, dear."

"And, I have heard about this lace that he brought."

Mieke brightened. "Oh, it's quite beautiful. I'll show you."

Antonio's mother, Signora di Brigo, had connections to the famous old island of Burano in the Venetian Lagoon of northern Italy, where they made the most amazing, delicate lace Mieke had ever seen. Completely handmade. The Signora had sent two pieces as a token of her gratitude, both of them pinned to black velvet and framed. Mieke selected the better of the two for herself (it was on prominent display in her guesthouse), and hung the other on one of the busy, decorated walls inside Big Joe's.

"Mrs. Campbell, is this your first time seeing this lace? Isn't it lovely?" Marge Tillman floated over the second they stopped in front of the frame, ready to spread around her own newly acquired knowledge of Burano lace. "I just love this, look at the detail. Mrs. Di Brigo was so kind…"

As another woman joined them, crooning over the lace, Mr. Campbell excused himself for a smoke. Mieke took her leave as well, heading for the bathroom. *Empty—thank goodness. A minute to myself.*

As she was washing her hands, another woman walked in whom she thought she recognized. Really just a girl, her long black hair was tied up in a high ponytail, and she had thick, cropped bangs. She was hard to forget in a small town like Shirley, especially in lieu of her habitual boldly patterned black and white, snuggly fitting clothing and red stilettos.

Mieke wished she could remember her name. "Hello. You're a member of Rotary International, aren't you?"

The young woman ran a finger under her black eyeliner to fix a smudge, and without looking away from the mirror, said, "Hello, Mieke."

Oh. Satisfied her own name was one people remembered, Mieke dove in, "I'm so glad more club members are attending than I saw at first. This isn't really a meeting, but it's not for just nosey townsfolk either, you know?"

"I do. Haven't seen Joe. I bet you have."

"Yes, he's home and doing well. He's not really up for a big event like this yet, though. He was excited to try the Italian food. I'll take him some dinner in a little while."

"You?"

"Mm-hm."

"I saw Pearl here. His son, even his grandson." She finally turned away from her reflection, her hair swinging over one shoulder, and delivered a piercing gaze.

"Well, you know. As the vice president, it's the least I can do for... the president—bring him dinner, that is," Mieke stammered. The woman watched her without comment. "Of course, he'll want to hear all about the success of our foreign exchange—"

"Oh, you don't need to explain things to me. Joe and I are good friends, too." She flicked her ponytail back in place, one side of her red lips raised in merriment, and she was out the door.

Mieke realized she had been drying her hands obsessively with her paper towel and threw it in the trash can. She remained in the bathroom for several minutes, reapplying her own lipstick, tidying her clothes and hair, wondering if she should feel offended by such an interaction. The woman hadn't actually said anything of substance, but why did she feel... threatened? Mocked? Deciding she was probably letting her imagination run away from her, she forced it out of her mind. *All the introductions and invitations must really be getting to me.*

As soon as she re-entered the dining room, Antonio made a beeline for her. "Mom!"

That was something to warm the heart. "Hi, sweetie."

"Can we make the speech now? I am hungry, but..." he grabbed his abdomen and made a sick face. "My stomach."

"Are you nervous, silly? You are so funny; let's get it over with then." Mieke could only imagine how nervous she would be if she had to give a speech in another language. She gave his shoulders a squeeze and pushed him out into the center of the dining room, clapping her hands and calling for everyone's attention. "This will be quick," she whispered in Antonio's ear and shoved his note cards into his hands. *We rehearsed together enough, he should be fine.*

Mieke reminded everyone of the real reason for such a fantastic party and gave Antonio a glowing introduction. He waved hello and read from his cards—haltingly, but with a friendly smile—and then formally present-ed his mother's gift of Burano lace and thanked them for their hospitality. She stayed close by while Antonio answered a few questions about the lace, his mother and his hometown in Italy. She knew he had a hard time with some of the accents in Shirley, so she translated when needed and explained what Antonio was trying to say in response. He kissed her cheek and made for the exit as soon as they were finished.

"Bye, Mom."

"Bye-bye, have fun, sweetie," she called after him, craning her neck to watch him head towards the patio buffet. Night had already fallen outside, and strings of lights were strewn along the ceiling rafters, casting the patio in pale gloom.

Antonio gave Mieke a final wave as he stepped into the dimness. He heard a quiet cough off to his right, down the stairs leading to the dirt path below the deck. "There you are," he said.

"Smoke?"

He trotted down the stairs without hesitation. "God, yes."

"Well, it wouldn't do for the town angel to be smoking around these parts."

"No."

"Let's get outta here then, partner," Charlotte Finley purred in his ear. She attached herself to his elbow and led him farther into the growing darkness. They skirted the raised platform deck, the party rolling on above their heads, and made their way down towards the river, hand in hand.

§

"Where you been?"

"Gawd, you scared me, Tyler," Charlotte hissed. She climbed the rocky path through the trees leading up to Buffalo Square, unsteady in her high-heels. The shindig died down hours ago and the courtyard was dark, paltry street lamps giving out small puffs of gnat-ridden incandescence. "Why can't people just leave some more porch lights on around here?"

"You went off with that foreigner, didn't you?" her cousin sulked. He was trying to seem tough, but he sounded like the bratty child he was. "Where'd you go?"

"Listen, I don't mind you sock-hoppin' along when I've got some business to attend to. But don't try to foxtrot, little brother."

"I ain't your brother, and you know it. We's just cousins. We could even get married, if we wanted."

"What?" Charlotte laughed, familiar with her cousin's little crush. "You're so cute, Ty." She bent to give him a kiss on his cheek, but he swatted her away.

"Stop it." He twisted away from her and stalked down the path to the river. She could hear him muttering about finding out what she'd been up to.

"Look, Buster Brown. You had better stay outta things that don't concern you."

"Stop baby-talking me!" he screeched, enraged.

"Stop throwing baby-tantrums, then."

His voice was smothered by forest undergrowth as he tramped towards the river in a string of muttered obscenities.

"Or I'll give you a spanking," it was mean, but she couldn't help it, "you little twerp." She heard him scream with fury in the distance, before silence fell around her again. "Oh, come on, Tyler. How you gonna get home?"

Charlotte waited, listening for his answer or the sound of returning footsteps. She hoisted herself up onto the low courtyard wall, pulled out a cigarette, and lit it. Her feet dangled, and she blew smoke into a cloud of gnats nearby, watching and waiting for Tyler to return.

chapter thirty-three

Candy watched wet clay blur into glassy smoothness as it rotated on the potter's wheel. She poked a thumb down into the center of the flattened ball to make a doughnut, then eased the hole out wider. Two fingers under the outside pinched a lip and she pulled up a thick, spinning wall between thumb and fingers. She dug her fingernail in and pressed with her thumb. Instant patterns encircled the cylinder. So graceful. When the clay wall became too thin to support its own weight, the tower began to buckle. Candy let her hands go limp and heavy, and the little structure was crushed. "Good-bye."

It was such a satisfying feeling. She cupped the mound of clay in both hands and braced her elbows against her knees. Her palms forced the rotating clay back into a smooth, centered ball, and she began again. She reached over into the bucket of slip sitting next to her stool and brought out a handful of water for sprinkling. Approving of the next song in her playlist, she shifted her hips to get more comfortable, and noticed her butt was starting to fall asleep.

Jeez, how long have I been throwing? Throwing pots settled her mind. Her insides felt calm and connected to the earth, enough that she could stop thinking for a while—stop beating herself up for saying all the wrong things to Sam. Stop feeling like an exposed nerve. A live wire. It was over two weeks since she spoke to Sam and she hadn't seen him once. The empty chasm his absence created felt dulled when she was calm, at least. The pain wasn't quite as sharp.

Louis bent sideways into her line of vision, hanging his head almost upside down, with his features twisted into a clown face.

"Is that supposed to be funny? You're freaking me out," she said over the music playing in her headphones.

Louis clamped his hands over his own ears and pretended to scream, to indicate she was yelling. She decided enough was enough. She wiped her hands on the towel in her lap and shut off her music.

"Candy's back on Earth. Are you coming to lunch, or are you going to work through it again?"

"No, I'm coming. Let me clean up." She dumped the bulk of her clay into her bucket and used a rubber rib to scrape the plate before flipping the switch under her wheel.

"Didn't get any good pieces, after a whole hour?" Louis asked.

"Huh?" Candy realized she hadn't saved any of her pots, though she'd pulled several beautiful specimens. "Oh…nah. I have all the pieces I need for this week's assignment already."

Louis frowned. "You're so gloomy lately, what's up?"

Candy shrugged, collecting her tools and not bothering to answer.

"Hey, you should come to youth group this Wednesday—that'll cheer you up. Pastor Dave even has a live band playing. Why won't you go anymore, girlfriend?"

"Maybe…" She couldn't think of anything less cheery than youth group.

"Your buddy Antonio played drums last week."

Candy walked over to one of the slop sinks to wash out her tools. She felt someone watching her and glanced up to find a couple of girls sitting together at one of the drawing tables. They had been studying her, but when Candy looked over, their eyes darted away and one of them made a shushing hand gesture. She looked at Louis, her mind fully alert. "What was that about?"

His face apologized for the two girls. "You haven't heard the rumors yet? Tell me it ain't true—you're supposed to be in love with me."

"What's not true? I have no idea what you're talking about, Louis."

"Someone's spreading the word that you're gay, darling."

"What?" Candy almost choked on the irony of it. There she was pining away for Sam, still weak in the knees with her memories, and people were saying that she was a lesbian? She snatched up her things and dragged Louis to the door. "That's ridiculous, who's saying that?"

"Some catty bimbo, some catty bimbo's friends?" He walked out into the hallway and she followed in a daze, her mind reeling.

"You know I don't think there's anything wrong with being gay," she stopped to face Louis. She wanted him to know she was not upset about the "gay" part. Louis had come out to her at the beginning of that summer; he felt out of place about it in Shirley County and she wanted him to feel comfortable with her. She was the only person who knew, though, so she checked herself in case the little birds were listening. "You know, my Aunt Melinda is gay."

He laughed and hugged her against him as they walked. "I know what you meant, Candy."

"If only I didn't care so much for stupid boys, honestly."

"I hope I'm not included in that assessment of the male gender."

"You know you're not. You're a man, not a boy." She stopped talking when a couple of girls ducked their heads into an open locker, giggling as she and Louis walked past. "Oh please. Gimme a break."

Louis scoffed in wholehearted agreement, then a female voice rang out behind them. "Hi, Tonio." Candy turned around to see Antonio striding past a pretty senior girl with long, curly blonde locks. He ignored the girl, his eyes fixed on Candy.

"There you are, honey." He gave Louis five, then took both of Candy's hands in his and kissed first her left cheek, then her right. The blonde suddenly decided she had forgotten something, and turned a clumsy pirouette. The gigglers gaped at each other in shock and dismay.

"'Nough of this bull-dookie. I'm starved, let's get lunch," Louis insisted.

Antonio held out his hand and said with remarkable fluidity, "Yeah, let's get outta here."

Candy accepted and the three of them made their way to the cafeteria. She glanced around for signs of Sam (fruitlessly, of course), simultaneously relishing the jealous eyes darting away in theatrical unconcern. The surprised appraisals of her apparent couple-hood with Antonio were easy to savor. Once in the cafeteria, he even pulled her chair out for her.

The Italian macho thing has its perks. She sank into the chair, trying to stifle her smile.

He sat down, saddle-style, and scooted his chair closer to hers. Louis made a hasty retreat. She didn't want Antonio to get the wrong idea, no matter how grateful she was of his chivalry. "Um, Antonio. Thanks for that back there, but you know I don't...I mean, we're not really..."

"We are just friends. I know this, Candy."

"Oh. Well. Good."

"Your heart belongs to another." His face revealed no ill feelings, only kindness.

"You know?"

"I know women." He leaned in closer and lowered his voice, his big brown eyes creasing at the corners. "You have the..." he gazed far away in the distance, clutching his chest with feigned desperation, "the look in your eyes."

Candy laughed. His imitation was probably spot-on. "Distant looks? Yeah, I guess I've been a little melodramatic lately. Don't know who it is, though, do you?"

He cocked his head and squinted, considering. "Not John." She shook her head, smiling. "Though your eyes, eh..." He mimed an explosion with his hands in front of his own eyes, searching for the right word.

"Light up?"

"Yes. Light up, when John is here."

"I love John, he always makes me happy. Well, usually…" She was still feeling the fool, after John dug up Sam's history and threw it in her face. She was mostly mad at herself for not knowing what to say in Sam's defense, though. John was always correct with the details, but he missed the point sometimes. "You're not disappointed or anything?"

"By love? Never. Seriously, you know I sign the contract?"

Candy swung her knees around to face him. "I heard about that, but I thought it was a joke. Like, you promised not to have 'relations' with under-aged girls or something?"

Antonio's maturity manifested in an instant. "Is no joke. Candy, I come here to learn. My studies are very important, yes?"

She thought about his work-study program in veterinary medicine the previous year, and considered the level of commitment necessary to undertake a year-long foreign language immersion program. He really did seem much older than most of her friends. "I understand. I'm sure they are."

"But, you are beautiful girl. I cannot tell you this?"

She searched his face for a few beats. He was being genuine. "Yes, you can. Thank you."

"You are welcome. And," he clapped his cheeks in mock surprise, as he rose from his seat, "Maybe, I have woman on the side, eh? You never know." Her eyebrows shot up in astonishment. He sauntered away towards the hot-lunch line, winking at the girls and making hip-level, shooting-gun gestures to the guys.

"Hey, Candy." She was jerked out of her reverie when Erica dumped her book bag and plopped down in the seat across the table. "I am so glad it's lunch time."

"Rough day, already?"

Erica groaned. "It's just that I already have so much homework, and we've only finished fourth period."

"Yeah, they're really piling it on this year." Candy agreed, but she wasn't in the mood to chat.

"My dad says if I don't get a better handle on it, then he won't let me go out on school nights anymore. Even open studios in Ender's—hey, where were you at the last one, by the way? You never miss First Thursdays."

"Eh."

Candy actually had attended, lingering in the outskirts and looking for Sam. After their fight at Rachel's that day, she skulked around the area for a while, trying to work up the courage to go back and apologize for blowing up on him. She lost the battle, but she went back for the open studios. When she didn't see any sign of Sam outside once the party started, she figured he was purposely making himself scarce and she took off.

"I saw Sam at Rachel's studio," Erica said, barely audible. "Last night."

Candy froze. Erica knew, of course she knew. She kept her eyes on her lunch bag, excavating its contents and placing sandwich, water bottle and apple before her with care. She wished Erica would say something and end the torturous silence. "You see him more than I do these days, then." She finally shrugged, trying for nonchalance. She knew it wouldn't work—Candy never wasted her time with stupid friends.

"I guess he was working. You know, doing Rachel's bidding," said Erica, testing the waters. "She keeps him busy."

Candy rolled her eyes, chopping on her sandwich. *I bet she does.*

"Well, I was done in my dad's workshop, so we talked for a while. He said Rachel helped him get enrolled into a work-study program, and he'll be doing that for the rest of the year." Erica seemed to want to add, "I'm sorry," to her revelation.

"That's nice to know."

"Yeah. I guess that's why he…hasn't been around much, lately." She trailed off awkwardly.

Candy tried to cool the blush that was surely blooming in her face. How infuriating that Erica had to tell her about the work-study—that she hadn't already known herself. She sighed, resigned to give up her pride for the reward of more information. "So…I guess he's doing really well with the glass apprenticeship?"

"I think he is, yeah. I heard Rachel say he really has a knack for it, and he's willing to work hard, and put in long hours."

"He's always worked a lot."

"Yeah, and Mr. Davis helped push the paperwork through, even though the school year had already started. That's weird for him to help like that—Mr. Davis is usually such a dick. You should have seen him lecturing his daughter, Missy, right in front of everyone the other day. Poor thing, she looked so embarrassed. I'm so glad my parents don't work at school."

"Well. I'm glad Sam's found something that he likes. He must be really happy?" ventured Candy. Erica had a tendency to get side-tracked. *Just a little more info, please?*

"Mmmm…" Erica screwed up her face in calculation as she chewed her lunch. "I don't know if he seemed happy, exactly."

"What do you mean?"

"Well, after everything was closing up, you know? Rachel lets my dad store his bigger instruments in her studio for the night sometimes—Dad was kinda toasted last night, and she has such a big space." Candy knitted her brows together in frustration. "Okay, okay. Sorry. I was putting Dad's stuff in the front room and I heard piano music coming from the back."

A prickle ran up Candy's spine, from a memory just at the edge of her consciousness. "Piano music?"

"Yeah. So, I kinda crept back there—"

"Why did you creep?"

"It just sounded…I don't know, like something no one else was supposed to hear. Private, somehow."

"Why?"

"Well, it was sort of…melancholy." She searched the ceiling with her eyes. "Really melancholy. Chopin, I think, but I don't know his music that well. A nocturne or something. Plus, it was pretty late and Ender's was deserted. Even Rachel had gone home."

"And it was Sam," Candy said flatly, certain of it. The memory of his odd behavior when they found that grand piano at the Buffalo Lodge finally clicked into place.

"Did you know he could play?"

She raised her brows and shoulders in defeated admittance. "He never told me he couldn't."

"He's very good. He played in the sort of way that a person does when they really love their instrument, and have been away from it for too long." Erica would know an accomplished musician when she heard one.

"What did he say when he saw you?"

"Oh, he didn't. No, I felt sure that he would not have liked me being there—like I had walked in on a personal moment. I crept back out as quiet as I could." Erica smiled at her own deviousness, proud to deliver an important chunk of information to her friend.

"Thanks, Erica." Oddly, Candy was unsurprised by the new piece of the Sam puzzle. She was almost comforted; Erica said the music was melancholy. Could he be missing her as much as she was missing him?

"You've really never heard him play?"

"Nope." How could she have heard something for which she had never bothered to listen?

"Here come the menfolk," Erica warned.

John and Antonio banged their cafeteria trays down, deeply involved in conversation about an imminent football game. She smiled but tuned them out, imagining how Sam would look playing Chopin. *She* knew that music and there was one that was her favorite: Ballade No. 1 in G Minor, Op 23. Was it sick to hope he was playing that one? It was the saddest song in the world.

Candy finished her food, nodding and smiling, her mind detached. A glance at her watch showed her the lunch hour was dragging by at a turtle's pace. She snapped to attention, however, when she noticed how red Erica's face had become. Her friend was smiling ear to ear and practically catching fire with embarrassed pleasure, averting her eyes from John. Conversation crept back into Candy's awareness. Had John just asked Erica to the Homecoming dance, after she complained of never going? Antonio was leaving his chair to bend a knee, next to hers.

"La mia bella amica, you would please to company me to the ball?"

Oh, shit. "Homecoming is over a month away, guys. Isn't it a little early for this?" She hesitated, looking for support, first at Erica who was still gushing, and then to John. His face was unreadable.

"Please, Candy." Antonio was wearing a brotherly smile. A dozen heads were turned toward their table in anticipation.

"Okay."

chapter thirty-four

Sam looked through the window on top of the sand blasting cabinet. He couldn't see a damn thing. The protective film covering the inside had been blasted along with the ornament. Again. He set the glass piece on the venting grate, pulled his hands free of the long rubber gloves, and opened the door for a better look. A fine cloud of sand and glass dust wafted out, and he was glad he'd kept his face-mask in place. Rachel was right; it was a hard, dirty job. But steady, and he liked that.

Dangerous, too. One day, when he'd been polishing the lips on a line of champagne flutes, he lost his grip and the grinding wheel yanked a glass out of his hand; it flew past his face and shattered on the wall behind him. Sometimes, pieces couldn't hold up to the blasting and would break apart in his hands. Or, he'd bump something delicate while pulling it out of the cabinet and it was broken glass everywhere. The concrete floors of the studio were often wet and slippery (everyone was too busy to stop and clean throughout the day, and it was messy work), and he'd lost his footing more than once. It all added up to the same thing: lot's of shit broken, all the time.

Rachel never complained. "It's glass, that's what happens. Bring it to the kiln and I'll have Caleb repair it."

He had the most contact at the shop with Caleb, and Caleb threw information as fast as Sam could catch it. Anything to lighten his own load. Resist masking. Photo emulsion. Oil painting. Sam hadn't gotten on the torch yet, but it was only a matter of time. The promise of learning more kept him coming back.

On his first day in the studio, when Caleb gave him the tour, he explained how tools worked and talked about the properties of glass. Sam was engaged but not fascinated. Then Caleb turned on a torch, picked up a long, thin borosilicate tube, and began rotating it over the flame with his bare hands. The small heated section glowed bright orange, and once the temperature was even, the glass condensed and turned to honey. Caleb pulled it to a point, making a taper, then took it out of the flame and talked while he let it cool. In fifteen seconds, the taper was solid again, and he snipped off the end. That end became a blowhole within minutes. He heated the other end to molten hot liquid, then put his mouth to the glass and blew a perfect bubble.

I want to do that. Sam knew without reservation.

"Quitting time." Rachel's voice echoed through the studio behind him. "Well past, love."

Sam went to check his watch reflexively, but his wrist was buried, his hands already back in the protective blue gloves. He turned to find the wall clock and saw Rachel sauntering toward him, swirling a glass of wine.

"How about I throw a couple steaks on the grill? You must be starving, Sam."

He had worked straight through lunch, and a look out the window into pitch-black night showed he'd missed dinner as well. His stomach clenched at the thought of steak, his nose picking up the scent of charcoal burning outside. She had already lit the grill.

"You're welcome to stay again, you know." She was close enough that he could smell her perfume, and a flick of his eyes confirmed that she had already changed. Slinky black dress, high-heels. His pulse quickened in memory of the previous night. She'd told him he didn't need to spend it alone and he was grateful for a respite from loneliness.

He pushed his paper mask down below his chin. "I should shower."

"You're welcome to that, too." She smiled over her shoulder as she walked towards the door, "You know where everything is. We'll eat after you clean up."

Sam wiped the sweat off of his forehead with his shirtsleeve and flinched at its griminess. *Guess I better bring some clothes from home.*

chapter thirty-five

Amanda started skipping when they got closer to the hidden passage. "Okay, so you look for the tree with the crazy, Martian-looking red lichen growing clear up one side, once you pass the turn off for Oak Court." She pulled Antonio with her, swinging their clasped hands between them. Lindsay followed behind with John; she had grabbed his hand in retaliation, once her friend stole Antonio away. It was either that, or sulk with her arms crossed against her chest, and Amanda had already chided her about that. Lindsay watched the side of John's face adoringly. He didn't really mind—Lindsay was pretty. But feeling like Amanda's pawn sucked.

Just past the lichen tree, they turned off the paved road, their shoes padding over a thick blanket of spongy fallen leaves, the topmost layer still sodden from a recent rain and cushioned by years of almost undisturbed decomposition. That section of the woods was uninhabited, and dense. Fallen trees and branches littered the forest floor, but Amanda seemed to know the way. She warned of muddy spots and poison oak, and pointed out a tiny, dilapidated wooden cabin the moment the view was clear.

"See? Just there, up ahead."

"The Shack?" John tried to take the edge off his voice, but he knew the place was Candy's hideout that she hadn't bothered to mention. The probable reason for her secrecy—that she had been with that creep Sam—was enough to make him almost lose his lunch. It had taken an enormous amount of will-power not to confront Candy about it. But, she seemed to be steering clear of Sam anyway lately, so why push it?

Oh, speak of the devil. John was unsurprised to find The Shack already inhabited once they finally reached their target and pulled aside the ratty curtain serving as a door.

"Sam—hi," Amanda sang. "What are you doing here?"

Sam and a friend were sitting across a makeshift table from each other, each holding a fan of playing cards to their chests, startled at the shrill voice. His buddy pulled his baseball cap farther down on his forehead to shade his eyes, then spit into a dip can next to his boot in reply. Sam snuffed out a joint under his heel and brought his cards to rest on his knee. He narrowed his eyes at the newcomers, blowing out his last puff of smoke with a provoked scowl.

"I hope we're not interrupting anything," Lindsay squeaked.

"Oh, please, Lindsay. This place belongs to everybody. I'm Amanda."

"Tyler," the other boy said, accepting Amanda's hand and letting his gaze linger over Lindsay's body, from the pigtails curling down either side of her breasts to her painted toenails in strappy leather sandals. "Thought this place was unbeknownst to most, but now we got football players and cheerleaders showin' up."

"I am not a cheerleader." Amanda plopped down on the loveseat next to Sam.

Lindsay was offended. "Well, just because I cheer doesn't mean I'm a prude or anything. It's a sport, you know."

"Hello, I am Antonio."

John internally derided his friend, watching him offer his hand affably to the shady characters. Couldn't he smell the pot? Sense the malice in them? *Nice place Candy.*

"What are you guys playing?" Amanda leaned against Sam's shoulder to peek at his cards with a mischievous smirk.

"Actually, I was just leaving." Sam collapsed his hand and passed the cards to her. He ran both hands through his hair and rose to go.

Tyler kept his nose buried in his cards. "Later."

John glowered at Sam and planted himself in front of the doorway to block his retreat. "Running off so fast? Too ashamed to be seen here?"

Sam straightened to his full height and met John's glare. He jutted his face close enough that their noses almost touched. "Get the fuck out of my way. I'm not ashamed of anything, pal."

"Make sure you're not." John, who had been leaning against the door-frame with his feet spread wide, unfurled vertically to impose the two or three inches he had on his adversary. Tense seconds passed in blood-rushing silence, before Sam rammed his shoulder into John hard, bulling past him and nearly knocking him off his feet. John righted himself and drove Sam sideways into the doorjamb. Chunks of debris fell from the ceiling. Sam grunted as he shoved free, an elbow in the gut to aid his passage. John let him go, eyes blazing after him.

The others sat in stunned silence; the only noise was John's panting breath and Sam's boots stomping away in the brush. The metallic slam of a truck door and the roar of an engine brought the party out of their stupor.

"You okay, man?"

"Wow."

"You guys are like, really mad at each other."

"That was so dramatic, what's going on?"

"Nothing," John mumbled, trying to shake it off.

Antonio put an arm around him, "You sure?"

"Yeah, forget it."

Amanda was unperturbed. "Well anyway. What were you guys playing?" John had a feeling she had been banking on some drama.

Tyler snickered, gathered up the cards, and shuffled expertly, clearly not feeling the need to leave. "We were playin' poker. Who's in?"

After all his friends asked to be dealt a hand, John rolled his shoulders loose and mumbled that a card game would be fabulous. He slouched into a musty seat, tenderly feeling his chest. A nasty bruise was on its way. Before he could blink, Amanda perched her cushy, scantily clad rear-end on his thigh and gave him a guileful look. "I don't really know all the rules. Can you help me, John?"

John glanced at Antonio, who was cuddled with Lindsay on the love-seat, taking direction from Tyler. Neither of them seemed to be familiar with the game, to the redneck's delight. *Please don't tell me they're betting money.*

Amanda leaned over to show him her hand of cards and spilled her cleavage in his face.

Why not? John knew she was teasing him and he wondered how fast she would rescind her offer. He circled his arm around her waist and ran his hand up the inside of her thigh. When she didn't shove him away, he thought he'd call her bet by snapping the hem of her panties or some other asshole move, but he jerked his hand back with a jolt when he didn't find any. "Damn you."

She chuckled. "Tsk, tsk. Bad boys should be able to backup naughty claims. You gonna help me win this, or not?"

"Not."

"Here, maybe you need a better look, my man," she sneered.

She tried to slide down his leg to sit fully on his lap, but John grabbed her around the middle and moved her into the seat next to him. "I've got to…"

Amanda sent daggers from her ignominious dismount. "What?"

John had to get out of there.

"Got to what?" she demanded.

"Piss."

As soon as he stepped under the drape and sucked in fresh air, he realized how stifling that cabin was—physically, mentally, not to mention sexually disturbing. God, what was going on with Candy? He looked up through the trees and saw blue sky streaked with high, thin clouds; a testament to the brisk, fresh breeze awaiting him if he could just get the hell away from The Shack. He walked aimlessly, first pretending he didn't care if he got lost. At least his head was clearing. But, after glancing back and seeing the cabin had disappeared among the trees, he admitted he didn't recognize one bush from the other. That could get dangerous in Shirley County. He gave up his bravado and sat down on a sizable boulder to let his brain finish settling.

"You just need to get out into the fresh air, son," his dad always insisted, usually between business calls, as each school year drew to a close. *"You don't know what that does for your mind, to unclutter it, to free your brain from all those worries you think you have."*

John relaxed back onto the rock in a sliver of sunshine. "Yeah, but when you *live* out in the fresh air, life has a way of crowding in anyway, doesn't it, Dad?" he said to the sky. Maybe that's why his father never returned to Shirley himself.

"Shit y'all, Come an' looka this!"

John raised his head, his brow furrowed. Something about the tone in that summons—it sounded like that Tyler guy—was too intense to ignore. He started backtracking to the cabin, aided by the general clamor of his friends tramping through the woods. They all seemed to be moving south of The Shack, their voices rising in amplitude. The air cooled and the unmistakable aroma of sulfur lingered in the air. When the trees cleared, John stopped short. He nearly tripped over some stones projecting from the ground and he grabbed a tree branch to avoid flailing headfirst into water. The whole crew was on the other side of a natural spring, Amanda disappearing into the towering rocks beyond.

"It's a cave," Lindsay said, waving John over as he emerged from the trees.

Tyler motioned to the water, "I's taken a wiz over here—"

"Tell me you didn't pee in the Blue Spring, Tyler."

"How come?"

"Oh my god."

"Why is it blue, anyway?" asked John, peering into the water, both intrigued and revolted. Did he see a green cloud in the pool, and smell Ode de Tyler mixed with the sulfur?

"It's a natural phenomenon," Lindsay said. "Didn't you guys learn about it in freshman history?"

"In Memphis?" John and Antonio looked at each other and laughed under their hands at the absurdity of Lindsay's belief in the wide-ranging importance of Shirley County's scientific wonders. "No word of it in Italy either?"

"No."

Lindsay put her hands on her hips. "It's some kind of rare algae or something. You definitely shouldn't pee in it."

"How do you know? Might be it's good for it," said Tyler defensively.

"It's sacred. Don't ever do that again." Amanda's voice echoed inside the chamber. If that wasn't enough to invite her friends into the more recently discovered, enticingly secret, natural phenomenon, Tyler Finley's murderous look in her direction was. First Lindsay, then Antonio, turned their backs to him and made their way inside.

John edged around the other side of the spring, keeping his eye on Tyler. There was something about that guy that made his skin crawl. *Wish he'd just take off.*

"Whoa, this is far out," Antonio breathed, peering around in the dim light inside. "I was hoping I find this…stuff here."

"Really?"

"What do you mean?" Lindsay sidled closer, helping herself to one of Antonio's arms, more cozily attired in his soft hoodie sweatshirt than her own bare biceps. The temperature dropped at least ten degrees inside the cave.

"Is famous, the mysterious of Appalachia? The caves."

"You seen that movie, The Descent?" asked Tyler. "Them monsters in the caves?"

"That was such a creepy movie, I saw it," said Lindsay.

Amanda shook her head in irritation. "Totally fictitious."

Can't you see this guy doesn't need more pissing off? John marveled at the foolish actions of otherwise intelligent people.

His eyes began to adjust to the gloom. He had always been interested in Shirley County caves growing up, and had visited some around the region, both north and south along the main mountain trail that ran through several states. He usually hit them with Candy's family, many of whom were devoted naturalists. Most were expert climbers, hikers and campers—even a few extreme spelunkers. Several close-by cave systems had been fitted with lights and railings, the more dangerous reaches closed off to casual visitors. John had never been scared to enter them, even as a child, because Candy was the scout. She always knew her way and was never scared. She laughed at the federally mandated warnings of the dangers involved in a gazillion tons of rock looming overhead, and joked about the admonitions of children lost forever after wandering off into uncharted nooks and crannies.

"There's more that goes back further…like, a lot more." Lindsay was leaning her face close to an inner wall and shining her cell phone light into a deep crack.

"What do you mean, like another room?"

"My mom always told me our dog hated to walk in this area," Lindsay chuckled. "No wonder. He hates the dark and won't even go into the basement, big chicken. You know how dogs are, with their sixth-sense. He must have known something like this was here."

"Something, like what?" Antonio offered his hand for her phone. "Mio Dio…"

John leaned in to look, and since he had the longest reach, Antonio gave him the phone for the best possible view of what lie beyond. The light was too weak, though, and they couldn't see much. "There's definitely a lot more back there."

Lindsay nodded. "You can hear our voices echoing far away. When the echo's long like that, it means the cave is really deep."

John felt a weakness in the wall as he leaned against it. It wasn't rock—it was more like fiber. "I think this is false rock here, look."

"That's so weird—what's behind it?" Amanda shouldered closer. "Can you break into it?"

John backed away. "I'm not sure that's such a good idea."

"Yeah." Tyler filled in. He pulled at the false rock, grunting with the effort. "I think so."

"There's a flimsy part here." Amanda helped Tyler ram through the structure, heedless of the billions of tons of stone overhead.

"Ew, gross. Is that a bone?" Their eyes followed Lindsay's trembling finger. She was pointing to a long and solid thing, hanging at an odd angle inside the wall.

John moved close again for a better look. It was definitely a bone. *Is this some kind of ancient burial site? Like the one under the restaurant?*

One of the girls screamed when something came loose and hit the floor with a heavy thud. They all jumped back and watched in stunned silence as a small, ceramic vessel rolled slowly towards their feet.

§

"It was right here." John knelt down and searched the darkest corners with the flashlight that he had insisted she bring. "Maybe it rolled into a corner or something, after we left."

Candy squatted down and helped him look. He had called her, thrilled with the news of an uncharted cave less than two miles from her house.

He was ranting about artifacts of unknown origin and said he'd be at her house to pick her up in two seconds.

Candy knew about the cave entrance; she'd visited it with her dad when she was a little kid. It used to have crude paintings on the walls inside that some said dated back to at least 500 or 600 CE. Dad wanted her to see them in their natural state before the university team removed them a couple years before. She hadn't known about the plastered-over corridor to a deeper system of tunnels beyond the main vestibule, however. Removing the paintings, and probably weakening the top layer of rock, hadn't been such a good idea after all. *Uncovered skeletal remains and pre-historic pottery--holy crap!* "You said it was a cup or a bowl? Cylindrical?"

"Yeah."

"Could have rolled off…"

"It was about this big," John cupped his hands together to indicate a vessel about the size of a coffee mug, "and it was brown with age, but it looked like it had been painted once." He scrubbed at his head and started pacing.

Candy let him fret and looked around the cave, trying to remember what the guide had told them when she was little. It was like a sitting room, similar to a modern formal living room in some houses, reserved for fancy guests and visiting aunts and uncles. Or maybe it was an eating space, like the family breakfast nook where everyone gathered. They probably drew pictures, told stories, played games together. She looked up. The ceiling was black with centuries of fire soot. She tried to recall what the cave paintings looked like, before the university removed them for preservation.

"We all agreed that the object shouldn't be touched. That it probably had archeological significance," John was saying to himself, more agitated than she had first realized. "It had these markings on it. Remember the symbols we saw in history class?"

"Huh?"

John snapped his fingers once or twice, irritated. "You know, the Mississippian Culture."

"Oh. Kind of. I didn't do too well on that test, actually."

"Would someone have taken it?" He was patrolling the room, muttering to himself. "Why?"

"Taken the cup thing?"

"We thought someone should call the university and have them come and look at it. I said I would. I told them that you would know who to talk to."

"Thanks."

"No. You don't understand. We stepped away and agreed that we shouldn't touch anything."

"Well. Maybe someone took it to the university themselves. I mean, that would be stupid. It should only be handled with gloves, by a profess—"

"Whoever took it didn't take it to the university," John barked.

Candy gaped at him. "How do you know that?"

"That little weasel probably doesn't even know what a university is."

"Who?"

John didn't answer. He crossed his arms over his chest and resumed pacing.

"Well," sighed Candy. "It's gone now. Let's get someone over to look at these bones, though, right?" She tried for upbeat. The painted cup meant more to John than he was willing to explain, obviously. If it really were that important, he would spill the beans sooner or later.

"Yeah, you're right." John jerked his cell phone out of his pocket, then started dialing as he walked away from her.

Candy suddenly understood that he meant to share something personal with her about the missing artifact before they called anyone. But she missed the beat.

chapter thirty-six

By the time Charlotte found the tree with the red lichen, the sun was already low in the sky. She hoped she could beat the sunset and get to The Shack before nightfall, but it was growing darker by the second. She parked just off the road and picked her way through the woods; the going was slow in the deepening gloom.

Antonio was so cute. He had called her the night before, all excited to show her the stupid cave. And the gross little cabin. She didn't mind entertaining a boy's fantasies, however. It could only pay off in her favor later. "If only I hadn't left my damn phone."

How had she been so careless as to leave her cell phone there? She didn't even realize it until she was stuck at work earlier that day. *But, the little Italian pervert wanted pictures.*

She just hoped she could find her way back in the dark. The smell of sulfur from the Blue Spring helped to guide her in the right direction.

"Only time I been thankful for that smell."

Her voice suddenly seemed too loud, the leaves crunching under her shoes as raucous as an alarm, and she slowed her pace, unsure why she felt the urge for stealth. A monotonous hum began to register in her ears. The tone flew to a higher pitch, like a wail, then picked up the hum once again.

Chanting?

It was definitely human. Charlotte realized why the forest felt so wrong seconds before: not a bird chirped, not a bug buzzed, not a squirrel scurried. The woods were eerily silent, except for the human voice coming from the direction of the spring. As she got closer to the sound, she sidled up next to the mountainside and slinked along as quietly as she could, her phone momentarily forgotten. The smell was overpowering.

She peeked around the side of a boulder, into the little inlet where the spring lie, and gasped at what she saw.

Tyler...

Her cousin was crouched at the edge of the water, naked. Guttural sounds were coming from his throat, his head fallen back at an impossible angle. She wondered if she should help him, but then his head snapped forward revealing a face twisted into a blind snarl, his eyes rolled back into his skull. The noises from his mouth coalesced back into the chant. *Some freaky demon language?*

Charlotte fell back behind the boulder, unable to watch. She tried to slow her breathing, wishing more than anything to remain unnoticed. *What in the hell is going on?*

The sounds by the spring became more frantic and she risked a look. She had to see. At first, she thought Tyler was masturbating, bouncing up and down on his haunches, his hands hidden between his legs. But then he began to retch and a stream of something flowed out of his mouth. Or was it flowing into his mouth? Charlotte felt like she might be sick herself.

She covered her cherry lips with her hand and slid back along the face of the overhanging cliff, promising herself not to look again. How fast could she get back to her car? What if Tyler heard her? She couldn't risk it. *Gonna have to wait it out. My gawd.*

As she knelt down in the dirt and tried to regain composure, her mind raced. What was "it?" After a few minutes, her curiosity overwhelmed her fear and she knew she'd have to stay until Tyler finally left. She had to go back and see what was over there at that damned spring.

A crackling sound—like something electric—erupted around the bend. There was a flash of blue light from the rocky inlet. Then the forest was silent.

Charlotte listened, barely daring to breathe. Gradually, she heard sounds of normalcy resume around her. An owl hooted. The crickets began to sing again. The wind picked up and rustled the branches overhead. Heavy boots scuffed through the underbrush and disappeared on the other side of the spring, and she knew Tyler was gone.

She waited for at least ten more minutes before emerging from her hiding spot and edging toward the spring. Had the smell of sulfur vanished, or was she just growing accustomed to it? Night had fallen and she wished for the foresight of retrieving her phone for a light first, before investigating the spring. But, as she got closer, she saw…there was nothing to see. A bird was drinking from the spring and took to the air as she approached. She didn't know what she had expected, but there was only plain old rocks and water in front of her.

Thought the water was gross before. A weird blue. She shrugged. "Looks clear now. Maybe just can't see it in the dark," She leaned over and saw her reflection looking back at her and dipped her finger into the pool to disrupt the mirror. The water wasn't cold anymore.

chapter thirty-seven

Homecoming Week was one of Stephanie Jameson's favorite times of year, even ranking above Christmas morning. She was cooking up a storm for her part in the Bake-A-Thon, a fundraiser which would take place in Andrew Jackson's courtyard, starting Monday morning and running throughout the week. The last-minute cash was perfect for buying the final decorations in the gymnasium, for the magical ending to the festivities on Saturday night. The dance.

Steph measured out her ingredients, mixing batter and turning out dough, humming along to her radio and thinking about the whirlwind of events in store. "Zippity do dah days," she sang, then giggled to herself. *I sound like a Disney princess or something. I'm so silly.*

Not only were there the themed days at the high school—Monday was Pajama's Day, Tuesday was Super Star Day, Thursday was Little Kid Day, and Friday was Spirit Day—but there were functions throughout the week, night and day. Wednesday would be for the intramural sports taking place on the football field all day long. Each class was pitted against the other and they fought it out, practically to the death. Of course, the games were rigged for the final score to be in the senior class's favor, and rightly so. They should enjoy that triumph in their last year.

All Friday, seniors took turns at the drums in the courtyard, chanting the Bobcatt theme. To finish, they organized a walking parade in the halls of the school building, luring all the kids out of class to join in with noise-makers, horns and pom-poms. That was always Steph's favorite school day event.

Friday night would be the actual Homecoming game. It was as joyous as any other game, with the roaring of the crowd and the crashing of helmets, to the background of a full live band. In any other setting but an outdoor football game, the trumpets, trombones and French horns, the clarinets, oboes and flutes, would have been overpowering and obnoxious. A wall of sound. But, there was something about the blending of that music with the smell of roasting hotdogs and buttered popcorn, with the girls leading the cheers alongside and the boys giving their hearts and souls to the game.

The Homecoming game would have the added bonus of a special half-time show, when the audience would enjoy an extended performance, including a choreographed dance of marching band members, baton twirlers and flagmen. There would be a special routine by the cheerleaders, complete with intricate pop-ups, tumbling and a pyramid formation. And then…the announcement of the Homecoming Court.

She knew that her friend Kerry would have chewed all her fingernails to the quick by the time the Queen was finally announced; terrified that it somehow wouldn't be her daughter, Ashley. Steph was feeling pretty bubbly about the likelihood of Tristan being named King, but not really worried. How could anyone except the star quarterback be chosen for such an honor, especially with his performance the past year? The Bobcatts were 6-0 so far, with no reason to think they wouldn't win their game on Homecoming night. Traditionally, the coaches would ensure victory by choosing a weak opponent for the occasion, but she didn't think they'd need it.

She bit her lip at one dark spot plaguing her mind. When Steph had suggested that Tristan take Ashley Davis to the dance, he ridiculed her and called her naïve. He was so mean; it still made her tummy rumble, "Come on, Mom. Like I'm gonna bring that tight-assed Puritan to the Homecoming dance. Her dad's probably already locked on the chastity belt in advance."

Steph was shocked, and she let him know it, "Tristan, my goodness. That's not a nice way to speak, and that's not what Homecoming is about."

"Yeah, right. You take Miss Grundy as just friends, then. I plan to get laid that night."

And then he asked Meg Shannon to the dance, just to drive home his point and enrage his mother—"get her panties in a wad," as Mike liked to say.

Meg was pretty, in a strange way, and seemed nice enough (though a little on the dumb side), but not even Steph could've ignored the rumors about her loose nature. The poor thing didn't have much going for her; she lived in the Southern Cove trailer park with a dozen raggedy step- and half-siblings, and a hard-working, but usually absent, mother. No father. People snickered that Meg would sleep with almost anyone to spend the night away from her own filthy, overrun trailer home. Everyone would know, of course, why Tristan had invited the girl to the dance.

She licked chocolate batter off her wooden spoon and thought she better talk to Mike about equipping Tristan with condoms, just in case. Her son probably wouldn't accept condoms from his mother. She'd never had to worry about that when he was dating Ashley.

"Oh, Tristan," she fumed. She thought about how debonair he would look in the tuxedo she picked out for him. She wanted nothing more than for him to enjoy the unique occasion, "He'll have a lovely boutonnière and matching corsage, no matter who he brings for a date."

Pouring batter into miniature Bundt pans, she looked across the kitchen to the family portraits decorating the hallway and found one of her recent favorites of Tristan, his senior photograph taken that summer. He was wearing a tuxedo dickey under a false jacket, like all the boys would have been, but his gorgeous, confident smile was the real decoration. Tristan inherited the best of both of his parents' features: Mike's thick, dark hair and striking jaw line, and Steph's bright blue eyes and full lips. She stopped pouring for a minute, adoring her son's image and chiding herself for feeling suspicious of his motives.

"Maybe he really does like the girl, how would I know?" she said to herself and shrugged. Ashley probably was a little too prudish, just like her mom, though she loved them both dearly.

Maybe Meg will turn into Cinderella. I'll help her pumpkin turn into a chariot. She nodded proudly, thinking of the limousine she hired for Tristan. Her pumpkin pies reached their peak in the hot oven and Steph chuckled at the sudden aroma. "What a coinkydink."

"What's a coinkydink?" asked Amanda, padding into the kitchen with her friend Jessica in tow, both of them still sleepy-eyed from their late night movie extravaganza. "You're up so early, Mom."

"Well, I've got a lot of baking to do. I'm a regular Keebler Elf today."

Steph popped two bagels into the double toaster and placed the cream cheese container and two paper plates in front of the girls, who sat at the bar overhanging the kitchen countertop.

"Thanks for getting us all the limo for the dance, Mrs. Jameson," Jessica said. "Amanda just told me, that's so cool."

"You're quite welcome, sweetheart."

"Musta been kinda difficult renting a limo to come all the way to Shirley from Tenakho Falls, huh?"

"You all are worth it," Steph winked. She pulled on her oven mitts to check her pies.

"Tristan gets it first, of course," Amanda complained, making a sour puss when Steph admonished her with one raised eyebrow.

"I don't care, works for me. I've never ridden in a limo."

"Thank you, Jessica. And neither has Amanda." The limo hadn't been difficult to rent and, although expensive, it was the right transportation for the star quarterback. The limo company sold large blocks of time to Shirley residents, so Steph was forced to pay for the whole evening or not at all. Amanda and her friends were the lucky beneficiaries of the rest of Tristan's rented time. "Are you girls still planning to go stag?"

"Definitely."

Steph frowned. "Y'all are so funny. You never stop surprising me."

"Well, there's absolutely no one of the male gender interesting to go with in our grade, Mom."

"Yeah," Jessica readily agreed, "Mrs. Jameson, all the boys in our class are immature. And most of our dads would freak out if we went with an older guy."

"Older guys," Steph chuckled at the very idea, rinsing her mixing bowls in the sink in preparation for a new recipe. They were all still babies. "Well, you girls just take care of each other."

"Hi, Daddy."

"Where's my sugar?" Mike snuck into the kitchen on Steph's blind side and spooned her in a hug.

"There's plenty of it in here." Steph laughed, but elbowed him away as he nipped her earlobe.

Amanda emitted audible disgust and Jessica whispered under her hand, "They're so cute."

"Did you make my special brownies yet?" Mike asked, ignoring his daughter and her friend, rooting through the refrigerator.

"Uh, no." Steph pointed her nose over at the girls, who were beginning to look bored.

"You two need a ride anywhere?"

"Thanks, Dad. But we've got stuff to do in my room for a while." Amanda slid off of her stool, motioning for Jessica to follow.

"Here, take your breakfast." Steph popped the bagels out of the toaster and spread cream cheese on both so fast a Fairy Godmother would be proud. "You want orange juice?"

"No, Mom."

Jessica shook her head. "Thanks, Mrs. Jameson."

"You're very welcome, sweetheart." Steph watched them disappear down the hallway. She heard Jessica ask if they would still have the house to themselves after the dance, as the pair turned into Amanda's room and closed the door. Steph heard the lock click in place and knitted her brows in irritation. "How many times have I told her I don't want doors locked in this house?"

"Secretive teenagers…" Mike yawned. He poured himself a cup of coffee and tucked the Sunday paper under his arm.

"Well, I don't like secrets, especially not with teenagers."

Her husband gave her a resigned expression and patted her rump as he passed by. He claimed the chair vacated by Amanda, spreading his newspaper open on the bar and adjusting his reading glasses on his nose.

Steph flipped on her handheld mixer and watched the yellow egg yolks swirl into the sugar and vegetable oil, the brown vanilla extract adding its own spirals. She breathed in deeply, trying to let the homey smell sooth her troubled mind. Amanda had been more secretive than usual lately. What were they doing in there that required a locked door? "Mike, maybe going to a hotel Saturday night isn't such a good idea, after all."

"Hhhmmm?" Mike was already absorbed in one of the cover news stories.

"Leaving the house to the kids, after the Homecoming dance."

"Thought it sounded great to me. Romantic." He trilled his 'r' with an Italian flourish, a new private joke between them.

Steph didn't laugh. "I'm not so sure anymore."

"Pussycat, after all the work you put in for Homecoming, you're gonna need the vacation and you know it. It'll be fun."

"Amanda and her friends going stag doesn't worry you? What do you think they're planning to do after the dance?"

Mike lifted a shoulder and kept his eyes on the paper. "Tristan will be in charge, not Mandy."

That idea made her nervous in a different way, remembering the gossip about Meg Shannon liking to try out other people's beds. Her bed, perhaps? "Well, what if they have some big party here, or something? What if they wreck the house, or some kids we don't know come over, and...I don't know, steal something?"

Mike snorted. "At the County Sheriff's house?"

"Or...or, root through my underwear drawer or something?"

"What?" Now she had his attention; he looked up from his paper, his eyes little slits of mirth. "Are you worried about high school boys sniffing your underwear?"

"No." She felt a little ridiculous when he put it like that. But she wasn't ready to give up. "I mean, think of what else I keep in that drawer?"

"Well, honey. We can make sure our bedroom door stays locked."

She sighed, frowning into her mixing bowl. "Okay..."

Mike put his elbows on the bar and cocked his head. "What is it really?"

"I don't know." She couldn't describe why she felt so apprehensive. She was probably just being silly.

"Look, I know you feel like you need to know everything that goes on in the world, especially when it comes to your kids." His attention slipped back to the news. "Trust me, you don't. There's lots going on that you don't want to see."

"Oh, it's the jaded cop routine now, is it, Sheriff Jameson?" she teased him, licking a sugary whisk with her cute-as-button routine.

He studied her over the top of his glasses. "You gonna give me one of those to lick, or not?"

chapter thirty-eight

Candy rang the doorbell at the Robinson house and stepped back out of the glaring porch light, readjusting her dress around her hips and twirling the ends of her hair. She realized her hands were trembling and she shook them, impatient with herself. Why was she so nervous? She was going to the dance with friends, two of whom she had known most of her life.

She caught her reflection in the window and hardly recognized herself. All the glittery princess stuff was what made her feel so weird. She heard a commotion within the house and peered inside. John's dad was scrambling around in the hall closet for something.

"Be right there," Grandma Pearl sang behind the door. Her face popped into view in the leaded glass. "Oh, it's just Candy—forget the roses, John."

Yeah, why bother with roses for ole' Candy? She turned around to scowl at her dad, still digging in the car trunk for something. "Dad, what are you doing? Come on."

"The correct lens makes all the difference, trust me." His voice was muffled, as he dug around with his head inside the back of the car. After several more thumps and clanks he found that urgent piece of photographic equipment, which Candy had never known he owned, and emerged triumphant. "Found it."

"Say cheese." A welcoming chorus sounded and a rush of air swept past her as one of the Robinsons flung the door open. She turned to them with a smile and was blinded by a flash of light. An old-fashioned camera clicked and whirred.

"I see someone else shares my dad's fondness for the classics," she said, blinking hard. She remembered not to rub her eyes, lest she smear the unfamiliar make-up and end up looking like a raccoon in the first few seconds of the evening.

Grandma Pearl held up her cell phone. "Don't worry. I'll shoot plenty too, just to be sure."

"Mom, these will be much better than anything you could take with a cell phone, trust me."

"You don't even know what you're taking with that, and I can see mine right away," replied Pearl, full of pride and wonderment at modern technology. She was one of those rare older ladies who always delighted in the next new device, even better if she could find an inexpensive version at the Discount Depot. She was constantly learning, though a little more slowly than younger generations, and sharing her revelations with anyone who would listen (even if they only pretended to listen). "Why bother to get film developed, when I can just look at the pictures on my phone? Developing film is a waste of time and money, Jamie."

"There's a pretty big difference in image quality when you use film, Mom."

"See, look—I can take as many as I want, and you can only take what? Twenty-four with one roll?" In illustration, she held down a button to use the rapid-fire function of her phone's camera app. Candy resisted the urge to hold her hands up in front of her face for protection, squeezing in sideways through the door and making for the sanctuary of John. He waved to her on the other side of the threshold like a policeman at a crime scene.

"Perfect example of why more isn't always better, Mom."

"Candy, hey." John leaned down to kiss her on the cheek.

"Whew. Hi."

"James, is that a Canon?" George Vale had finally gathered his gear. He bounded up the porch steps with all his paraphernalia dangling from straps around his neck. "EOS?"

"How's it going, George. Yeah, EOS 10."

Her dad whistled, accepting James camera for inspection while handing over his own. "EOS ELAN II, right there."

"Candy, you look beautiful, my dear." Pearl gave her a quick peck on the forehead, careful not to disturb any make-up or hair, before bustling back down the hallway. "I made lemonade, you thirsty?"

"Oh, thank you. But...I'd rather not...mess anything up. Lipstick and all," Candy said, feeling girly and impolite for not accepting the offered refreshment.

"I understand, dear." Pearl's voice died away and then echoed more loudly as she entered the kitchen. "You're a woman now."

Candy's cheeks burned with embarrassment, and she looked to the guys, expecting them to burst into laughter. Her dad and Mr. Robinson were deep in conversation, trading facts about shooting styles and detachable lenses. John wore a crooked smile, full of empathy. He grabbed her hand to pull her into the quiet of an adjoining room.

"You really do look beautiful, Candy."

"Oh. Heh, thanks."

"I'm speechless."

He held her fingers in his hands and pulled her arms out for an appraisal of her dress. She had to admit she loved the dress. Her Aunt Shelby, who had mothered three sons and longed for the opportunity to go dress shopping, had taken Candy on a special trip to Tenakho Falls for the occasion. She helped her pick out a dress that perfectly flattered both her figure and her personal style. The simple, black velvet A-line hit her shapely legs mid-thigh and was hemmed with a ring of fuzzy black feathers. The bust was snug yet modest, with velvet spaghetti straps. Elegant satin high-heels set off the old-fashioned black seam running up the back of her legs in shear black stockings. The "milky white" expanse of her chest (her aunt had insisted it was one of her sexiest features) was left bare, with long, sparkling crystal earrings dropping down either side of her neck.

Maybe the effect worked a little too well. John's eyes were glued to that particular area. "Come on, you're never speechless."

He shrugged and smiled, continuing to admire her with unnerving frankness.

"You look good, too." Candy had never seen him so dressed up before, and though John always looked nice (even in gym clothes, somehow), she hadn't noticed how genuinely handsome he was until then.

"Thanks, you think?" He turned around once for appraisal. He wasn't finished dressing, but had already donned black tuxedo pants with satin piping and patent leather shoes. A stark white shirt, vest and tie set off his tan, the fanciness in contrast to the adorable freckles sprinkling his nose. His hair was freshly washed and neatly styled, darker than when he was little, but sun kissed with golden streaks. It was beginning to curl at the ends.

"Curls are coming back. You're growing it out, I'm glad."

"Yeah," he went to run a hand through his hair automatically, but pulled it back laughing. "This took an effort, and quite a bit of 'product.'"

"Me too," she agreed, motioning to her own head.

He walked around her to check out the back. "Very pixie-like. It's pretty."

Candy circled him in turn, nodding approval. "I like the white-on-white thing."

"Don't worry, the jacket's black." John pulled his tuxedo jacket off the back of a chair and slipped into it. He filled it out well.

"Having trouble with that tie?" Candy gestured to his neck, where his tie was hanging loose under the collar, still open at the throat.

"Oh, yeah. I found a video, but it's a little hard to follow."

"Your dad's no help?"

"No—he's been digging out camera stuff for hours."

"Oh my god, mine, too." They both laughed, gently breaking through the mood that had settled between them.

"Crazy fools. Well, special occasion and all."

"It is. Wow, Erica's roses are beautiful," Candy motioned toward a bouquet lying on a table by the front window. *No roses for Candy.* "Did you choose yellow for friendship?"

"Does yellow stand for friendship? She said her dress was cream and gold, so yellow seemed like it would harmonize well. The white roses seemed a little too…"

"Meant for a wedding?"

"Yes."

"Good call."

"And…" John reached a hand behind the table lamp looming over the bouquet and produced a single red country rose, fully bloomed. Its spindly stem was still dripping, the sharp thorns all carefully removed. "You get red, of course."

Candy gasped. "It's gorgeous." She dug her nose into the center and breathed deeply, satisfaction washing over her. "Smells like heaven." She held it up to John's nose and he sniffed dutifully. Candy was sure he already knew what it smelled like; he probably selected it especially for its heavy fragrance, knowing how much she loved the smell of country roses.

His smile was shy. "I'm glad you like it."

"Divine," she said, honestly touched, and smirked inwardly at Grandma Pearl's earlier remark. "Thank you."

"Headlights everyone," Pearl's voice rang throughout the house, as if on cue.

John's dad came into the living room to peer outside, kneeling on the cushioned window seat and cupping his hands against the glass to cut the glare from the lights in the house. "Who drives an SUV, Erica's dad or Mieke Walsh?"

"Ugh. Mieke Walsh does," Pearl said, her tone dripping with disappointment. She walked closer to the entrance to the den and bellowed, "Grandpa, it's time to make your appearance, dear."

John muttered, "Good, maybe Antonio can help me with this tie."

"Son, I'm sorry. I forgot I was going to get to that."

The new guests rolled in at an angle to the house and the car's length became apparent. "Does Mrs. Walsh have a stretch Hummer?" asked Candy.

"What? No."

"Cool, she must have rented it." Candy beamed at John and they bounded to the door together, as the Hummer came to a stop. A uniformed driver got out, tipped his hat to them, and walked around the passenger side to open the doors.

"Hi, everybody," Mieke Walsh cheered from inside the limousine. Antonio, rejecting the helping hand of the driver, hopped down first and then turned to offer assistance to his adopted parent. She descended demurely, in a plain T-shirt, jeans and sneakers.

Antonio let go of Mrs. Walsh's hand with a kiss, then turned to his friends. "Hello, Candy. John." He spread his arms wide, indicating the vast expanse of their chariot. "Is fabulous, no?"

John was already inspecting the cabin, his voice muffled inside. "Amazing."

"Thank you, Mrs. Walsh, honestly," said Candy.

"Well, you kids are worth it."

Antonio hugged her around the waist and gave her a half-spin. "I love my Mamma Americano."

"Oh, Antonio!" She laughed and swatted at him playfully until he put her down. "Okay, now the evening is yours. Everything is set, including the tip." Mieke was full of pride and merriment. She straightened her T-shirt and hair without much thought, waving the driver over. "Randall, Antonio is in charge for the rest of the evening. You have my number, in case anything comes up. And other than that…" She clasped her hands to her chest, gazing at the group of friends affectionately, "have fun, you guys."

"There she is," Grandma Pearl sounded from the porch. She produced grunting sounds as she heaved her husband's wheelchair over the threshold. "About time."

"Mom, I'll do that. Don't ask Mieke to—"

"I'm not talking about her, James. I'm talking about the lady of the hour, John's companion to the ball."

"Is Erica here?" Candy wheeled around toward the road and saw headlights approaching, the glare mostly blocked by the expansive Hummer.

"John, get the roses."

"On my way, Grandma."

"Wait, wait. Let me get the flash for the outside. I didn't think it would be so dark," said John's dad, rushing back inside.

Her dad followed him inside, offering advice. "What kinda film you got, Jamie?"

"Speaking of roses…" Antonio's voice was close and gentle, his aftershave suddenly apparent and his words tickling Candy's bare neck. He pulled her away from the fuss to the other side of the limo, where voices were muffled and the moonlight lent a soft glow to the darkening front lawn. He appraised her figure in the flattering luminescence and ran a finger down her jaw. "They write poetry about women as you."

"Uh." Candy felt awkward, bewildered by all the attention to her appearance and the yearning male gazes. She already felt strained by playing the princess. She wanted to be polished and polite for the occasion and she knew she wasn't. "You got me roses?"

"Sei bella come una rosa."

She understood enough to translate that to her being as beautiful as a rose. "Oh. I don't know what to say…"

"Just say 'thank you,' honey. Live with the compliment." And to accentuate, he slapped her velvety buttocks hard and let out a ridiculous, lupine howl, "Let's party."

"Do *not* smack my butt again."

"Don't worry, no roses for you, honey." He snatched up her hand and towed her back to the bedlam ensuing on the other side of the front lawn.

"Oh no, of course not. Not for Candy." She reminded herself to grab the one that John had given her before they left.

"Candy," Erica's voice emitted from a shapely, elegant form in a clinging satin gown, and Candy stifled her surprise. Normally one to hide her body in frumpy flannel shirts under baggy overalls, with her mousy brown hair slicked back in tight plaits and bulky glasses covering most of her eyes, Erica was the quintessential ugly duckling turned beautiful swan. Candy looked over her shoulder to check for hidden filmmakers producing a reality TV, after-school special.

"Erica, wow." She went on tip-toe to hug her friend and whispered in her ear, "Didn't know you were so stacked, girlfriend." She had a stunning figure hiding under all those clothes.

Erica flicked a strand of hot-rolled curls over her shoulder. "Well, with a date on the Homecoming Court, I figured I had to step it up a little, you know?" She winked a catlike eye, and Candy could see that she had expert help with her make-up. Her friend usually never wore a smudge of it, but that night her eyes were artfully enhanced, her cheeks were rosy, her lips were glossy and her spots of acne were hidden.

"Are you wearing contacts?"

"Yes, I hate them." Erica grimaced, glanced at encroaching parents and escorts, and added, "And how do people live with thongs up their butts every day?"

"My dear girl, you are a vision." Grandma Pearl (who had left her husband camped on the porch, helpless in front of the stairs) advanced on Erica and kissed her lightly on each cheek.

"'At's my boy, John," said the marooned Grandpa Joe, in a voice so unlike the bellow Candy expected from the enormous man. She worried how honest his family was being about the state of his health, before her face burned at the sight of John next to him. John was exiting the house with an armful of roses.

Grandma Pearl barked orders. Erica gushed her thank-you's. John posed beside her with one arm around her waist, while his dad fumbled with the Canon. Pearl held down the shutter button on her phone and snapped off dozens of shots with a smug expression. Candy watched and tried not to roll her eyes, wishing it would just end. Then her dad shoved Antonio against her and started shooting. Antonio remembered the macho act and let his hands roam. Pearl decided to shoot some video, too. It was miserable.

"All the kids together," said Mieke. She pulled out a compact camera and corralled the group in front of what she thought was the best background. While the adults argued about lighting and rearranged their subjects according to height and partnerships, Candy found herself smashed into John's chest. When he rested his hand possessively on her hip, she felt her pilot light flaring with anger, deep within her gut.

"How many roses did you pick up today?" she whispered up into his face, sweetly mocking. "I'm sure Charice Hawkins got hers, too."

He looked down into her eyes coolly, unsurprised by her jealous challenge. She felt ashamed, even as she had said it. "Nice of you to wonder about that. Thanks for showing up to watch the parade."

"I'm sure you enjoyed yourself plenty, without me."

"Riding in a mint condition '57 Bel Air Convertible, next to a pretty girl telling me how wonderful I am, was a horrible experience, in fact." He held her glare as the group was rearranged for more photos.

Candy fumed at the thought of John in the stupid Homecoming Court parade. She imagined him, waggling a pompous, presidential wave at the crowd. The whole town had probably turned out to ogle the beautiful people, riding in the meticulously refurbished and highly buffed classic cars that their owners trotted out every year for Homecoming Week. As Mieke shoved and pulled here and there, to arrange the kids into a new configuration, John sucked in to slip past Candy without touching her. She glanced up to see him gazing fiercely past the camera lenses, willing himself to breath slowly and probably counting to ten in his head.

He was right. She should have gone to see the parade. She did every year with her dad, ever since she was a little kid; the cars were the best part, especially when Dad entered one of his own. When she was a child, she thought the pretty girls were all princesses and their consorts, princes.

As she grew older, however, she became better acquainted with the type of people who were usually elected to serve on "the Court"—mindless bobble-headed girls and arrogant, glazed-ham guys. She was as different as could be from those people. Then, her own John had been elected as the junior male representative the night of the Homecoming game. She was nothing short of devastated.

"The parade wasn't just the Homecoming Court. That was only a small part," John whispered, as the adults finished up their snapping and everyone began to disperse. "Every club had a float—I know you worked on the Art Club one. I rode on the Drama Club float, too. Louis was there—we did Shakespeare, for crying out loud. Erica was there in the marching band. And you missed it all."

Candy looked away, begging her chin not to tremble.

"You were *missed*," he emphasized, pointing his eyes at Erica, who seemed more like her awkward self suddenly. She was letting her mother help tuck in her strapless bra, while juggling her bouquet in her gangly arms. "Erica, let me help you with those. Sorry, what was I thinking?"

"No, I love them."

Erica's mom spoke around the safety pin in her mouth, "John, they are lovely. That was very thoughtful. Erica, sweetheart, I'll take them home and put them in a vase for you."

"Molly, aren't you coming to The Kitchen?" asked John's dad.

"Yeah, a bunch of us parents are having our own little shindig." Candy's dad was carefully stowing his Canon in its case. He felt Candy watching him and smiled, "Don't worry, no more pictures allowed."

Erica's mom was unsure, as awkward as her daughtert in social situations. "Well, that sounds lovely, George…"

"Yeah, Mom. Go party down with the old folks. You'd worry a lot less if you did." Erica shoved her mother towards the group of parents, missing the scowl that transformed Mieke Walsh's face after the "old folks" comment.

"I'll watch those roses for ya," Joe Robinson said, in a pained voice that turned every head. He added, trying for humor, "All I can do these days is watch, I guess."

Candy's dad was clueless as ever. "Joe, you should come out, too."

"Absolutely not, dear," Pearl snapped. "You are staying right here."

"I'll stay, too, then," said Mieke.

"Mieke, I thought you're riding with me?"

"Candy, come here." Antonio grabbed her hand and urged her towards their waiting limousine. "Time to bolt."

She was willing her insides to simper down and Antonio's strange mixt of dated American slang and sexy Italian accent helped. She grinned and let him tow her along. He climbed in first and gave her a hand up into the spacious cabin, spilling back with her onto the luxurious, wrap-around leather couches. The first thing she noticed was an arrangement of wild-flowers, exploding with orange mums, red daisies, yellow sunflowers, purple berries, blue eucalyptus, and more textures and vibrant autumn colors that she could name or count. The whole car was flooded with their delectable fragrance. The flowers sat securely in a vase set into the central table; her flowers would be the Hummer's crowning glory throughout their evening festivities. All for her. Beaming, Candy sprung into Antonio's arms. "I love them, thank you! They're absolutely perfect, Antonio."

"So this is how I win Candy's heart? I see."

"I've been trying to solve that mystery for over ten years, man. Forget it." John climbed in and slid onto the seat across from them. He reached over and patted her knee, as if comforting a small child, "All better, now?"

She openly admired her flowers, kicking off her heels on the fluffy carpet. "Yes."

"Brat," John murmured.

She was about to retort, but then she saw her rose tucked into his front pocket. She forgot it inside, but he went back for it. *Oh no. And he just watched me rave over Antonio's flowers—I'm such a jerk.* But when she found John's eyes, they were smiling. He plucked the rose from his tuxedo and handed it to her.

Erica popped her head in. "Whoa, those are gorgeous," she grunted, struggling into the cabin in her snug, ankle-length dress. John stepped out to help her inside, and ended up supporting most of her weight while she snaked in sideways and he tried to keep his hands away from delicate areas. She finally achieved a seat, flushed with the effort. "Let's get out of here fast, before I rip something."

"Dancing is next, I can't wait." Candy ignored Erica's groan and clapped her hands, her mood considerably brightened. She loved to dance and all the bad stuff was over.

chapter thirty-nine

"*Blech*, that's nasty." Lindsay gagged, but held the syrupy beverage down. "What's sloe gin, anyway? It tastes like cough medicine."

"It's good for you, insurance for a healthy party tonight." Amanda took another sip from the stainless steel flask and tried to hand it back. Lindsay shook her head and made a puking motion, so she screwed the top back on and stashed the booze in her sequined handbag.

"Where's Jessica? Wasn't this her idea?"

Amanda held a finger up to her lips, listening for noises outside in the main washroom, then unhooked the latch and stepped out cautiously. "We already came in here before I got you. It would be too suspicious for us all to huddle in a bathroom stall at once." She walked past each stall, checking under their doors, before calling to Lindsay in a normal voice, "Alright, it's still clear."

Lindsay ran over to the mirror and spun around to check her figure in her beaded dress once again. "Whoo-hoo, that stuff does hit the spot pretty fast, huh?"

"Told ya."

The girls brought out their compacts and lipsticks to perfect their faces.

"So, are you gonna make your move on Antonio tonight, or what?"

"Amanda, he's here with Candy Vale."

"Antonio told me himself that they're only friends, Lindsay. I told you she's a lesbian. I don't know why you can't see this is just a cover-up."

"I don't know…John Robinson is actually much cuter."

"John Robinson is mine," Amanda said flatly. Lindsay's eyes snapped to hers in the mirror, defiant, but she remained mute. Amanda held the gaze until Lindsay dropped it and started digging around in her purse for something.

She brought out a new gloss, which she studiously applied, before finally giving in. "Well, when did you talk to Antonio?"

"Just now, right before I found you to come in here. God, you should have seen how gaga he was over you in that dress." Amanda gave Lindsay's hindquarters a lascivious look; she knew how proud her she was of her tight derriere.

"Really? What else did he—"

The bathroom exploded into a chorus of gabbing underclassmen. They saw the contemptuous looks of the two sophomore girls and scampered into stalls. Amanda smiled at Lindsay's reflection and they recommenced primping, letting an uncomfortable silence settle in the room and grunting with derision at the delicate tinkling sound the younger girls were unable to stifle. They pressed together to block access to the sink as the freshman rushed out of the bathroom one by one.

"Look, Lindsay. Antonio is totally into you, trust me."

"He actually said that?"

"Come on, it's obvious." Amanda scrutinized her friend's reaction. Full of giddy expectation, just as she hoped. Every girl at Jackson wanted to be the Italian Stallion's object of desire, no matter if she desired *him* or not. Such novelty was a dream for the bovine masses. "We have to get him to my house tonight, at all costs. My parents have left the whole place to us—when else are we going to have this kind of freedom?"

"My mom said Tristan's in charge, though. That's the only reason she thinks it's okay for me to spend the night at your place, with your mom gone."

"Yeah, Tristan's in charge," Amanda snorted, "of making sure we don't bother him in the master bedroom."

"What?"

"Are you kidding? All he cares about is getting off. Well, that and football. Why do you think he invited Meg Shannon to the dance? At least he won't have to worry about her fighting him off, like Ashley Davis did."

"What do you mean?"

"Come on, why do you think Ashley broke up with him?"

"I just always figured *he* dumped *her*," Lindsay shrugged. "Tristan's the hottest guy in school, why would she break up with him?"

"Let's just say I wouldn't want to be in a parked car, alone in an empty field, with my brother."

"Are you saying, he actually…"

"I'm not going to say the word, Lindsay. He *is* my brother, read between the lines."

Lindsay looked at her, aghast.

"I mean, I don't know if there was actually penetration—"

"Penetration? Gross, Amanda."

Lindsay plugged her ears and clamped her eyes shut.

"Oh, don't like that word?" Amanda pinched her friend on the belly, and then on the rump, when she twisted away laughing. "I won't say 'penetration' again, don't worry your delicate little ears."

More girls trouped into the lavatory en masse and Amanda declared it was time to rejoin the party. Out on the main gymnasium floor, a live band was playing a version of The Beatles's "Twist and Shout," the emcee encouraging more students to get out on the dance floor and "Shake it up, baby!" Friends and dates were grabbing hands and either running onto the dance floor or running off of it, most of them shouting in riotous delirium within the fractured, spinning light of the crystal ball overhead.

"But, yes," Amanda hollered into Lindsay's ear over the cacophony. "He actually said he likes you."

"Really?"

"Would I lie to you?"

"Yes," Lindsay laughed.

Amanda's face lost all traces of humor, and she stepped back to reproach Lindsay, showing her wounds. "That's not funny. That really hurts my feelings."

"I'm sorry." Lindsay tried to take her hand, but Amanda yanked it back.

"You know you're not just my cousin, you're my best friend, too. I would never lie to you, never."

"Oh, Amanda. Come on, I was just teasing."

"No, I know how you and Jessica like to joke around, tossing insults back and forth, but I'm not into that. Sometimes I think you two are really serious when you say mean stuff to each other. But, I don't insult my friends." Amanda turned to walk away, but she let Lindsay pull her back that time.

"Look, I really am sorry. I trust you." Lindsay moved her face around in front of Amanda's when she looked away. "Come on. Okay?"

"Okay," Amanda accepted her friend's hug. *Lindsay is so easy.*

"Let's just forget about it, and have fun." The whine in her cousin's voice was palpable. Begging. "We'll make this night one we won't forget. I promise, Amanda."

Amanda finally relented, allowing a shy smile to spread across her features. The two grasped hands and bounded towards the dance floor, fully primped and buzzing with both sloe gin and the promise of thrills awaiting.

"We'll burn this night to the ground."

"What?" Lindsay turned around in question, but Amanda shook her ahead. *Nothin'.*

They wove through gyrating bodies to find a good spot. Amanda squeezed Lindsay's arm when she located her prize. "Lookie there," she nodded across the room where Antonio was dancing in a crowd of other Bobcatts. Candy Vale was there, too, dancing close to John Robinson. *How predictable.*

"Here comes the She-Devil," John shouted to Candy, motioning towards Amanda Jameson's approaching form in the undulating light.

"Huh?"

"Nothin'," he shook his head and urged her farther into a knot of people, closer to Antonio and Erica. They were doubled over in merriment and grabbing their aching sides from attempting to keep up with the twisting dance the emcee was demonstrating onstage. The song was coming to a close, with a distinctly different beat fading in. It was the old house classic, "Jump Around."

"Who is this guy?" Candy hollered to John over the whistling tempo and thudding base. "First, 'The Electric Slide,' then 'Twist and Shout,' and now this?"

"Weird mix, but good for a dance party."

"What's he gonna play next, the 'Chicken Dance'?" Erica cheered, exultant with the fun despite herself.

As the song neared its chorus, Erica sliced a hand across her throat towards her date, communicating, "no way," and John seized Candy by the waist instead. He hoisted her from behind, into the air with the *Jump! Jump!* chant of the song. Several nearby able-bodied fellows followed his cue to assist the closest fun-loving girl, whether date, friend or acquaintance. The bulk of the less hardy crowd sang along, clapping and hooting. Candy felt like she was flying, as small as she was in relation to John's normally larger frame, beefed up from all his recent football training. He propelled her up higher, with the momentum of her own jump, and each time she left his grip for a split second and had spectacular view of a joyous crowd, roaring approval. She was laughing so hard that she could hardly breathe, and before long she was limp in John's arms, trying in vain to express, "stop, stop," even though stopping was the last thing in the world she wanted to do.

John gaped at her legs; her dress had been rucked up so far the tops of her thigh-highs were visible. He tugged her hemline down, "My god, I'm sorry…"

"It's okay," she said and smothered him in a hug. She felt sweat trickling off of his hair onto her neck, and pulled back making a face. "Am I that heavy?"

"Are you crazy? You're light as a feather." He clapped a hand on his chest in mock surprise. "Oh that's right—Fair Feather."

"You're so strong." She squeezed one of his biceps in jest, but when he flexed with a grin, she pulled her hand back like she'd touched a hot stove. She hadn't realized how muscular his arms had gotten, and it made her body notice his body. Too much. "Well, anyway. You made me feel weightless."

He watched her, bemused, and she looked away. She felt him chuckle next to her and she cast around for Erica or Antonio, something to help her feel normal again.

"Something's happening," John murmured.

"What do you mean?"

When she stared at him, he smiled and nodded towards the stage.

He was right, the music was dying down. She felt her hair self-consciously, not used to maintaining gel and hairspray through physical exertion, and John tucked an errant strand behind her ear. "Thanks."

"Anything for you, Candy-cane." He wiped a bead of sweat from her forehead, then he took her hand and held it between them. They watched the stage together.

"Alright, alright everybody. We have more music from DJ Doubletake in the funnel, kids. But we have a few announcements first, y'all." Principal Warren had taken the stage and was brandishing both hands towards his audience in a dampening gesture. "First of all, we need the Homecoming Court to assemble by the equipment lockers for formal photographs."

Candy felt like she had been slapped. She missed the rest of their headmaster's speech—muted as it was in her buzzing skull—but she tried to appear calm. When was all this "Court" crap going to end? They already announced Queen Ashley and King Tristan like it was their wedding day. Mr. Davis had stopped patrolling and checking the punch for signs of spiking for a few minutes to admire his beautiful princess of a daughter while she performed the first dance. Ashley and Tristan simply shifted weight from one foot to the other, spinning in slow circles. "That's not dancing," Candy had smirked, remembering how the real thing felt in Sam's hands.

And again, more accolades. On and on. Why can't this night belong to everyone, instead of the select few? The damn beautiful people. She felt one of the beautiful people monitoring her from the corner of his eye. "Well, I'll just hang out with Erica. Come find us when you're done with the pictures. Make sure you smile, I want one of those." At least her friend had come to stand with her, in her hour of need.

"Er…" Erica fumbled, imploring John with her eyes. "They asked that the dates be present for photos, as well."

John gestured for Erica to head to the assigned location. As Erica squeezed her shoulder in passing and John pressed Candy's fingers harder, his face full of burdened concern, Candy had to restrain herself from whacking them both.

"You know what? It's really hot in here." Candy freed herself from John's grip and fanned her neck with both hands. "I just feel like getting outside for a minute, I need some fresh air."

"Look Candy, if you don't want me to—"

"I'm fine, really. I just need to cool off."

John held her gaze with agonizing sympathy, before finally releasing her, "Okay, I'll find you in a few minutes."

"Okay."

"This shouldn't take long."

"I'm fine," Candy insisted, punctuating her lie with a kiss on his cheek.

She kept her pace steady and her stride stately until she reached the perpendicular hallway leading outside and out of view. Then she stomped her high-heels in a rage and let out her best un-ladylike roar, before ripping the bra-stuffers out of her bust line and flinging them against the wall. She would have lobbed her princess slippers across the parking lot as she stalked away from the gymnasium, but she had neglected to pack flip-flops into her sparkling little bitch-bag.

chapter forty

The Pumpkin Festival was a sister celebration to Andrew Jackson High's Homecoming Week, and in Candy's opinion, the former was far superior to the latter in almost every way. For one thing, it was a larger event, bringing in folks from neighboring counties and a good share of tourists as well. At first it was just a county fair to judge produce and livestock, but Pumpkin Fest had blossomed over the years into a full carnival. Natural accompaniments to the judging were pony rides and a petting zoo for the little ones and seasonal delicacies for everyone. Of course, one could find anything and everything pumpkin—pumpkin tarts and pies, pumpkin breads and jams, pumpkin ice cream and smoothies, and lately, stranger options from serious entrepreneurs, like pumpkin ravioli and pumpkin pasta sauce. The aroma of Candy's favorite dish (pumpkin funnel cake), wafting across neighboring Fairbrother Field, lifted her spirits considerably as she wove through the school parking lot.

She let herself be swallowed by the crowds, milling around flashing, whirling, zooming carny rides. A serendipitous meeting at the edge of the field knocked off the remaining crumbs of the chip on her shoulder; her cousin Sean and his jolly hound dog were closing up the pony trailers for the day. The dog might have been even happier to see Candy than she was to see him, judging by the pouncing and rapturous licking she received, so she gave him a good rub-down in gratitude.

Moving into the thick of the carnival, she lingered by craft tables and artists' tents that she had never seen at Pumpkin Fest before. She lamented her decision to shun that afternoon's events in her effort to stay clear of the Homecoming Parade. Most of the best stuff was probably already bought out.

"Candy, hey. Out here in all your finery?" She turned to see Erica's dad hailing her from across his folding table of dulcimers.

"Hi, Mr. Norman." Walking over closer, she was glad to see that he had apparently already made a killing; there were very few instruments left to sell.

"Where's Erica?"

"Oh, they're doing the professional pictures—you know, for the Homecoming Court thing."

Mr. Norman winced. "She was real nervous about being up to par. After John was elected during half-time on Friday and all. She doing okay?"

"Nervous?" Candy scoffed, feeling guilty about her resentfulness; the image of her homely friend, holding the bouquet of roses outside John's house, flashed through her mind. "She shouldn't be. She looked absolutely gorgeous tonight, and no one I saw at that dance could have topped her."

"Well, that's real nice of you to say. I'm glad she could go with good friends this year. And if anyone deserved to represent your class more than John, I don't know who it is."

"Really?" Candy had missed most of the games so far.

"Shit, that boy rushes his ass off on the field, and the season ain't half over." Mr. Norman's assistant burst into the conversation, bringing four more dulcimers from their storage trailer to lay out for display. Maybe they hadn't sold as many as Candy thought.

"Language please, Nick. There's a lady present."

"Well, I guess so." Nick pretended to see Candy for the first time, his grin lecherous as he surveyed her body. "Candy, I didn't know you was even a girl."

"Nice to see you, too, Nick. Don't worry, Mr. Norman. Erica's having fun."

"I'm glad, honey. Thanks." His countenance was lit with pride. He cut off any further remarks from his subordinate by barking instructions, as Candy sidled away.

She moseyed through the stalls and tents, trying to decide whether or not to indulge in some fried fair food. It would be greasy and plentiful, thereby messy and wonderful in equal measure. Just when she made up her mind that she didn't care about her make-up anymore, and supposed that even velvet dresses could be dry-cleaned, she rounded a food cart at the end of one aisle and her heart jumped into her throat. Across a small clearing, there was a flare of bright blue fire spitting around a glowing orb of orange glass, lighting up the faces of onlookers. Rachel usually arranged such demos to draw interest and encourage sales during the most lucrative art fairs, a status which Pumpkin Fest had finally obtained. But the person performing the demo, gripping the glass tube on either side of the molten bubble, spinning and turning it to heat it and bend it just right, was not Rachel.

The glass artist's back was to her, with his boots spread wide and his knees soft in raggedy blue jeans. His tank top was damp with hours of grueling, sweaty work at the torch. A mirror had been hung at an angle over his workbench, to give his audience a better view of the flame-working process. Candy could see his forehead, smoothed in concentration. Dark sunglasses shaded his eyes from the glare and his hair was pulled out of his face, under a bandana. But there was no mistaking Sam's jaw line.

She dodged back behind the food cart and rooted for her compact in the bitch-bag, smiling at the irony. How handy a mirror was, all of a sudden. Checking her eyes and hair, she dabbed some powder on her nose and—looking around to make sure no one was watching—she reapplied her lipstick in two swipes. Heart pounding, she sauntered around the corner towards Rachel's tent and quietly joined Sam's audience.

She watched him work for about fifteen minutes (which felt like fifteen hours), before she saw Sam glance around as he finished a bead. He spotted her and smiled to himself. Her pulse raced. She hoped beyond hope that she saw kindness there, instead of satisfaction. He checked his watch, then called into the tent, "Last one, Caleb."

Overjoyed, Candy's mind raced with what she would say to him—if he wanted to talk to her. She watched his triceps flex with the turning motion of his wrists; the howling wolf tattoo that raced down from his right shoulder danced on the surface of his skin. She tried to calm her nerves by mesmerizing herself with the stylized black swirls of fur, claws and teeth encircling Sam's upper-arm.

Be cool. Be calm. Be confident. She flinched. *If he still wants you, don't ever let him go.*

Then he was slapping Caleb on the shoulder as he took his turn at the torch, grabbing the rag hanging from his belt to wipe the sweat off of his face. He rubbed the stubble along his chin, looking around for Candy. She stepped away from the crowd to wave at him timidly. To her immense relief, Sam's face broke into a grin and he spread his arms wide. "Hey," he drawled, obviously tired.

She skipped around the demo audience and leapt into his arms, certainly less cool than she had counseled herself to be. But definitely happy. "It's so good to see you, Sam." She buried her face against him before she started to cry.

"I probably stink," he said, without attempting to pull away. His arms tightened around her.

"I like it." Sam's chest rumbled under her ear in a quiet laugh. "I missed it," she said, finally pulling back from him enough to look into his face. "I'm sorry, Sam."

He watched her for a few thundering heartbeats and seemed about to speak. Candy held her breath.

"That was a fantastic performance, son." A bustling man in a baseball cap and "Members Only" jacket burst forth. The man clapped Sam on the shoulder, somehow oblivious to the intimate reunion he was interrupting.

"Thank you, sir." Sam drew back from her and the man grabbed his hand for a congratulatory shake. He dug around in a fanny pack and slipped Sam a few folded bills.

"Wonderful, you made it." Rachel swept in from the shadows at the rear of her tent, taking control of the uncouth tourist with grace. She angled him toward her more expensive display cases. "Now that you've seen the basics of glass art in action, let me show you something to knock your socks off…"

Candy and Sam exchanged looks of relief and made haste to exit the public arena through a backdoor flap, into the alleyway. In the muffled quiet behind the carnival tents and stalls, they looked at each other anew, completely alone. And suddenly bashful.

Candy flapped a hand toward the tent. "You're really getting good at the torch, I'm impressed."

"Thanks."

"That sure was fast. I mean, you're a real apprentice now already, huh?"

Sam thumbed his nose and shrugged. "I work at it a lot."

"So…I should just call you Sam, right? I'm not trying to be snarky or anything." Candy begged herself to stop rambling.

"Yeah." He let out his breath in a whistle. "Yeah, call me Sam."

"Well…I'm glad we got that make-up bit over with." Candy tried to laugh, but it sounded like a sob. "Let's move on, right?"

"Please." Sam reached for her hand and pulled her close. He leaned over to press his forehead against hers, willing her to just *be* for a few moments, and she allowed herself to savor it. A soft, lingering kiss left the flavor of lipstick on both of their lips, and he pulled back, his eyes alight with humor. "So, I guess you went to the dance after all?"

"Yeah."

"Have a hot date?" he teased.

"We just went as friends. The foreign exchange student, Antonio—"

"Antonio di Brigo, I know."

"Oh. You heard about that, huh?"

"Small town, everybody's heard about that." He stepped back a few paces to sit down on an upright barrel stacked beside Rachel's storage trailer. He pulled out a cigarette and the butane flame lit up his face. He squinted against the smoke. "Be hearing about that dress for a while, too, I bet."

Candy spun around and kicked one high-heel up behind her, sticking out her tushie and putting her fingers to her lips in a shocked Betty Boop rendition. "You likey?"

"Smokin'." He slipped his palm around the top of her thigh and urged her closer. "But I think you're beautiful in whatever you wear." She tittered off-balance and braced herself against his shoulders. "Or don't wear."

Her country rose, which she had threaded into her purse chain, bumped into Sam's cheek. He looked down at it and touched the limp petals.

"Poor thing stood up pretty well to all the abuse." Candy felt guilty for slinging her purse around in frustration with the rose onboard, and she gently freed its delicate stem. When she looked up, Sam was watching her. "John gave it to me. What?"

"John."

"Don't get the wrong idea—me and John are just friends."

"Friends," repeated Sam, taking the rose from her and bringing it to his nose. He let the petals fall onto his face, brushing his lips against the velvety tickle. "Then how does he know that you're as soft as rose petals?"

A hot blush shot up her neck. "It's not like that. He just knows I've loved them since I was little. And red: my hair, my fiery temper."

"Fireworks come to mind before roses."

"I know I have a short fuse." She shrugged, still ashamed of her outburst at The Palace that day. And at Rachel's studio. *Might have been one or two more...*

"Fireworks are gorgeous." Sam reached up and pressed two fingers against her forehead, to smooth away her troubled brow. He looked at her with sincerity, then his teeth gleamed in a wide smile, "Just not when someone lets them off in your face."

"Okay ... okay, I get it." Candy threw one leg across his lap to straddle his hips.

Sam shook his head, resisting her sidelining technique. "Girls like you can get away with anything."

"Girls like me?"

"Beautiful girls."

Me? The beautiful people? No, that can't be what he means.

"Why are you always fighting me, Candy? I'm on your side."

"What side am I on?" She had never been sure.

"Mine." It was a question, an invitation. She watched his eyes, her heart pounding. That was all she wanted. The wind picked up, whistling through the tent flaps around them. A shutter ran through Sam, then through her.

"Gettin' pretty chilly."

Candy rubbed her palms over his shoulders in an attempt at warming them, but he sucked in with a hiss, "Your hands are freezing."

"Sorry, I guess I'm pretty cold, too. Darn girlie dress."

"Yeah, I was gonna say—it's pretty short." He leaned back to gaze at the top of her stockings, where he ran his thumb over a garter clipped to the hem. "Those are nice."

"Not slutty?"

"That's why they're nice." They both tried to laugh, but shivered instead. "I have Rachel's truck tonight." Sam hooked his finger around a dress strap and pulled her face closer to his. "Let's get out of here."

"I thought you'd never ask."

Sam said he had some quick clean-up to do, but not much, since Rachel's crew would be at it again in the morning. He gave her a quick kiss with the promise of more, then went to it. Candy was elated. She wandered back to the front of the exhibition tent like she was in a dream. She had never hoped the night would end so miraculously. Leaving with Sam. She could hardly contain her happiness.

I don't know how I lost him, but I am never going to make that mistake again. She sat on a packing crate in front of Rachel's tent, grinning ear to ear.

"There she is." She startled to hear Antonio's voice. Lindsay Yates and Amanda Jameson were huddled against each of his arms like parentheses. Candy cursed them privately, but smiled and waved them over, as if she too had been looking for her date.

"Hey, guys," she called, choking back her suspicion about who had been spreading the lame rumors about her all year.

"We're so over the 'Bunny Hop,'" Amanda said in disdain.

Lindsay, always the peppy cheerleader: "Whatcha doin' over here, Candy?"

"I was just…"

"Hi." Sam appeared from between two tents without warning, and Candy watched as Amanda's face froze into a black glower. Candy warmed from head to toe as Sam held out his bomber jacket for her to shrug into.

"Hello, again." Antonio stepped forward, stretching out his hand to Sam and offering Candy an expression full of understanding and acceptance.

"Sorry about last time, man."

"Last time?" Candy wondered.

Sam shook his head resolutely: forget it.

"So, Sam. I heard you're doing the glass thing now," Amanda said, faking magnanimity. Candy knew better and enjoyed the spectacle, watching Amanda make a big show of asking all about glass blowing. Candy sat on her crate, enveloped inside the smell of Sam in his cozy, wool-lined jacket. She felt more peaceful than she had in weeks.

Antonio sauntered away from the group and sat down next to her, perched on one side of the crate. "So this is the one, who gets the... distance looks," he whispered. "This is happy Candy?"

"Yeah, it is," she admitted.

"I am glad to see this."

"Thanks, Antonio." She twisted around to embrace him. "I'm sorry. I was supposed to be your date tonight."

"Not necessary, honey. I am liking you happy," he said. He squeezed her, then let her go and rose with his hands outstretched, striding over to the others. "Ladies, ladies—let us find another party."

"Looks like we found the best party in town." John's voice rang out behind her, and Candy's spine stiffened. Sam's head jerked towards John, his eyes steel.

Erica complained, "Candy, we've been looking all over for you."

"We thought you left without us," John's voice was light, but Candy didn't believe it. He was as tight as a bowstring ready to be loosed, if she knew him at all.

Erica plopped down next to her. "Do you think it would be rude for me to go home with my dad? I just saw him, and he said he brought me some sweats to change into, just in case. I think he could probably use an extra hand..."

Candy looked at her like she was crazy. "Of course. Are you kidding?"

"I mean, I don't want to insult anybody. But I am really ready to get out of this dress, you know?"

"Erica, it's okay, don't worry about it." Seeing her poor friend wrenching her trembling blue fingers with the decision, her heart almost exploded. "I totally agree, by the way."

"You do? Oh, thank you. I already mentioned it to John, and he said he wouldn't mind. He's so polite. He even offered me his jacket, but I think I just want to go home. Is that nerdy?"

Candy peeked around to see Antonio standing off to the side with one arm draped over John's shoulders, speaking reassuringly into his ear. John looked resigned, nodding agreement. She met Sam's eyes. He looked towards the sky; not thrilled, but willing to keep the peace. What run-in had she missed?

"No, go get into your sweats," Candy insisted, bringing her attention back to Erica. "Seriously."

"Are you sure? I don't want to desert you."

Candy buried her guilt; she was planning to do just that to Erica only moments before. "I'm sure."

"Thanks, Candy." Erica hugged her and offered air-kisses to the others, before exclaiming with delight, "Bye, everybody," and bolting for her father's tent. She rubbed her bare arms for warmth as she disappeared through the crowd.

I'm not half the friend she is. Candy watched her go. Erica had always been a good friend and just the person she claimed to be. No more, no less. Candy considered how rare that was and brought her attention back to the present with reluctance.

"Tyler said you guys hitchhike on the train all the time," Amanda was whining to Sam.

"Well, I wouldn't recommend it." Sam was holding up his hands, glaring at Tyler Finley. When had that guy shown up? "Look, we were just taking off."

Candy saw John snap to attention and she jumped up from her seat, realizing some smoothing was in order, tout de suite. "We were just going for a walk."

Sam's shoulders slumped.

"Well, we'll go with you guys," Amanda chirped. "We have things that need…less of an audience. Right, Ty?"

"You could say that," Tyler sniggered, clearing his throat and miming smoking a joint.

"Excellent, yes," Antonio agreed, probably having written "get high" on his American bucket list.

"You guys are coming back to Amanda's house after, right? Her parents are out of town," Lindsay chimed in. Candy and Sam met eyes reflexively. They hadn't discussed where they planned on heading, after their immediate decision to simply leave. The night was way too cold for The Palace.

"Well then, why don't we just smoke it there?" John asked.

Candy was surprised. *John's okay with smoking pot?*

"No way, you know my dad's the County Sheriff, right? Amanda *Jameson?*"

"Oh right."

"But we can walk down south of here where it's plenty deserted, then hop on the train back to my house," offered Amanda.

"We're not hopping on any trains."

§

John rolled his sleeves back down and turned his shirt collar up against the chill. He wondered again how he ended up walking south along the railroad tracks, in the cold, heading deeper into the canyons and farther away from a comfortable stretched limousine.. Far ahead, Amanda was wearing his tuxedo jacket, plucked off of his hooked finger as soon as they left Fairbrother Field. She was holding hands and skipping with Lindsay, in front of Antonio and that creep Tyler. John blamed the lengthening of their outing on him; after they had all passed the joint back and forth, plenty far enough away from the festival crowd, Tyler produced a flask of some kind of vile moonshine. The others were sharing it as they strolled along the river, but John had no desire to more fully pollute his brain. He wanted to regain some control. At least Candy and Sam stopped holding hands once John took position at the rear. They were bumping shoulders, apparently deep in conversation, Candy laying her head against his shoulder and gazing adoringly up into his face now and again.

John flexed his knuckles and rubbed his temples, tried to clear his head. He looked around at the countryside. It was as beautiful as Candy promised when she cajoled him into walking farther along the river. Yet, the cliffs were rising steadily higher, turning the sky into a line of unearthly blue. The sides of the cliffs squeezed against them like a vice inching closed. A harvest moon illuminated the rocky layers of sandstone and limestone, casting eerie, stark shadows. The coarse clumps of granite jutting out of the canyon walls formed bizarre faces and anthropomorphic figures that seemed to watch their passage. The gutter between the two mountain ridges was becoming so tight that John could feel cold spray from the river on the other side of the tracks, to his right, and the road to their left had become a single dirt lane. Surely, they would come to the junction, where the road climbed into the mountains and the train headed through a tunnel, where the river turned and hurtled down a waterfall. They'd be forced to turn back then. *How long since we've even seen a car pass?* It was almost ten o'clock. He groaned with irritation when he read at his cell phone's warning, *"Out Of Service Area."*

"You okay, John?" Candy called back to him.

"I think it's time to turn back." His voice was swallowed by the sudden blare of a train whistle, echoing out of the ravine ahead.

"What?"

"Hold on a minute…" He waved her over to shelter against the rock wall on the other side of the dirt road, as far away from the train tracks as possible. A headlight streamed around a stony corner, and John could see that the rest of their group was still walking along the tracks, heedless of the approaching train. "You guys, get out of the way," he yelled, but they couldn't have heard him. He sat down on an outcrop and leaned his back against the stone, aware that he'd just have to wait it out.

When he looked up, he saw his friends running alongside the train. *What?*

They were intent on matching its speed.

My god, what are they thinking?

John watched helplessly as Tyler leapt, making contact with an opened boxcar. He turned to haul a female form in a slinky dress up after him.

Lindsay!

John stepped into the road. "What are you doing?"

Candy raised her hands to John in question, then clapped them over her ears in pain; the train whistle sounded again, rebounding off of stone and water all around them. Metal screeched against metal. John jabbed his finger past her, pointing towards their foolish companions a few hundred yards down the tracks. She spun around in a daze and Sam shot an arm out to steady her.

John watched in horror, as Antonio sprang for the boxcar next. His foot slipped in the gravel, and he hung on with one hand for several seconds, before he lost his grip. He spun once or twice before something large and solid made impact—the next boxcar. His body was thrown backwards, and his legs crumpled under him as he fell to the earth.

"Shit!" John bolted down the dirt road, Candy and Sam racing ahead of him.

"Tyler…help me," Lindsay wailed. Her desperation streamed past John as the train sped past. He looked back to see that Tyler had jumped from the train and left Lindsay alone onboard, disappearing fast around the bend.

John sprinted back the way he had come, his hands cupped around his mouth, "Lindsay, don't jump off."

"Help me!"

"Stay on the train and keep your phone on—I'll come get you where you stop."

"I'm scared, John…" her reply was lost in the distance.

John picked up his speed.

"Lindsay?"

Nothing.

He could only hope that she understood, and that the next scheduled train stop wasn't too far away. It was all he could do for her just then. He threw up his hands and turned back, rushing towards where Antonio had fallen, the bile rising in his throat from fear of what awaited him. His mind went blank as he ran—horror blocked the vivid image of Antonio crumpling to the ground, like a marionette with its strings snipped. He slowed to a jog as he drew nearer, panting and gripping his side, taking in the details. Tyler was pacing back and forth chewing his nails and Amanda stood frozen with her hands over her mouth. But, Antonio was moving—not dead, thank god—and seemed relatively quiet. Sam was on the ground with one arm under him for support, cradling his head. Candy was holding one of Antonio's hands to her chest. John saw that he gripped a black satin high-heel in his other hand, and realized that he must have been holding Lindsay's shoes for her as she ran.

"Let me take that, man." John knelt down to pull the shoe out of his grip, and Antonio groaned in agony. His hand, his arm, all the way up the right side of his torso seemed to be unable to move, and John sickened as he noticed the odd angle of his arm to his body. He could hardly discern a shoulder. The shoe dropped with a thud.

As if the movement had loosened something inside, Antonio lurched forward to grasp at Candy's neck. John could see angry fingernail gouges on her pale skin. Sam grabbed Antonio's hand to keep him from choking Candy, and Antonio howled.

"Sorry, buddy." Sam's fingers encircled his wrist instead, and he held it to his own chest. "I think your hand is broken."

Candy was mumbling incoherent prayers and snuffling, tears and mascara streaming down both cheeks. She looked at John. "I think he's trying to tell me something."

"Candy, I'll take him—" John began, but Antonio heaved towards her and produced an explosive cough, sending splatters of blood against her chest. Red against white. He babbled something in Italian—*pericolo?*—struggling to breathe, choking and sending up blood from his lungs in a torrent that stained his crisp, pleated tuxedo shirt. He fell back against Sam again, crying in pain.

"John." Sam barked, urgent. "Go get help. I've got this here."

"It's okay, honey. It's okay. It'll be okay," Candy prayed, cupping Antonio's cheek with her hand and stroking his face.

Antonio trembled against Sam's arm. His body jerked with uncontrollable spasm, his whine animal.

Sam glared at John. "John. Run."

With one last look into Antonio's large, terrified eyes that saw nothing and everything at once, John took off up the tracks, heading for civilization as fast as his legs would allow. He yanked his cell phone out of his pocket. No reception.

"Come on come on come on."

Antonio's cries became a scream of torment. John closed his eyes, pounding the dirt with every ounce of strength he had.

"One bar, just one bar. Come on."

The scream choked and coughed, searching for a gasp of breath. A long, low moan bellowed from deep inside his pain.

John pushed harder, his muscles seizing and his lungs burning. "Hold on, man. Just hold on—"

POP!

He nearly tripped over his feet as the gunshot sounded behind him and the canyon went silent.

chapter forty-one

Mieke twirled her spoon in her chamomile tea, well past the point that the honey was dissolved. She picked up a lemon wedge. It had already been juiced more than once, so she dropped it on the saucer again. She traced the edge of her spoon against the teacup, heard the tinkling shake of her nerves in the motion, and plunked it down. Silver clanked against china. The damn thing could chip for all she cared.

"Are you absolutely certain the boy hasn't been seen or heard from in over twenty-four hours?" a young deputy asked, clipping his pen back into his shirt pocket and flipping his note pad closed before she answered.

"I haven't seen Antonio since Saturday night and it's Monday morning. Where is the confusion here?" Mieke slapped her hand down on the glass table with a satisfactory sting. "Why is your office not more concerned about a missing person?"

"Honey…" Ian tried to placate his wife, but fell silent at her withering look.

"Mrs. Walsh, there was a lot going on that night. The kids had a lot of free reign, and kids can be kids."

"Well, Sheriff Jameson," replied Mieke, "that's interesting that Antonio is now just a 'kid' to you, after your wife had such a fit about his adult status a few months ago." The two law enforcement officers shifted in their seats. Mieke picked up her spoon and stirred her tea some more.

The sheriff cleared his throat. "All I'm asking is, are you sure that he knew he was supposed to be home by Saturday night? You've told us that he had the use of the limousine for the evening, and you would've been asleep when he got home. You said you liked to give him his privacy—"

"The driver said he dropped Antonio home before eleven o'clock."

Ian laid his hand on her shoulder. "No, hon. The driver said he picked up four kids and he dropped off four kids. He didn't study their faces."

She shrugged out from underneath his touch. "But who would he have dropped off here, if not Antonio?"

"Well, Mrs. Walsh," the half-grown deputy chuckled, his Adam's apple bobbing in his throat. "Teenagers have been known to pull a fast one, from time to time. How well do you really know this kid—guy?"

"Very well. Antonio would never have been dishonest with me." Mieke almost slapped the doubtful look off of his pimpled face, wondering how far past his teen years the deputy was himself.

"Is there another place that he would have gone, to keep the party going?" Mike asked.

"And miss school this morning?"

"Has he?" Mike checked his watch. "School hasn't even started yet; it's only 6:30 a.m."

"Oh, well I am so sorry to have gotten you out of bed early," Mieke spat, uncrossing and re-crossing her legs. "Shouldn't you be more worried about a crime being reported, than getting enough beauty sleep?"

"Believe me, Mrs. Walsh—"

"Mieke!"

"Mieke, I was already at the office at dawn, just like I am every morning that I'm on duty. And I am always concerned about crime in my own home town." Mike reached to grab her hand. She wanted to snatch it away, but that was no way to get help for Antonio. She let Mike squeeze her fingers and forced her face to soften. "But I can't accept a crime report, until I am positive that a crime has been committed. Wouldn't you rather find Antonio first and talk to him, before embarrassing the boy with a lot of dramatics?" Mieke noted the tone in his voice: patronizing with a hint of fear. Hysterical women do that to men. She watched his mouth move, devising a way make him listen. "Did he have a girlfriend? Did he have a place that he liked to go for privacy? You mentioned that you liked to give him privacy. Was he a private person?"

"Well," Ian ventured, "remember, you did find that…uh…"

Mieke exhaled loudly in irritation.

"What did you find?" asked the deputy, like it was so much town gossip.

"When she was cleaning the guesthouse, she found a—"

"I found an opened condom wrapper under the bed in the guesthouse, after he had moved into the main house with us." She heard her voice going shrill again, and tried to steady her tone. "It could have been Aaron's."

"Don't bring Aaron into this, Mieke," Ian warned her under his breath, asserting himself between her and his family—his *real* family never seemed to include her, even though they were married.

The young officer perked up. "Aaron's in town?"

"Yeah," said Ian. "But he went camping for a few days."

"Tell him I said hey when he gets back, I'd love to see him."

"Sure will—"

"Excuse me," snapped Mieke with a look to kill.

Her husband blanched and the deputy blushed.

Mike sighed. "Did you question him about it, the condom? Did you ever see a female visitor, or a male visitor for that matter?" He spread his palms out for patience at the communal groan from the menfolk, "I'm just covering all the bases. Someone who he might have gone to see after the dance."

Mieke flicked her hands up. "I don't know. Who a person is intimate with is his or her own business. I didn't 'question' him."

The deputy and Ian exchanged knowing looks and Mike clapped his hat on his head. The message was clear: interview over.

"Let's just wait and see," Mike said, rising from the kitchen table. Ian stood to escort the officers to the front door. "Let me know if you remember anything else."

Mieke sat clicking her fingernails against the glass table, struggling with her next move. She knew in her bones that Antonio was not missing, felt it in her blood. Something had happened. Those country bumpkins would scoff at the idea of women's intuition, and Mieke had gone all her life thinking she had no nurturing capacity, always marveling at the elusive female instinct. Since Antonio had come into her life she had felt it herself, though, and she knew it was real. She was a mama bear and proud of it. She made her decision.

She sprung out of her chair, hurried through the garage door and out onto the walkway along the side of the house. The deputy was already in the cruiser and Mike was waving good-bye to Ian as he went back inside.

"Mike," Mieke called, waving him over. "I did remember something else."

He glanced at Ian's back and sauntered over, a smile playing on his lips. "What's that?"

"I know something has happened to Antonio." She lowered her voice, stepping close enough to whisper in his ear. "You find out what happened, or your little wife will find out what happened in that janitor's closet."

chapter forty-two

Aaron Walsh rolled over in his down-filled sleeping bag and stretched the length of his tent. The tips of his fingers brushed against the zipper head, locked tight against the dissolving night. He had awoken hours earlier, to the sound of prowling coywolves, the notorious hybrid between the Eastern Wolf and coyotes. He was prepared to meet any type of animal common to Shirley County, be it deer, hawk or bear, but the strange yip-howl of the coywolves spooked him. That weird call—a bizarre blend of a childlike cry and the howl of a wolf—was apt to cause anxiety in humans, especially those alone in the dark woods. A fat harvest moon, round and lazy, had hung low in the sky and Aaron lie awake most of the night, his imagination running wild.

The smell of the morning approaching, mist settling into dew as the air stilled for dawn, was more welcome than cinnamon buns in the oven. The forest around him grew silent as the nightwalkers made for their dens, and Aaron had to say a little prayer of thanks. "Hello, daybreak."

Right on time, an American Robin broke into her, "Cheer up, cheer up, cheerily," whistle not a hundred yards away, and Aaron decided to quit his tent for an early start.

He unzipped the door flaps and ducked out into the fresh morning air, then reached back inside for his coat, shocked at the drop in temperature. Feeling the yawn in his abdomen, he considered breakfast, but since the sun wasn't up yet, it would be a hassle in the dark. Instead, he sat down on the blanket of fallen pine leaves outside his front door, tugged on his boots, and decided to sit out the sunrise with a better vantage point closer to the river. He inspected his jeep as he passed for any signs of bear ran-sacking, but seeing nothing amiss, he ambled toward the rim of the bluff.

The stroll was easy through towering pine trees, their high plumes of needles overhead floating over the forest floor like thunderheads. He could barely see the stars, much less the blossoming horizon to the east, but he knew the giant trees would stand aside for maples, dogwoods and holly bushes along the edge of the cliffs. The heavens would open up for a gorgeous sunrise over the southern canyon. He heard the rapid, stuttering trill and then low, buzzing tones of a warbler in the distance, announcing the dawn. Aaron picked up his pace. Near the edge of the forest, he slowed down to navigate a thicket of mountain laurel and rhododendron. He heard more birdsongs announcing survival of the night and warning enemies of nests still protected, and Aaron worried he might miss the sunrise.

But the canopy above cleared abruptly, and he was kissed by the fresh air of the open ravine, with an earthy smell of fast moving water churning up the riverbed below. He could just discern a delicate lavender wash seeping across the sky into the western blackness, the stars beginning to wink out with the advance of light. Aaron collapsed to the ground, leaned back in relief and dangled his boots over the side of the bluff, his palms damp on the cool, crusty granite. He thought about the healing power of a new day—of every new day—and admitted that he was starting to accept his friend Henri's death.

"Bye, little buddy."

The burst of sunfire was spectacular, perfect for Henri's requiem. Bright pinks and oranges flared and rippled amongst feathers of clouds. Aaron's face warmed as the sun rose and the pageant faded and the sky gradually fused back together in a cool, peaceful blue. It was morning, fair and full of promise.

He rose to depart, dusting his hands on his wool pajama pants. With one last look over the side of the bluff into the river, a strange motion caught his eye. He peered down into the canyon. Thankful now for the chill that caused him to don his hunting coat; he unclipped his binoculars from their utility hook and focused in on the object below.

"What the…"

There was a large mass of some sort of waterlogged fabric or plastic caught on roots or rocks at the river's edge; the bundle had ebbed over into a nook and was bobbing there, apparently too heavy or too well entangled to be dislodged by the current. It was floating in and out of his line of sight.

"Well, darn."

He'd to have to loosen it himself, or it would just sit there and rot in the water.

"Probably a sack of garbage," he muttered, resigning himself to one more wilderness errand before returning to civilization. "Dang tourist campers."

He whistled his own tune in honor of the songbirds as he wound down the steep mountainside to the water, knowing his bustling human presence would scare off anymore singing from wildlife. He didn't care. He was feeling downright sunny; his heart was lighter than it had felt in weeks. Healed, or on his way. Drawing nearer to where he figured the garbage was wedged, he glanced around to get his bearings.

"Now, where'd you go?"

With a shock, he saw a wolf struggling with the bundle, attempting to pull it onto land. One of his brothers offered aid, but the first turned and snapped. A skirmish ensued, while a third opportunist lunged at the prize.

"What is that?" Aaron crouched down beside a scrubby bush and pulled his binoculars up to his eyes again. Closer now, and with the light strengthening, he could see a bare human foot.

The wolves had torn the shoe off tugging the human body to shore and were fighting over the shoe. Aaron leapt from his hiding place. He fumbled his handgun out of his coat pocket—not sure what to do, but he had to do something before the wolves remembered the body and dropped that shoe—and fired several shots into the air. His ears rang as he sprinted to the water. The wolves scattered, sprinting up the shoreline and disappearing into the brush.

"Get outta here!" he shouted after them.

Nearing the body, whose head and arms were still partially submerged, Aaron's mind raced. He needed to retrieve this person and defend his body from the elements, as a respect befitting any human being. Yet, as he approached the bundle, he winced at the odor of rot and steeled himself for death. He had no idea how the person died, and he wasn't sure he wanted to know.

"What the heck am I gonna do with a dead body?" He edged closer so he might see the corpse's face, still bobbing in the water. "Be damned if I know what to do with a——." Aaron let out an anguished wail. He jammed his knuckles into his mouth. He looked around, desperate for help, tears springing to his eyes.

The last thing he was prepared for was recognizing the face.

His eye caught the blackened silhouette of a bird circling high in the sky above. *Is that an eagle or a vulture?* He patted his jacket pockets, frantic. *No cell phone service out here.* He mopped at his brow. *Think, Aaron.*

He forced himself to breathe, slow and steady.

"The CB."

There was a radio in his jeep. If he could get to it, he could get the sheriff. But what if the wolves came back while he was gone? The vultures? How fast could he get to the jeep and back? He looked at Antonio's bloated face. Gruesome as it was, he was still the sweet young kid Aaron had done his best to ignore, shunning him while he and Dad bonded.

"Sweet Jesus."

Soft brown curls wafted around the baby face, and his head nodded in the undulating current of the little inlet. Aaron tasted blood on his lip and whispered an apology to the dead boy's foot, his throat aching. He turned away with tightness in his chest. *I'll have to leave him. All alone.*

Aaron prayed that he would find the body intact when he came back with help. He shot three more warning shots into the air, and raced back to his campsite.

chapter forty-three

"Inhibited olfactory sensation is one of my most fortunate shortcomings on a day like today." Sometimes, Zenée Abney really didn't know how she would do her job, if not for that little genetic quirk.

As a medical examiner, she was generally used to foul smells, but even *she* winced as she unzipped the bag containing the late Antonio di Brigo. There were several deputies and the Shirley County Sheriff waiting in the hospital lobby upstairs, conjecturing and gossiping, but she insisted that her examination be performed without observers. Her pretext was fear of further contamination of evidence, but truthfully, she couldn't stand men in her personal space, hovering over her and breathing audibly, when she needed to concentrate. As if to compensate for a deviated nasal septum, broken at birth, the gods had gifted Zenée with an extremely sensitive set of ears.

She scrutinized the form for several minutes, circumnavigating the examination table, taking in the entire body before focusing on any one apparent injury.

"Well, this one's a doozie," she murmured, having already detected four plausible trauma sites. She had seen violently maimed corpses before, but not many since the transfer from her residency in New York to the quiet mountain town of Tenakho Falls. There was the odd accident-befallen camper, and more than a proportionate share seemed to issue from Shirley County. This new body was a special case—probably a murder victim—and she couldn't help but feel a twinge of excitement.

She began with the least serious damage first. Zenée snapped her latex gloves at the wrist and switched on her digital recorder.

"Multiple phalangeal fractures in the right hand…" She lifted the hand and pressed into the flesh, feeling along each joint. "On the index: fracture of the distal and middle phalanges, and…also the inter-phalangeal joint. Distal phalanx fractured on the middle finger and fourth finger."

She turned the hand over, examining bruises. "Metacarpals have been crushed by a flat, heavy object, with considerable force. Maybe stepped on. Contusions indicate a pre-mortem injury." She placed the hand back on the table, palm up.

"Pruning of the hands and feet, as well as bloating…" she picked a wet leaf from between the waterlogged fingers of the other hand, "and debris from the river. I estimate the body has been fully or partially submerged in water for approximately two days."

She walked towards the victim's head.

"I would place time of death shortly before submersion."

Most of the blood had been washed away, but Zenée had been told that the clothing was profusely stained, blood still apparent even after a decent washing in the elements. She carefully pried the subject's jaws apart. Her pin light shone on a bloated tongue, and she pressed it flat to see deeper inside. "Blood still apparent in the oral cavity."

She felt along the left side of the torso. "Extensive contusions on the subcutaneous tissue overlying the left ribcage. Multiple rib fractures on that side, indicating severe blunt-force trauma."

Zenée would have bet her life savings that she would find lacerations of the parenchyma, with diffuse hemorrhaging (that he had breathed in blood and lots of it), but she would have to open him up for a look at his lungs once she finished her cursory examination.

But that wasn't how you died, was it, Mr. Di Brigo? She gently fingered the bullet hole in the middle of his forehead. "Gun powder detected near entrance wound on the frontal cranial bone."

Someone finished you off, didn't they? She crouched down low and lifted the skull, and eyeing the larger hole on the back of the head that indicated a bullet's exit. She turned the head sideways for a better view.

"Any progress report, ma'am? Those fellas upstairs are feeling mighty anxious." A timid voice echoed through Zenée's concentration.

She directed her gaze towards the offending owner, who was lingering just inside the doorway to the morgue, then continued her exploration of the posterior lesion. "Where was the bullet recovered?"

"Recovered?"

"Yes, the bullet would have entered the frontal bone here, and exited through the occipital bone at the base of the skull, there. According to the probable state of health at the time, I would say the body would have been lying prostrate, most likely on a plane lower than the weapon." She straightened. Mimed holding a handgun, pointed at the floor. "The angle of the bullet path through the skull indicates the body was likely propped against something or someone when the shooter fired. I certainly hope Mr. Di Brigo's friend made out better than he did. So, where was the bullet lodged?"

"That's police business, Ms. Abney."

"*Dr.* Abney, Sheriff Jameson."

"My apologies. Doctor."

Zenée raised her recorder to show him it was still running and fixed him with sarcastic gratitude. She moved around to the other side of the table and leaned over the subject's midsection. "Jagged, incised wound traversing the abdomen indicates a dull blade was employed. Switch-blade or pocketknife. Evisceration of the intestines, liver, spleen. No hemorrhaging apparent, implying the damage was post-mortem and possibly post-submersion—"

"Excuse me, doctor. Did you say 'switch-blade or pocketknife'?"

"Yes, the body has been disemboweled," she stated, waving her hand across the expanse of empty body cavity in illustration.

"The witness who discovered the boy said the wolves had been at him."

"Well, unless a wolf eats with a fork and knife, Sheriff..."

Dumbfounded was a phrase made for people like Sheriff Jameson. His lips moved, but nothing came out. Zenée waited for him to regain control of his vocal chords. "You are certain this boy's...innards were removed by a person? Not an animal?"

"That depends on your definition of animal, I suppose."

"Why would a person have done that?"

"Ritual? Trophy? The heart would make a more likely trophy, but that would have been harder to reach and the culprit was clearly not an expert surgeon. He would have needed to understand that the diaphragm must be incised first, before locating the heart." Zenée continued with her survey, holding up one leg for inspection of the gluteus. She glanced up and paused to see the sheriff's pale face. "You don't have a queasy stomach, do you? If so, you had better exit through there. You'll find a bathroom two doors down."

"I'm not sick, Doctor," the sheriff said, his voice so quiet it sounded like a secret. He watched the victim's face instead of hers. "I knew this boy. Only slightly, but I knew him."

"Oh." Zenée shut off the recorder. "Well, I'm sorry for your loss, Sheriff Jameson. I certainly hope this will be reported to the Committee for Safety of Foreign Exchange Students. Immediately."

"I'll take care of it." He kept his head down and let her get back to work.

chapter forty-four

Have a sudden urge to do some laundry, son? James eyed John's crouching form, bent over and sorting clothes in the laundry room that was just off the kitchen. Busy as a bee.

Sheriff Jameson sat across from him, and James leaned close with his voice lowered, "Listen, Mike. John has already made his statement to your deputy. All the kids were dropped home before midnight Saturday, and Antonio was fine the last time he saw him. Ours would've been the first house on the route, but there's no reason Antonio wouldn't have made it safely home within fifteen or twenty minutes after John got home. I saw John come in, and I saw him to bed."

James made no mention of the fact that he heard his son sneak out of his room shortly after that. Through a darkened window, he had watched him put his car in neutral, roll it out to the road, and turn the ignition once he was clear down the drive. James hadn't thought the secretive behavior was of concern; he himself had snuck out more than once when he was John's age, and teenage boys needed some freedom. After Antonio had turned up missing, though, he had to ask. John confessed to meeting with Lindsay Yates (whom James remembered to be quite pretty). He said he didn't wanted to shame his date to the dance by leaving with another girl, and apparently, Lindsay had invited John to visit her at the Jameson's house. Did Mike know the girls had visitors while he and Stephanie were away for the night? John insisted that Antonio wasn't a part of the after-party, and though James trusted his son, he sensed the need to tread lightly with the sheriff.

"Well," Mike grunted, leaning back against the back of the booth, "that's the information that we have from the limo driver, too." He seemed about to say more, then hesitated, as if unsure whether or not to divulge his thoughts.

"Has anyone been able to ascertain whether or not Antonio left the Walsh house that night? Well, clearly he did. But any idea why, or where he went?" James hinted, fishing for mention of the party at the Jameson house.

Mike narrowed his eyes. "Thing is, Jamie. I have in my possession Antonio's personal notebook."

'I' have in 'my' possession; not 'we,' the police force.

"Aaron Walsh was the man who found the body. Know him?"

"Slightly."

"Good fella. Has a real thing for the hounds. When he watched them scenting around the crime scene, he invited us to the Walsh house straight away. Let us look wherever we pleased, let the dogs sniff where they would, and the notebook turned up right quick. Under the boy's bed."

"And, you've read it?"

"What do you think?"

James rubbed the scruff on his chin with both hands. "I'm surprised it wasn't in Italian."

"Looks like he was practicing English. One part would be in Italian, then the next in English."

"That makes sense," James said. He tried to shrug, but he was tense from his ears to his toenails.

"I'll be honest with you, Jamie. John was mentioned quite a bit, and we all know boys will be boys."

James had no choice but to hold Mike's gaze, unreadable as it was. He had to return the challenge, "The two were pretty good friends. John told me Amanda had recently joined their little crew, as well." He watched Mike flinch, almost imperceptibly.

"No, Amanda was never mentioned in the notebook." Mike recovered his composure in an instant. "She only knew the boy in passing."

And who could prove otherwise, Mike? Since no one shall ever see Antonio's writings, but you? "John must have been mistaken," James offered magnanimously. "He's still getting to know everybody, you know."

"John's a good kid. I understand."

James sensed that Mike's subtext was, "We understand each other," and he shifted in his seat, dreading where the conversation might be headed. What was James "understanding," exactly?

"Look, Jamie," Mike rapped his knuckles on the table between them. "You and I go back a long time. Our families go back a long time. We're on the same team. Neither one of us wants our kids mixed up in something as serious as this murder case."

James felt the subtle threat in Mike's unblinking eyes and it pissed him off. But he sympathized with his need to protect his daughter as certainly as James would defend his son. Leaning back he nodded—yes.

"There's a punk mentioned several times in the journal, name of Sam Castle. Been up to his share of trouble. Sound familiar?" Mike asked, finally seeming to arrive at the crux of his mission to the Robinson household.

"Another kid from Andrew Jackson?"

"Dropped out of Jackson, I guess. This Castle kid lives down in Finley Hollow."

"You're talking about the Southern Cove Mobile-Home Park." James corrected the slur. He had no patience for the old warring families theme, and didn't find any humor in the joke that so many members of the Finley family were poor that they might as well name the lower-valued properties in town after them. "What does the boy's neighborhood have to do with it, Mike?"

"I've had more than enough calls down there, made enough arrests in the hollows, to know unsavory events happen there. More drugs, more drunks, more of just about everything we don't want in Shirley, friend."

"What makes you think this Sam kid is involved with Antonio's murder, though?"

"Things I've heard. My daughter may not have known Antonio di Brigo very well, but she seems to have known plenty about Sam Castle. Wouldn't say much, but I get the idea he's not a good guy. Does John know him?"

"Wait a minute, Mike. We're talking about kids here. 'Not a good guy,' maybe, but how does that correlate with killing someone?"

"Does John know him?" Mike repeated.

"I have no idea. Why do you suspect him?"

"Just a hunch. Let's say something I read," he murmured, then turned his head toward the kitchen and hollered, "Hey John, that you skulkin' around back there?"

John had been loitering close enough to appear within seconds, padding around the corner in bare feet, politely curious. "Sir?"

"You have any dealings with a boy named Sam Castle? Used to go to Andrew Jackson." Mike rose from his seat to stand in front of John, cocking his head in the manner of one listening to a small child.

"I've talked to him once or twice, but we're not really friends." John used the new air of forced unconcern that James noticed had settled over his son during the past few days.

"What do you think of him?"

"I don't," he shrugged, and then amended his statement to sound more kind, when Mike snickered and clapped him on the shoulder. "I mean, I don't really know him. He seems alright."

"You be up for a trip down to Finley Hollow, to talk to him? You and your dad?"

John looked to his dad.

"Is that really necessary, Mike?" *There's something else there. What is it, son?* "We don't want to get involved in law enforcement activities."

Mike's pitch rose in humorous defense, "I just want to ask a few questions, clear up some foggy details."

John bristled. "Am I a foggy detail?"

James gave his son a warning look.

"Ho! Fiesty, I like that." Mike let loose a stilted guffaw and wrestled John around the neck, adding a noogie that deepened his scowl.

"Relax," James mouthed to his son's sour mug, strangled in Mike's bicep.

"You Robinson's, I love you guys," Mike laughed, hanging an arm around James next as he rose to stand. "You all follow me, this won't take long."

"We'll take the Mercedes, meet you around front," James called after him, motioning towards the garage. "Son, grab your coat, it's getting chilly."

"Mercedes. You Robinson's…" Mike chuckled, disappearing through the front door.

John shoved his feet into a pair of flip-flops, then headed for the garage without bothering to get a jacket. "At least he didn't handcuff us and toss us into in the back of his cruiser," he muttered.

"Should he have, son?" John jerked one shoulder up as he pushed past him. "The more you tell me, the more I can help you, John," James hissed, resisting the urge to grab the top of his arm and yank him back to look his father in the face.

"Yeah, like you'd listen." He opened the car door and flounced into the passenger seat, then settled with his arms folded, staring straight ahead and affecting boredom.

James closed his eyes and prayed for patience, reminding himself that John had just lost a friend—probably a close one, and in a terrible way. Descending into his seat, he watched the side of his son's face and wondered how much John actually knew about the details of Antonio's death.

"Have I not been listening?" he asked. When James didn't get an answer, he sighed and punched the button on the garage door remote. "Have you been trying to tell me something?" His son sat as still as a statue next to him. "Is there something that you want to tell me now, John?"

John turned away to gaze out the car window in reply, and James noticed with a groan that a deputy had been waiting in the police cruiser to accompany them. He'd hoped that it would just be the three of them—and that the Castle house would be empty when they arrived. But so far the errand was ratcheting in drama, instead of fading into a non-event. The two officers waved as James slowed to a stop and let the cruiser take the lead down their long driveway.

Please don't turn on any sirens, Mike. He didn't, and James relaxed a fraction, as they turned onto Riverbend Road.

When they came to the intersection with the state road, he glanced at John, contemplating the countryside. He looked disinterested, but his brain was likely buzzing with activity. James resigned himself to a long, apprehensive ride, and began sorting through the events of the past few weeks in his mind, trying to remember when his habitually cheerful son had become so glum. He thought he could trace it back to well before Antonio's death.

John broke the silence after they had only driven a short distance, to James's surprise. "Have you ever felt like this place is…I don't know, a little off?"

"Small towns are all a bit weird, I think."

"No, not weird."

"How would you describe it?" James ventured, fearing his son would lapse back into the personal censorship that he had been practicing for the last several days—the last several weeks really. He hadn't been trying to ignore John's moodiness, just unsure of how to react.

John thought for a while before replying. He watched the cows in the fields, clumps of elm trees, the sunset in the distance—turned just enough away so his dad couldn't see his face. "I don't know. Sort of dangerous. Somehow."

"Dangerous?" After several minutes of dead air, James prodded, "I suppose when a good friend is killed like Antonio was, the world seems a lot more dangerous than it used to."

"I'm not only talking about Antonio. Something…unsettling is going on. More than unsettling. I think I felt it when I was little, but I just couldn't recognize what my instinct was telling me. Now that I've been gone for a while and came back, though. Or maybe because I'm older now…" He shrugged and looked at his hands. "It's stronger now."

"You are older now, son. Things can get pretty jumbled in your head, at your age. I understand why you feel confused."

"I don't feel confused, Dad, I feel protective. Aggressively protective."

James cleared his throat and began, "Well—"

"It's not hormones that I'm talking about."

"Why do you think I would mention hormones?" James chuckled.

"Because you cleared your throat and squeezed the steering wheel in exactly the same way when I asked you what a condom was. When I was ten?"

You remember that from when you were ten? James didn't remember a condom discussion, but he was certain that John could recite every one of his father's embarrassed sexual context blunders, word for word.

"I worry about Candy, yes. But not because of why you think."

"Well, you both experienced your share of danger when you were little here, John. When Candy was kidnapped, well, that was something no child should ever have to think about. You, or her." James shuddered at the memory, rising so unwelcomed into his mind. "You saved her from probably a very horrible outcome, though, John. You should be proud of that."

"I didn't save her."

The words were bitten out, and James glanced over to see that John had his fist jammed against his mouth in a grimace of anguish, his eyes lost beyond the racing fields outside.

"Of course you—"

"I'm not just talking about Candy either. It's more than that. Don't you care about those drawings that Grandpa made in the hospital? Do you think that's normal?"

James racked his brain for the "drawings," knowing he was in trouble if he couldn't remember something. He had been working so much since he got there, taking over Dad's business and simultaneously keeping his own afloat remotely.

"They weren't just drawings." John finally turned towards him, gesturing with his whole arms. "I don't know why I know that, but I do."

"Okay, I understand."

"No, you don't. There was a giant release when Antonio died, like something was…I don't know, satisfied. For a minute. I felt it in the air and in the ground. Like a sigh."

"Were you there, when Antonio died?"

John's face fell, and he turned away. He was sullen, closed again.

"John, *were* you?"

James watched him fume for several seconds, glaring out through the front windshield, before he finally answered. "No."

"Well, I'm glad. If that's true. The boy died horribly." He breathed a sigh of relief, but something that his son said left him worried. He had to ask, "Do you know how he died?"

"He was shot."

"Yes."

"In the face," John said, so bluntly that he almost sobbed the words.

James's jerked his head in reaction; he couldn't remember the last time John had cried. His suspicions returned to the possibility that he had witnessed at least some part of the macabre scene. *No, that's insane. How could my own son have been involved with a murder? In any way?*

It was unthinkable. He forced the possibility out of his mind.

"I don't know how much you know, but the shooting wasn't the worst of it, John," he began, bracing himself for what needed to be said, before the news was all over town. "Someone, well…"

"I know about the rest. You and Sheriff Jameson weren't as quiet as you thought you were."

"Oh." James ran a hand through his hair, embarrassed. *Did he hear everything? My god…* "I'm sorry about that, son."

John lapsed back into silence and James turned his focus to the taillights of Mike's cruiser, wary of the deepness of the night falling around them. He wondered how to prepare himself or his son for the confrontation that lay ahead. Mike obviously wanted John there as a decoy for his schoolmate. A pawn. What was the consequence for John, then? For that matter, what was the consequence for this poor kid, Sam? James rubbed the bridge of his nose, wishing the drive would last a few minutes longer. Way before he was ready, Southern Cove came into view.

The rusted welcome sign across the entrance to the trailer park was rimmed with old-fashioned light bulbs, oddly reminiscent of the oldest section of Las Vegas. Many of the bulbs were burned out and several sputtered on and off at the end of life. Gnarled, scrubby bushes framed the sign, illuminated from below by a spotlight pointing heavenward, highlighting the twisted ugliness of the needled shrubs. Their car rolled down a narrow lane, lined with mobile houses and broken-down cars mounted on cinderblocks. Several residents sat on stoops or folding chairs in front of their homes, and James felt the heat of their stares. A visit from Sheriff Jameson seemed ordinary, but not popular.

The cruiser stopped in front of a nondescript mobile home and James parked alongside. He turned off his headlights with trepidation. *Here we go.*

"Maybe the Benz wasn't such a great idea, Dad." John's voice was full of teenage scorn, as he got out of the car. He eased his door closed, embarrassed.

James's cheeks burned as he realized the truth of his son's words; the abject poverty surrounding them glared brighter than the shine on his Mercedes. There was nothing for it, though. He shut his car door as quietly as John had and turned to face the Castle residence. Light shone dimly behind small, curtained windows, and he could hear the rise and fall of a television laugh-track as they approached the door. "John, I think we should let the officers go first."

"If they're going to use me to get to Sam, I'm not going to cower in the background," John said, striding ahead with purpose.

"I'll do the talkin', son." Mike met him on the steps and rapped on the door.

Brave John. James was willing to linger behind the others. John had never been one to hide from responsibility or shy from a challenge. That part of his nature was what gnawed at James as he watched his son; he had never seen John look so unsure before. What did he mean about danger? In Shirley County? All James could do was wait for him to open up again, since pushing would have the opposite effect.

A woman's muffled answer sounded from inside the door after Mike's second, more insistent, knock. James steeled himself for the unknown, as he heard her grappling with the latch on the other side.

"...second..."

Mike turned back to exchange a knowing look with his deputy. When the woman inside finally conquered the door handle, she stumbled over the threshold with the force of the swing, still hanging onto the latch. "Damn thing," she mumbled.

"Mrs. Castle?" Mike's voice was louder than it needed to be. He leaned down and craned his neck to place his face in her line of vision.

"Yes, tha's me." The woman brought her eyes together with an effort. When she realized she was talking to a sheriff, she snapped to as much attention as she could muster.

"Oop, there we go," Mike teased, resuming his full height as she wiped her mouth and produced a dutiful smile.

"Can I hep you?"

"I think you may need a little help yourself there, Mrs. Castle. You doing alright?" Mike turned back to grin at James, who remained stone-faced. The deputy snickered, but John held his composure. "Okay, okay," Mike chuckled. "You Robinson's... Mrs. Castle, we'd like to have a word with your son, Sam. He home?"

"Sam?"

"Your son. Sam Castle is your son, is he not?"

"Yes, he is." She looked behind her, confused. "He's not here?"

"That's what I'm asking you, darlin'."

"Yes. No, I mean he isn't..." She looked behind her again, peering into the house as if she hadn't thought to check whether or not her son was home before that moment.

"Mind if we have a look around, sweetheart?" Mike asked. He mounted the step to tower over her diminutive form.

"No, nah a all, ociffer."

James smiled and eased past her through the doorway. His chest swelled with pride as he heard his son's quiet, "Thank you, ma'am."

James was surprised to find the house well-kept and clean, sparely appointed and sparsely furnished as it was. He suspected Mrs. Castle to be the kind of addict who scoured the house clean with guilt after a binge. He had known several of that variety in his time, and had even dated a few. There didn't appear to be much else to see but an unfortunate woman with a bad habit, if the kid wasn't home. James wanted to reassure his son that their errand was almost over, and he tried to catch his eye, but John was staring at the floor, concentrating on his thoughts. Curious about the nature of his son's relationship with this Castle boy, James realized he probably wasn't going to tell him if he asked, so he let it go and began to wander through the tiny house.

"...have any idea where he is tonight?" Mike was asking, standing closer to the woman than he needed to. James felt his shoulders recommence their tensing. "Rick, shut off that television. Don't keep a very good watch on your son, do you?"

"Well, I think e's working."

"Working?" Mike motioned to his deputy, who pulled a notepad from his shirt pocket and began scribbling. "Where does he work?"

"I think..."

"Where does he work?" Mike repeated.

"I think he works on a delivy truck. De-liv-er-y truck," she said, slowing down to tackle the longer word. James squeezed the bridge of his nose between his thumb and forefinger.

"So late at night?"

"Yep."

Mike shook his head at the deputy. He scratched his last line out and replaced the notebook in his pocket, rolling his eyes in disgust and sauntering away to snoop through the rest of the house.

"When was the last time you saw Sam?"

"Mmmmm..."

"Haven't seen him in a while, huh?"

"Who?"

"Sam. Your son."

"Sam's here?"

"Sheriff. I think you'll want to see this," the deputy called, leaning out of the doorway to an adjacent room.

"Tha's Sam's room." Mrs. Castle lit up, pleased to offer relevant information. She jumped off her perch in the living area and followed the men into her son's bedroom.

The room was a typical teenage boy's room. Dirty clothes were flung here or there, and shoes and a skateboard tumbled out of an open closet door. The bed was a simple mattress on the floor piled with pillows and blankets. There was a bookshelf against one wall with a surprising number of books lined up on two shelves, and various knick-knacks of mysterious importance scattered on the other. A pretty nice electric keyboard. A small chest of drawers sat perpendicular to that, with a drawer pulled open, the clothes rifled through but mostly organized. Shelving had been hung high above the furniture, probably to make more storage space in such a small room, but the shelves lay empty. Those were all the normal things one might expect to see in a kid's room, but the walls were where normality ended.

James had wandered in with his eyes cast down, scanning the floor basically uninterested, but he caught his breath when he looked up. The largest expanse of open wall space, over the bed, was covered with densely drawn black figures; some were lunging forward, some were falling back, and others were simply standing, staring back at the viewer or screaming at another figure. It was difficult for James to discern whether or not the figures were humanoid, but they struck a familiar chord, albeit one of terror. They were fantastical and alien—more than he could comprehend, with strange, extra appendages and body parts that morphed into inanimate forms. The overlapping, the detail, and the depth were fascinating and almost beautiful, if not for the basic savagery. There was anger and pain laid bare, so raw that James could feel the emotion of the drawings starting to take over. He looked away for relief.

"God, those are intense..." he murmured.

He heard John's intake of breath, as he entered the room.

Shit. James worried whether or not his son should be seeing such gruesome, morbid imagery so soon after the death of his friend.

"Sam likes to draw," Mrs. Castle supplied.

"Holy Mary, we hit the jackpot," Mike breathed.

James was instantly alarmed at Mike's elation. "What do you mean?"

"Iss like a richal for 'im."

"It's a ritual? Sam likes to draw satanic imagery?" Mike asked.

"Satanic?" She looked at the wall again, as if seeing the drawings for the first time.

James examined the figures; he hadn't seen anything devilish or evil, but he had to admit that he could understand if another person had. "Mike, she probably means that making art is a ritual for him. It is for a lot of artists."

"What's with all the blood? Did Sam kill something? Somebody?"

"Wha you mean blood?"

"Mike, it's red paint. Come on," James reasoned.

"Looks like blood to me. Why'd your son smear red all over the walls?"

Mrs. Castle gaped at the wall for several seconds, seeming to sober up with a dose of fear—more likely fear of the sheriff than fear of the otherworldly imagery. James wondered if she was finally beginning to understand her situation through the haze.

She whispered weakly, "Sam's color blind."

"*Color blind?*" Mike hollered. "Is that your answer?"

"Mike…"

"Shut up, James. Is that your answer?"

"Sam can't see red. That red must be a mistake."

Mike chortled. "Oh, I don't think this is a mistake, sweetheart. Rick, get some pictures of this. Look, get this swastika here. Kids probably a freakin' Nazi skinhead."

"That's not a Nazi Swastika," John whispered, and James turned to see his son transfixed by the drawings.

"It does look like one, son," he said, moving closer to the wall and pointing out the area that the sheriff had asked to have photographed, "…unfortunately. Looks like there are more of them, too." He sighed, wondering how much drawings really had to do with a crime, as disturbing as they looked. All kids carry around their share of angst. He glanced back and saw that John had left the room.

"Mike, I think John's upset. I'm going to go talk to him, okay?"

Mike directed his reply to the pinched up face of Mrs. Castle. "Yeah, I can see why he would be upset."

"John?" James called, wandering through the tiny trailer. He peeked around open doors leading into separate rooms, but the place was empty. He ducked back into the boy's room. "I think he went outside. I'll be right back."

"Sure, go 'head," Mike waved him on, still focused on the kid's poor mother.

I don't know what more he thinks he can get from her. James took a final glance at the deputy, furiously snapping pictures from every angle possible in the cramped space. He looked at Mrs. Castle and the sheriff seated together on the bed, shook his head with pity and annoyance, and looked forward to the fresh air. "Any mother would protect her son," he said to the empty hallway.

James left the trailer and stood on the steps breathing deeply for several minutes, stretching his neck from side to side and trying to calm his nerves. Surprised John wasn't sitting in the car; he walked farther away from the house to scan the area. After a full circuit of the mobile home, he registered an urgent voice, lowered in stealth, coming from the darkness of a sprawling oak tree nearby.

"...disemboweled...It means his guts were cut out!...Yeah, I know he wasn't like that when we left..."

It was John. He was pacing with his cell phone; James could see the glow lighting up his cheek as he walked back and forth on the other side of the tree.

"I'm here with them, and trust me, it looks really bad...Sam's not here, do you know where he is?"

Silence, while he listened to the other end.

"You have to tell him...No, just get over there..."

James cleared his throat as he walked nearer, but John didn't hear his warning.

"They might know about that, too. You have to get rid of it. Now."

"John."

John stopped in his tracks and rearranged his features into a mask of indifference.

"Candy, I've got to go." He hung up and stuffed his phone into the back pocket of his jeans, then tucked his hands under his arms and stalked in James's direction. "It's colder than I thought; can we get out of here?"

"I told you you'd need more than a T-shirt tonight."

"Thanks. Are we done now?" John strode past James and headed for the car. "Would you tell Sheriff Mike that I have school tomorrow? How 'bout I get home and do some homework?"

James couldn't have agreed more. "It's late, you're right. I'll go let him know we need to get home."

"We're not arrested, are we?" John asked, sliding into the passenger seat and shutting the door on a reply.

"No, we're not arrested," James answered to the closed door. He considered whether or not he needed to clear their exit with Mike. As much as he hated to leave that woman alone with the officers, he had been finished with the outing before it began. He decided to text Mike instead, and headed for the car himself.

chapter forty-five

Candy parked her bike in a stand of trees well up the road from the turn-off to The Palace. On second thought, she laid it on the ground and covered it with some loose branches, then skulked along the dimly lit street without emerging fully from the underbrush. Her ears pricked and her eyes wide, she searched the woodland for signs of clandestine observation. When she reached the footpath marked with the Christmas wreath lichens, she strained her eyes to look ahead and proceeded, wary as a cat. John wasn't sure whether or not the sheriff was aware of this place (it was only a matter of time), and she didn't want to be caught sneaking up to it. She had to move the gun, though.

If they found *that*. Well, who knew where it might lead or who could be implicated.

She spotted the corroded roofline of the little cabin. Light of the waning moon peeked through the trees and sprinkled silver glitter over the rotting wood. Candy felt a tug of nostalgia. *Wonder if there'll be yellow police tape all over it the next time I see it.*

There was no light in the cabin, but as she drew nearer, a puff of blue smoke caught the moonlight as it drifted up from under the narrow roof. A tiny red ember glowed and then danced down and to the side, as its owner paced in the pitch-black doorway.

"Sam," she whispered.

He growled an expletive, tossed his cigarette, and left the porch to meet her. He pulled her to his chest as soon as their hands were stretched within reach of each other. "I'm glad you called."

"Thank you for meeting me."

"Of course, baby."

Baby. Her heart lurched, but Candy knew it wasn't that simple, and so did he. All of them were trying to act normal at school and at home, and that meant avoiding Sam. Sam fell somewhere into the cracks of anomalous and delinquent in Shirley County and it was too risky to be seen with him, mostly for his sake. She had been afraid that he would be unfairly targeted, but she never would've guessed at the hysterical conclusions being drawn. Satanic drawings, John said. It was almost laughable, if not for the real danger it posed to Sam. She grabbed his face and smothered him with a kiss.

The last thing she wanted was to stop, but she had to. "We probably don't have much time," she said, their lips barely parted.

"Oh, come on…" He gathered her in closer and found her mouth again.

Yes, please…no, wait! "Sam, what about the jacket?"

"Loved that jacket," he murmured against her neck.

So did I, it smelled like you. He had found another one—leather—and he wrapped her into it and himself. She breathed in deep. "Sam, you're not being serious."

"Okay, let's get serious. I missed you."

The space between them became a cozy jumble of persuasive hands and soft kisses. "And my dress?"

"Loved that dress, too." He slid his palm down the small of her back, under the place where her jeans gaped loose.

How were his hands always so warm, even on a chilly night? It was like he carried around some of those little hot massage stones in his pockets or something. Candy was in a daze, intoxicated by his body all round her. "But it was covered in blood."

"Don't worry, I burned them both," he whispered and turned her face to nuzzle against the back of her ear. His hair hung against her neck and tickled her shoulder.

Burn…like me, right now. "Wait—Sam. Really, I'm serious. We don't have time."

He relented with a sigh; his head slumped against her shoulder, "Alright."

She took his hand and pulled him towards the cabin, holding the drapery aside and glancing around once more before shoving him inside. He knelt down to light the kerosene lamp by the door and the room leapt into dancing golden gloom from below.

"So. It's bad, right? You said the sheriff was at my house?"

"They saw your drawings and freaked out, Sam. They're saying the drawings are some kind of Satanic ritual or something."

"What?" He frowned into his laugh. "You're kidding, why?"

"Because they're small-minded, ignorant rednecks," Candy hissed, feeling her skin tingling with the injustice.

Sam plopped down on the loveseat. "Hmph. I never really thought they were that good."

"This isn't funny, Sam." But of course he had no way of knowing the damage to Antonio's body—the disemboweling after they dumped his body in the river. He must have been staying clear of everyone, hiding in the backwoods up there. "Do you know how bad it looks that you haven't been going home? Like you're on the run? We've all given statements."

"I haven't slept at home in weeks—before all this shit even." He let his head roll onto the back of the couch and gazed up through the ceiling. "I'm a vagabond. I just stay wherever I can hang my hat, between working my ass off, night and day." He rubbed his temples, more tired than Candy had realized. "Besides, why would they even think I was involved?"

She sat down next to him and took his hand. "Antonio wrote in a journal or something, and you were in it. This place could've been mentioned. You were with him here, right? And the drawings all over the walls here, too…" Sam's face lost some of its color, then, and the urgency of her errand rushed back, "Look, we have to move that gun, before someone finds it."

He stood with alarm—the gun. "And get out of here."

They wrestled the loveseat away from the wall, knelt down, and brought the light closer to a gaping hole in the floor.

"Sam, there's more," Candy began. She watched his back as he bent over to reach an arm under the floorboards, unsure how to describe how Antonio's body had been discovered. The image in her mind made her sick to her stomach. "The reason the cops think your drawings were like a ritual, why Satan-anything had even been brought up, I think…"

"It's gone." Sam straightened up to face her, indignation darkening his features.

"What? No—"

A car door slammed in the distance and they both went erect.

Candy grabbed his shoulders and squeezed. "Sam, you have to go!"

"Right." He gave her the handle of the kerosene lantern.

"Do you have Rachel's truck?"

"Yeah, I parked it on Fern, on the other side of the woods," he grunted, shoving the couch back over the hole.

"Good. Go out the back."

"What about you?"

"Don't worry about me. They want you."

He kissed her hard. Both of them were aware of the question hanging between them.

"Sam, where will I find you? No—don't tell me."

He hoisted himself up onto a window ledge in the back of the cabin and swung his legs outside. Candy grabbed his shirt and pulled him back for a final, urgent embrace. Sam whispered, "I'll find you," and then disappeared into blackness.

She watched the empty window, holding her breath and listening for the sound of approaching police officers. No dogs, no shouting or flashlights. After a few minutes, she guessed Sam had reached a safe distance and she collapsed onto the little couch, gasping with relief.

Wait... Footsteps approached outside, but they sounded like the quick, slapping gait of someone running in flip-flops, instead of the heavy tread of a uniformed officer. She sat perched on the edge of the cushions, her heart hammering in her chest.

"Candy?" came John's voice, breathless.

"John." She flopped back down. "Oh, thank god it's you."

He shoved the thin curtain of their makeshift door aside so hard she heard it rip. "Did you hide the gun? Where's Sam? Did he meet you here?"

"The gun's gone." She leaned back and closed her eyes, emotionally exhausted.

"The bloody jacket? The dress?"

"Burned." She flapped her hand in the air in affirmation. "He said he burned them."

"So you saw him? He was here?"

"He was here, but he left. I told him to get out of here, just in case."

"Oh. I was hoping to catch him."

Candy opened her eyes and narrowed them in suspicion. "Why?"

He shrugged, but he was still holding the curtain in his fists. "I just wanted to talk to him. Well, anyway…that's good he's gone. You're safe."

"What?" Didn't John have any clue how much it was killing her that Sam was gone *again*? And for who knew how long? Why was he so obsessed with keeping her away from Sam? "John, stop trying to save me. I don't need saving."

He dropped the curtain and moved in front of her. "Yes. You do."

"What's that supposed to mean?"

"And you have since the first day that I met you, Candy."

She sat bolt upright and met his glare with fire in her eyes. "How dare you bring that up. Right, now? How dare you, John."

"Why not now? I think it's perfect timing, since you don't seem to understand the danger you're in now, any better than you did then. What are you going to let happen this time, if I don't stop it?"

"I told you, nothing happened last time." She sprang to her feet and shoved her face into John's, furious that at her full height, she was still forced to look up at him like a child. "What—do you think I'm lying?"

"No, I think you don't remember. Your uncle got you all the way into another state and they didn't find you until the next day, in a motel room. Your mother killed herself when she found out who you were with—"

"Nobody knows why she jumped in that river, John!"

"You were only seven! How could nothing have happened?" His voice thundered, and he leaned down to meet her at close range. "Maybe I couldn't do anything then, but I'll die before I let anything like that happen again."

"Nothing happened!" Candy shouted.

They stood glowering at each other, both of them seething. Candy balled her fists so tight that her fingernails dug into her sweaty palms. She felt the sting and looked at her hands, then shook them out, embarrassed. John relaxed his shoulders and averted his eyes.

Candy put up her hands and made for the door. "Look, I'm not talking about this anymore." When she swung through the exit, she ducked her head back inside to find John heading in the same direction. "Do. Not. Follow me."

She stomped back through the trees headed for her bike. Not bothering to conceal her progress as she had on the way to the cabin, she slapped branches out of her face in disgust. Anguish rumbled deep in her chest and she let it erupt into a roar, but it was a paltry release. At least the closeness of the forest helped her to feel less exposed, less naked. She breathed the woods in and tried to calm her rushing blood.

Candy knew her family—and too many people in town—remembered the abduction. Like John, many thought her Uncle Brian molested her when he took her. Candy didn't even want to think about what her mom believed, why she had…done what she had done.

She squeezed her eyes shut. *No, that wasn't my fault.* That's what she insisted to herself over and over through the years.

After they found her in that motel, a shrink spent hours talking with her about it. He groomed her for days, trying to force her confession that there had been "sexual misconduct." That would have beefed up the trial. But all she could remember was sitting around watching television re-runs of Mr. Ed and Denis the Menace, eating potato chips and Oreo cookies. Could she have blocked something else out?

I can't believe John thinks I just forgot. "No," she said, gritting her teeth.

Considering how repugnant anything like that would have been to her, she was certain she didn't just forget. And the fact that people still imagined those things made her feel violated more than the mythical event ever could have. *Do they actually picture scenes—with my body parts—in their minds?* The possibility of that made her hate the speculators even more than the suspect.

"Not John." She could never hate John. But her mind felt completely boggled. She pounded her fists against her skull trying to clear it.

Crap, did I go too far? She stopped walking and looked around, regaining her bearings. *Better head towards the road...*

"Hey, Candy."

She jumped nearly out of her skin, and spun around to find Tyler Finley, leaned against a tree with an eely grin sliding from under his baseball cap.

"God, you scared me, Tyler." She grasped her chest and looked at him with distaste. "Were you following me?"

"Where'd you put my gun?"

"Huh?" Candy was genuinely surprised. "It was gone when we got there. I figured you took it already."

His voice was icy. "No. Where is it?"

"You idiot, you're the one who got us into this in the first place."

"I's doin' him a favor. He was already dead."

"You don't know that," she snapped. She was revolted by the sleaze bag, and furious about what he had done. "You didn't need to sh—" She couldn't even get the words out—in the face, he shot him in the face! But Antonio was in so much pain. It was excruciating, even to watch. He was dying, and they all knew it was true.

"He should'n a been messin' with my girl."

"What?"

"Sam took my gun, didn't he? Playin' Mr. Authority again, like he has a right."

"He was just trying to keep us all from getting arrested that night, Tyler. Someone had to take charge—"

"It's my gun!" Tyler screeched, his face contorted. Candy gasped, horrified by the change, like a glimpse of the demon inside Tyler Finley. Just as suddenly, he backed away and smoothed his features. In a voice quiet with menace, he said, "It's my gun and I want it back. Now."

"Look, we don't have it, I already told you." She tried to sound reasonable, but she checked behind her to make sure of the terrain for a quick exit.

"Slip it to Sam, did ya? 'Fore he took off? Bet you slipped him sumpin' else, too." He gyrated his hips towards her, humping the air and making a high-pitched, mocking moan. "For the road, huh?"

"You're disgusting, leave me alone." She wheeled away from the creep, but froze when she heard the unmistakable metallic, sliding click of a switchblade. She saw the blade glinting from the corner of her eye, and tore off through the trees. The undergrowth was so thick, though, that she had only run a few paces before she was forced to dodge and slow down. He was right behind her.

Tyler lunged forward, grabbed a handful of her hair, and yanked it hard. Her neck snapped back and he slammed his body against hers.

The blade slid under her chin. "You're a quick lil' vixen, ain't ya?"

His foul breath huffed against the back of her head, blowing wisps of her hair. She braced herself and felt the knife dig deeper into her flesh. All he had to do was whip it to one side to slit her throat. She stilled herself, barely daring to breathe.

"You been given that ole' Sam goodies all along, wasn't you? Think it's 'bout time I took some for me," he snickered. Candy squeezed her eyes shut in revulsion. "Or, might be I should try again." He moved his hand down to pat her belly with the flat of the blade. "Maybe it works better when you's screamin'."

Is he talking about Antonio? Candy thought wildly. She suddenly knew, without a doubt, that it was Tyler who cut him up. *He went back later, and cut Antonio to pieces.*

"Heck, maybe I do both. We got to bring her back."

"Bring who back?"

"Shut your mouth, you little slut." He ran his tongue up her ear.

The heat rose so fast in Candy she felt dizzy. How dare he. She tried to catch her breath over her fury. But, she knew where his filthy mouth was. She had a better idea where his eyes were, right behind her cheek. And as he struggled against the buttons of her jeans with his knife-hand, the point of the blade swung away from her. Candy Vale hadn't grown up wrestling against three older brothers without learning how to deliver a few sucker-punches. She rammed two fingers backwards and felt at least one make squishy, wet contact with an eyeball. Tyler howled, and when he raised the switchblade, she grabbed his wrist and bit down as hard as she could. She tasted blood and heard the knife thud to the ground. He was still hanging onto her arm with his other hand, but he was leaning over in pain. She cracked her head against the bridge of his nose. He fell down, hollering in agony. She broke free, but tripped over a tree root.

"Shit!" As she scrambled to her feet she could hear Tyler on the move behind her. He grabbed her ankle and wrenched her back to the ground, twisting her leg so that she landed hard on her elbows. Her bones jarred to the top of her head.

"You bitch!" he screamed, blood spurting from his nose.

She saw her opportunity, partially blinded as he was with his own blood, and she wrenched herself around to grab his head in both her hands, delivering her rage through her palms with a howl. She had planned to knee him in the face, but he yanked his head back so violently she lost her grip. He wailed like a banshee and flailed away from her. His eyes rolled back in his head and his body convulsed.

"Aahnaah…" Tyler sat up, in control of his limbs again. His voice came out in a moan, "Ahnaanvwodi." The last two syllables were produced deep within his mouth, guttural, but Candy understood the meaning perfectly.

"Where?" she stuttered, bewildered. He was gaping at her. "Me? I'm not the…"

He lunged at her, ripping at her shirt, her face. He tore at her hair in a frenzy, like he would claw his way inside.

"Get off—get off me!"

She kicked him away as hard as she could. A hulking shadow loomed over Tyler from behind, raised both arms overhead with a club held high. The club came down on Tyler's head with a dull whack. His body crumpled to the ground like a sack of potatoes. She gaped at him in horror, not daring to take her eyes off the filthy beast.

A flip-flop clad foot kicked the switchblade away, and it skittered across the ground. "Are you alright?"

Candy sat up and turned to stare dumbly at her savior.

"Candy, are you hurt?"

The adrenaline coursed through her body. "Is he d-dead?"

John knelt down next to the stilled heap, feeling for a pulse. "No, just passed out. But, I think he's going to wish he were dead when he comes to."

"M-my g-g-god…"

Candy accepted John's hand to help her rise, wincing in pain when she put weight on her left ankle. She bore the pain to administer a sharp kick to Tyler's midsection, and ended up hissing and hopping on her good foot.

"The cup," John breathed. He bent over to pick something up as it rolled away from the body.

The shakes were setting in, and Candy felt like she might collapse. "Can we g-get the hell out of h-here, before he wakes up?"

"Yeah." John stuffed whatever he found in the pocket of his hoodie and reached out his hand again, "Come here, Candy."

He wrapped an arm around her waist for support, but when she fell into him, sobbing and trembling, he hoisted her up with both arms. She looped her legs around him and held onto his neck, clinging to him like a scared monkey. He threaded his hands under her bum—exactly the way the Child Services officer had carried her away from the crime scene when she was seven. She had watched over the officer's shoulder; her Uncle

Brian was sprawled face-down on the pavement, the policemen shouting over him. Guns were trained on his head.

"Let's get you home." John kissed her forehead, stepping gingerly through the undergrowth.

"I d-don't want. Want to. Go h-home," she spluttered and hiccupped. Home was lonely; her dad droned on about his issues, if he was even there instead of hanging around the shop, gabbing with whomever. She didn't want to go home, not that night. She blurted in a rush, "I don't wanna be alone."

"Spend the night at our place then. Grandma Pearl's got plenty of room."

"Okay." Her blubbering increased with her gratitude, and John made quiet shushing sounds as they left the woods. His Mustang was parked up the road under an umbrella of elm trees. She snuffled wetly into his neck, "I had him, John."

"Alright. It's alright."

"I don't need s-saving." Tears flowed and she pounded his broad back with a weak fist. "I don't."

"You could have fooled me, Candy-cane," he sighed. She hugged him tighter. "You sure could have fooled me."

epilogue

John sat in the breakfast nook staring at the table top. Looking up meant meeting more conciliatory ogling—sad eyes waiting to find his and search his expression. They sent sympathy like telepathy.

What a strange custom. He listened to the funeral after-party. His grandmother's endless recital of the last days before Grandpa Joe died droned on and on. Her story was filled with doctor comments, bodily details that should have been private, and her described shock of the "unforeseen."

"We all thought he was doing better." And then the final, terminal dig, "But I knew Joe wasn't one to watch his health." John hadn't seen her tears once, even at the funeral. But who was he to question that? He hadn't shed one either.

He watched Candy through the doorway to the front room, talking with his Aunt Beth. Candy wept freely throughout most of the service. In fact, her face was still puffy; she looked like she'd been crying all afternoon and could start up again at any moment. John was surprised at first, until he realized that she was crying not for Grandpa Joe, but for Antonio. It was a fair exchange: Antonio didn't even receive a memorial service. Probably already en route from Europe, his parents had arrived soon after his body was found in the river. The poor mother was inconsolable, the father angry and frustrated. They insisted on a private cremation and went back to Italy, taking their son's ashes with them.

After they left, John made inquiries about an honorary service in Antonio's memory, but he was met with stone faces and locked jaws; no one wanted to recognize anything. The school staff was humiliated, the sheriff's office was defensive and the Rotary Club was devastated. Mieke Walsh, in particular. John had spoken with her at Grandpa's funeral, and judging from her red eyes and utter lack of grooming, she had done her share of mourning. Between the dual tragedies of both Antonio's and Joe Robinson's deaths, John could hardly blame her. She probably felt as bad as he did. When she started talking, he wasn't sure whether she was looking to give or receive, but she needed some kind of confirmation.

"Whatever you may think," she had said, smoothing and re-crumpling a wad of soaked tissues and glancing suspiciously at fellow mourners. "I loved your grandfather dearly. He loved you more than you probably realize."

"I know he loved me." John had looked away, unsure where the sentiment might've led.

"He thought of you as his savior."

He hadn't expected that. "Savior?"

"He was having those horrible visions."

Then John snapped to attention, ready to listen. But he had to correct her, out of his own fear, "Nightmares."

"Oh, you know? He told me he saw them while he was awake, too. They scared the shit out of him."

"He actually said that?"

Mieke laughed bitterly, "Oh we weren't 'close' like everyone likes to gossip. But we were very good friends, as hard as that is for the people of Shirley County to believe." She narrowed her eyes at several of those people standing around the sanctuary vestibule. Then she cocked her head, thoughtful. "But you're not 'of' Shirley at all, are you?"

"No."

"Those nightmares stopped the night that you arrived and he never saw another vision. He felt like that was because of you, and he was grateful. More than you know."

And John remembered that his own peculiar dreams began that same night, right before school started. Yes, it was all very interesting information, but what the hell did it mean? He reached for the newspaper across the table again; he had already read the front-page article three times, "Sendalee Nation Advances Claims to Big Joe's." He studied the young man in the accompanying picture, his jet black hair, his Armani suit, and the surety in his expression. In the text, Michael Wright talked of surety of purpose: his conviction that sacred Sendalee grounds be returned to their Nation. He was confident that, now that the tyrant was dead, the Robinson's "stolen property" might fall into the hands of a more reasonable, "more forward-thinking individual." Subtext: John's grandfather was an asshole and his dad was a pantywaist.

John was angry, not because of the man's words or intentions, or out of fear that his threat might be real. He was angry with himself for having missed such important information, an integral part of his family history. He was ashamed that his power of observation had failed him so miserably. The article had come out that morning, headline splashed across the Sunday paper, and the funeral was buzzing with the news. That was one more reason that the after-party farce was driving him crazy—he would have to bide his time until everyone left and Grandma Pearl took a Valium to pass out for the night (she had already mentioned doing so several times) before he could investigate.

The wait was maddening, but at least he had secured one critical piece of the puzzle, and an avenue towards understanding it. The painted cup that fell out of the cave wall was locked in a metal box in the back of his closet upstairs, safe from Tyler Finley, and his meeting with a university student on the Native American Archeological Research team was in two days. He knew the dreams, the drawings, and the cup were somehow related; once he got a better look at the cup, he confirmed that the tri-lobe motif and the Swastika were almost certainly included in the crumbling, painted ceramic veneer. The girl at the research lab could tell him for sure. And the Sendalee guy's interest in the Big Joe's property couldn't be coincidental. His dad called it The Kitchen now, but John called it The Mound in his head.

He refolded the newspaper and turned it over in disgust. He did that each time he read it, and each time he was confronted with the mug shot of Sam Castle at the bottom of the page. "Missing Youth, Still Wanted For Questioning." A thirteen-year-old Sam glared at readers from an old juvie hall photo, next to a more recent snapshot, probably provided by his mother. He'd already turned eighteen, from the birth date on the mug shot. That was too bad; he was legally an adult, so things would be legally worse for him.

"Sam…"

He was beginning to feel differently about that guy, yet still conflicted. Sam had the symbols on his bedroom walls, and John couldn't believe that was a coincidence either. Also, he was indebted to him for the way he handled things, after Antonio was injured. John was used to being the only levelheaded person in a trauma, but Sam had kept his cool, too.

Too well, actually. Not only did he retain the presence of mind to give orders, he knew exactly what orders to give. As if that weren't the first time for him. John was sure he would deny it, but he noticed tears in Sam's eyes. The sadness in his face and the tenderness in his voice were well beyond what he could have felt for Antonio, whom he barely knew. No, Sam was remembering. He had watched someone close to him die before, probably just as violently.

"Don't look at that." Candy snatched up the newspaper, tossed it into the garbage, and plopped down opposite John. "You okay?"

John finally looked up from the table. Candy's was the only face he wanted to see and he felt comfortable having her close, after the episode with Tyler. He had looked up the Italian word Antonio was struggling to say at the end, "pericolo." The pain he must've endured to get that word out meant he was desperate for Candy to hear it. And the word translates as "danger." *No kidding, Antonio.* Candy was spending her nights at Grandma Pearl's, and none of the adults were confused as to why, once the news of "the foreign boy's" tortured corpse spread like wildfire. Better to stay in pairs.

"Yeah, I'm okay. You?"

She shrugged. Just past her, he saw a woman crossing the kitchen in their direction and he let out a tired groan. But Candy's face brightened. "It's Rachel."

Oh, the glass artist. John figured he'd let Candy handle it and zoned out.

After a few pleasantries and the predictable offer of condolence, Rachel skipped to the goal of her mission. "He's safe," she whispered, one eyebrow raised, then dropped something in Candy's hand and walked away without another word.

Candy stared at it, her mouth hanging open. The little object Rachel gave her was roundish and colorful, smooth like a large river pebble or a worry stone.

"What's that?" John plucked it out of her hand and saw that it was glass, with tiny strands of color streaking from the center. Gold, magenta, orange, red. It was like a tiny fireworks display exploding in his palm. "Pretty neat." Then he saw the covetous expression on Candy's face, her eyes glued to the treasure, and he dropped it on the table like he was holding a live cockroach. *Sam made it.*

Candy caught the glass stone before it bounced to the floor and tucked it into her pocket with a scowl.

"Well, now we know where he is," he said. "That wasn't very smart."

"It was if you keep your mouth shut, John," she snapped. "He trusts me, and I trust you. I *can*, right?"

He put up his hands in defense. "Don't worry, Candy—I don't want his location revealed any more than you do."

She scrutinized him doubtfully and kept her hand in her pocket, protecting Sam's gift.

"Look, I have no intention of giving him away." He reached for her other hand, but the two of them were interrupted again.

"You guys, how are you doing?" Amanda Jameson was standing in the entrance to the dining nook. Candy looked to John, letting him take care of that one.

"Holding up," he said, figuring he couldn't go wrong with a cliché in a mourning environment. Even with Amanda.

"I know how you feel," she said. "His picture is still in the paper, and it bothers me every time I see it."

"Um—" Candy started, confused. Amanda ducked in to give her a hug before she could say more. Stiff arms returned the embrace, fingers tapping her back in reluctant obligation.

"We could all use an extra hug right now," Amanda said. She turned to offer one to John. "Don't worry, guys. I know they'll catch that creep Sam Castle." Inexplicably, she choked on a sob and wiped a tear, then turned and left the room.

John and Candy stared at each other for several seconds, speechless.

"I thought you said—" John was bewildered. When he had run back along the tracks that night and found Antonio shot dead, it was obvious that Tyler pulled the trigger, even though Sam was holding the gun. Candy confirmed that Sam took it from him (forcibly, by the look on Tyler's face), and John was relieved to know the gun was out of play. But there was so much going on at once that night. "You said Sam didn't..."

But the next words wouldn't come.

Candy nodded. "I did. I did say that."

"Tyler sh—" John stuttered. "Tyler w-was... Shit!"

"I know," Candy nodded fervently. "You can't say it now, can you? I can't talk about it either, John."

Watching her face scrunched in vexation, John realized he wasn't imagining the reason for the tongue-tied past few days. He had tried to pretend his trouble with words was due to reticence or indecision. They were all sworn to secrecy, because anyone could've been implicated in Antonio's death. John knew it was stupid to get rid of the body in the river—it hadn't worked anyway. He was ashamed that he agreed to it, but Candy's dress was soaked with blood, her neck gouged by Antonio's fingernails. She was desperate to protect Sam, whose "evidence" was all over Antonio, since he had held him in his arms and bunched his jacket under him for cushion. Amanda was frantic with thoughts of her father's involvement—the damn sheriff. John wanted to find Lindsay before something happened to *her*. In fact, the train had taken her all the way to Tenakho Falls and it took John half the night to get her to Amanda's house. The whole thing was a clusterfuck.

But, after Tyler attacked Candy in the woods, that animal had to be restrained. John went to his father first, which was fortunate, since that decision saved him from making a fool of himself at the sheriff's office. When he tried to speak of the event with Dad, the words wouldn't come.

"When I tried to say something after that disgusting creep pounced on me, it was like I went dumb," Candy said, echoing his thoughts. "I tried to tell my dad, but I couldn't."

"I did the exact same thing," John laughed, though there was nothing funny about the chill creeping up his spine.

"You don't think it was the stupid 'binding spell'? That thing Amanda made us do?"

John understood the horror in her expression; he couldn't fathom being held under Amanda's spell either. That night by the river, she insisted that they all prick their fingers and shake hands while promising to keep silent, and as ridiculous as that seemed to most of them, the fact that her father was sheriff carried weight. When they put their hands together (John kept his bloody digit clear and washed his hands in the river later), he was annoyed to hear her chanting something under her breath about "binding." He repressed a tense smile when Candy jerked her hand away in revulsion.

"No," he shook his head. He thought Amanda was just as tied as they were. She wouldn't like being silenced, and by the dark circles under her eyes, John guessed she hadn't been sleeping much. "From the conversation I overheard between her dad and mine, she hasn't said anything. I think if she could turn someone in, she would. She obviously has plans for Sam. Poor guy."

Candy's face went crimson with that comment, then her eyes widened. "What's going on, John? I don't want to sound melodramatic, but when I try to say anything about…" and she pounded her fist on the table in frustration, unable to produce the name or concept she needed, "…anything specific. It's like someone—something—reaches in and takes the words right out of my mouth. I can almost feel it."

Terror wafted off of her. John studied him palms, hating what he had to say—he hated to see her so scared, but he knew he could protect her against anything. He had to. And he needed to be honest with her, because they had to figure it out together or not at all.

"Candy, it's the same for me." He looked up from his hands with apology in his eyes, and watched the blood drain from her face. She was looking past him.

"Oh my god…"

"What?" John tried to turn around to see what she was looking at, but she clutched his forearm with an iron grip.

She partially shielded her mouth with the pretense of fixing her over-long bangs. "Don't turn around. Just act natural. Look at me."

He frowned at her and watched a brittle grin crack over her face. Not even close to natural.

He strained his eyes as far as he could to the side, hoping for some hint of what lay behind him. "What's going on?" he whispered.

Candy clawed his arm tighter, her fingernails nearly piercing flesh. "Shhhh!"

John stared at the table—he couldn't bear to see the anxiety etched in Candy's face—as seconds ticked by. Finally, her grip loosened and she leaned in to whisper, "Okay, she's looking the other way. Turn around slowly and look at Charlotte Finley's feet."

"Her feet?" It was the last thing he expected to hear, but he did as he was told. He found her easily; she was the only person dressed in anything but solid black. Her black and white harlequin patterned dress shouted through the mournful gathering. John's eyes fell to her feet. "Oh fuck."

Charlotte was standing with her back to the kitchen, nodding at something Grandma Pearl was saying. Her long ponytail swayed back and forth with sympathy, one hand reaching out to console a shoulder. And on her feet were Lindsay's black satin shoes—shoes last seen in Antonio's death grip.

§

Steph tossed her car keys into a wooden bowl on the side table and closed her front door, exhausted. She had stayed up late the night before, preparing a tuna casserole for Pearl, then woke up early that morning to make apple cinnamon muffins for Joe's funeral reception. Afterwards, she'd lingered late at the Robinson's to help clean up, to boot.

"You girls want some dinner?" She groaned at the thought of more cooking, but she could whip up some chili mac in a jiffy. When she turned a tired face in the direction of her daughter's room, however, Amanda and Lindsay had already disappeared inside and closed the door.

She sighed hard, pausing in the act of hanging up her purse, then followed their rude departure instead. "Enough is enough," she muttered, starting down the hallway before even kicking her shoes off her sore feet.

Amanda and Lindsay had been inseparable since they heard about that train accident. That would've been understandable, since a fellow Bobcatt had been horribly killed. And everyone in town was feeling strange about that awful rumor of a Satanic ritual...well, Steph didn't like to think about that part. But constant locked doors and meal refusals were starting to drive her batty. She had a mind to stop it right then and there. *We're all mourning for Pete's sake.*

She stopped outside Amanda's door, about to knock, when she heard snippets of one half of a phone conversation. Figuring she might nibble a crumb or two of information from her highly secretive daughter, she decided to listen instead. Steph pressed her ear to the door.

"…sure as hell did. What was that supposed to be, a threat, Tyler? We want those shoes back."

Lindsay snuffled in agreement.

"I already told you I sent my dad in the other direction. Didn't you see the paper this morning? Or do you even read?"

Lindsay whimpered through a half-hearted laugh, her voice shaky.

"I can't out and out accuse anybody, and you know why—"

"Hallelujah! Hallelujah!"

Oh, fiddlesticks! Steph clapped her hand over her purse to quiet her cellphone and hurried away from the door grasping at her chest. She was beginning to reconsider using the "Hallelujah Chorus" as her new ringtone, no matter how excited she was about Christmas. It startled the dickens out of her every time.

As soon as she was out of earshot, she answered the call, "Hello?"

"Mrs. Jameson, please."

"Yes, speaking."

"This is Ricky Mendez, from The Kitchen?"

The Kitchen? Oh, that's right. Steph chuckled at Jamie's new name for the restaurant. "Well, hi there, Ricky. What can I help you with?"

Ricky cleared his throat and seemed to shuffle through papers. "We've been asked to clear a few things from the schedule, and…" There was a click interrupting his voice, "I'm sorry, could you hold for one moment?"

"Sure," she said, annoyed. Why was the stock boy calling her, and who was he to make her wait on the line? She hung up her purse and put her shoes in the closet, then stood waiting with her arms crossed over her chest.

"Sorry about that, ma'am."

"Fine. What is it?"

"We need to cancel your breakfast that you scheduled for December, Mrs. Jameson."

Steph's mouth fell open. "Pancakes With Santa? Why?"

Pancakes With Santa was the kick-off event for the Christmas season. She hosted it every year since she could remember, on the Saturday morning right after Thanksgiving. It was one of Steph's favorite holiday parties—she had the most adorable fur-lined, green velvet elf dress that she wore with candy-cane tights.

"She said to take it off the calendar," said Ricky, unapologetic.

"But it's over a month away," whined Steph—she couldn't help it. Was it because Pearl felt a festive event would be inappropriate, so soon after her husband's death? Joe had played Santa once or twice, but lots of other grandpas in town took turns. And Jamie had been running Big Joe's for months. "Pearl wouldn't have to be involved at all. I'll take care of everything, like I always do."

"Mrs. Robinson wasn't the one who canceled it."

"Oh. Jamie did?" *I thought he said 'she' wanted it off the calendar.*

"No, Mrs. Walsh."

Steph blinked in stunned silence for several beats, then found a chair and sat down. "Mieke Walsh?"

"Yeah, the new owner," Ricky said, like it should have been obvious.

"Of...the restaurant?" Steph spluttered.

"Of the whole compound."

keep reading

Remember Stephanie Jameson's reservations about her son's date to the Homecoming Dance? She thought Meg Shannon was pretty, in a strange way, and seemed nice enough (though a little on the dumb side), but not even Steph could've ignored the rumors about her loose nature. The poor thing didn't have much going for her; she lived in the Southern Cove trailer park with a dozen raggedy step- and half-siblings, and a hard-working, but usually absent, mother. No father. People snickered that Meg would sleep with almost anyone to spend the night away from her own filthy, overrun trailer home. Everyone would know, of course, why Tristan had invited the girl to the dance.

But Steph doesn't know as much as she thinks she does. Meet the real Meg Shannon in my new serial novel, Catchpenny...

catchpenny

PART ONE: Wicked LOVER

SARAH WATHEN

chapter one

I stepped off the school bus, my brain still foggy and my eyes still sleepy. But when I saw the janitor re-painting my locker again, my early morning funk was slapped right off my face. Someone must have used spray paint that time, or maybe a permanent marker—not so easily cleaned as lipstick or a simple splatter of oozing garbage. My eyes scanned the lockers on either side of mine, all faded and chipped orange paint, while mine was a bright beacon of fresh lacquer. I wondered what graffiti Henry had seen that morning on his 5 a.m. arrival to campus. Maybe just a word: "slut." Maybe something more creative, like the enormous penis, complete with pubic hair and a little squirt coming from the tip, that had been drawn on my locker door a few weeks ago. Luckily, most sharpie-wielding dipshits at my high school weren't so clever. Clever was remembered better.

It looked like Henry was almost finished covering whatever new allusion to my reputation had been left for me to find. I didn't need to guess whether or not anyone else saw the graffiti before it had been painted over—darting eyes and stifled giggles nearby told me they had. Thankful that I already had the book I needed, I changed direction, and headed for my first period class instead of my locker.

How did people even get into the school at night? I walked to class, keeping my gaze focused straight ahead and my face expressionless. Who had I newly pissed off—and how? Whose boyfriend had been caught with his eyes glued to my ass as I passed? Or, maybe a jealous underclassman brat hadn't developed quite as well as I had yet? I had been the first girl to grow breasts in grade school, years ago, and it hadn't escaped anyone's notice, no matter how baggy the shirt I wore was. Those babies just kept growing over the years, while the rest of me stretched out tall and lean. Most guys can't help but stare, and most girls hate me for it.

But I don't wear baggy shirts anymore. I pushed my shoulders back and straightened my spine, the shock and embarrassment of morning graffiti already wearing off. It never took long to remember who I was, and shrug off the ridicule of who people thought I was. Who they needed me to be. I readjusted my backpack and fluffed my hair. Screw them.

A pair of eyes locked onto mine. Tristan Jameson, Andrew Jackson's star quarterback, was walking down the hallway in my direction, staring at me. He was holding the strap of his backpack over one shoulder, the other hand in the pocket of his jeans, strolling slowly with a half-smile playing on his lips.

"Hi," he said in a low voice as he passed, so close we almost bumped shoulders.

"Hi." I glanced back. He was looking back at me.

"Watch it!"

"Oh, sorry." I stopped short just before slamming into the oncoming student traffic. Several girls were walking together like a wall of bodies, chatting and laughing. I shot my elbows in front of me for protection, and accidentally toppled the books from one of the girl's hands.

"Why don't you look where you're going?" She stooped down to gather her things, tugging the hem of her miniskirt down and muttering under her breath.

"Here. Sorry." She snatched the book I held out for her and pushed past me with a scowl, running to catch up with the herd.

"Why don't you get a backpack?" I mumbled, watching her bustle away in the direction Tristan had been headed. He was already gone.

§

I sat on my favorite table in the outdoor courtyard, my feet propped on the back of a conjoined concrete bench. The yard was all brick and concrete, with a lone tree springing up from the center, a square space open to the sky where four school buildings met. The tables were mostly empty, with only a few guys loitering by the doors to the cafeteria. The cafeteria was where the bulk of the student body preferred to eat. I prefer solitude. I leaned back on my hands and closed my eyes, knowing that extending my tan was hopeless. I let the late morning sun warm my shoulders and face, soaking it in with greed. It was the last of the summer heat, the days already shortening and the shadows lengthening into autumn.

A burst of laughter erupted nearby as a group of girls swarmed around one of the empty tables, flinging their purses and book bags on top, and my moment of peace vanished. I opened up Tolstoy's *Anna Karenina*, the pages blue after letting my closed eyes bake in the sun. I had been slog-ging through the book for days, and I thought once again about seeing the movie before I finished. I hate that seeing a movie changes the way a character looks in my mind, but I detest how much a movie stinks after I've already read the book. I thumbed a few pages forward to see where the chapter ended, not really in the mood for reading, but always more comfortable to have a book in hand at lunchtime.

"Meg?"

I gasped. He was standing just behind me, his head cocked to one side, looking over my shoulder at the Tolstoy.

"Hi, I'm Tristan."

He was squinting into the sun, and it was hard to tell if he was smiling or frowning.

"Yeah, I know who you are."

He shaded his eyes and laughed. Didn't everyone know who he was? He was on the billboard in front of the football field, for god's sake, his arm cocked back to throw a winning pass. *Go Bobcatts!*

"What are you reading?" His voice was soft and curious, and he squint-ed to read the pages I held open in my lap.

"Uh…" I stammered. The sun shone through his light irises like glass, shocking against his dark hair. His black polo shirt was gathered loosely around one hip, the hand in his pocket pushing it up casually over the waistband of his jeans. A slice of flesh was made visible. He stood in perfect contrapposto, a bookbag slung over his shoulder like Michelangelo's David holding the slingshot. I closed my book and tossed it onto the table, pretending not to notice how his jeans hung, low and delicious on slender hips. "Just something for English Lit."

"Man, that's a fat book. We never have to read stuff like that in my class."

"Aren't you a senior, too?"

"Yeah. What English class are *you* in?"

"AP," I shrugged.

"AP. What's that stand for?"

"Advanced Placement."

He furrowed his brow.

"Based on college reading lists." I held up my "fat" book in illustration. "You take a test at the end and get college credits, depending on how well you do."

"Oh, wow."

I could tell he was surprised I had a brain. Most guys were. I wasn't sure what to say next, so I held his gaze, challenging him to ask me more about books.

"How can you read out here? It's so bright."

Because I'd rather read a book than sit alone with no one talking to me. "I heard that people with light eyes have a harder time adjusting to bright light."

"Really?"

He stepped closer to me, shifting his weight and putting his back to the sunlight. The color of his eyes reminded me of Halls Mentho-Lyptus cough drops after I'd sucked on one for a while and the zing got too strong to keep it in my mouth—icy blue and transparent.

"I don't want to bother you or anything," he said, dropping his voice lower, since we were face to face then. He smelled like soap and clean laundry, with something gritty underneath. Something undeniably male.

"No, I—" I cleared my throat. He was even better looking up close. "I'm not busy."

He glanced back over his shoulder and the group of girls who had been watching suddenly picked up their conversation again, all of them talking at once and fumbling with their lunches. I was waiting with as much anticipation as they had been—why on earth was he talking to *me*?

"I'll let you get back to your book, but I just wanted to ask you something."

"Sure. What's up?" Those eyes.

"Would you be my date for Homecoming this weekend?"

"Cough drop—" I spluttered.

"Huh?"

I slapped my chest and choked out a cough. "I mean...uh, the dance?"

"Yeah, the dance."

"In five days?" It was Tuesday and the dance was Saturday. I hadn't planned on going, for many reasons.

"Four. Depending on how you count it," he said, a blinding smile spreading across his face. "Today's halfway through."

"I guess it is."

"And Saturday would only be a half-day, since the dance is that night." He was daring me to accept the challenge. I could never refuse a dare, especially one with such an irresistible smile attached.

"Wait. Don't you have a girlfriend?" I wasn't exactly buddies with anyone in the popular crowd at Andrew Jackson, nowhere close. But everyone knew that the star quarterback and the head cheerleader had been together since freshman year. Sugary sweet.

"No. I don't have a girlfriend." That smile again, but with an undercurrent in his voice.

The neighboring table had gone silent once more, the bombshell news of Tristan's single status freezing them all mid-prattle.

"Absolutely." I grinned over his shoulder—a present for our shocked audience.

"Absolutely, you'll go with me?"

Did he really think I would say no? The curiosity itself was enough for me to agree.

"Sure. Why not?" I shrugged, like it was nothing to me. Yeah, right.

"Great. Okay, lemme just get your number." He handed me his phone and I punched my number in, wondering what kind of psychedelic rabbit hole I had accidentally wandered through. Had somebody drugged my orange juice that morning? He took his phone back and saved, whispering, "Meg…Shannon," as he typed. "I'll call you, so you'll have mine."

"I don't have a cellphone. That's the number at my house."

"Oh."

I felt my cheeks getting hot, and nothing to do with the sun. Was I the only person at school without a cellphone or something?

"Okay. Well, I'll see you around, then?"

"Yeah, see ya." I resisted the urge to bite down on my knuckles.

He winked at me and waved over his shoulder as he turned back to the courtyard entrance. His jeans looked even nicer from behind, snug around his well-shaped glutes and muscular thighs. "Bye, Meg."

"Bye."

I picked my book up again, refusing to gaze at his retreating form in concert with the other females. A wink—what did that mean? Maybe it was just the bright light on his Mentho-Lyptus eyes. I opened *Anna Karenina* again and pretended to concentrate for the rest of lunch. But I couldn't read another word.

Find Catchpenny on Amazon, and other online retailers!

a note from the author

There is nothing like connecting with readers! I hope that you will join me on my website, www.sarahwathen.com. There, you will find my contact information and links to all of my social media outlets: I would love to hear from you!

Also, did you know that The Tramp has a full-length musical soundtrack album, composed and performed by the band Her Last Boyfriend? Music and art is at the heart of all my stories, and I highly encourage readers to listen to The Tramp Soundtrack. It's more than just awesome alternative rock—it's a concept album that follows the story from beginning to end, with lyrics and instrumentation specifically designed for my characters. Go to my website to find links to the album, as well as artwork featured in The Tramp, character playlists, and videos I used in my research for the book.

www.ingramcontent.com/pod-product-compliance
Lightning Source LLC
Chambersburg PA
CBHW072117250626
47159CB00007B/2477